Also available
in Random House Large Print

Pandora
Violin
Servant of the Bones

THE

VAMPIRE
ARMAND

by

ANNE RICE

Published by Random House Large Print
in association with Alfred A. Knopf, Inc.
New York   1998

Library of Congress Cataloging-in-Publication Data
Rice, Anne, 1941–
The vampire Armand / Anne Rice.
p.   cm. — (Vampire chronicles)
ISBN 0-375-70415-9
1. Vampires—Fiction.   2. Large type books.   I. Title.
II. Series: Rice, Anne, 1941– Vampire chronicles.
[PS3568.I265V25   1998b]
813'.54—dc21   98-26240
CIP

Random House Web Address: http://www.randomhouse.com/
Printed in the United States of America
FIRST LARGE PRINT EDITION

This Large Print Book carries the
Seal of Approval of N.A.V.H.

For
Brandy Edwards,
Brian Robertson
and
Christopher and Michele Rice

Jesus, speaking to Mary Magdalene:

Jesus saith unto her, Touch me not;
for I am not yet ascended to my Father:
but go to my brethren, and say unto them,
I ascend unto my Father, and your Father;
and to my God, and your God.

THE GOSPEL
ACCORDING TO ST. JOHN 20:17

PART I

BODY and BLOOD

1

THEY SAID a child had died in the attic. Her clothes had been discovered in the wall.

I wanted to go up there, and to lie down near the wall, and be alone.

They'd seen her ghost now and then, the child. But none of these vampires could see spirits, really, at least not the way that I could see them. No matter. It wasn't the company of the child I wanted. It was to be in that place.

Nothing more could be gained from lingering near Lestat. I'd come. I'd fulfilled my purpose. I couldn't help him.

The sight of his sharply focused and unchanging eyes unnerved me, and I was quiet inside and full of love for those nearest me—my human children, my dark-haired little Benji and my tender willow Sybelle—but I was not strong enough just yet to take them away.

I left the chapel.

I didn't even take note of who was there. The whole convent was now the dwelling place of vampires. It was not an unruly place, or a neglected place, but I didn't notice who remained in the chapel when I left.

Lestat lay as he had all along, on the marble floor of the chapel in front of the huge crucifix, on his side, his hands slack, the left hand just below the right hand, its fingers touching the marble lightly, as if with a purpose, when there was no purpose at all. The fingers of his right hand curled, making a little hollow in the palm where the light fell, and that too seemed to have a meaning, but there was no meaning.

This was simply the preternatural body lying there without will or animation, no more purposeful than the face, its expression almost defiantly intelligent, given that months had passed in which Lestat had not moved.

The high stained-glass windows were dutifully draped for him before sunrise. At night, they shone with all the wondrous candles scattered about the fine statues and relics which filled this once sanctified and holy place. Little mortal children had heard Mass under this high coved roof; a priest had sung out the Latin words from an altar.

It was ours now. It belonged to him—Lestat, the man who lay motionless on the marble floor.

Man. Vampire. Immortal. Child of Darkness. Any and all are excellent words for him.

Looking over my shoulder at him, I never felt so much like a child.

That's what I am. I fill out the definition, as if it were encoded in me perfectly, and there had never been any other genetic design.

I was perhaps seventeen years old when Marius made me into a vampire. I had stopped growing by that time. For a year, I'd been five feet six inches. My hands are as delicate as those of a young woman, and I was beardless, as we used to say in that time, the years of the sixteenth century. Not a eunuch, no, not that, most certainly, but a boy.

It was fashionable then for boys to be as beautiful as girls. Only now does it seem something worthwhile, and that's because I love the others—my own: Sybelle with her woman's breasts and long girlish limbs, and Benji with his round intense little Arab face.

I stood at the foot of the stairs. No mirrors here, only the high brick walls stripped of their plaster, walls that were old only for America, darkened by the damp even inside the convent, all textures and elements here softened by the simmering summers of New Orleans and her clammy crawling winters, green winters I call them because the trees here are almost never bare.

I was born in a place of eternal winter when one compares it to this place. No wonder in sunny Italy I forgot the beginnings altogether, and fashioned my life out of the present of my years with Marius. "I don't remember." It was a condition of loving so much vice, of being so addicted to Italian wine and sumptuous meals, and even the feel of the warm marble under my bare feet when the rooms of the palazzo were sinfully, wickedly heated by Marius's exorbitant fires.

His mortal friends . . . human beings like me at that time . . . scolded constantly about these expenditures: firewood, oil, candles. And for Marius only the finest candles of beeswax were acceptable. Every fragrance was significant.

Stop these thoughts. Memories can't hurt you now. You came here for a reason and now you have finished, and you must find those you love, your young mortals, Benji and Sybelle, and you must go on.

Life was no longer a theatrical stage where Banquo's ghost came again and again to seat himself at the grim table.

My soul hurt.

Up the stairs. Lie for a little while in this brick convent where the child's clothes were found. Lie with the child, murdered here in this convent, so say the rumormongers, the vampires who haunt these halls now, who have come to see the great Vampire Lestat in his Endymionlike sleep.

I felt no murder here, only the tender voices of nuns.

I went up the staircase, letting my body find its human weight and human tread.

After five hundred years, I know such tricks. I could frighten all the young ones—the hangers-on and the gawkers—just as surely as the other ancient ones did it, even the most modest, uttering words to evince their telepathy, or vanishing when they chose to leave, or now and then even making the building tremble with their power—an interesting accomplishment even with these walls eighteen inches thick with cypress sills that will never rot.

He must like the fragrances here, I thought. Marius, where is he? Before I had visited Lestat, I had not wanted to talk very much to Marius, and had spoken only a few civil words when I left my treasures in his charge.

After all, I had brought my children into a menagerie of the Undead. Who better to safeguard them than my beloved Marius, so powerful that none here dared question his smallest request.

There is no telepathic link between us naturally—Marius made me, I am forever his fledgling—but as soon as this occurred to me, I realized without the aid of this telepathic link that I could not feel the presence of Marius in the building. I didn't know what had happened in that brief interval when I knelt down to look at Lestat. I didn't know where Marius was. I couldn't catch the familiar human scents of Benji or Sybelle. A little stab of panic paralyzed me.

I stood on the second story of the building. I leaned against the wall, my eyes settling with determined calm on the deeply varnished heart pine floor. The light made pools of yellow on the boards.

Where were they, Benji and Sybelle? What had I done in bringing them here, two ripe and glorious humans? Benji was a spirited boy of twelve, Sybelle, a womanling of twenty-five. What if Marius, so generous in his own soul, had carelessly let them out of his sight?

"I'm here, young one." The voice was abrupt, soft, welcome.

My Maker stood on the landing just below me, having come up the steps behind me, or more truly, with his powers, having placed himself there, covering the preceding distance with silent and invisible speed.

"Master," I said with a little trace of a smile. "I was afraid for them for a moment." It was an apology. "This place makes me sad."

He nodded. "I have them, Armand," he said. "The city seethes with mortals. There's food enough for all the vagabonds wandering here. No one will hurt them. Even if I weren't here to say so, no one would dare."

It was I who nodded now. I wasn't so sure, really. Vampires are by their very nature perverse and do wicked and terrible things simply for the sport of it. To kill another's mortal pet would be a worthy entertainment for some grim and alien creature, skirting the fringes here, drawn by remarkable events.

"You're a wonder, young one," he said to me smiling. Young one! Who else would call me this but Marius, my Maker, and what is five hundred years to him? "You went into the sun, child," he continued with the same legible concern written on his kind face. "And you lived to tell the tale."

"Into the sun, Master?" I questioned his words. But I myself did not want to reveal any more. I did not want to talk yet, to tell of what had happened, the legend of Veronica's Veil and the Face of Our Lord emblazoned upon it, and the morning when I had given up my soul with such perfect happiness. What a fable it was.

He came up the steps to be near me, but kept a polite distance. He has always been the gentleman, even before there was such a word. In ancient Rome, they must have had a term for such a person, infallibly good mannered, and considerate as a point of honor, and wholly successful at common courtesy to rich and poor alike. This was Marius, and it had always been Marius, insofar as I could know.

He let his snow-white hand rest on the dull satiny banister. He wore a long shapeless cloak of gray velvet, once perfectly extravagant, now downplayed with wear and rain, and his yellow hair was long like Lestat's hair, full of random light and unruly in the damp, and even studded with drops of dew from outside, the same dew clinging to his golden eyebrows and darkening his long curling eyelashes around his large cobalt-blue eyes.

There was something altogether more Nordic and

icy about him than there was about Lestat, whose hair tended more to golden, for all its luminous highlights, and whose eyes were forever prismatic, drinking up the colors around him, becoming even a gorgeous violet with the slightest provocation from the worshipful outside world.

In Marius, I saw the sunny skies of the northern wilderness, eyes of steady radiance which rejected any outside color, perfect portals to his own most constant soul.

"Armand," he said. "I want you to come with me."

"Where is that, Master, come where?" I asked. I too wanted to be civil. He had always, even after a struggle of wits, brought such finer instincts out of me.

"To my house, Armand, where they are now, Sybelle and Benji. Oh, don't fear for them for a second. Pandora's with them. They are rather astonishing mortals, brilliant, remarkably different, yet alike. They love you, and they know so much and have come with you rather a long way."

I flushed with blood and color; the warmth was stinging and unpleasant, and then as the blood danced back away from the surface of my face, I felt cooler and strangely enervated that I felt any sensations at all.

It was a shock being here and I wanted it to be over.

"Master, I don't know who I am in this new life," I said gratefully. "Reborn? Confused?" I hesitated, but there was no use stopping it. "Don't ask me to stay here just now. Maybe some time when Lestat is himself again, maybe when enough time has passed—. I don't know for certain, only that I can't accept your kind invitation now."

He gave me a brief accepting nod. With his hand he made a little acquiescent gesture. His old gray cloak had slipped off one shoulder. He seemed not to care about it. His thin black wool clothes were neglected, lapels and pockets trimmed in a careless gray dust. That was not right for him.

He had a big shock of white silk at his throat that made his pale face seem more colored and human than it otherwise would. But the silk was torn as if by brambles. In sum, he haunted the world in these clothes, rather than was dressed in them. They were for a stumbler, not my old Master.

I think he knew I was at a loss. I was looking up at the gloom above me. I wanted to reach the attic of this place, the half-concealed clothing of the dead child. I wondered at this story of the dead child. I had the impertinence to let my mind drift, though he was waiting.

He brought me back with his gentle words:

"Sybelle and Benji will be with me when you want them," he said. "You can find us. We aren't far. You'll hear the *Appassionata* when you want to hear it." He smiled.

"You've given her a piano," I said. I spoke of golden Sybelle. I had shut out the world from my preternatural hearing, and I didn't want just yet to unstop my ears even for the lovely sound of her playing, which I already missed overly much.

As soon as we'd entered the convent, Sybelle had seen a piano and asked in a whisper at my ear if she could play it. It was not in the chapel where Lestat lay, but off in another long empty room. I had told her it wasn't quite proper, that it might disturb Lestat as he lay there, and we couldn't know what he thought, or what he felt, or if he was anguished and trapped in his own dreams.

"Perhaps when you come, you'll stay for a while," Marius said. "You'll like the sound of her playing my piano, and maybe then we'll talk together, and you can rest with us, and we can share the house for as long as you like."

I didn't answer.

"It's palatial in a New World sort of way," he said with a little mockery in his smile. "It's not far at all. I have the most spacious gardens and old oaks, oaks far older than those even out there on the Avenue, and all the windows are doors. You know how I like it that way. It's the Roman style. The house is open to the spring rain, and the spring rain here is like a dream."

"Yes, I know," I whispered. "I think it's falling now, isn't it?" I smiled.

"Well, I'm rather spattered with it, yes," he said almost gaily. "You come when you want to. If not tonight, then tomorrow . . ."

"Oh, I'll be there tonight," I said. I didn't want to offend him, not in the slightest, but Benji and Sybelle had seen enough of white-faced monsters with velvet voices. It was time to be off.

I looked at him rather boldly, enjoying it for a moment, overcoming a shyness that had been our curse in this modern world. In Venice of old, he had gloried in his clothes as men did then, always so sharp and splendidly embellished, the glass of fashion, to use the old graceful phrase. When he crossed the Piazza San Marco in the soft purple of evening, all turned to watch him pass. Red had been his badge of pride, red velvet—a flowing cape, and magnificently embroidered doublet, and beneath it a tunic of gold silk tissue, so very popular in those times.

He'd had the hair of a young Lorenzo de' Medici, right from the painted wall.

"Master, I love you, but now I must be alone," I said. "You don't need me now, do you, Sir? How can you? You never really did." Instantly I regretted it. The words, not the tone, were impudent. And our minds being so divided by intimate blood, I was afraid he'd misunderstand.

"Cherub, I want you," he said forgivingly. "But I can wait. Seems not long ago I spoke these same words when we were together, and so I say them again."

I couldn't bring myself to tell him it was my season for mortal company, how I longed just to be talking away the night with little Benji, who was such a sage, or listening to my beloved Sybelle play her sonata over and over again. It seemed beside the point to explain any further. And the sadness came over me again, heavily and undeniably, of having come to this forlorn and empty convent where Lestat lay, unable or unwilling to move or speak, none of us knew.

"Nothing will come of my company just now, Master," I said. "But you will grant me some key to finding you, surely, so that when this time passes . . ." I let my words die.

"I fear for you!" he whispered suddenly, with great warmth.

"Any more than ever before, Sir?" I asked.

He thought for a moment. Then he said, "Yes. You love two mortal children. They are your moon and stars.

Come stay with me if only for a little while. Tell me what you think of our Lestat and what's happened. Tell me perhaps, if I promise to remain very quiet and not to press you, tell me your opinion of all you've so recently seen."

"You touch on it delicately, Sir, I admire you. You mean why did I believe Lestat when he said he had been to Heaven and Hell, you mean what did I see when I looked at the relic he brought back with him, Veronica's Veil."

"If you want to tell me. But more truly, I wish you would come and rest."

I put my hand on top of his, marveling that in spite of all I'd endured, my skin was almost as white as his.

"You will be patient with my children till I come, won't you?" I asked. "They imagine themselves so intrepidly wicked, coming here to be with me, whistling nonchalantly in the crucible of the Undead, so to speak."

"Undead," he said, smiling reprovingly. "Such language, and in my presence. You know I hate it."

He planted a kiss quickly on my cheek. It startled me, and then I realized that he was gone.

"Old tricks!" I said aloud, wondering if he were still near enough to hear me, or whether he had shut up his ears to me as fiercely as I shut mine to the outside world.

I looked off, wanting the quiet, dreaming of bowers suddenly, not in words but in images, the way my old mind would do it, wanting to lie down in garden beds among growing flowers, wanting to press my face to earth and sing softly to myself.

The spring outside, the warmth, the hovering mist that would be rain. All this I wanted. I wanted the swampy forests beyond, but I wanted Sybelle and Benji, too, and to be gone, and to have some will to carry on.

Ah, Armand, you always lack this very thing, the will. Don't let the old story repeat itself now. Arm yourself with all that's happened.

Another was nearby.

It seemed so awful to me suddenly, that some immortal whom I didn't know should intrude here on my random private thoughts, perhaps to make a selfish approximation of what I felt.

It was only David Talbot.

He came from the chapel wing, through the bridge rooms of the convent that connect it to the main building where I stood at the top of the staircase to the second floor.

I saw him come into the hallway. Behind him was the glass of the door that led to the gallery, and beyond that the soft mingled gold and white light of the courtyard below.

"It's quiet now," he said. "And the attic's empty and you know that you can go there, of course."

"Go away," I said. I felt no anger, only the honest wish to have my thoughts unread and my emotions left alone.

With remarkable self-possession he ignored me, then said:

"Yes, I am afraid of you, a little, but then terribly curious too."

"Oh, I see, so that excuses it, that you followed me here?"

"I didn't follow you, Armand," he said. "I live here."

"Ah, I'm sorry then," I admitted. "I hadn't known. I

suppose I'm glad of it. You guard him. He's never alone." I meant Lestat of course.

"Everyone's afraid of you," he said calmly. He had taken up a position only a few feet away, casually folding his arms. "You know, it's quite a study, the lore and habits of the vampires."

"Not to me," I said.

"Yes, I realize that," he said. "I was only musing, and I hope you'll forgive me. It was about the child in the attic, the child they said was murdered. It's a tall story, about a very small little person. Maybe if your luck is better than that of everyone else, you'll see the ghost of the child whose clothes were shut up in the wall."

"Do you mind if I look at you?" I said. "I mean if you're going to dip your beak into my mind with such abandon? We met some time ago before all this happened—Lestat, the Heavenly Journey, this place. I never really took stock of you. I was indifferent, or too polite, I don't know which."

I was surprised to hear such heat in my voice. I was volatile, and it wasn't David Talbot's fault.

"I'm thinking of the conventional knowledge about you," I said. "That you weren't born in this body, that you were an elderly man when Lestat knew you, that this body you inhabit now belonged to a clever soul who could hop from living being to living being, and there set up shop with his own trespassing soul."

He gave me a rather disarming smile.

"So Lestat said," he answered. "So Lestat wrote. It's true, of course. You know it is. You've known since you saw me before."

"Three nights we spent together," I said. "And I

never really questioned you. I mean I never really even looked directly into your eyes."

"We were thinking of Lestat then."

"Aren't we now?"

"I don't know," he said.

"David Talbot," I said, measuring him coldly with my eyes, "David Talbot, Superior General of the Order of Psychic Detectives known as the Talamasca, had been catapulted into the body in which he now walks." I didn't know whether I paraphrased or made it up as I went along. "He'd been entrenched or chained inside it, made a prisoner by so many ropey veins, and then tricked into a vampire as a fiery unstanchable blood invaded his lucky anatomy, sealing his soul up in it as it transformed him into an immortal—a man of dark bronzed skin and dry, lustrous and thick black hair."

"I think you have it right," he said with indulgent politeness.

"A handsome gent," I went on, "the color of caramel, moving with such catlike ease and gilded glances that he makes me think of all things once delectable, and now a potpourri of scent: cinnamon, clove, mild peppers and other spices golden, brown or red, whose fragrances can spike my brain and plunge me into erotic yearnings that live now, more than ever, to play themselves out. His skin must smell like cashew nuts and thick almond creams. It does."

He laughed. "I get your point."

I had shocked myself. I was wretched for a moment. "I'm not sure I get myself," I said apologetically.

"I think it's plain," he said. "You want me to leave you alone."

I saw the preposterous contradictions in all this at once.

"Look," I whispered quickly. "I'm deranged," I whispered. "My senses cross, like so many threads to make a knot: taste, see, smell, feel. I'm rampant."

I wondered idly and viciously if I could attack him, take him, bring him down under my greater craft and cunning and taste his blood without his consent.

"I'm much too far along the road for that," he said, "and why would you chance such a thing?"

What self-possession. The older man in him did indeed command the sturdier younger flesh, the wise mortal with an iron authority over all things eternal and supernaturally powerful. What a blend of energies! Nice to drink his blood, to take him against his will. There is no such fun on Earth like the raping of an equal.

"I don't know," I said, ashamed. Rape is unmanly. "I don't know why I insult you. You know, I wanted to leave quickly. I mean I wanted to visit the attic, and then be out of here. I wanted to avoid this sort of infatuation. You are a wonder, and you think me a wonder, and it's rich."

I let my eyes pass over him. I'd been blind to him when we met last, that was most true.

He dressed to kill. With the cleverness of olden times, when men could preen like peacocks, he'd chosen golden sepia and umber colors for his clothes. He was smart and clean and fretted all over with careful bits of pure gold, in a wristband timepiece and buttons and a slender pin for his modern tie, that tailored spill of color men wear in this age, as if to let us grab them all the more easily by its noose. Stupid ornament. Even his shirt of polished cotton was tawny and full of something of the sun and the warmed earth. Even his shoes were brown, glossy as beetles' backs.

He came towards me.

"You know what I'm going to ask," he said. "Don't wrestle with these unarticulated thoughts, these new experiences, all this overwhelming understanding. Make a book out of it for me."

I couldn't have predicted that this would be his question. I was surprised, sweetly so, but nevertheless taken off guard.

"Make a book? I? Armand?"

I went towards him, turned sharply and fled up the steps to the attic, skirting the third floor and then entering the fourth.

The air was thick and warm here. It was a place daily baked by the sun. All was dry and sweet, the wood like incense and the floors splintery.

"Little girl, where are you?" I asked.

"Child, you mean," he said.

He had come up behind me, taking a bit of time for courtesy's sake.

He added, "She was never here."

"How do you know?"

"If she were a ghost, I could call her," he said.

I looked over my shoulder. "You have that power? Or is this just what you want to say to me right now? Before you venture further, let me warn you that we almost never have the power to see spirits."

"I'm altogether new," David said. "I'm unlike any others. I've come into the Dark World with different faculties. Dare I say, we, our species, vampires, have evolved?"

"The conventional word is stupid," I said. I moved further into the attic. I spied a small chamber with plaster and peeling roses, big floppy prettily drawn Victorian roses with pale fuzzy green leaves. I went into the chamber. Light came from a high window out of which a child could not have seen. Merciless, I thought.

"Who said that a child died here?" I said. All was clean beneath the soil of years. There was no presence. It seemed perfect and just, no ghost to comfort me. Why should a ghost come from some savory rest for my sake?

So I could cuddle up perhaps to the memory of her, her tender legend. How are children murdered in orphanages where only nuns attend? I never thought of women as so cruel. Dried up, without imagination perhaps, but not aggressive as we are, to kill.

I turned round and round. Wooden lockers lined one wall, and one locker stood open, and there the tumbled shoes were, little brown Oxfords, as they called them, with black strings, and now I beheld, where it had been behind me, the broken and frayed hole from which they'd ripped her clothes. All fallen there, moldy and wrinkled they lay, her clothes.

A stillness settled on me as if the dust of this place were a fine ice, coming down from the high peaks of haughty and monstrously selfish mountains to freeze all living things, this ice, to close up and stop forever all that breathed or felt or dreamed or lived.

He spoke in poetry:

" 'Fear no more the heat of the sun,' "he whispered. " 'Nor the furious winter's rages. Fear no more . . .' "

I winced with pleasure. I knew the verses. I loved them.

I genuflected, as if before the Sacrament, and touched her clothes. "And she was little, no more than five, and she didn't die here at all. No one killed her. Nothing so special for her."

"How your words belie your thoughts," he said.

"Not so, I think of two things simultaneously. There's a distinction in being murdered. I was murdered. Oh, not by Marius, as you might think, but by others."

I knew I spoke soft and in an assuming way, because this wasn't meant for pure drama.

"I'm trimmed in memories as if in old furs. I lift my arm and the sleeve of memory covers it. I look around and see other times. But you know what frightens me the most—it is that this state, like so many others with me, will prove the verge of nothing but extend itself over centuries."

"What do you really fear? What did you want from Lestat when you came here?"

"David, I came to see him. I came to find out how it was with him, and why he lies there, unmoving. I came—." I wasn't going to say any more.

His glossy nails made his hands look ornamental and special, caressive, comely and lovely with which to be touched. He picked up a small dress, torn, gray, spotted with bits of mean lace. Everything dressed in flesh can yield a dizzying beauty if you concentrate on it long enough, and his beauty leapt out without apology.

"Just clothes." Flowered cotton, a bit of velvet with a puffed sleeve no bigger than an apple for the century of bare arms by day and night. "No violence at all surrounding her," he said as if it were a pity. "Just a poor child, don't you think, and sad by nature as well as circumstance."

"And why were they walled up, tell me that! What sin did these little dresses commit?" I sighed. "Good God, David Talbot, why don't we let the little girl have her romance, her fame? You make me angry. You say you can see ghosts. You find them pleasant? You like to talk with them. I could tell you about a ghost—."

"When will you tell me? Look, don't you see the trick of a book?" He stood up, and dusted off his knee with his right hand. In his left was her gathered dress. Something about the whole configuration bothered me, a tall creature holding a little girl's crumpled dress.

"You know, when you think of it," I said, turning away, so I wouldn't see the dress in his hand, "there's no good reason under God for little girls and little boys. Think of it, the other tender issue of mammals. Among puppies or kitten or colts, does one find gender? It's never an issue. The half-grown fragile thing is sexless. There is no determination. There is nothing as splendid to look at as a little boy or girl. My head is so full of notions. I rather think I'll explode if I don't do something, and you say make a book for you. You think it's possible, you think . . ."

"What I think is that when you make a book, you tell the tale as you would like to know it!"

"I see no great wisdom in that."

"Well, then think, for most speech is a mere issue of

our feelings, a mere explosion. Listen, note the way that you make these outbursts."

"I don't want to."

"But you do, but they are not the words you want to read. When you write, something different happens. You make a tale, no matter how fragmented or experimental or how disregarding of all conventional and helpful forms. Try this for me. No, no, I have a better idea."

"What?"

"Come down with me into my rooms. I live here now, I told you. Through my windows you can see the trees. I don't live like our friend Louis, wandering from dusty corner to dusty corner, and then back to his flat in the Rue Royale when he's convinced himself once more and for the thousandth time that no one can harm Lestat. I have warm rooms. I use candles for old light. Come down and let me write it, your story. Talk to me. Pace, and rant if you will, or rail, yes, rail, and let me write it, and even so, the very fact that I write, this in itself will make you make a form out of it. You'll begin to . . ."

"What?"

"To tell me what happened. How you died and how you lived."

"Expect no miracles, perplexing scholar. I didn't die in New York that morning. I almost died."

He had me faintly curious, but I could never do what he wanted. Nevertheless he was honest, amazingly so, as far as I could measure, and therefore sincere.

"Ah, so, I didn't mean literally. I meant that you should tell me what it was like to climb so high into the sun, and suffer so much, and, as you said, to discover in your pain all these memories, these connecting links. Tell me! Tell me."

"Not if you mean to make it coherent," I said crossly. I gauged his reaction. I wasn't bothering him. He wanted to talk more.

"Make it coherent? Armand, I'll simply write down what you say." He made his words simple yet curiously passionate.

"Promise?"

I flashed on him a playful look. Me! To do that.

He smiled. He wadded up the little dress and then dropped it carefully so it might fall in the middle of the pile of her old clothes.

"I'll not alter one syllable," he said. "Come be with me, and talk to me, and be my love." Again, he smiled.

Suddenly he came towards me, much in the aggressive manner in which I'd thought earlier to approach him. He slipped his hands under my hair, and felt of my face, and then he gathered up the hair and he put his face down into my curls, and he laughed. He kissed my cheek.

"Your hair's like something spun from amber, as if the amber would melt and could be drawn from candle flames in long fine airy threads and let to dry that way to make all these shining tresses. You're sweet, boylike and pretty as a girl. I wish I had one glimpse of you in antique velvet the way you were for him, for Marius. I wish I could see for one moment how it was when you dressed in stockings and wore a belted doublet sewn with rubies. Look at you, the frosty child. My love doesn't even touch you."

This wasn't true.

His lips were hot, and I could feel the fangs under them, feel the urgency suddenly in his fingers pressing against my scalp. It sent the shivers through me, and my body tensed and then shuddered, and it was sweet beyond prediction. I resented this lonely intimacy, resented it enough to transform it, or rid myself of it utterly. I'd rather die or be away, in the dark, simple and lonely with common tears.

From the look in his eyes, I thought he could love without giving anything. Not a connoisseur, just a blood drinker.

"You make me hungry," I whispered. "Not for you but for one who is doomed and yet alive. I want to hunt. Stop it. Why do you touch me? Why be so gentle?"

"Everyone wants you," he said.

"Oh, I know. Everyone would ravage a guilty cunning child! Everyone would have a laughing boy who knows his way around the block. Kids make better food than women, and girls are all too much like women, but young boys? They're not like men, are they?"

"Don't mock me. I meant I wanted only to touch you, to feel how soft you are, how eternally young."

"Oh, that's me, eternally young," I said. "You speak nonsense words for one so pretty yourself. I'm going out. I have to feed. And when I've finished with that, when I'm full and hot, then I'll come and I'll talk to you and tell you anything you want." I stepped back just a little from him, feeling the quivers through me as his fingers released my hair. I looked at the empty white window, peering too high for the trees.

"They could see nothing green here, and it's spring outside, southern spring. I can smell it through the walls.

I want to look just for a moment on flowers. To kill, to drink blood and to have flowers."

"Not good enough. Want to make the book," he said. "Want to make it now and want you to come with me. I won't hang around forever."

"Oh, nonsense, of course you will. You think I'm a doll, don't you? You think I'm cute and made of poured wax, and you'll stay as long as I stay."

"You're a bit mean, Armand. You look like an angel, and talk like a common thug."

"Such arrogance! I thought you wanted me."

"Only on certain terms."

"You lie, David Talbot," I said.

I headed past him for the stairs. Cicadas sang in the night as they often do, to no clock, in New Orleans.

Through the nine-pane windows of the stairwell, I glimpsed the flowering trees of spring, a bit of vine curling on a porch top.

He followed. Down and down we went, walking like regular men, down to the first floor, and out the sparkling glass doors and into the broad lighted space of Napoleon Avenue with its damp, sweet park of green down the middle, a park thick with carefully planted flowers and old gnarled and humble, bending trees.

The whole picture moved with the subtle river winds, and wet mist swirled but would not fall into rain itself, and tiny green leaves drifted down like wilting ashes to the ground. Soft soft southern spring. Even the sky seemed pregnant with the season, lowering yet blushing with reflected light, giving birth to the mist from all its pores.

Strident perfume rose from the gardens right and

left, from purple Four O'Clocks, as mortals call them here, a rampant flower like unto weed, but infinitely sweet, and the wild irises stabbing upwards like blades out of the black mud, throaty petals monstrously big, battering themselves on old walls and concrete steps, and then as always there were roses, roses of old women and roses of the young, roses too whole for the tropical night, roses coated with poison.

There had been streetcars here once on this center strip of grass. I knew it, that the tracks had run along this wide deep green space where I walked ahead of him, slumward, riverward, deathward, bloodward. He came after me. I could close my eyes as I walked, never losing a step, and see the streetcars.

"Come on, follow me," I said, describing what he did, not inviting him.

Blocks and blocks within seconds. He kept up. Very strong. The blood of an entire Royal Vampire court was inside him, no doubt of it. Count on Lestat to make the most lethal of monsters, that is, after his initial seductive blunders—Nicolas, Louis, Claudia—not a single one of the three able to take care of themselves alone, and two perished, and one lingering and perhaps the weakest vampire yet walking in the great world.

I looked back. His tight, polished brown face startled me. He looked lacquered all over, waxed, buffed, and once again I thought of spicy things, of the meat of candied nuts, and delicious aromas, of chocolates sweet with sugar and dark rich butterscotch, and it seemed a good thing suddenly to maybe grab ahold of him.

But this was no substitute for one rotten, cheap, ripe

and odoriferous mortal. And guess what? I pointed. "Over there."

He looked as I directed him. He saw the sagging line of old buildings. Mortals everywhere lurked, slept, sat, dined, wandered, amid tiny narrow stairs, behind peeling walls and under cracked ceilings.

I had found one, most perfect in his wickedness, a great flurry of hateful embers, of malice and greed and contempt smoldering as he waited for me.

We'd come to Magazine Street and passed it, but we were not at the river, only almost, and this was a street I had no recollection of, or knowledge of, in my wanderings of this city—their city, Louis's and Lestat's—just a narrow street with these houses the color of driftwood under the moon and windows hung with makeshift coverings, and inside there was this one slouching, arrogant, vicious mortal fixed to a television set and guzzling malt from a brown bottle, ignoring the roaches and the pulsing heat that pressed in from the open window, this ugly, sweating, filthy and irresistible thing, this flesh and blood for me.

The house was so alive with vermin and tiny despicable things that it seemed no more than a shell surrounding him, crackling and friable and the same color in all its shadows as a forest. No antiseptic modern standards here. Even the furniture rotted in the trashy clutter and damp. Mildew covered the grinding white refrigerator.

Only the reeky personal bed and rags gave off the clue to reigning domesticity.

It was a proper nest in which to find this fowl, this

ugly bird, thick rich pluckable, devourable sack of bones and blood and shabby plumage.

I pushed the door to one side, the human stench rising like a swirl of gnats, and thereby put it off its hinges, but not with much sound.

I walked on newspapers strewn on painted wood. Orange peels turned to brownish leather. Roaches running. He didn't even look up. His swollen drunken face was blue and eerie, black eyebrows thick and unkempt, and yet he looked quite possibly a bit angelic, due to the light from the tube.

He flicked the magic plastic twanger in his hand to make the channels change, and the light flared and flickered soundlessly, and then he let the song rise, a band playing, a travesty, people clapping.

Trashy noises, trashy images, like the trash all around him. All right, I want you. No one else does.

He looked up at me, a boy invader, David too far off for him to see, waiting.

I pushed the television set to the side. It teetered, then fell onto the floor, its parts breaking, like so many jars of energy were inside, and now splinters of glass.

A momentary fury overcame him, charging his face with sluggish recognition.

He rose up, arms out, and came at me.

Before I sank my teeth, I noticed that he had long tangled black hair. Dirty but rich. He wore it back by means of a knotted bit of rag at the base of his neck and then straggling down his checkered shirt in a thick tail.

Meantime, he had enough syrupy and beer-besotted blood in him for two vampires, delicious, ugly, and a raging fighting heart, and so much bulk it was like riding a bull to be on him.

In the midst of the feed, all odors rise to sweetness, even the most rancid. I thought I would quietly die of joy, as always.

I sucked hard enough to fill my mouth, letting the blood roll over my tongue, and then to fill my stomach, if I have one, but above all just to stanch this greedy dirty thirst, but not hard enough to slow him down.

He swooned and fought, and did the stupid thing of tearing at my fingers, and then the most dangerous and clumsy thing of trying to find my eyes. I shut them tight and let him press with his greasy thumbs. It did him no good. I am an impregnable little boy. You can not blind the blind. I was too full of blood to care. Besides it felt good. Those weak things that would scratch you do only stroke you.

His life went by as if everyone he ever loved were riding a roller coaster under snazzy stars. Worse than a Van Gogh painting. You never know the palette of the one you kill until the mind disgorges its finest colors.

Soon enough he sank down. I went with him. I had my left arm all the way around him now, and I lay childlike against his big muscular belly, and I drew the blood out now in the blindest gushes, pressing everything he thought and saw and felt down into only color, just give me color, pure orange, and just for a second, as he died—as the death passed me by, like a big rolling ball of black strength which turns out to be nothing actually, nothing but smoke or something even less than that—as this death came into me and went out again like the wind, I thought, Do I by crushing everything that he is deprive him of a final knowing?

Nonsense, Armand. You know what the spirits know, what the angels know. The bastard is going home! To Heaven. To Heaven that would not have you, and might never.

In death, he looked most excellent.

I sat beside him. I wiped my mouth, not that there was a drop to wipe. Vampires slobber blood only in motion pictures. Even the most mundane immortal is far too skilled to spill a drop. I wiped my mouth because his sweat was on my lips and on my face, and I wanted it to go away.

I admired him, however, that he was big and wondrously hard for all his seeming roundness. I admired the black hair clinging to his wet chest where the shirt had been so inevitably torn away.

His black hair was something to behold. I ripped the knotted cloth that tied it. It was as full and thick as a woman's hair.

Making sure he was dead, I wrapped its length around my left hand and purposed to pull the whole mass from his scalp.

David gasped. "Must you do this?" he asked me.

"No," I said. Even then a few thousand strands had ripped loose from the scalp, each with only its tiny blooded root winking in the air like a tiny firefly. I held the mop for a moment and then let it slip out of my fingers and fall down behind his turned head.

Those unanchored hairs fell sloppily over his coarse cheek. His eyes were wet and wakeful-seeming, dying jelly.

David turned and went out into the little street. Cars roared and clattered by. A ship on the river sang with a steam calliope.

I came up behind him. I wiped the dust off me. One blow and I could have set the whole house to falling down, just caving in on the putrid filth within, dying softly amid other houses so no one indoors here would even know, all this moist wood merely caving.

I could not get the taste and smell of this sweat gone.

"Why did you so object to my pulling out his hair?" I asked. "I only wanted to have it, and he's dead and beyond caring and no one else will miss his black hair."

He turned with a sly smile and took my measure.

"You frighten me, the way you look," I said. "Have I so carelessly revealed myself to be a monster? You know, my blessed mortal Sybelle, when she is not playing the Sonata by Beethoven called the *Appassionata*, watches me feed all the time. Do you want me to tell my story now?"

I glanced back at the dead man on his side, his shoulder sagging. On the windowsill beyond and above him stood a blue glass bottle and in it was an orange flower. Isn't that the damnedest thing?

"Yes, I do want your story," David said. "Come, let's go back together. I only asked you not to take his hair for one reason."

"Yes?" I asked. I looked at him. Rather genuine curiosity. "What was the reason then? I was only going to pull out all his hair and throw it away."

"Like pulling off the wings of a fly," he offered seemingly without judgment.

"A dead fly," I said. I deliberately smiled. "Come now, why the fuss?"

"I wanted to see if you'd listen to me," he said. "That's all. Because if you did then it might be all right between us. And you stopped. And it is." He turned around and took my arm.

"I don't like you!" I said.

"Oh, yes, you do, Armand," he answered. "Let me write it. Pace and rail and rant. You're very high and mighty right now because you have those two splendid little mortals hanging on your every gesture, and they're like acolytes to a god. But you want to tell me the story, you know you do. Come on!"

I couldn't stop myself from laughing. "Have these tactics worked for you in the past?"

Now it was his turn to laugh and he did, good-naturedly. "No, I suppose not," he said. "But let me put it to you this way, write it for them."

"For whom?"

"For Benji and Sybelle." He shrugged. "No?"

I didn't answer.

Write the story for Benji and Sybelle. My mind raced forwards, to some cheerful and wholesome room, where we three would be gathered years hence—I, Armand, unchanged, boy teacher—and Benji and Sybelle in their mortal prime, Benji grown into a sleek tall gentleman with an Arab's ink-eyed allure and his favorite cheroot in his hand, a man of great expectation and opportunity, and my Sybelle, a curvaceous and full regal-bodied woman by then, and an even greater concert pianist than she could be now, her golden hair framing a woman's oval face and fuller womanish lips and eyes full of *entsagang* and secret radiance.

Could I dictate the story in this room and give them the book? This book dictated to David Talbot? Could I, as I set them free from my alchemical world, give them this book? Go forth my children, with all the wealth and guidance I could bestow, and now this book I wrote so long ago for you with David.

Yes, said my soul. Yet I turned, and ripped the black scalp of hair from my victim and stomped on it with a Rumpelstiltskin foot.

David didn't flinch. Englishmen are so polite.

"Very well," I said. "I'll tell you my story."

His rooms were on the second floor, not far from where I'd paused at the top of the staircase. What a change from the barren and unheated hallways! He'd made a library for himself and with tables and chairs. A brass bed was there, dry and clean.

"These are her rooms," he said. "Don't you remember?"

"Dora," I said. I breathed her scent suddenly. Why, it was all around me. But all her personal things were gone.

These were his books, they had to be. They were new spiritual explorers—Dannion Brinkley, Hilarion, Melvin Morse, Brian Weiss, Matthew Fox, the Urantia book. Add to this old texts—Cassiodorus, St. Teresa of Avila, Gregory of Tours, the Veda, Talmud, Torah, Kama Sutra—all in original tongues. He had a few obscure novels, plays, poetry.

"Yes." He sat down at the table. "I don't need the light. Do you want it?"

"I don't know what to tell you."

"Ah," he said. He took out his mechanical pen. He opened a notebook with startlingly white paper scored with fine green lines. "You will know what to tell me." He looked up at me.

I stood hugging myself, as it were, letting my head fall as if it could drop right off me and I would die. My hair fell long about me.

I thought of Sybelle and Benjamin, my quiet girl and exuberant boy.

"Did you like them, David, my children?" I asked.

"Yes, the first moment I saw them, when you brought them in. Everyone did. Everyone looked lovingly and respectfully at them. Such poise, such charm. I think we all dream of such confidants, faithful mortal companions of compelling grace, who aren't screaming mad. They love you, yet they are neither terrified nor entranced."

I didn't move. I didn't speak. I shut my eyes. I heard in my heart the swift, bold march of the *Appassionata*, those rumbling, incandescent waves of music, full of throbbing and brittle metal, *Appassionata*. Only it was in my head. No golden long-limbed Sybelle.

"Light the candles that you have," I said timidly. "Will you do that for me? It would be sweet to have many candles, and look, Dora's lace is hanging still on the windows, fresh and clean. I am a lover of lace, that is Brussels point de gaze, or very like it, yes, I'm rather mad for it."

"Of course, I'll light the candles," he said.

I had my back to him. I heard the sharp delicious crack of a small wooden match. I smelt it burn, and then came the liquid fragrance of the nodding wick, the curling wick, and the light rose upwards, finding the cypress boards of the stripped wooden ceiling above us. Another crack, another series of tiny sweet soft crackling sounds, and the light swelled and came down over me and fell just short of brightness along the shadowy wall.

"Why did you do it, Armand?" he said. "Oh, the Veil has Christ on it, in some form, no doubt of it, it did seem to be the Holy Veil of Veronica, and God knows, thousands of others believed it, yes, but why in your case, why? It was blazingly beautiful, yes, I grant you that, Christ with His thorns and His blood, and His eyes gazing right at us, both of us, but why did you believe it so completely, Armand, after so long? Why did you go to Him? That's what you tried to do, didn't you?"

I shook my head. I made my words soft and pleading.

"Back up, scholar," I said, turning around slowly. "Mind your page. This is for you, and for Sybelle. Oh, it's for my little Benji too. But in a way, it's my symphony for Sybelle. The story begins a long time ago. Maybe I've never truly realized how long ago, until this very moment. You listen and write. Let me be the one to cry and to rant and to rail."

2

I LOOK AT MY HANDS. I think of the phrase "not made by human hands." I know what this means, even though every time I ever heard the phrase said with emotion it had to do with what had come from my hands.

I'd like to paint now, to pick up a brush and try it the way I did it then, in a trance, furiously, once and for only, every line and mass of color, each blending, each decision final.

Ah, I'm so disorganized, so browbeaten by what I remember.

Let me choose a place to begin.

Constantinople—newly under the Turks, by that I mean a Moslem City for less than a century when I was brought there, a slave boy, captured in the wild lands of his country for which he barely knew the proper name: the Golden Horde.

Memory had already been choked out of me, along with language, or any capacity to reason in a consistent way. I remember the squalid rooms that must have been Constantinople because other people talked, and for the first time in forever, since I'd been ripped out of what I couldn't remember, I could understand what people said.

They spoke Greek, of course, these traders who dealt in slaves for brothels in Europe. They knew no religious allegiance, which was all I knew, pitifully devoid of detail.

I was thrown down on a thick Turkey carpet, the fancified rich floor covering one saw in a palace, a display rug for high-priced goods.

My hair was wet and long; someone had brushed it enough to hurt me. All those personal things that were mine had been stripped from me and from my memory. I was naked beneath an old frayed tunic of gold cloth. It was hot and damp in the room. I was hungry, but having no hope of food, I knew this to be a pain that would spike and then, of its own, die away. The tunic must have given me a castoff glory, the shimmer of a fallen angel. It had long bell sleeves and came to my knees.

When I got to my feet, which were bare of course, I saw these men and knew what they wanted, that this was vice, and despicable, and the price of it was Hell. Curses of vanished elders echoed down on me: too pretty, too soft, too pale, eyes far too full of the Devil, ah, the devilish smile.

How intent these men were on their argument, their bargaining. How they looked at me without ever looking into my eyes.

Suddenly I laughed. Things here were being done so hastily. Those who had delivered me had left me. Those who had scrubbed me had never left the tubs. I was a bundle thrown down on the carpet.

For one moment, I had an awareness of myself as having been sharp-tongued once and cynical, and keenly aware of the nature of men in general. I laughed because these merchants thought I was a girl.

I waited, listening, catching these bits and pieces of talk.

We were in a broad room, with a low canopied ceiling, the silk of it sewn with tiny mirrors and the curlicues so loved by the Turks, and the lamps, though smoky, were scented and filled the air with a dusky hazy soot that burned my eyes.

The men in their turbans and caftans weren't unfamiliar to me any more than the language. But I only caught dashes of what they said. My eyes looked for an escape. There was none. There were heavy, brooding men slouching near the entrances. A man far off at a desk used an abacus for counting. He had piles and piles of gold coins.

One of the men, a tall lean one, all cheekbones and jaw, with rotted-out teeth, came towards me and felt of my shoulders and my neck. Then he lifted up the tunic. I stood stock-still, not enraged or consciously fearful, merely paralyzed. This was the land of the Turks, and I knew what they did to boys. Only I had never seen a picture, nor heard a real story of it, or known anyone who had ever really lived in it, penetrated it and come back home.

Home. Surely I must have wanted to forget who I was. I must have. Shame must have made it mandatory. But at that moment, in the tentlike room with its flowered carpet, among the merchants and slave traders, I strained to remember as if, discovering a map in myself, I could follow it out of here and back to where I belonged.

I did recollect the grasslands, the wild lands, lands where you don't go, except for—. But that was a blank. I'd been in the grasslands, defying fate, stupidly but not unwillingly. I'd been carrying something of the utmost importance. I got off my horse, ripped this big bundle loose from the leather harness and ran with the bundle clutched against my chest.

"The trees!" he shouted, but who was he?

I knew what he had meant, however, that I had to reach the copse and put this treasure there, this splendid and magical thing that was inside the bundle, "not made by human hands."

I never got that far. When they grabbed hold of me, I dropped the bundle and they didn't even go after it, at least not as I saw. I thought, as I was hoisted into the air: It isn't supposed to be found like that, wrapped in cloth like that. It has to be placed in the trees.

They must have raped me on the boat because I don't remember coming to Constantinople. I don't remember being hungry, cold, outraged or afraid.

Now here for the first time, I knew the particulars of rape, the stinking grease, the squabbling, the curses over the ruin of the lamb. I felt a hideous unsupportable powerlessness.

Loathsome men, men against God and against nature.

I made a roar like an animal at the turbaned merchant, and he struck me hard on the ear so that I fell to the ground. I lay still looking up at him with all the contempt I could bring into my gaze. I didn't get up, even when he kicked me. I wouldn't speak.

Thrown over his shoulder I was carried out, taken through a crowded courtyard, past wondrous stinking camels and donkeys and heaps of filth, out by the harbor where the ships waited, over the gangplank and into the ship's hold.

It was filth again, the smell of hemp, the rustling of the rats on board. I was thrown on a pallet of rough cloth. Once again, I looked for the escape and saw only the ladder by which we'd descended and above heard the voices of too many men.

It was still dark when the ship began to move. Within an hour I was so sick, I wanted simply to die. I curled up on the floor and lay as still as possible, hiding myself entirely under the soft clinging fabric of the old tunic. I slept for the longest time.

When I awoke an old man was there. He wore a different style of dress, less frightening to me than that of the turbaned Turks, and his eyes were kindly. He bent near me. He spoke a new language which was uncommonly soft and sweet, but I couldn't understand him.

A voice speaking Greek told him that I was a mute, had no wits and growled like a beast.

Time to laugh again, but I was too sick.

The same Greek told the old man I hadn't been torn or wounded. I was marked at a high price.

The old man made some dismissing gestures as he shook his head and talked a song in the new speech. He laid his hands on me and gently coaxed me to my feet.

He took me through a doorway into a small chamber, draped all in red silk.

I spent the rest of the voyage in this chamber, except for one night.

On that one night—and I can't place it in terms of the journey—I awoke, and finding him asleep beside me, this old man who never touched me except to pat or console me, I went out, up the ladder, and stood for a long time looking up at the stars.

We were at anchor in a port, and a city of dark blue-black buildings with domed roofs and bell towers tumbled down the cliffs to the harbor where the torches turned beneath the ornamented arches of an arcade.

All this, the civilized shore, looked probable to me, appealing, but I had no thought that I could jump ship and get free. Men wandered beneath the archways. Beneath the arch nearest to me, a strangely garbed man in a shiny helmet, with a big broad sword dangling on his hip, stood guard against the branching fretted column, carved so marvelously to look like a tree as it supported the cloister, like the remnant of a palace into which this channel for ships had been rudely dug.

I didn't look at the shore much after this first long and memorable glimpse. I looked up at Heaven and her court of mythical creatures fixed forever in the all powerful and inscrutable stars. Ink black was the night beyond them, and they so like jewels that old poetry came back to me, the sound even of hymns sung only by men.

As I recall it, hours passed before I was caught, beaten fiercely with a leather thong and dragged back down in the hold. I knew the beating would stop when the old man saw me. He was furious and trembling. He gathered me to him, and we bedded down again. He was too old to ask anything of me.

I didn't love him. It was clear to the witless mute that this man regarded him as something quite valuable, to be preserved for sale. But I needed him and he wiped my tears. I slept as much as I could. I was sick every time the waves were rough. Sometimes the heat alone sickened me. I didn't know real heat. The man fed me so well that sometimes I thought I was a being kept by him like a fatted calf to be sold for food.

When we reached Venice, it was late in the day. I had no hint of the beauty of Italy. I'd been locked away from it, down in this grime pit with the old keeper, and being taken up into the city I soon saw that my suspicions about the old keeper were perfectly right.

In a dark room, he and another man fell into bitter argument. Nothing could make me speak. Nothing could make me indicate that I understood anything that was happening to me. I did, however, understand. Money changed hands. The old man left without looking back.

They tried to teach me things. The soft caressing new language was all around me. Boys came, sat beside me, tried to coax me with soft kisses and embraces. They pinched the nipples on my chest and tried to touch the private parts which I'd been taught not even to look at on account of the bitter occasion of sin.

Several times I resolved to pray. But I discovered I couldn't remember the words. Even the images were indistinct. Lights had gone out forever which had guided me through all my years. Every time I drifted deep into thought, someone struck me or yanked at my hair.

They always came with ointments after they hit me. They were careful to treat the abraded skin. Once, when a man struck me on the side of the face, another shouted and grabbed his upraised hand before he could land the second blow.

I refused food and drink. They couldn't make me take it. I couldn't take it. I didn't choose to starve. I simply couldn't do anything to keep myself alive. I knew I was going home. I was going home. I would die and go home. It would be an awful painful passage. I would have cried if I'd been alone. But I was never alone. I'd have to die in front of people. I hadn't seen real daylight in forever. Even the lamps hurt my eyes because I was so much in unbroken darkness. But people were always there.

The lamp would brighten. They sat in a ring around me with grimy little faces and quick pawlike hands that wiped my hair out of my face or shook me by the shoulder. I turned my face to the wall.

A sound kept me company. This was to be the end of my life. The sound was the sound of water outside. I could hear it against the wall. I could tell when a boat passed and I could hear the wood pylons creaking, and I lay my head against the stone and felt the house sway in the water as if we were not beside it but planted in it, which of course we were.

Once I dreamed of home, but I don't remember what it was like. I woke, I cried, and there came a volley of little greetings from the shadows, wheedling, sentimental voices.

I thought I wanted to be alone. I didn't. When they locked me up for days and nights in a black room without bread or water, I began to scream and pound on the walls. No one came.

After a while, I fell into a stupor. It was a violent jolt when the door was opened. I sat up, covering my eyes. The lamp was a menace. My head throbbed.

But there came a soft insinuating perfume, a mixture of the smell of sweet burning wood in snowing winter and that of crushed flowers and pungent oil.

I was touched by something hard, something made of wood or brass, only this thing moved as if it were organic. At last I opened my eyes and saw that a man held me, and these inhuman things, these things that felt so like stone or brass, were his white fingers, and he looked at me with eager, gentle blue eyes.

"Amadeo," he said.

He was dressed all in red velvet and splendidly tall.

His blond hair was parted in the middle in a saintly fashion and combed richly down to his shoulders where it broke over his cloak in lustrous curls. He had a smooth forehead without a line to it, and high straight golden eyebrows dark enough to give his face a clear, determined look. His lashes curled like dark golden threads from his eyelids. And when he smiled, his lips were flushed suddenly with a pale immediate color that made their full careful shape all the more visible.

I knew him. I spoke to him. I could have never seen such miracles in the face of anyone else.

He smiled so kindly at me. His upper lip and chin were all clean shaven. I couldn't even see the scantest hair on him, and his nose was narrow and delicate though large enough to be in proportion to the other magnetic features of his face.

"Not the Christ, my child," he said. "But one who comes with his own salvation. Come into my arms."

"I'm dying, Master." What was my language? I can't say even now what it was. But he understood me.

"No, little one, you're not dying. You're coming now into my protection, and perhaps if the stars are with us, if they are kind to us, you'll never die at all."

"But you are the Christ. I know you!"

He shook his head, and in the most common human way he lowered his eyes as he did, and he smiled. His generous lips parted, and I saw only a human's white teeth. He put his hands beneath my arms, lifted me and kissed my throat, and the shivers paralyzed me. I closed my eyes and felt his fingers on top of them, and heard him say into my ear, "Sleep as I take you home."

When I awoke, we were in a huge bath. No Venetian

ever had such a bath as this, I can tell you that now from all the things I saw later, but what did I know of the conventions of this place? This was a palace truly; I had seen palaces.

I climbed up and out of the swaddling of velvet in which I lay—his red cloak if I'm not mistaken—and I saw a great curtained bed to my right and, beyond, the deep oval basin of the bath itself. Water poured from a shell held by angels into the basin, and steam rose from the broad surface, and in the steam my Master stood. His white chest was naked and the nipples faintly pink, and his hair, pushed back from his smooth straight forehead, looked even thicker and more beautifully blond than it had before.

He beckoned to me.

I was afraid of the water. I knelt at the edge and put my hand into it.

With amazing speed and grace, he reached for me and brought me down into the warm pool, pushing me until the water covered my shoulders and then tilting back my head.

Again I looked up at him. Beyond him the bright-blue ceiling was covered in startlingly vivid angels with giant white feathery wings. I had never seen such brilliant and curly angels, leaping as they did, out of all restraint and style, to flaunt their human beauty in muscled limbs and swirling garments, in flying locks. It seemed a bit of madness this, these robust and romping figures, this riot of celestial play above me to which the steam ascended, evaporating in a golden light.

I looked at my Master. His face was right before me. Kiss me again, yes, do it, that shiver, kiss—. But he was of the same ilk as those painted beings, one of them, and this some form of heathen Heaven, a pagan place of Soldiers' gods where all is wine, and fruit, and flesh. I had come to the wrong place.

He threw back his head. He gave way to ringing laughter. He lifted a handful of water again and let it spill down my chest. He opened his mouth and for a moment I saw the flash of something very wrong and dangerous, teeth such as a wolf might have. But these were gone, and only his lips sucked at my throat, then at my shoulder. Only his lips sucked at the nipple as I sought too late to cover it.

I groaned for all this. I sank against him in the warm water, and his lips went down my chest to my belly. He sucked tenderly at the skin as if he were sucking up the salt and the heat from it, and even his forehead nudging my shoulder filled me with warm thrilling sensations. I put my arm around him, and when he found the sin itself, I felt it go off as if an arrow had been shot from it, and it were a crossbow; I felt it go, this arrow, this thrust, and I cried out.

He let me lie for a while against him. He bathed me slowly. He had a soft gathered cloth with which he wiped my face. He dipped me back to wash my hair.

And then when he thought I had rested enough, we began the kisses again.

Before dawn, I woke against his pillow. I sat up and saw him as he put on his big cloak and covered his head. The room was full of boys again, but these were not the sad, emaciated tutors of the brothel. These boys were handsome, well fed, smiling and sweet, as they gathered around the bed.

They wore brightly colored tunics of effervescent colors, with fabrics carefully pleated and tight belts that gave them a girlish grace. All wore long luxuriant hair.

My Master looked at me and in a tongue I knew, I knew perfectly, he said that I was his only child, and he would come again that night, and by such time as that I would have seen a new world.

"A new world!" I cried out. "No, don't leave me, Master. I don't want the whole world. I want you!"

"Amadeo," he said in this private tongue of confidence, leaning over the bed, his hair dry now and beautifully brushed, his hands softened with powder. "You have me forever. Let the boys feed you, dress you." You belong to me, to Marius Romanus, now.

He turned to them and gave them their commands in the soft singing language.

And you would have thought from their happy faces that he had given them sweets and gold.

"Amadeo, Amadeo," they sang as they gathered around me. They held me so that I couldn't follow him. They spoke Greek to me, fast and easily, and Greek for me was not so easy. But I understood.

Come with us, you are one of us, we are to be good to you, we are to be especially good to you. They dressed me up hastily in castoffs, arguing with one another about my tunic, was it good enough, and these faded stockings, well, it was only for now! Put on the slippers; here, a jacket that was too small for Riccardo. These seemed the garments of kings.

"We love you," said Albinus, the second in command to Riccardo, and a dramatic contrast to the black-haired Riccardo, for his blond hair and pale green eyes.

The other boys, I couldn't quite distinguish, but these two were easy to watch.

"Yes, we love you," said Riccardo, pushing back his black hair and winking at me, his skin so smooth and dark compared to the others. His eyes were fiercely black. He clutched my hand and I saw his long thin fingers. Here everyone had thin fingers, fine fingers. They had fingers like mine, and mine had been unusual among my brethren. But I couldn't think of this.

And eerie possibility suggested itself to me, that I, the pale one, the one who made all the trouble, the one with the fine fingers, had been spirited away to the good land where I belonged. But that was altogether too fabulous to believe. My head ached. I saw wordless flashes of the stubby horsemen who had captured me, of the stinking hold of the ship in which I'd been brought to Constantinople, flashes of gaunt, busy men, men fussing as they had handled me there.

Dear God, why did anyone love me? What for? Marius Romanus, why do you love me?

The Master smiled as he waved from the door. The hood was up around his head, a crimson frame for his fine cheekbones and his curling lips.

My eyes filled with tears.

A white mist swirled around the Master as the door closed behind him. The night was going. But the candles still burned.

We came into a large room, and I saw that it was full of paints and pots of color and brushes standing in earthen jars ready to be used. Great white squares of cloth—canvas—waited for the paint.

These boys didn't make their colors with the yoke of an egg in the time-honored manner. They mixed the bright fine ground pigments directly with the amber-colored oils. Great glossy gobs of color awaited me in little pots. I took the brush when they gave it to me. I looked at the stretched white cloth on which I was to paint.

"Not from human hands," I said. But what did these words mean? I lifted the brush and I began to paint him, this blond-haired man who had rescued me from darkness and squalor. I threw out the hand with the brush, dipping the bristles into the jars of cream and pink and white and slapping these colors onto the curiously resilient canvas. But I couldn't make a picture. No picture came!

"Not by human hands!" I whispered. I dropped the brush. I put my hands over my face.

I searched for the words in Greek. When I said them, several of the boys nodded, but they didn't grasp the meaning. How could I explain to them the catastrophe? I looked at my fingers. What had become of—. There all recollection burnt up and I was left suddenly with Amadeo.

"I can't do it." I stared at the canvas, at the mess of colors. "Maybe if it was wood, not cloth, I could do it."

What had it been that I could do? They didn't understand.

He was not the Living Lord, my Master, the blond one, the blond one with the icy blue eyes.

But he was my Lord. And I could not do this thing that was meant to be done.

To comfort me, to distract me, the boys took up their brushes and quickly astonished me with pictures that ran like a stream out of their quick applications of the brush.

A boy's face, cheeks, lips, eyes, yes, and reddish-golden hair in profusion. Good Lord, it was I . . . it was not a canvas but a mirror. It was this Amadeo. Riccardo took over to refine the expression, to deepen the eyes and work a sorcery on the tongue so I seemed about to speak. What was this rampant magic that made a boy appear out of nothing, most natural, at a casual angle, with knitted brows and streaks of unkempt hair over his ear?

It seemed both blasphemous and beautiful, this fluid, abandoned fleshly figure.

Riccardo spelled the letters out in Greek as he wrote them. Then he threw the brush down. He cried:

"A very different picture is what our Master has in mind." He snatched up the drawings.

They pulled me through the house, the "palazzo" as they called it, teaching me the word with relish.

The entire place was filled with such paintings—on its walls, its ceilings, on panels and canvases stacked against each other—towering pictures full of ruined buildings, broken columns, rampant greenery, distant mountains and an endless stream of busy people with flushed faces, their luxuriant hair and gorgeous clothing always rumpled and curling in a wind.

It was like the big platters of fruit and meats that they brought out and set before me. A mad disorder, an abundance for the sake of itself, a great drench of colors and shapes. It was like the wine, too sweet and light.

*   *   *

IT WAS LIKE the city below when they threw open the windows, and I saw the small black boats—gondolas, even then—in brilliant sunlight coursing through the greenish waters, when I saw the men in their sumptuous scarlet or gold cloaks hurrying along the quays.

Into our gondolas we piled, a troop of us, and suddenly we traveled in graceful darting silence among the facades, each huge house as magnificent as a Cathedral, with its narrow pointed arches, its lotus windows, its covering of gleaming white stone.

Even the older, sorrier dwellings, not too ornate but nevertheless monstrous in size, were plastered in colors, a rose so deep it seemed to come from crushed petals, a green so thick it seemed to have been mixed from the opaque water itself.

Out into the Piazza San Marco we came, amid the long fantastically regular arcades on both sides.

It seemed the very gathering place of Heaven as I stared at the hundreds milling before the distant golden domes of the church.

Golden domes. Golden domes.

Some old tale had been told to me of golden domes, and I had seen them in a darkling picture, had I not? Sacred domes, lost domes, domes in flames, a church violated, as I had been violated. Ah, ruin, ruin was gone, laid waste by the sudden eruption all around me of what was vital and whole! How had all this been born out of wintry ashes? How had I died among snows and smoking fires and come to rise here beneath this caressing sun?

Its warm sweet light bathed beggars and tradesmen; it shone on princes passing with pages to carry their ornate velvet trains behind them, on the booksellers who spread their books beneath scarlet canopies, lute players who vied for small coins.

The wares of the wide diabolical world were displayed in the shops and market stalls—glassware such as I have never beheld, including goblets of all possible colors, not to mention little figurines of glass including animals and human beings and other filmy shining trinkets. There were marvelously bright and beautifully turned beads for rosaries; magnificent laces in grand and graceful patterns, including even snowy white pictures of actual church towers and little houses with windows and doors; great feathery plumes from birds I couldn't name; other exotic species flapping and screeching in gilt cages; and the finest and most magnificently worked multicolored carpets only too reminiscent of the powerful Turks and their capital from which I'd come. Nevertheless, who resists such carpets? Forbidden by law to render human beings, Moslems rendered flowers, arabesques, labyrinthian curlicues and other such designs with bold dyes and awe-inspiring exactitude. There were oils for lamps, tapers, candles, incense, and great displays of glistering jewels of indescribable beauty and the most delicate work of the goldsmiths and silversmiths, in plate and ornamental items both newly made and old. There were shops that sold only spices. There were shops that sold medicines and cures. There were bronze statues, lion heads, lanterns and weapons. There were cloth merchants with the silks of the East, the finest woven wools dyed in miraculous tints, cotton and linen and fine specimens of embroidery, and ribbons galore.

Men and women here appeared immensely wealthy, feasting casually on fresh meat tarts in the cookshops, drinking clear red wine and eating sweet cakes full of cream.

There were booksellers offering the new printed books, of which the other apprentices told me eagerly, explaining the marvelous invention of the printing press, which had only lately made it possible for men far and wide to acquire not only books of letters and words but books of drawn pictures as well.

Venice already had dozens of small print shops and publishers where the presses were hard at work producing books in Greek as well as Latin, and in the vernacular tongue—the soft singing tongue—which the apprentices spoke amongst themselves.

They let me stop to glut my eyes on these wonders, these machines that made pages for books.

But they did have their chores, Riccardo and the others—they were to scoop up the prints and engravings of the German painters for our Master, pictures made by the new printing presses of old wonders by Memling, Van Eyck, or Hieronymus Bosch. Our Master was always in the market for them. Such drawings brought the north to the south. Our Master was a champion of such wonders. Our Master was pleased that over one hundred printing presses filled our city, that he could throw away his coarse inaccurate copies of Livy and Virgil and have now corrected printed texts.

Oh, it was such a load of information.

And no less important than the literature or paintings of the universe was the matter of my clothes. We had to get the tailors to stop everything to dress me properly according to small chalk drawings which the Master had made.

Handwritten letters of credit had to be taken to the banks. I was to have money. Everyone was to have money. I had never touched such a thing as money.

Money was pretty—Florentine gold or silver, German florins, Bohemian groschens, fancy old coins minted under the rulers of Venice who were called the Doges, exotic coins from the Constantinople of old. I was given a little sack of my own clinking clanking money. We tied our "purses" to our belts.

One of the boys bought me a small wonder because I stared at it. It was a ticking watch. I couldn't grasp the theory of it, this tiny ticking thing, all encrusted with jewels, and not all the hands pointed at the sky would teach me. At last with a shock I realized: It was, beneath its filigree and paint, its strange glass and bejeweled frame, a tiny clock!

I closed my hand on it and felt dizzy. I had never known clocks to be anything but great venerable things in bell towers or on walls.

"I carry time now," I whispered in Greek, looking to my friends.

"Amadeo," said Riccardo. "Count the hours for me."

I wanted to say that this prodigious discovery meant something, something personal. It was a message to me from some other too hastily and perilously forgotten world. Time was not time anymore and never would be. The day was not the day, nor the night the night. I couldn't articulate it, not in Greek, nor any tongue, nor even in my feverish thoughts. I wiped the sweat from my forehead. I squinted into the brilliant sun of Italy. My eyes clapped upon the birds who flew in great flocks across the sky, like tiny pen strokes made to flap in unison. I think I whispered foolishly, "We are in the world."

"We are in the center of it, the greatest city of it!" Riccardo cried, urging me on into the crowds. "We shall see it before we get locked up in the tailor's, that's for damned sure."

But first it was time for the sweetshop, for the miracle of chocolate with sugar, for syrupy concoctions of unnameable but bright red and yellow sweets.

One of the boys showed to me his little book of the most frightening printed pictures, men and women embraced in carnality. It was the stories of Boccaccio. Riccardo said he would read them to me, that it was in fact an excellent book to teach me Italian. And that he would teach me Dante too.

Boccaccio and Dante were Florentines, said one of the other boys, but all in all the two weren't so bad.

Our Master loved all kinds of books, I was told, you couldn't go wrong spending your money on them, he was always pleased with that. I'd come to see that the teachers who came to the house would drive me crazy with their lessons. It was the *studia humanitatis* that we must all learn, and it included history, grammar, rhetoric, philosophy and ancient authors . . . all of this so much dazzling words that only revealed its meaning to me as it was often repeated and demonstrated in the days to come.

We could not look too good for our Master either, that was another lesson I must learn. Gold and silver chains, necklaces with medallions and other such trinkets were bought for me and laid over my neck. I needed rings, jeweled rings. We had to bargain fiercely with the jewelers for these, and I came out of it wearing a real emerald from the new world, and two ruby rings carved with silver inscriptions which I couldn't read.

I couldn't get over the sight of my hand with a ring. To this very night of my life, some five hundred years after, you see, I have a weakness for jeweled rings. Only during those centuries in Paris when I was a penitent, one of Satan's discalced Children of the Night, during that long slumber only, did I give up my rings. But we'll come to that nightmare soon enough.

For now, this was Venice, I was Marius's child and romped with his other children in a manner that would be repeated for years ahead.

On to the tailor.

As I was measured and pinned and dressed, the boys told me stories of all those rich Venetians who came to our Master seeking to have even the smallest piece of his work. As for our Master, he, claiming that he was too wretched, sold almost nothing but occasionally did a portrait of a woman or man who struck his eye. These portraits almost always worked the person into a mythological subject—gods, goddesses, angels, saints. Names I knew and names I'd never heard of tripped off the boys' tongues. It seemed here all echoes of sacred things were swept up in a new tide.

Memory would jolt me only to release me. Saints and gods, they were one and the same? Wasn't there a code to which I should remain faithful that somehow dictated these were but artful lies? I couldn't get it clear in my head, and all around me was such happiness, yes, happiness. It seemed impossible that these simple shining faces could mask wickedness. I didn't believe it. Yet all pleasure to me was suspect. I was dazzled when I could not give in, and overcome when I did surrender, and as the days followed I surrendered with ever greater ease all the time.

This day of initiation was only one of hundreds, nay, thousands that were to follow, and I don't know when I started to understand with any preciseness what my boy companions said. That time came, however, and rather quickly. I do not remember being the naive one very long.

On this first excursion, it was magic. And high above the sky was the perfect blue of cobalt, and the breeze from the sea was fresh and moist and cool. There above were massed the scudding clouds I had seen so wondrously rendered in the paintings of the palazzo, and there came my first hint that the paintings of my Master were no lie.

Indeed when we entered, by special permission, the Doges' chapel, San Marco, I was caught by the throat by its splendor—its walls of gleaming tessellated gold. But another shock followed hard upon my finding myself virtually entombed in light and in riches. Here were stark, somber figures, figures of saints I knew.

These were no mystery to me, the almond-eyed tenants of these hammered walls, severe in their straight careful drapery, their hands infallibly folded in prayer. I knew their halos, I knew the tiny holes made in the gold to make it glitter ever more magically. I knew the judgment of these bearded patriarchs who gazed impassively on me as I stopped, dead in my tracks, unable to go on.

I slumped to the stone floor. I was sick.

I had to be taken from the church. The noise of the piazza rose over me as if I were descending to some awful denouement. I wanted to tell my friends it was inevitable, not their fault.

The boys were in a fluster. I couldn't explain it. Stunned, sweating all over and lying limp at the base of a column, I listened dully as they explained to me in Greek that this church was only part of all I had seen. Why should it frighten me so? Yes, it was old, yes, it was Byzantine, as so much in Venice was. "Our ships have traded with Byzantium for centuries. We are a maritime empire." I tried to grasp it.

What came clear in my pain was only that this place had not been a special judgment upon me. I had been taken from it as easily as I had been brought into it. The sweet-voiced boys with the gentle hands who surrounded me, who offered me cool wine to drink and fruit to eat that I might recover, they did not hold this place in any terrible dread.

Turning to the left of me, I glimpsed the quays, the harbor. I ran towards it, thunderstruck by the sight of the wooden ships. They stood at anchor four and five deep, but beyond them was enacted the greatest miracle: great galleons of deep ballooning wood, their sails collecting the breeze, their graceful oars chopping the water as they moved out to sea.

Back and forth the traffic moved, the huge wooden barks dangerously close to one another, slipping in and out of the mouth of Venice, while others no less graceful and impossible at anchor disgorged abundant goods.

Leading me stumbling to the Arsenale, my companions comforted me with the sight of the ships being built by ordinary men. In days to come I would hang about at the Arsenale for hours, watching the ingenious process by which human beings made such immense barks that to my mind should rightly sink.

Now and then in snatches I saw images of icy rivers, of barges and flatboats, of coarse men reeking of animal fat and rancid leather. But these last ragged tidbits of the winter world from which I'd come faded.

Perhaps had this not been Venice, it would have been a different tale.

In all my years in Venice, I never tired of the Arsenale, of watching the ships being built. I had no problem gaining access by means of a few kind words and coins, and it was ever my delight to watch these fantastical structures being constructed of bowed ribs, bent wood and piercing masts. Of this first day, we were rushed through this yard of miracles. It was enough.

Yes, well, it was Venice, this place that must erase from my mind, at least for a while, the clotted torment of some earlier existence, some congestion of all truths I would not face.

My Master would never have been there, had it not been Venice.

Not a month later he would tell me matter-of-factly what each of the cities of Italy had to offer him, how he loved to watch Michelangelo, the great sculptor, hard at work in Florence, how he went to listen to the fine teachers in Rome.

"But Venice has an art of a thousand years," he said as he himself lifted his brush to paint the huge panel before him. "Venice is in itself a work of art, a metropolis of impossible domestic temples built side by side like waxen honeycombs and maintained in ever flowing nectar by a population as busy as bees. Behold our palaces, they alone are worthy of the eye."

As time passed he would school me in the history of Venice, as did the others, dwelling on the nature of the Republic, which, though despotic in its decisions and fiercely hostile to the outsider, was nevertheless a city of "equal" men. Florence, Milan, Rome—these cities were falling under the power of small elites or powerful families and individuals, while Venice, for all her faults, remained governed by her Senators, her powerful merchants and her Council of Ten.

On that first day, an everlasting love for Venice was born in me. It seemed singularly devoid of horrors, a warm home even for its well-dressed and clever beggars, a hive of prosperity and vehement passion as well as staggering wealth.

And in the tailor shop, was I not being made up into a prince like my new friends?

Look, had I not seen Riccardo's sword? They were all noblemen.

"Forget all that has gone before," said Riccardo. "Our Master is our Lord, and we are his princes, we are his royal court. You are rich now and nothing can hurt you."

"We are not mere apprentices in the ordinary sense," said Albinus. "We are to be sent to the University of Padua. You'll see. We are tutored in music and dance and manners as regularly as in science and literature. You will have time to see the boys who come back to visit, all gentlemen of means. Why, Giuliano was a prosperous lawyer, and one of the other boys was a physician in Torcello, an island city nearby.

"But all have independent means when they leave the Master," explained Albinus. "It's only that the Master, like all Venetians, deplores idleness. We are as well off as lazy lords from abroad who do nothing but sample our world as though it were a dish of food."

By the end of this first sunlighted adventure, this welcome into the bosom of my Master's school and his splendid city, I was combed, trimmed and dressed in the colors he would forever choose for me, sky blue for the stockings, a darker midnight blue velvet for a short belted jacket, and a tunic of an even fairer shade of azure embroidered with tiny French fleur-de-lis in thick gold thread. A bit of burgundy there might be for trimming and fur; for when the sea breezes grew strong in winter, this paradise would be what these Italians called cold.

By nightfall, I pranced on the marble tile with the others, dancing for a while to the lutes played by the younger boys, accompanied by the fragile music of the Virginal, the first keyboard instrument I had ever seen.

When the last of twilight had died beautifully into the canal outside the narrow pointed arched windows of the palazzo, I roamed about, catching random glances of myself in the many dark mirrors that rose up from the marble tile to the very ceiling of the corridor, the salon, the alcove, or whatever beautifully appointed room I should find.

I sang new words in unison with Riccardo. The great state of Venice was called the Serenissima. The black boats of the canals were gondolas. The winds that would come soon to make us all crazy were called the Sirocco. The most high ruler of this magical city was the Doge, our book tonight with the teacher was Cicero, the musical instrument which Riccardo gathered up and played with his plucking fingers was the lute. The great canopy of the Master's regal bed was a baldaquin trimmed each fortnight with new gold fringe.

I was ecstatic.

I had not merely a sword but a dagger.

Such trust. Of course I was lamblike to these others, and pretty much a lamb to myself. But never had anyone entrusted to me such bronze and steel weapons. Again, memory played its tricks. I knew how to throw a wooden spear, how to . . . Alas, it became a wisp of smoke, and there lay in the air around it that I'd been committed not to weapons, but to something else, something immense which exacted all I could give it. Weapons were forbidden for me.

Well, no more. No more, no more, no more. Death had swallowed me whole and thrown me forth here. In the palazzo of my Master, in a salon of brilliantly painted battle scenes, with maps upon the ceiling, with windows of thick molded glass, I drew my sword with a great singing sound and pointed it at the future. With my dagger, after examining the emeralds and rubies of its handle, I sliced an apple in two with a gasp.

The other boys laughed at me. But it was all friendly, kind.

Soon the Master would come. Look. From room to room the youngest fellows among us, little boys who had not come out with us, now moved quickly, lifting their tapers to torches and candelabra. I stood in the door, looking to yet another and another and another. Light burst forth soundlessly in each of these rooms.

A tall man, very shadowy and plain, came in with a tattered book in his hand. His long thin hair and plain wool robe were black. His small eyes were cheerful, but his thin mouth was colorless and belligerently set.

The boys all groaned.

High narrow windows were closed against the cooler night air.

In the canal below, men sang as they drove their long narrow gondolas, voices seeming to ring, to splash up the walls, delicate, sparkling, then dying away.

I ate the apple to the last juicy speck of it. I had eaten more in this day of fruit, meat, bread, sweets and candy than a human being could possibly eat. I wasn't human. I was a hungry boy.

The teacher snapped his fingers, then took from his belt a long switch and cracked it against his own leg. "Come now," he said to the boys.

I looked up as the Master appeared.

All the boys, big and tall, babyfied and manly, ran to him and embraced him and clung to his arms as he made his inspection of the painting they had done by the long day.

The teacher waited in silence, giving the Master a humble bow.

Through the galleries we walked, the entire company, the teacher trailing behind.

The Master held out his hands, and it was a privilege to feel the touch of his cold white fingers, a privilege to catch a part of his long thick trailing red sleeves.

"Come, Amadeo, come with us."

I wanted one thing only, and it came soon enough.

They were sent off with the man who was to read Cicero. The Master's firm hands with their flashing fingernails turned me and directed me to his private rooms.

It was private here, the painted wooden doors at once bolted, the burning braziers scented with incense, perfumed smoke rising from the brass lamps. It was the soft pillows of the bed, a flower garden of stenciled and embroidered silk, floral satin, rich chenille, intricately patterned brocade. He pulled the scarlet bed curtains. The light made them transparent. Red and red and red. It was his color, he told me, as blue was to be mine.

In a universal tongue he wooed me, feeding me the images:

"Your brown eyes are amber when the fire catches them," he whispered. "Oh, but they are lustrous and dark, two glossy mirrors in which I see myself even as they keep their secrets, these dark portals of a rich soul."

I was too lost in the frigid blue of his own eyes, and the smooth gleaming coral of his lips.

He lay with me, kissed me, pushing his fingers carefully and smoothly through my hair, never pulling a curl of it, and brought the shivers from my scalp and from between my legs. His thumbs, so hard and cold, stroked my cheeks, my lips, my jaw so as to make the flesh quicken. Turning my head from right to left, he pressed his half-formed kisses with a dainty hunger to the inner shells of my ears.

I was too young for a wet pleasure.

I wonder if it was more what women feel. I thought it couldn't end. It became an agony of rapture, being caught in his hands, unable to escape, convulsing and twisting and feeling this ecstasy again and again and again.

He taught me words in the new language afterwards, the word for the cold hard tile on the floor which was Carrara marble, the word for the curtains which was spun silk, the names of the "fishes" and "turtles" and the "elephants" embroidered onto the pillows, the word for the lion sewn in tapestry on the heavy coverlet itself.

As I listened, rapt, to all details both large and small, he told me the provenance of the pearls sewn into my tunic, of how they had come from the oysters of the sea. Boys had dived into the depths to bring these precious round white treasures up to the surface, carrying them in their very mouths. Emeralds came from mines within the earth. Men killed for them. And diamonds, ah, look at these diamonds. He took a ring from his finger and put it on mine, his fingertips stroking my finger gently as he made sure of the fit. Diamonds are the white light of God, he said. Diamonds are pure.

God. What is God! The shock went through my body. It seemed the scene about me would wither.

He watched me as he spoke, and it seemed now and then I heard him clearly, though he had not moved his lips or made a sound.

I grew agitated. God, don't let me think of God. Be my God.

"Give me your mouth, give me your arms," I whispered. My hunger startled and delighted him.

He laughed softly as he answered me with more fragrant and harmless kisses. His warm breath came in a soft whistling flood against my groin.

"Amadeo, Amadeo, Amadeo," he said.

"What does this name mean, Master?" I asked. "Why do you give it to me?" I think I heard an old self in my voice, but maybe it was only this newborn princeling gilded and wrapped in fine goods that had chosen this soft respectful but nevertheless bold voice.

"Beloved of God," he said.

Oh, I couldn't bear to hear this. God, the inescapable God. I was troubled, panic-stricken.

He took my outstretched hand and bent my finger to point to a tiny winged infant etched in glittering beads on a worn square cushion that lay beside us. "Amadeo," he said, "beloved of the God of love."

He found the ticking watch in the heap of my clothes at bedside. He picked it up and smiled as he looked at it. He had not seen many of these at all. Most marvelous. They were expensive enough for Kings and Queens.

"You shall have everything you want," he said.

"Why?"

Again came his laughter in answer.

"For reddish locks such as these," he said caressing my hair, "for eyes of the deepest and most sympathetic brown. For skin like the fresh cream of the milk in the morning; for lips indistinguishable from the petals of a rose."

In the small hours, he told me tales of Eros and Aphrodite; he lulled me with the fantastic sorrow of Psyche, beloved by Eros and never allowed to see him by the day's light.

I walked beside him through chilly corridors, his fingers clasping my shoulders, as he showed me the fine white marble statues of his gods and goddesses, all lovers—Daphne, her graceful limbs turned into the branches of the laurel as the god Apollo desperately sought her; Leda helpless within the grip of the mighty swan.

He guided my hands over the marble curves, the sharply chiseled and highly polished faces, the taut calves of nubile legs, the ice-cold clefts of half-opened mouths. And then to his own face he lifted my fingers. He did seem the very living and breathing statue, more marvelously made than any other, and even as he lifted me with powerful hands, a great heat came out of him, a heat of sweet breath in sighs and murmured words.

By the end of the week, I couldn't even remember one word of my Mother Tongue.

In a storm of proffered adjectives I stood in the piazza and watched spellbound as the Great Council of Venice marched along the Molo, as the High Mass was sung from the altar of San Marco, as the ships moved out on the glassy waves of the Adriatic, as the brushes dipped to gather up their colors and mix them in the earthen pots—rose madder, vermilion, carmine, cerise, cerulean, turquoise, viridian, yellow ocher, burnt umber, quinacridone, citrine, sepia, Caput Mortuum Violet— oh, too lovely—and of a thick lacquer, the name Dragon's blood.

At dancing and fencing, I excelled. My favorite partner was Riccardo, and I fast realized I was close to this elder in all skills, even surpassing Albinus, who had held that place until I came, though now he showed me no ill will.

These boys were like my brothers to me.

They took me to the home of the slender and

beautiful courtesan, Bianca Solderini, a lithesome and incomparable charmer, with Botticelli-style wavy locks and almond-shaped gray eyes and a generous and kindly wit. I was the fashion in her house whenever I wanted to be, among the young women and men there who spent hours reading poetry, talking of the foreign wars, which seemed endless, and of the latest painters and who would get what commission next.

Bianca had a small, childlike voice which matched her girlish face and tiny nose. Her mouth was a mere budding rose. But she was clever, and indomitable. She turned away possessive lovers coldly; she preferred that her house be full of people at all hours. Anyone in proper dress, or carrying a sword, was admitted automatically. Almost no one but those who wanted to own her were ever turned away.

Visitors from France and Germany were common at the home of Bianca, and all there, both from afar and from home, were curious about our Master, Marius, a man of mystery, though we had been schooled never to answer idle questions about him, and could only smile when asked if he intended to marry, if he would paint this or that portrait, if he would be home on such and such a date for this person or that to call.

Sometimes I fell asleep on the pillows of the couch at Bianca's or even on one of the beds, listening to the hushed voices of the noblemen who came there, dreaming to the music which was always of the most lulling and soothing kind.

Now and then, on the most rare occasions, the Master himself appeared there to collect me and Riccardo, always causing a minor sensation in the portego, or main salon. He would never take a chair. He stood always with his hooded cloak over his head and shoulders. But he smiled graciously to all the entreaties put to him, and did sometimes offer a tiny portrait that he had done of Bianca.

I see these now, these many *tiny* portraits that he gave her over the years, each encrusted with jewels.

"You capture my likeness so keenly from memory," she said as she went to kiss him. I saw the reserve with which he held her aloof from his cold hard chest and face, planting kisses on her cheeks that conveyed the spell of softness and sweetness which the real touch of him would have destroyed.

I read for hours with the aid of the teacher Leonardo of Padua, my voice perfectly in time with his as I grasped the scheme of Latin, then Italian, then back to Greek. I liked Aristotle as much as Plato or Plutarch or Livy or Virgil. The truth was, I didn't much comprehend any of them. I was doing as the Master directed, letting the knowledge accumulate in my mind.

I saw no reason to talk endlessly, as Aristotle did, about things that were made. The lives of the ancients that Plutarch told with such spirit made excellent stories. I wanted to know people of the now, however. I preferred to doze on Bianca's couch rather than argue about the merits of this or that painter. Besides, I knew my Master was the best.

This world was one of spacious rooms, decorated walls, generous fragrant light and a regular parade of high fashion, to which I grew accustomed completely, never seeing much of the pain and misery of the poor of the city at all. Even the books I read reflected this new realm in which I had been so securely fixed that nothing could take me back to the world of confusion and suffering that had gone before.

I learned to play little songs on the Virginal. I learned to strum the lute and to sing in a soft voice, though I would only sing sad songs. My Master loved these songs.

We made a choir now and then, all the boys together, and presented the Master with our own compositions and sometimes our own dances as well.

In the hot afternoon, we played cards when we were supposed to be napping. Riccardo and I slipped out to gamble in taverns. We drank too much once or twice. The Master knew it and put a stop to it at once. He was particularly horrified that I'd fallen drunk into the Grand Canal, necessitating a clumsy and hysterical rescue. I could have sworn he went pale at the account, that I saw the color dance back from his whitening cheeks.

He whipped Riccardo for it. I was full of shame. Riccardo took it like a soldier without cries or comment, standing still at a large fireplace in the library, his back turned to receive the blows on his legs. Afterwards, he knelt and kissed the Master's ring. I vowed I'd never get drunk again.

I got drunk the next day, but I had the sense to stagger into Bianca's house and climb under her bed, where I could fall asleep without risk. Before midnight the Master pulled me out. I thought, Now I'll get it. But he only put me to bed, where I fell asleep before I could apologize. When I woke once it was to see him at his writing desk, writing as swiftly as he could paint, in some great book which he always managed to hide before he left the house.

When others did sleep, including Riccardo, during the worst afternoons of summer, I ventured out and hired a gondola. I lay on my back in it staring skyward, as we floated down the canal and to the more turbulent breast of the gulf. I closed my eyes as we made our way back so that I might hear the smallest cries from the quiet siesta-time buildings, the lap of the rank waters on rotting foundations, the cry of seagulls overhead. I didn't mind the gnats or the smell of the canals.

One afternoon I didn't go home for work or lessons. I wandered into a tavern to listen to musicians and singers, and another time happened upon an open drama on a trestle stage in a square before a church. No one was angry with me for my comings and goings. Nothing was reported. There were no tests of my learning or anyone else's.

Sometimes I slept all day, or until I was curious. It was an extreme pleasure to wake up and find the Master at work, either in the studio, walking up and down the scaffolding as he painted his larger canvas, or just near me, at his table in the bedroom, writing away.

There was always food everywhere, glistening bunches of grapes, and ripe melons cut open for us, and delicious fine-grained bread with the freshest oil. I ate black olives, slices of pale soft cheese and fresh leeks from the roof garden. The milk came up cool in the silver pitchers.

The Master ate nothing. All knew this. The Master was always gone by day. The Master was never spoken of without reverence. The Master could read a boy's soul. The Master knew good from evil, and he knew deceit. The boys were good boys. There was some hushed mention now and then of bad boys who had been banished from the house almost at once. But no one ever spoke even in a trivial way about the Master. No one spoke about the fact that I slept in the Master's bed.

At noon each day, we dined together formally on roasted fowl, tender lamb, thick juicy slabs of beef.

Three and four teachers came at any one time to instruct the various small groups of apprentices. Some worked while others studied.

I could wander from the Latin class to the Greek class. I could leaf through the erotic sonnets and read what I could until Riccardo came to the rescue and drew a circle of laughter around his reading, for which the teachers had to wait.

In this leniency I prospered. I learnt quickly, and could answer all the Master's casual questions, offering thoughtful questions of my own.

The Master painted four out of the seven nights a week, and usually from after midnight until his disappearance at dawn. Nothing interrupted him on these nights.

He climbed the scaffold with amazing ease, rather like a great white monkey, and, letting his scarlet cloak drop carelessly, he snatched up the brush from the boy who held it for him and painted in such a fury that the paint splattered on all of us as we watched aghast. Under his genius whole landscapes came to life within hours; gatherings of people were drawn with the greatest detail.

He hummed aloud as he worked; he announced the names of the great writers or heroes as he painted their portraits from his memory or his imagination. He drew our attention to his colors, the lines he chose, the tricks with perspective that plunged his groupings of palpable and enthusiastic subjects into real gardens, rooms, palaces, halls.

Only the fill-in work was left to the boys to do by morning—the coloring of drapery, the tinting of wings, the broad spaces of flesh to which the Master would come again to add the modeling while the oily paint was still mobile, the shining flooring of sometime palaces which after his final touches looked like real marble receding beneath the flushed chubby feet of his philosophers and saints.

The work drew us naturally, spontaneously. There were dozens of unfinished canvases and walls within the palazzo, all so lifelike they seemed portals to another world.

Gaetano, one of the youngest of us, was the most gifted. But any of the boys, except me, could match the apprentice painters of any man's workshop, even the boys of Bellini.

Sometimes there was a receiving day. Bianca was then jubilant as she would receive for the Master, and came with her servants to be lady of the house. Men and women from the finest houses in Venice came to view the Master's paintings. People were astonished at his powers. Only from listening to them on these days did I realize my Master sold almost nothing, but filled his palazzo with his own work, and that he had his own versions of most famous subjects, from the school of

Aristotle to the Crucifixion of Christ. Christ. This was the curly-haired, ruddy, muscular and human-looking Christ, their Christ. The Christ who was like Cupid or Zeus.

I didn't mind that I couldn't paint as well as Riccardo and the others, that I was half the time content to hold the pots for them, to wash the brushes, to wipe clean the mistakes that had to be corrected. I did not want to paint. I did not want to. I could feel my hands cramp at the thought of it, and there would come a sickness in my belly when I thought of it.

I preferred the conversation, the jokes, the speculation as to why our fabulous Master took no commissions, though letters came to him daily inviting him to compete for this or that mural to be painted in the Ducal Palace or in one or another of the thousand churches of the isle.

I watched the color spreading out by the hour. I breathed in the fragrance of varnishes, the pigments, the oils.

Now and then a stuporous anger overcame me, but not at my lack of skill.

Something else tormented me, something to do with the humid, tempestuous postures of the painted figures, with their glistening pink cheeks and the boiling sweep of cloudy sky behind them, or the fleecy branches of the dark trees.

It seemed madness, this, this unbridled depiction of nature. My head hurting, I walked alone and briskly along the quays until I found an old church, and a gilded altar with stiff, narrow-eyed saints, dark and drawn and rigid: the legacy of Byzantium, as I had seen it in San Marco on my first day. My soul hurt and hurt and hurt as I gazed worshipfully at these old proprieties. I cursed when my new friends found me. I knelt, stubborn, refusing to show that I knew they were there. I covered my ears to shut out the laughter of my new friends. How could they laugh in the hollow of the church where the tortured Christ bled tears like black beetles leaping from His fading hands and feet?

Now and then I fell asleep before antique altars. I had escaped my companions. I was solitary and happy on the damp cold stones. I fancied I could hear the water beneath the floor.

I took a gondola to Torcello and there sought out the great old Cathedral of Santa Maria Assunta, famous for its mosaics which some said were as splendid in the antique way as the mosaics of San Marco. I crept about under the low arches, looking at the ancient gold Iconostasis and the mosaics of the apse. High above, in the back curve of the apse there stood the great Virgin, the Theotokos, the bearer of God. Her face was austere, almost sour. A tear glistened on her left cheek. In her hands she held the infant Jesus, but also a napkin, the token of the Mater Dolorosa.

I understood these images, even as they froze my soul. My head swam and the heat of the island and the quiet Cathedral made me sick in my stomach. But I stayed there. I drifted about the Iconostasis and prayed.

I thought sure no one could find me here. Towards dusk, I became truly sick. I knew I had a fever, but I sought a corner of the church and took comfort in only the cold of the stone floor against my face and my out-stretched hands. Before me, if I raised my head I could see terrifying scenes of the Last Judgment, of souls con-demned to Hell. I deserve this pain, I thought.

The Master came for me. I don't remember the jour-ney back to the palazzo. It seemed that somehow in a matter of moments he had put me in bed. The boys bathed my forehead with cool cloths. I was made to drink water. Someone said that I had "the fever" and someone else said, "Be quiet."

The Master kept watch with me. I had bad dreams which I couldn't bring with me into my waking state. Before dawn, the Master kissed me and held me close to him. I had never loved so much the chill hardness of his body as I did in this fever, wrapping my arms around him, pushing my cheek against his.

He gave me something hot and spiced to drink from a warm cup. And then he kissed me, and again came the cup. My body was filled with a healing fire.

But by the time he returned that night my fever was bad again. I did not dream so much as I wandered, half asleep, half awake, through terrible dark corridors unable to find a place that was either warm or clean. There was dirt beneath my fingernails. At one point, I saw a shovel moving, and saw the dirt, and feared the dirt would cover me, and I started to cry.

Riccardo kept watch, holding my hand, telling me it would soon be nightfall, and that the Master would surely come.

"Amadeo," the Master said. He hoisted me up as if I were truly still a small child.

Too many questions formed in my mind. Would I

die? Where was the Master taking me now? I was wrapped in velvet and furs and he carried me, but how?

We were in a church in Venice, amid new paintings of our time. The requisite candles burned. Men prayed. He turned me in his arms and told me to look up at the giant altarpiece before me.

Squinting, my eyes hurting, I obeyed him and saw the Virgin on high being crowned by her beloved Son, Christ the King.

"Look at the sweetness of her face, the natural expression to her," the Master whispered. "She sits there as one might sit here in the church. And the angels, look at them, the happy boys clustered around the columns beneath her. Look at the serenity and the gentleness of their smiles. This is Heaven, Amadeo. This is goodness."

My sleepy eyes moved over the high painting. "See the Apostle who whispers so naturally to the one beside him, as men might at such a ceremony. See above, God the Father, gazing down so contentedly on all."

I tried to form questions, to say it was not possible, this combination of the fleshly and the beatific, but I couldn't find eloquent words. The nakedness of the boy angels was enchanting and innocent, but I could not believe it. It was a lie of Venice, a lie of the West, a lie of the Devil himself.

"Amadeo," he continued, "there is no good that is founded in suffering and cruelty; there is no good that must root itself in the privation of little children. Amadeo, out of the love of God grows beauty everywhere. Look at these colors; these are the colors created by God."

Secure in his arms, my feet dangling, my arms about

his neck, I let the details of the immense altarpiece sink into my consciousness. I went back and forth, back and forth, over those small touches I loved.

I raised my finger to point. The lion there, just sitting so calmly at the feet of St. Mark, and look, the pages of St. Mark's book, the pages are actually in motion as he turns them. And the lion is tame and gentle as a friendly fireside dog.

"This is Heaven, Amadeo," he said to me. "Whatever the past has hammered into your soul, let it go."

I smiled, and slowly, gazing up at the saints, the rows and rows of saints, I began to laugh softly and confidentially in the Master's ear.

"They're all talking, murmuring, talking amongst themselves as if they were the Venetian Senators."

I heard his low, subdued laughter in answer. "Oh, I think the Senators are more decorous, Amadeo. I've never seen them in such informality, but this is Heaven, as I said."

"Ah, Master, look there. A saint holds an ikon, a beautiful ikon. Master, I have to tell you—." I broke off. The fever rose and the sweat broke out on me. My eyes felt hot, and I couldn't see. "Master," I said. "I am in the wild lands. I'm running. I have to put it in the trees." How could he know what I meant, that I spoke of that long-ago desperate flight out of coherent recollection and through the wild grasses with the sacred bundle in my keep, the bundle that had to be unwrapped and placed in the trees. "Look, the ikon."

Honey filled me. It was thick and sweet. It came from a cold fount, but it didn't matter. I knew this fount. My body was like a goblet stirred so that all that was bitter dissolved in the fluids of it, dissolved in a vortex to leave only honey and a dreamy warmth.

When I opened my eyes, I was in our bed. I was cool all over. The fever was gone. I turned over and pulled myself up.

My Master sat at his desk. He was reading over what he had apparently just written. He had tied back his blond hair with a bit of cord. His face was very beautiful, unveiled as it were, with its chiseled cheekbones and smooth narrow nose. He looked at me, and his mouth worked the miracle of the ordinary smile.

"Don't chase these memories," he said. He said it as if we'd been talking all the while that I slept. "Don't go to the church of Torcello to find them. Don't go to the mosaics of San Marco. In time all these harmful things will come back."

"I'm afraid to remember," I said.

"I know," he answered.

"How can you know?" I asked him. "I have it in my heart. It's mine alone, this pain." I was sorry for sounding so bold, but whatever my guilt, the boldness came more and more often.

"Do you really doubt me?" he asked.

"Your endowments are beyond measure. We all know it, and we never speak of it, and you and I never speak of it."

"So why then don't you put your faith in me instead of things you only half recall?"

He got up from the desk and came to the bed.

"Come," he said. "Your fever's broken. Come with me."

He took me into one of the many libraries of the

palazzo, messy rooms in which the manuscripts lay helter-skelter, and the books in stacks. Seldom if ever did he work in these rooms. He threw his purchases there to be cataloged by the boys, taking what he needed back to the writing desk in our room.

He moved among the shelves now until he found a portfolio, a big flopping thing of old yellowed leather, frayed at the edges. His white fingers smoothed a large page of vellum. He laid it down on the oak study table for me to see.

A painting, antique.

I saw there drawn a great church of gilded domes, so beautiful, so majestic. Letters were blazoned there. I knew these letters. But I couldn't make the words come to my mind or my tongue.

"Kiev Rus," he said. *Kiev Rus.*

An unsupportable horror came over me. Before I could stop myself, I said, "It's ruined, burnt. There is no such place. It's not alive like Venice. It's ruined, and all is cold, and filthy and desperate. Yes, that's the very word." I was dizzy. I felt I saw an escape from desolation, only it was cold and dark, this escape, and it led by twists and turns into a world of eternal darkness where the raw earth gave the only smell to one's hands, one's skin, one's clothes.

I pulled back and ran from the Master.

I ran the full length of the palazzo.

I ran down the stairs, and through the dark lower rooms that opened on the canal. When I came back, I found him alone in the bedroom. He was reading as always. He had his favorite book of late, *The Consolation of Philosophy* by Boethius, and he looked up from it patiently when I came in.

I stood thinking of my painful memories.

I couldn't catch them. So be it. They scurried into the nothingness rather like the leaves in the alleyways, the leaves that sometimes tumble down and down the stained green walls from the little gardens whipped in the wind up there on the rooftops.

"I don't want to," I said again.

There was but one Living Lord. My Master.

"Some day it will all come clear to you, when you have the strength to use it," he said. He shut his book. "For now, let me comfort you."

Ah, yes, I was all too ready for this.

3

OH, HOW LONG the days could be without him. By nightfall, I clenched my fists as the candles were lighted.

There came nights when he didn't appear at all. The boys said he had gone on most important errands. The house must run as if he were there.

I slept in his empty bed, and no one questioned me. I searched the house for any personal trace of him. Questions plagued me. I feared he would never come back.

But he always came back.

When he came up the stairs, I flew into his embrace. He caught me, held me, kissed me and only then let me fall gently against his hard chest. My weight was nothing to him, though I seemed to grow taller and heavier every day.

I would never be anything but the seventeen-year-old boy you see now, but how could a man so slight as he heft me with such ease? I am not a waif and never have been. I am a strong child.

I liked it best—if I had to share with the others—when he read to us aloud.

Surrounding himself with candelabra, he spoke in a hushed and sympathetic voice. He read *The Divine Comedy* by Dante, the *Decameron* by Boccaccio, or in French *The Romance of the Rose* or the poems of François Villon. He spoke of the new languages we must understand as well as we understood Greek and Latin. He warned us that literature would no longer be confined to the classic works.

We sat in silence around him, on pillows, or on the naked tile. Some of us stood near him. Others rested back on their heels.

Sometimes Riccardo played the lute for us and sang those melodies he'd learned from his teacher, or even the wilder ribald tunes he'd picked up in the streets. He sang mournfully of love and made us weep over it. The Master watched him with loving eyes.

I had no jealousy. I alone shared the Master's bed.

Sometimes, he even had Riccardo sit outside the bedroom door and play for us. Obedient Riccardo never asked to come inside.

My heart raced as the curtains closed around us. The Master pulled open my tunic, sometimes even ripping it playfully, as if it were no more than a castoff thing.

I sank into the satin quilted down beneath him; I opened my legs and let my knees caress him, numbed and vibrating from the graze of his knuckles against my lips.

Once I lay half asleep. The air was rosy and golden. The place was warm. I felt his lips on mine, and his cold tongue move serpentlike into my mouth. A liquid filled my mouth, a rich and burning nectar, a potion so exquisite that I felt it roll through my body to the very tips of my outstretched fingers. I felt it descend through my torso and into the most private part of me. I burned. I burned.

"Master," I whispered. "What is this trick now which is sweeter than kissing?"

He laid his head down on the pillow. He turned away.

"Give it to me again, Master," I said.

He did, but only when he chose, in droplets, and with red tears he now and then let me lick from his eyes.

I think a whole year passed before I came home one evening, flushed from the winter air, dressed in my very finest dark blue for him, with sky blue stockings and the most expensive gold enameled slippers that I could find in all the world, a year before I came in that night and threw my book into the corner of the bedroom with a great world-weary gesture, putting my hands on my hips and glaring at him as he sat in his high thick arch-back chair looking at the coals in the brazier, putting his hands over them, watching the flames.

"Well, now," I said cockily and with my head back, a very man of the world, a sophisticated Venetian, a prince in the Marketplace with an entire court of merchants to wait on him, a scholar who had read too much.

"Well, now," I said. "There's a great mystery here and you know it. It's time you told me."

"What?" he asked obligingly enough.

"Why do you never . . . Why do you never feel anything! Why do you handle me as if I were a poppet? Why do you never . . . ?"

For the first time ever I saw his face redden; I saw his eyes gloss and narrow and then widen with reddish tears.

"Master, you frighten me," I whispered.

"What is it you want me to feel, Amadeo?" he said.

"You're like an angel, a statue," I said, only now I was chastened and trembling. "Master, you play with me and I'm the toy that feels all things." I drew nearer. I touched his shirt, sought to unlace it. "Let me—."

He took my hand. He took my fingers and put them to his lips, and drew my fingers inside his mouth, caressing them with his tongue. His eyes moved so that he was looking up at me.

Quite enough, said his eyes. I feel quite enough.

"I'd give you anything," I said imploringly. I put my hand between his legs. Oh, he was wonderfully hard. That was not uncommon, but he must let me take him further; he must trust me.

"Amadeo," he said.

With his unaccountable strength he drew me back with him to the bed. You could hardly say he'd risen from the chair. It seemed we were there one moment and now fallen amongst our familiar pillows. I blinked. It seemed the curtains closed around us without his touching them, some trick of the breeze from the open windows. Yes, listen to the voices from the canal below. How voices sing out and up the walls in Venice, the city of palaces.

"Amadeo," he said, his lips on my throat as they'd come a thousand times, only this time there came a sting, sharp, swift and gone. A thread stitched into my heart was jerked all of a sudden. I had become the thing between my legs, and was nothing but that. His mouth nestled against me, and again that thread snapped and again.

I dreamed. I think I saw another place. I think I saw the revelations of my sleeping hours which never stayed for me when I awoke. I think I trod a road into those bursting fantasies I knew in sleep and sleep alone.

This is what I want of you.

"And you must have it," I said, words propelled to the near forgotten present as I floated against him, feeling him tremble, feeling him thrill to it, feeling him shudder, feeling him whip these threads from inside me, quickening my heart and making me nearly cry out, feeling him love it, and stiffen his back and let his fingers tremble and dance as he writhed against me. Drink it, drink it, drink it.

He broke loose and lay to the side.

I smiled as I lay with closed eyes. I felt my lips. I felt the barest bit of that nectar still gathered on my lower lip, and my tongue took it up and I dreamed.

His breathing was heavy and he was somber. He shivered still, and when his hand found me it was unsteady.

"Ah," I said smiling still, and kissing his shoulder.

"I hurt you!" he said.

"No, no, not at all, sweet Master," I answered. "But I hurt you! I have you, now!"

"Amadeo, you play the devil."

"Don't you want me to, Master? Didn't you like it? You took my blood and it made you my slave!"

He laughed. "So that's the twist you put on it, isn't it?"

"Hmmm. Love me. What does it matter?" I asked.

"Never tell the others," he said. There was no fear or weakness or shame in it.

I turned over and drew up on my elbows and looked at him, at his quiet profile turned away from me.

"What would they do?"

"Nothing," he answered. "It's what they would think and feel that matters. And I have no time or place for it." He looked at me. "Be merciful and wise, Amadeo."

For a long time I said nothing. I merely looked at him. Only gradually did I realize I was frightened. For one moment it seemed that fear would obliterate the warmth of the moment, the soft glory of the radiant light swelling in the curtains, of the polished planes of his ivory face, the sweetness of his smile. Then some higher graver concern overruled the fear.

"You're not my slave at all, are you?" I whispered.

"Yes," he said, almost laughing again. "I am, if you must know."

"What happened, what did you do, what was it that—."

He laid his finger on my lips.

"Do you think me like other men?" he asked.

"No," I said, but the fear rose in the word and strangled out the wound. I tried to stop myself, but before I could I embraced him and tried to push my face into his neck. He was too hard for such things, though he cradled my head and kissed the top of it, though he gathered back my hair, and let his thumb sink into my cheek.

"Some day I want you to leave here," he said. "I want you to go. You'll take wealth with you and all the learning I've been able to give you. You'll take your grace with you, and all the many arts you've mastered, that you can paint, that you can play any music I ask of you—that you can do already—that you can so exquisitely dance. You'll take these accomplishments and you'll go out in search of those precious things that you want—."

"I want nothing but you."

"—and when you think back on this time, when in half-sleep at night you remember me as your eyes close on your pillow, these moments of ours will seem corrupt and most strange. They'll seem like sorcery and the antics of the mad, and this warm place might become the lost chamber of dark secrets and this might bring you pain."

"I won't go."

"Remember then that it was love," he said. "That this indeed was the school of love in which you healed your wounds, in which you learnt to speak again, aye, even to sing, and in which you were born out of the broken child as if he were no more than an eggshell, and you the angel, ascending out of him with widening, strengthening wings."

"And what if I never go of my own free will? Will you pitch me from some window so that I must fly or fall? Will you bolt all shutters after me? You had better, because I'll knock and knock and knock until I fall down dead. I'll have no wings that take me away from you."

He made a study of me for the longest time. I never had such an unbroken feast on his eyes myself, and had never been let to touch his mouth with my prying fingers for such a spell.

Finally he rose up next to me and pressed me gently down. His lips, always softly pink like the inner petals of blushing white roses, turned slowly red as I watched. It was a gleaming seam of red that ran between his lips and then flowed through all the fine lines of which his lips were made, perfectly coloring them, as wine might do, only it was so brilliant, this fluid, that his lips shimmered, and when he parted them, the red burst as if it were a curled tongue.

My head was lifted. I caught it with my own mouth.

The world moved out from under me. I listed and drifted, and my eyes opened and saw nothing as he shut his mouth over mine.

"Master, I die from this!" I whispered. I tossed under him, seeking to find some firm place in this dreamy intoxicating void. My body churned and rolled with pleasure, my limbs tightening then floating, my whole body issuing from him, from his lips, through my lips, my body his very breath and his sigh.

There came the sting, there came the blade, tiny and sharp beyond measure, puncturing my soul. I twisted on it as if I'd been skewered. Oh, this could teach the gods of love what love was. This was my deliverance if I could but survive.

Blind and shaking I was wed to him. I felt his hand cover my mouth, and only then heard my cries as they were muffled away.

I wrapped my hand around his neck, pressing him against my throat all the harder, "Do it, do it, do it, do it!"

When I awoke, it was day.

He was long gone, as was his infallible custom. I lay alone. The boys had not yet come.

I climbed out of bed and went to the high narrow window, the kind of window which is everywhere in Venice, locking out the fierce heat of summer and sealing off the cold Adriatic winds when they inevitably come.

I unbolted the thick glass panels and looked out on the walls across from my safe place as I had often done.

A common serving woman shook her cloth mop from a far balcony above. Across the canal, I watched her. Her face seemed livid and crawling, as if some tiny species of life covered her, some rampage of ants. She didn't know! I laid my hands on the sill and looked ever more keenly. It was only the life inside her, the workings of the flesh in her that made the mask of her face seem to move.

But horrid her hands seemed, knuckled and swollen, and the dust from her broom engraving every line.

I shook my head. She was too far from me for these observations.

In a faraway room, the boys talked. Time for work.

Time to get up, even in the palazzo of the night Lord who never checks or prods by day. Too far away for me to hear them.

And this velvet now, this curtain made of the Master's favorite fabric, this was like fur to my touch, not velvet, I could see each tiny fiber! I dropped it. I went for the looking glass.

The house had dozens of them, great ornate mirrors, all with fancified frames and most replete with tiny cherubs. I found the tall mirror in the anteroom, the alcove behind warped yet beautifully painted doors where I kept my clothes.

The light of the window followed me. I saw myself. But I was not a seething corrupt mass, such as this woman had seemed. My face was baby smooth and starkly white.

"I want it!" I whispered. I knew.

"No," he told me.

This is when he came that night. I ranted and paced and cried out to him.

He didn't give me long explanations, no sorcery or science, either of which would have been so easy for him. He told me only I was a child still, and there were things to be savored which would be lost forever.

I cried. I didn't want to work or paint or study or do anything in the world.

"It's lost its savor for a little while," he said patiently. "But you'd be surprised."

"At what?"

"At how much you'll lament it when it's gone utterly, when you are perfect and unchangeable like me,

and all those human mistakes can be triumphantly sup-
planted by a new and more stunning series of failures.
Don't ask for this, not again."

I would have died then, curled up, black and furious
and too bitter for words.

But he wasn't finished.

"Amadeo," he said, his voice thick with sorrow.
"Say nothing. You don't have to. I'll give it to you
quickly enough when I think the time has come."

At that I went to him, running, childlike, flinging
myself at his neck, kissing his icy cheek a thousand
times despite his mock-disdainful smile.

At last his hands became like iron. There was to be
no blood play this night. I must study. I must make up the
lessons I had scorned by day.

He had to see to his apprentices, to his tasks, to the
giant canvas on which he'd been working, and I did as
he said.

But well before morning, I saw him change. The
others had long gone to bed. I was turning the pages of
the book obediently when I saw him staring, beastlike,
from his chair, as if some ravener had come into him and
banished all his civilized faculties and left him thus,
hungry, with glazed eyes and reddening mouth, the glittering blood finding its myriad little paths over the silky
margin of his lips.

He rose, a drugged thing, and came towards me with
a rhythm of movements that was alien and struck the
coldest terror in my heart.

His fingers flashed, closed, beckoned.

I ran to him. He lifted me in both hands, clutching

my arms ever so gently, and tucked his face against my neck. From the soles of my feet up my back through my arms and my neck and scalp, I felt it.

Where he flung me I didn't know. Was it our bed or some hasty cushions he found in another closer salon? "Give it to me," I said sleepily, and when it came into my mouth, I was gone.

4

HE SAID THAT I must go to the brothels, learn what it meant to couple properly—not merely in play, as we did among the boys.

Venice had many such places, very well run and devoted to pleasure in the most luxurious environment. It was firmly held that such pleasures were little more than a venial sin in the eyes of the Christ, and the young men of fashion frequented these establishments without hiding it.

I knew of a house of particularly exquisite and skilled women, where there were tall, buxom, very pale-eyed beauties from the North of Europe, some whose blond hair was almost white, deemed to be somewhat different from the shorter Italian women's which we saw every day. I don't know that difference was such a high priority with me, as I'd been somewhat dazzled by the beauty of Italian boys and women since I had come. Swan-necked Venetian girls in their fancy cushion-head dresses with abundant translucent veils were very nearly irresistible to me. But then the brothel had all kinds of women, and the name of the game was to mount as many as I could.

My Master took me to this place, paid for me, a fortune in ducats, and told the buxom enchanting mistress that he would collect me in a matter of days.

Days!

I was pale with jealousy and on fire with curiosity, as I watched him take his leave—the usual regal figure in his familiar crimson robes, climbing into the gondola and giving me his clever wink as the boat took him away.

I spent three days, as it turned out, in the house of the most voluptuous available maidens in Venice, sleeping late in the morning, comparing olive skin to blond skin and indulging myself in leisurely examinations of the nether hair of all beauties, distinguishing the more silken from the wiry and more tightly curled.

I learned little niceties of pleasure, such as how sweet it was to have one's nipples bitten (lightly, and these weren't vampires) and to have the hair under one's arms, of which I had just a little, tugged affectionately at the appropriate moments. Golden honey was painted on my nether parts only to be licked away by giggling angels.

There were other more intimate tricks, of course, including bestial acts which were strictly speaking crimes but which were in this house merely various extra accouterments to overall wholesome and tantalizing feasts. All was done with grace, the steamy hot perfumed baths came frequently in large deep wooden tubs, flowers floating on the surface of the rose-tinted water, and I lay back sometimes at the mercy of a bevy of soft-voiced women who cooed over me like birds in the eaves as they licked me like so many kittens and combed my hair around their fingers to make curls.

I was the little Ganymede of Zeus, an angel tumbled out of Botticelli's more ribald paintings (many of which by the way were in this brothel, having been rescued from the Bonfires of the Vanities erected in Florence by the adamant reformer Savonarola, who had urged the great Botticelli to just . . . burn up his beautiful work!), a little cherub fallen off the ceiling of a Cathedral, a Venetian prince (of which there were none in the Republic technically) delivered into their hands by his enemies to be rendered helpless with desire.

I grew hotter in desire. If one had to be human for the rest of one's life, this was great fun, tumbling among Turkish cushions with nymphs such as most men only glimpse through magical forests in their dreams. Each soft and downy cleft was a new and exotic envelope for my romping spirit.

The wine was delicious and the food quite marvelous, including sugared and spiced dishes from the Arabs, and being altogether more extravagant and more exotic than the fare served by my Master at home.

(When I told him, he hired four new chefs.)

I wasn't awake, apparently, when my Master arrived to collect me, and I was spirited home by him, in his mysterious and infallible manner, and found myself again in my bed.

I knew I wanted only him when my eyes opened. And it seemed the fleshy repasts of the last few days had only made me more hungry, more inflamed and more eager to see if his enchanted white body would respond to the more tender tricks I'd learned. I threw myself on him when he finally came in behind the curtains, and I unloosed his shirt and sucked his nipples, discovering that for all their disturbing whiteness and coldness they were soft and obviously intimately connected in a seemingly natural way to the root of his desires.

He lay there, graceful and quiet, letting me play with him as my women teachers had played with me. When he finally gave me the blood kisses, all memories of human contact were obliterated, and I lay helpless as always in his arms. It seemed our world then was not merely one of the flesh, but of a mutual spell to which all natural laws gave way.

Towards morning on the second night, I sought him out where he was painting by himself in the studio, the scattered apprentices fallen asleep like the unfaithful Apostles in Gethsemane.

He wouldn't stop for my questions. I stood behind him and locked my arms around him and, climbing on tiptoe, I whispered my questions in his ear.

"Tell me, Master, you must, how did you gain this magic blood inside you?" I bit his earlobes and ran my hands through his hair. He wouldn't stop painting. "Were you born into this state, am I so wrong about this as to suppose that you were transformed . . ."

"Stop it, Amadeo," he whispered, and continued to paint. He worked furiously on the face of Aristotle, the bearded, balding elder of his great painting, *The Academy*.

"Is there ever a loneliness in you, Master, that

pushes you to tell someone, anyone, to have a friend of your own mettle, to confide your heart to one who can comprehend?"

He turned, startled for once by my questions.

"And you, spoiled little angel," he said, lowering his voice to maintain its gentleness, "you think you can be that friend? You're an innocent! You'll be an innocent all of your days. You have the heart of an innocent. You refuse to accept truth that doesn't correspond with some deep raging faith in you which makes you ever the little monk, the acolyte—."

I stepped backwards, as angry as I'd ever been with him. "No, I won't be such!" I declared. "I'm a man already in the guise of a boy, and you know it. Who else dreams of what you are, and the alchemy of your powers? I wish I could drain a cupful of your blood from you and study it as the doctors might and determine what is its makeup and how it differs from the fluid that runs through my veins! I am your pupil, yes, your student, yes, but to be that, I must be a man. When would you tolerate innocence? When we bed together, you call that innocence? I am a man."

He burst into the most amazed laughter. It was a treat to see him so surprised.

"Tell me your secret, Sir," I said. I put my arms around his neck and laid my head on his shoulder. "Was there a Mother as white and strong as you were who brought you forth, the God-Bearer, from her celestial womb?"

He took my arms and moved me back away from him, so that he could kiss me, and his mouth was insistent and frightening to me for a moment. Then it moved over my throat, sucking at my flesh and causing me to become weak and, with all my heart, willing to be anything he wished.

"Of the moon and the stars, yes, I'm made, of that sovereign whiteness which is the substance of clouds and innocence alike," he said. "But no Mother gave birth to me, you know that's so; I was a man once, a man moving on in his years. Look—." He lifted my face with both hands and made me study his face. "You see here remnants of the lines of age which once marked me, here at the corners of my eyes."

"Merely nothing, Sir," I whispered, thinking to console him if this imperfection troubled him. He shone in his brilliance, his polished smoothness. The simplest expressions flashed in his face in luminescent heat.

Imagine a figure of ice, as perfectly made as Pygmalion's Galatea, thrown into the fire, and sizzling, and melting, and yet the features all wondrously intact still . . . well, such was my Master when human emotions infected him, as they did now.

He crushed my arms deliciously and kissed me again.

"Little man, manikin, elf," he whispered. "Would you be so for eternity? Haven't you lain with me often enough to know what I can and cannot enjoy?"

I won him over, captive to me, for the last hour before he was off.

But the next night he dispatched me to a more clandestine and even more luxurious house of pleasure, a house which kept for the passions of others only young boys.

It was got up in Eastern style, and I think it blended

the luxuries of Egypt with those of Babylon, its small cells made up of golden latticework, and colonnettes of brass studded with lapis lazuli holding up the salmon-colored drapery of the ceilings over tasseled couches of gilt wood and damask-covered down. Incense made the air heavy, and the lights were soothingly low.

The naked boys, well fed, nubile, smooth and rounded of limb, were eager, strong, tenacious, and brought to the games their own rampant male desires.

It seemed my soul was a pendulum that swung between the hearty pleasure of conquest and the swooning surrender to stronger limbs, and stronger wills, and stronger hands that tossed me tenderly about.

Captive between two skilled and willful lovers, I was pierced and suckled, pummeled and emptied until I slept as soundly as ever I had without the Master's magic at home.

It was only the beginning.

Sometime in my drunken sleep, I woke to find myself surrounded by beings that seemed neither male nor female. Only two of them were eunuchs, cut with such skill they could raise their trusty weapons as well as any boy. The others merely shared the taste of their companions for paint. All had eyes lined in black and shaded in purple, with lashes curled and glazed to give their expressions an eerie fathomless aloofness. Their rouged lips seemed tougher than those of women and more demanding, pushing at me in their kisses as if the male element which had given them muscles and hard organs had given them as well a virility to their very mouths. They had the smiles of angels. Gold rings decorated their nipples. Their nether hair was powdered with gold.

I made no protest when they overcame me. I feared no extreme, and even let them bind my wrists and ankles to the bed, so they could better work their craft. It was impossible to fear them. I was crucified with pleasure. Their insistent fingers would not even allow me to close my eyes. They stroked my lids, they forced me to look. They brought soft thick brushes down over my limbs. They rubbed oils into all my skin. They sucked from me, as if it were nectar, the fiery sap I gave forth, over and over, until I cried out vainly that I could give no more. A count was kept of my "little deaths" with which to taunt me playfully, and I was turned over and cuffed and pinioned as I tumbled down into rapturous sleep.

When I awoke I knew no time or worry. The thick smoke of a pipe rose into my nostrils. I took it and sucked on it, savoring the dark familiar smell of hemp.

I stayed there for four nights.

Again, I was delivered.

This time I found myself, groggy and in dishabille, barely covered by a thin torn cream-colored silk shirt. I lay on a couch brought from the very brothel, but this was my Master's studio, and there he sat, not far away, painting my picture obviously, at a small easel from which he took his eyes only to dart glances at me.

I asked the time of day and what night it was. He didn't answer.

"And so you're angry that I enjoyed it?" I asked.

"I told you to lie still," he said.

I lay back, cold all over, and hurt suddenly, lonely perhaps, and wanting like a child to hide in his arms.

Morning came and he left me, having said nothing else. The painting was a gleaming masterpiece of the obscene. I was in my sleeping posture cast down on a riverbank, a fawn of sorts, over which a tall shepherd, the Master himself, in priestly robes stood watch. The woods around us were thick and richly realized with the peeling tree trunks and their clustered dusty leaves. The water of the stream seemed wet to the touch, so clever was the realism of it, and my own figure appeared guileless and lost in sleep, my mouth half-open in a natural way, my brow obviously troubled by uneasy dreams.

I threw it on the floor, in a rage, meaning to smear it.

Why had he said nothing? Why did he force me to these lessons which drove us apart? Why his anger at me for merely doing what he had told me? I wondered if the brothels had been a test of my innocence, and his admonitions to me to enjoy all of it had been lies.

I sat at his desk, picked up his pen and scribbled a message to him.

> You are the Master. You should know all things. It's unsupportable to be Mastered by one who cannot do it. Make clear the way, shepherd, or lay down your staff.

The fact was, I was wrung out from the pleasure, from the drink, from the distortion of my senses, and lonely just to be with him and for his guidance and his kindness and his reassurance that I was his.

But he was gone.

I went out roaming. I spent all day in the taverns, drinking, playing cards, deliberately enticing the pretty girls who were fair game, to keep them at my side as I played the various games of chance.

Then when night came, I let myself be seduced, ho-hum, by a drunken Englishman, a fair freckle-skinned noble of the oldest French and English titles, of which this one was the Earl of Harlech, who was traveling in Italy to see the great wonders and utterly intoxicated with its many delights, including buggery in a strange land.

Naturally, he found me a beautiful boy. Didn't everyone? He was not at all ugly himself. Even his pale freckles had a kind of prettiness to them, especially given his outrageous copper hair.

Taking me back to his rooms in an overstuffed and beautiful palazzo, he made love to me. It was not all bad. I liked his innocence and his clumsiness. His light round blue eyes were a marvel; he had wondrously thick and muscular arms and a pampered but deliciously rough-pointed orange beard.

He wrote poems to me in Latin and in French, and re-cited them to me with great charm. After an hour or two of playing the vanquishing brute, he had let on that he wanted to be covered by me. And this I had very much enjoyed. We played it that way after that, my being the conquering soldier and he the victim on the battlefield, and sometimes I whipped him lightly with a doubled-up leather belt before I took him, which sent us both into a tidy froth.

From time to time, he implored me to confess who I really was and where he might afterwards find me, which of course I wouldn't.

I stayed there for three nights with him, talking about the mysterious islands of England with him, and reading Italian poetry aloud to him, and even sometimes playing the mandolin for him and singing any number of the soft love songs I knew.

He taught me a great deal of rank gutter-tramp English, and wanted to take me home. He had to regain his wits, he said; he had to return to his duties, his estates, his hateful wicked adulterous Scottish wife whose father was an assassin, and his innocent little child whose paternity he was most certain of, due to its orange curly hair so like his own.

He would keep me in London in a splendid house he had there, a present from His Majesty King Henry VII. He could not now live without me, the Harlechs to a man had to have what they must have, and there was nothing for me to do but yield to him. If I was the son of a formidable nobleman I should confess it, and this obstacle would be dealt with. Did I hate my Father, perchance? His was a scoundrel. All the Harlechs were scoundrels and had been since the days of Edward the Confessor. We would sneak out of Venice this very night.

"You don't know Venice, and you don't know her noblemen," I said kindly. "Think on all this. You'll be cut to pieces for giving it a try."

I now perceived that he was fairly young. Since all older men seemed old to me, I had not thought about it before. He couldn't have been more than twenty-five. He was also mad.

He leapt on the bed, his bushy copper hair flying, and pulled his dagger, a formidable Italian stiletto, and stared down into my upturned face.

"I'll kill for you," he said confidentially and proudly, in the Venetian dialect. Then he drove the dagger into the pillow and the feathers flew out of it. "I'll kill you if I have to." The feathers went up into his face.

"And then you'll have what?" I asked.

There was a creaking behind him. I felt certain someone was at the window, beyond the bolted wooden shutters, even though we were three stories above the Grand Canal. I told him so. He believed me.

"I come from a family of murderous beasts," I lied. "They'll follow you to the ends of the Earth if you think of taking me out of here; they'll dismantle your castles stone by stone, chop you in half and cut out your tongue and your private parts, wrap them in velvet and send them to your King. Now calm down."

"Oh, you bright, saucy little demon," he said, "you look like an angel and hold forth like a tavern knave in that sweet crooning mannish voice."

"That's me," I said gaily.

I got up, dressed hastily, warning him not to kill me just yet, as I would return as soon as I possibly could, longing to be nowhere but with him, and kissing him hastily, I made for the door.

He hovered in the bed, his dagger still tightly clutched in his hand, the feathers having settled on his carrot-colored head and on his shoulders and on his beard. He looked truly dangerous.

I'd lost count of the nights of my absence.

I could find no churches open. I wanted no company.

It was dark and cold. The curfew had come down. Of course the Venetian winter seemed mild to me after the snowy lands of the north, where I'd been born, but it was nevertheless an oppressive and damp winter, and though cleansing breezes purified the city, it was inhospitable and unnaturally quiet. The illimitable sky vanished in thick mists. The very stones gave forth the chill as if they were blocks of ice.

On a water stairs, I sat, not caring that it was brutally wet, and I burst into tears. What had I learned from all this?

I felt very sophisticated on account of this education. But I had no warmth from it, no lasting warmth, and it seemed my loneliness was worse than guilt, worse than the feeling of being damned.

Indeed it seemed to replace that old feeling. I feared it, being utterly alone. As I sat there looking up at the tiny margin of black Heaven, at the few stars that drifted over the roofs of the houses, I sensed how utterly terrible it would be to lose both my Master and my guilt simultaneously, to be cast out where nothing bothered to love me or damn me, to be lost and tumbling through the world with only those humans for companions, those boys and those girls, the English lord with his dagger, even my beloved Bianca.

It was to her house that I went. I climbed under her bed, as I'd done in the past, and wouldn't come out.

She was entertaining a whole flock of Englishmen, but not, fortunately, my copper-haired lover, who was no doubt still stumbling around in the feathers, and I thought, Well, if my charming Lord Harlech shows up, he won't risk shame before his countrymen in making a fool out of himself. She came in, looking most lovely in her violet silk gown with a fortune of radiant pearls around her neck. She knelt down and put her head near mine.

"Amadeo, what's the matter with you?"

I had never asked for her favors. To my knowledge no one did such a thing. But in my particular adolescent frenzy, nothing seemed more appropriate than that I should ravage her.

I scrambled out from under the bed and went to the doors and shut them, so the noise of her guests would leave us alone.

When I turned around she knelt on the floor, looking at me, her golden eyebrows knotted and her peach-soft lips open in a vague wondering expression that I found enchanting. I wanted to smash her with my passion, but not all that hard, of course, assuming all the while that she'd come back together again afterwards as if a beautiful vase, broken into pieces, could pull itself together again from all the tiniest shards and particles and be restored to its glory with an even finer glaze.

I pulled her up by the arms and threw her down on her bed. It was quite an affair, this marvelous coffered thing in which she slept alone, as far as all men knew. It had great gilded swans at its head, and columns rising to a framed canopy of painted dancing nymphs. Its curtains were spun gold and transparent. It had no winter aspect to it, like my Master's red velvet bed.

I bent down and kissed her, maddened by her sharp, pretty eyes which stared coolly at me as I did it. I held her wrists and then, swinging her left wrist over with her right, entrapped both her hands in one so that I was free to rip open her fine dress. I ripped it carefully so that all the little pearl buttons flew off the side of it, and her girdle was opened and underneath was her fine whalebone and lace. This I broke open as if it were a tight shell.

Her breasts were small and sweet, far too delicate and youngish for the brothel where voluptuousness had been the order of the day. I meant to pillage them nevertheless. I crooned against her, humming a bit of a song to her, and then I heard her sigh. I swooped down, still clutching her wrists firmly, and I sucked hard at her nipples in quick order and then drew back. I slapped her breasts playfully, from left to right until they turned pink.

Her face was flushed and she had her little golden frown still, the wrinkles almost incongruous in her smooth white forehead.

Her eyes were like two opals, and though she blinked slowly, near sleepily, she didn't flinch.

I finished my work on her fragile clothes. I ripped open the ties of her skirt and pushed it down away from her and found her splendidly and daintily naked as I had supposed she would be. I really had no idea what was beneath the skirts of a respectable woman in the way of obstacles. There was nothing except the small golden nest of her pubic hair, all feathery beneath her very slightly rounded little belly, and a dampness gleaming on her inner thighs.

I knew at once she favored me. She was hardly helpless. And the sight of the glittering down on her legs drove me mad. I plunged into her, amazed at her smallness and the way that she cringed, for she was not very well used, and it hurt her just a little.

I worked her hard, delighting to see her blush. My own weight I held up above her with my right arm, because I wouldn't let go of her wrists. She tossed and turned, and her blond tresses worked themselves out of her pearl and ribbon coif, and she became moist all over and pink and gleaming, like the inner curve of a great shell.

At last I couldn't contain myself any longer, and it seemed when I would give up the timing, she gave herself up to the final sigh. I spent with it, and we rocked together, as she closed her eyes, turned blood red as if she were dying and tossed her head in a final frenzy before going limp.

I rolled over and covered my face with both my arms, as if I were about to be slapped.

I heard her little laughter, and she did slap me suddenly, hard on my arms. It was nothing. I made as if I were weeping with shame.

"Look what you've done to my beautiful gown, you dreadful little satyr, you secret conquistador! You vile precocious child!"

I felt her weight leave the bed. I heard her dressing. She sang to herself.

"What's your Master going to think of this, Amadeo?" she asked.

I removed my arms and looked to find her voice. She dressed behind her painted paneled screen, a gift from Paris, if I recalled, given her by one of her favorite French poets. She appeared quickly, clothed as splendidly as before in a dress of pale spring green, embroidered with the flowers of the field. She seemed a very garden of delight with these tiny yellow and pink blooms so carefully made in rich thread over her new bodice and her long taffeta skirts.

"Well, tell me, what is the great Master going to say when he finds out his little lover is a veritable god of the wood?"

"Lover?" I was astonished.

She was very gentle in her manner. She sat down and began to comb out her tousled hair. She wore no paint and her face was unmarred by our games, and her hair came down around in a glorious hood of rippling gold. Her forehead was smooth and high.

"Botticelli made you," I whispered. I often said this to her, because she was so like his beauties. Indeed everyone thought so, and they would bring her small copies of this famous Florentine's paintings from time to time.

I thought on it, I thought on Venice and this world in which I lived. I thought on her, a courtesan, receiving those chaste yet lascivious paintings as if she were a saint.

Some echo came to me of old words that I had been told long ago, when I knelt in the presence of old and burnished beauty, and thought myself at the pinnacle, that I must take up my brush and I must paint only "what represented the world of God."

There was no tumult in me, only a great mixing of currents, as I watched her braid her hair again, stringing the fine ropes of pearls in with it, and the pale green ribbons, the ribbons themselves sewn with the same pretty little flowers that decorated her gown. Her breasts were blushing, half-covered beneath the press of her bodice. I wanted to rip it open again.

"Pretty Bianca, what makes you say this, that I'm his lover?"

"Everyone knows it," she whispered. "You are his favorite. Do you think you've made him angry?"

"Oh, if only I could," I said. I sat up. "You don't know my Master. Nothing makes him lift his hand to me. Nothing makes him even raise his voice. He sent me forth to learn all things, to know what men can know."

She smiled and nodded. "So you came and hid under the bed."

"I was sad."

"I'm sure," she said. "Well, sleep now, and when I come back, if you're still here, I'll keep you warm. But need I tell you, my rambunctious one, that you will never utter one careless word of what happened here? Are you so young that I have to tell you this?" She bent down to kiss me.

"No, my pearl, my beauty, you needn't tell me. I won't even tell *him*."

She stood and gathered up her broken pearls and wrinkled ribbons, the remnants of the rape. She smoothed the bed. She looked as lovely as a human swan, a match for the gilded swans of her boatlike bed.

"Your Master will know," she said. "He's a great magician."

"Are you afraid of him? I mean in general, Bianca, I don't mean on account of me?"

"No," she said. "Why should I fear him? Everyone knows not to anger him or offend him or break his solitude or question him, but it's not fear. Why do you cry, Amadeo, what's wrong?"

"I don't know, Bianca."

"I'll tell you then," she said. "He has become the world to you as only such a great being can. And you are out of it now and longing to return to it. A man such as that becomes all things to you, and his wise voice becomes the law by which everything is measured. All that lies beyond has no value because he doesn't see it, and he doesn't declare that it is valuable. And so you have no choice but to leave the wastes that lie outside his light and return to it. You must go home."

She went out, closing the doors. I slept, refusing to go home.

The next morning, I breakfasted with her, and spent all day with her. Our intimacy had given me a radiant sense of her. No matter how much she talked of my Master, I had eyes only for her just now, in these quarters of hers which were perfumed with her and full of all her private and special things.

I will never forget Bianca. Never.

I told her, as one can do with a courtesan, all about the brothels to which I'd been. Perhaps I remember them in such detail because I told her. I told her with delicate words, of course. But I told her. I told her how my Master wanted me to learn everything and had taken me to these splendid academies himself.

"Well, that's fine, but you can't linger here, Amadeo. He's taken you to places where you'll have the pleasure of much company. He may not want you to remain in the company of one."

I didn't want to go. But when nightfall came, and the house filled with her English and French poets, and the music started, and the dancing, I didn't want to share her with all the admiring world.

For a while I watched her, confusingly conscious that I had had her in her secret chamber as none of these, her admirers, had or might have, but it gave me no solace.

I wanted something from my Master, something final and conclusive and obliterating, and maddened by this desire, suddenly fully aware of it, I got drunk in a tavern, drunk enough to be nervy and nasty, and I went blundering home.

I felt bold and defiant and very independent for having stayed away from my Master and all his mysteries for so long.

He was painting furiously when I returned. He was high on the scaffold, and I figured he was attending to the faces of his Greek philosophers, working the alchemy by which vivid countenances came out of his brush, as though uncovered rather than applied.

He wore a bedraggled gray tunic that hung down to his feet. He didn't turn to look at me when I came in. Every brazier in the house it seemed had been crammed into the room to give him the light he wanted.

The boys were frightened at the speed with which he covered the canvas.

I soon realized, as I staggered into the studio, that he wasn't painting on his Greek Academy.

He was painting a picture of me. I knelt in this picture, a boy of our time, with my familiar long locks and a quiet suit of clothing as if I had taken leave of the high-toned world, and seemingly innocent, my hands clasped in prayer. Around me were gathered angels, gentle-faced and glorious as they always appeared, only these had been graced with black wings.

Black wings. Great black feathery wings. Hideous they seemed, the more I looked upon this canvas.

Hideous, and he had almost completed it. The auburn-haired boy seemed real as he looked unchallengingly to Heaven, and the angels appeared avid yet sad.

But nothing therein was as monstrous as the spectacle of my Master painting this, of his hand and brush whipping across the picture, realizing sky, clouds, broken pediment, angel wing, sunlight.

The boys clung to one another, certain of his madness or his sorcery. Which was it? Why did he so carelessly reveal himself to those whose minds had been at peace?

Why did he flaunt our secret, that he was no more a man than the winged creatures he painted! Why had he the Lord lost his patience in such a manner as this?

Suddenly in a rage, he threw a pot of paint at the far corner of the room. A splatter of dark green disfigured the wall. He cursed and cried in a language none of us knew.

He hurled the pots down, and the paint spilt in great shiny splashes from the wooden scaffold. He sent the brushes flying like arrows.

"Get out of here, go to your beds, I don't want to see you, innocents. Go. Go."

The apprentices ran from him. Riccardo reached out to gather to him the smaller boys. All hurried out the door.

High up on the scaffold, he sat down, his legs dangling, and merely looked at me as I stood beneath him, as if he didn't know who I was.

"Come down, Master," I said.

His hair was disheveled and matted here and there

with paint. He showed no surprise that I was there, no start at the sound of my voice. He had known I was there. He knew all such things. He could hear words spoken in other rooms. He knew the thoughts of those around him. He was pumped full of magic, and when I drank from that magic, I reeled.

"Let me comb your hair out for you," I said. I was insolent, I knew it.

His tunic was stained and filthy. He'd wiped his brush on it over and over again.

One of his sandals fell with a clatter to the marble. I picked it up.

"Master, come down. Whatever I said to worry you, I won't say it again."

He wouldn't answer me.

Suddenly all my rage came up in me, my loneliness to have been separated from him for days on end, obeying his injunctions, and now to come home and find him staring at me wild and unconfiding. I would not tolerate his staring off, ignoring me as if I weren't there. He must admit that I was the cause of his anger. He must speak.

I wanted suddenly to cry.

His face became anguished. I couldn't watch this; I couldn't think that he felt pain as I did, as the other boys did. I was in wild revolt.

"You frighten everyone selfishly, Lord and Master!" I declared.

Without regarding me, he vanished in a great flurry, and I heard his footsteps rushing through the empty rooms.

I knew he had moved with a speed men couldn't

master. I hurried after him, only to hear the bedroom doors slammed shut against me, to hear the lock slid closed before I reached out to grab the latch.

"Master, let me in," I cried. "I went only because you told me to." I turned around and around. It was quite impossible to break these doors. I pounded on them with my fists and kicked them. "Master, you sent me to the brothels. You sent me on damnable errands."

After a long time, I sat down at the foot of the door, my back against it, and wept and wailed. I made a riotous amount of noise. He waited until I stopped.

"Go to sleep, Amadeo," he said. "My rages have nothing to do with you."

Impossible. A lie! I was infuriated and insulted, and hurt and cold! This whole house was damnably cold.

"Then let your peace and calm have to do with me, Sir!" I said. "Open the damned door."

"Go to bed with the others," he said quietly. "You belong with the others, Amadeo. They are your loved ones. They are your kind. Don't seek the company of monsters."

"Ah, is that what you are, Sir?" I asked contemptuously and crossly. "You that can paint like Bellini or Mantegna, who can read all words and speak all tongues, who has love without end and patience to match it, a monster! Is that it? A monster spreads the roof over our head and feeds us our daily supper from the kitchens of the gods! Oh, indeed, a monster."

He didn't answer.

I was further enraged. I went down to the lower floor. I took a great battle-ax from the wall. It was one of many weapons on display in the house which I'd scarcely ever noticed. Well, it was time for it, I thought. I've had enough of this coldness. I can't stand it. I can't stand it.

I went upstairs and heaved the battle-ax at the door. Of course it went through the brittle wood, shattering the painted panel, cracking through the old lacquer and the pretty yellow and red roses. I pulled it back and smashed it into the door again.

This time the lock was broken. I kicked the shattered frame with my foot and it fell back.

In utter amazement he sat in his large dark oak chair looking at me, his hands clutching the two lion's head arms. Behind him loomed the massive bed with its rich red baldaquin trimmed in gold.

"How dare you!" he said.

He stood before me in an instant, took the ax and hurled it with ease so that it crashed into the stone wall opposite. Then he picked me up and threw me towards the bed. The entire bed shivered, baldaquin and draperies as well. No man could have made me span that distance. But he had done it. With arms and legs flying, I landed on the pillows.

"Despicable monster!" I said. I turned over, steadied myself and drew up on my left side, glaring at him, one knee crooked.

He stood with his back to me. He had been about to close the inner doors of the apartment, which had been open before and therefore were not broken. But he stopped. He turned. A playful expression came over him.

"Oh, what a vile temper we have for such an angelic countenance," he said mildly.

"If I'm an angel," I said, drawing back from the edge of the bed, "paint me with black wings."

"You dare knock down my door." He folded his arms. "Need I tell you why I will not tolerate such from you, or from anyone?"

He stood gazing at me with raised eyebrows.

"You torture me," I said.

"Oh, indeed, how and since when?"

I wanted to bawl. I wanted to say, "I love only you." Instead I said, "I detest you."

He couldn't help but laugh. He lowered his head, his fingers curled under his chin, as he stared at me.

Then he extended his hand and snapped his fingers.

I heard a rustling from the rooms beyond. I sat up petrified with amazement.

I saw the long switch of the teacher come slithering along the floor as if a wind had sent it hither, and then it twisted and turned and rose and dropped into his waiting hand.

Behind him, the inner doors slammed shut and the bolt slipped into place with a loud metallic clatter.

I drew back in the bed.

"It's going to be a pleasure to whip you," he said, smiling sweetly, his eyes almost innocent. "You may chalk it up as another human experience, rather like cavorting with your English lord."

"Do it. I hate you," I said. "I'm a man and you deny it."

He looked superior and gentle but not amused.

He came towards me, and grabbed at my head, and threw me face down on the bed.

"Demon!" I said.

"Master," he replied calmly.

I felt the nudge of his knee in the small of my back and then down came the switch across my thighs. Of course I wasn't wearing anything but the thin stockings that fashion decreed, so I might as well have been naked.

I cried out in pain and then shut my mouth tight. When the next few blows came, walloping my legs, I swallowed all noise, furious to hear myself make a careless impossible groan.

Again and again, he brought the switch down, whipping my thighs and then my lower legs as well. Enraged, I struggled to get up, pushing vainly on the covers with the heels of my hands. I couldn't move. I was pinioned by his knee, and he whacked away without the slightest deterrent.

Suddenly as rebellious as I'd ever been, I decided to play games with this. I'd be damned if I'd lie there crying, and the tears were coming up in my eyes. I closed my eyes shut, gritted my teeth and decided that each blow was the divine color red and that I liked, and that the hot crashing pain I felt was red, and that the warmth swelling up in my leg after was golden and sweet.

"Oh, that's lovely!" I said.

"You make a fool's bargain, little boy!" he said.

He whipped me harder and faster. I couldn't keep my pretty visions. It hurt, it bloody hurt.

"I'm not a boy!" I cried.

I felt a wetness on my leg. I knew I was bleeding.

"Master, you mean to disfigure me?"

"There's nothing worse than for a fallen saint to be a horrid devil!"

More blows. I knew I was bleeding from more than

one place. I would surely be bruised all over. I wouldn't be able to walk.

"I don't know what you mean! Stop!"

To my astonishment, he did. I curled my arm up under my face and I sobbed. I sobbed for a long moment, and my legs burned as if the switch were still hitting them. It seemed the blows were being laid on over and over, but they weren't. I kept hoping, Let this pain die away to something warm again, something tingling and nice, the way it felt the first couple of times. That would be all right, but this is terrible. I hate it!

Suddenly I felt him cover me. I felt the sweet tickling of his hair on my legs. I felt his fingers as he grabbed the torn cloth of the stockings and ripped it, tearing it off both my legs very quickly, leaving them bare. He reached up under my tunic and tore loose the remnants of the hose.

The pain throbbed, grew worse, then a little better. The air was cool on my bruises. When his fingers touched them, I felt such terrible pleasure that all I could do was moan.

"You going to break down my door again?"

"Never," I whispered.

"You going to defy me in any way in particular?"

"Never in any way ever."

"Further words?"

"I love you."

"I'm sure."

"But I do," I said sniffling.

The stroking of his fingers on my hurt flesh was insupportably delicious. I didn't dare raise my head. I pressed my cheek against the scratchy embroidered coverlet, against the great picture of the lion stitched into it, and I sucked in my breath and let my tears flow. I felt calm all over; this pleasure robbed me of any control of my limbs.

I closed my eyes, and there came his lips on my leg. He kissed one of the bruises. I thought I would die. I would go to Heaven, that is, some other higher more delicious Heaven even than this Venetian Heaven. Beneath me, my groin was alive with thankful and desperate and isolated strength.

The burning blood flowed over the bruise. The slightly rough stroke of his tongue touched it, lapped at it, pressed it, and the inevitable tingling made a fire in my closed eyes, a blazing fire across a mythical horizon in the darkness of my blind mind.

To the next bruise he went, and there came the trickles of the blood and the lap of his tongue, and the hideous pain departed and there was nothing but a throbbing sweetness. And as he went to the next, I thought, I cannot bear this, I will simply die.

He moved fast, from bruise to bruise, depositing his magical kiss and the stroke of his tongue, and I quivered all over and moaned.

"Some punishment!" I suddenly said with a gasp.

It was a dreadful thing to say! Instantly, I regretted it, the sassiness of it.

But his hand had already come down with a fierce slap on my backside.

"I didn't mean it," I said. "I mean, I didn't mean it to sound so ungrateful. I mean, I'm sorry I said it!" But there was another slap as hot as the first.

"Master, have pity on me. I'm mixed up!" I cried.

His hand lay on me, on the warm surface that he had slapped, and I thought, Oh, now he's going to beat me till I'm unconscious.

But his fingers only gently clasped the skin, which was not broken, only warm as the first welts from the switch had been.

I felt his lips again on the calf of my left leg, and the blood, and his tongue. The pleasure moved all through me, and helpless, I let the air escape my lips in a rosary of sighs.

"Master, Master, Master, I love you."

"Yes, well, that's not so unusual," he whispered. He didn't stop his kissing. He lapped at the blood. I writhed under the weight of his hand on my backside. "But the question is, Amadeo, why do I love you? Why? Why did I have to go into that stinking brothel and look upon you? I am strong by nature . . . whatever my nature . . ."

He greedily kissed a large bruise on my thigh. I could feel his sucking at it, and then the tongue lapping it, eating the blood, and then his blood coming down into it. The pleasure sent shock after shock through me. I saw nothing, though I thought that my eyes were now open. I struggled to make certain that my eyes were open, but nothing came visible, only a golden haze.

"I love you, I do love you," he said. "And why? Quick-witted, yes, beautiful, yes, and inside you, the burnt-up relics of a saint!"

"Master, I don't know what you're saying to me. I was never a saint, never, I don't claim to be a saint. I'm a wretched disrespectful and ungrateful being. Oh, I adore you. It's so delicious to be helpless and at your mercy."

"Stop mocking me."

"But I don't," I said. "I want to speak, the truth, I want to be a fool for the truth, a fool for—. I want to be a fool for you."

"No, I don't guess you do mean to mock me. You mean it. You don't realize the absurdity of it."

He had finished his progress. My legs had lost any shape they possessed in my mist-filled mind. I could only lie there, my whole body vibrating from his kisses. He laid his head on my hips, against the warm place that he had smacked with his hand, and I felt his fingers come up under me and touch the most private part of me.

My organ hardened in his fingers, hardened with the infusion of his searing blood, but all the more with the young male in me who had so often mingled pleasure with pain at his will.

Harder and harder I grew, and bucked and pumped beneath his head and shoulders as he lay on my backside, as he held tight to the organ, and then into his slippery fingers I gave forth in violent unsurpassed spasms a great gush.

I rose on my elbow and looked back at him. He was sitting up, staring at the pearly white semen that clung to his fingers.

"Good God, is that what you wanted?" I asked. "To see the viscous whiteness in your hand?

He looked at me with anguish. Oh, such anguish.

"Doesn't it mean?" I asked, "that the time has come?"

The misery in his eyes was too much for me to question him anymore.

Drowsy and blind, I felt him turn me over and rip off

my tunic and jacket. I felt him lift me and then came the sting of his assault into my neck. A fierce pain gathered itself around my heart, slackening just when I feared it, and then I sank down beside him into the perfumed cleft of the bed; and against his chest, warm under covers that he pulled up over us, I slept.

It was still thick and heavy night when I opened my eyes. I had learnt with him to feel the coming of morning. And morning was not yet really near.

I looked around for him. I saw him at the foot of the bed. He was dressed in his finest red velvet. He wore a jacket with slashed sleeves and a heavy tunic with a high collar. This cloak of red velvet was trimmed in ermine.

His hair was thoroughly brushed and very slightly oiled so that it gave off its most civilized and artful shimmer, swept back from his clean straight hairline and turning in mannered curls on his shoulders. He looked sad.

"Master, what is it?"

"I have to go for a few nights. No, it's not out of anger at you, Amadeo. It's one of those journeys I have to make. I'm long overdue for it."

"No, Master, not now, please. I'm sorry, I beg you, not now! What I—."

"Child. I go to see Those Who Must Be Kept. I have no choice in this."

For a moment I said nothing. I tried to understand the denotation of the words he'd spoken. His voice had dropped, and he had said the words halfheartedly.

"What is that, Master?" I asked.

"Some night perhaps I'll take you with me. I'll ask permission . . ." His voice trailed off.

"For what, Master? When have you ever needed anyone's permission for anything?"

I had meant this to be simple and candid, but I knew now it had an impertinent sound.

"It's all right, Amadeo," he said. "I ask permission now and then from my Elders, that's all. Who else?" He looked weary. He sat beside me and leaned down next to me and kissed my lips.

"Elders, Sir? You mean Those Who Must Be Kept—these are creatures like you?"

"You be kind to Riccardo and the others. They worship you," he said. "They wept for you the whole time you were away. They didn't quite believe me when I told them you were coming home. Then Riccardo spied you with your English lord and was terrified I'd break you in little pieces, yet afraid the Englishman would kill you. He has quite the reputation, your English lord, slamming down his knife on the board in any tavern he chooses. Do you have to consort with common murderers? You have a nonpareil here when it comes to those who take life. When you went to Bianca, they didn't dare to tell me, but made fancy pictures in their minds so I couldn't read their thoughts. How docile they are with my powers."

"They love you, my Lord," I said. "Thank God that you forgive me for the places I went. I'll do whatever you wish."

"Good night then." He rose to go.

"Master, how many nights?"

"Three at most," he said over his shoulder. He made for the door, a tall gallant figure in his cloak.

"Master."

"Yes."

"I'll be very good, a saint," I said. "But if I'm not will you whip me again, please?"

The moment I saw the anger in his face I regretted this. What made me say such things!

"Don't tell me you didn't mean it!" he said, reading my mind and hearing the words before I could get them out.

"No. It's just I hate it when you go. I thought maybe if I taunted you, you wouldn't."

"Well, I will. And don't taunt me. As a matter of policy, don't taunt me."

He was out the door before he changed his mind and returned. He came towards the bed. I expected the worst. He was going to slap me and then not be around to kiss the bruise.

But he didn't.

"Amadeo, while I'm gone, *think on it,*" he said.

I was sobered, looking at him. His very manner made me reflect before I uttered a word.

"On everything, Sir?" I asked.

"Yes," he said. Then he came again to kiss me. "Will you be this forever?" he asked. "This man, this young man, that you are now?"

"Yes, Master! Forever, and with you!" I wanted to tell him that there was nothing I couldn't do that a man could do, but this seemed most unwise, and also it would not seem true to him.

He laid his hand fondly on my head, pushing my hair back.

"For two years, I've watched you grow," he said. "You've reached your full height, but you're small, and your face is a baby's face, and for all your good health, you're slight and not the robust man yet that you are surely meant to be."

I was too enthralled to interrupt him. When he paused, I waited.

He sighed. He looked off as if he couldn't find words.

"When you were gone, your English lord drew his dagger on you, but you weren't afraid. Do you remember? It wasn't two days ago."

"Yes, Sir, it was stupid."

"You could easily have died then," he said with a raise of his eyebrow. "Easily."

"Sir, please open up these mysteries to me," I said. "Tell me how you came to your powers. Entrust these secrets to me. Lord, make it so that I can be with you forever. I don't care anything for my own judgment of such things. I yield to yours."

"Ah, yes, you yield if I fulfill your request."

"Well, Sir, that is a form of yielding, to give myself up to you, your will and your power, and yes, I would have it and be like you. Is that what you promise, Master, is that what you hint at, that you can make me like you? You can fill me with this blood of yours that makes a slave out of me, and it will be accomplished? It seems at times I know this, Master, that you can do it, and yet I wonder if I know it only because you know it, and you are lonely to do it to me."

"Ah!" He put his hands to his face, as though I had displeased him totally.

I was at a loss.

"Master, if I offended, hit me, beat me, do anything

to me but don't turn away. Don't cover your eyes that would look on me, Master, because I can't live without your gaze. Explain it to me. Master, take away what divides us; if it be only ignorance then take away that."

"Oh, I will, I will," he said. "You are so clever and deceiving, Amadeo. You would be the fool for God all right, as you were told a long time ago that a saint should be."

"You lose me, Sir. I am no saint, and a fool, yes, because I conjecture it's a form of wisdom and I want it because you prize wisdom."

"I mean that you appear simple, and out of your simplicity comes a clever grasp. I am lonely. Oh, yes, I am lonely, and lonely to tell my woes if nothing else. But who would burden one so young as you with my woes? Amadeo, what age do you think I am? Gauge my age with your simplicity."

"You have none, Sir. You neither eat nor drink, nor change with time. You need no water to wash you clean. You are smooth and resistant to all things of nature. Master, we all know this. You are a clean and fine and whole thing."

He shook his head. I was distressing him when I wanted just the opposite.

"I have done it already," he whispered.

"What, my Lord, what have you done?"

"Oh, brought you to me, Amadeo, for now—." He stopped. He frowned, and his face was so soft and wondering that it made me ache. "Ah, but these are just self-serving delusions. I could take you, with a heap of gold, and plant you down in a distant city where—."

"Master, kill me. Kill me before you do this, or make

sure your city is beyond the compass of the known world, because I will journey back! I will spend the last ducat of your heap of gold to journey here and beat on your doors."

He looked wretched, more a man than I'd ever seen him, in pain and trembling as he looked off, deep into the endless dark divide that separated us.

I clung to his shoulder and kissed him. There was a stronger, more virile intimacy due to my crude act of hours ago.

"No, no time for such comforts," he said. "I have to be gone. Duty calls me. Ancient things call to me, things which have been my burden for so very long. I am so weary!"

"Don't go tonight. When the morning comes, take me with you, Master, take me to where you conceal yourself from the sun. It is from the sun that you must hide, isn't it, Master, you who paint blue skies and the light of Phoebus more brilliantly than those who see it, you never see it—."

"Stop," he begged me, pressing his fingers about my hand. "Stop your kisses and your reason, and do as I say."

He took a deep breath, and for the first time in all my life with him, I saw him take a handkerchief from his coat and pat the moisture on his own forehead and his lips. The cloth was faintly red. He looked at it.

"I want to show you something before I go," he said. "Dress yourself, quickly. Here, I'll help you."

I was fully dressed for the cold winter night in less than a few minutes. He put a black cape over my shoulders, and gave me gloves trimmed in miniver, and put a black velvet cap on my head. The shoes he chose were black leather boots, which he never wanted me to wear before. To him the ankles of the boys were beautiful, and he did not favor boots, though he did not mind if we wore them by day when he could not see.

He was so troubled, so distressed, and all his face, despite its blanched cleanliness, was so infused with it, that I couldn't keep from embracing him and kissing him, just to make his lips part, just to feel his mouth locking onto mine.

I closed my eyes. I felt his hand cover up my face and cover my eyelids.

There was a great noise around me, as of the flapping of the wooden doors, and the flying about of the broken fragments of that door I'd shattered, and of draperies billowed and snapped.

The cold air of outside surrounded me. He set me down, blind, and I knew my feet were on the quay. I could hear the water of the canal near me, lapping, lapping, as the winter wind stirred it and drove the sea into the city, and I could hear a wooden boat knocking persistently against a dock.

He let slip his fingers, and I opened my eyes.

We were far from the palazzo. I was abashed to see us at such a distance, though I was not really surprised. He could do wonders, and so he let me know this now. We were in back alleyways. We stood on a small landing by a narrow canal. I had never ventured into this mean district where workmen lived.

I saw only the back porches of houses, and their ironclad windows, and a general squalor and blindness,

and a rankness as refuse floated on the water of the dipping, splashing winter-blown canal.

He turned and drew me with him away from the water's edge, and for a moment I couldn't see. His white
hand flashed out. I beheld one finger pointed and then I
beheld a man sleeping in a long rotted gondola that had
been drawn up out of the water and set on workmen's
blocks. The man stirred and threw back his covering. I
saw his hulking fussing shape as he grumbled and
cursed at us that we dared to disturb his sleep.

I reached for my dagger. I saw the flash of his blade.
The white hand of the Master, glowing like quartz,
seemed only to touch the man's wrist and send the
weapon flying and rolling on the stones. Befuddled and
enraged, the man charged my Master in a great clumsy
bid to knock my Master off his feet.

My Master caught him easily, as if he were no more
than a great swaddling of evil-smelling wool. I saw my
Master's face. His mouth opened. There came two tiny
sharp teeth, like daggers unto themselves, as he bit down
into the man's throat. I heard the man cry out, but only
for an instant, and then his stinking body went still.

Astonished and enthralled, I watched as my Master
closed his smooth eyes, his golden eyelashes seeming
silvery in the dimness, and I heard a low wet sound,
barely audible but horribly suggestive of the flow of
something, and that something had to be the man's
blood. My Master pressed himself ever more closely to
his victim, his plainly visible white fingers coaxing the
life fluid from the dying body, as he gave off a long sweet
savoring sigh. He drank. He drank, and there was no
mistaking it. He even twisted his head a little as if to

bring the last draught all the more quickly, and at this the man's form, now seemingly frail and plastic, shuddered all over, as if the man had gone into a final convulsion, and then was still.

The Master drew himself up and ran his tongue over his lips. There was not a drop of blood to be seen. But the blood was visible. It was visible inside my Master. His face took on a florid gleam. He turned and looked at me, and I could make out the vivid flush of his cheeks, the ruddy glister of his lips.

"This is where it comes from, Amadeo," he said. He shoved the corpse towards me, the filthy clothes brushed all against me, and as the heavy head fell back in death, he pushed it even closer so that I had to look down at the doomed man's coarse and lifeless face. He was young, he was bearded, he was not beautiful, and he was pale and he was dead.

A seam of white showed beneath each limp and expressionless eyelid. A greasy spittle hung from his decaying yellowed teeth, his breathless and colorless mouth.

I was speechless. Fear, loathing, these things had no part in it. I was simply amazed. If I thought, I thought it was wondrous.

In a sudden fit of seeming anger, my Master hurled the man's body to his left and out into the water where it fell with a dull splashing and bubbling sound.

He snatched me up, and I saw the windows falling past me. I almost screamed as we rose above the roofs. His hands clamped over my mouth. He moved so swiftly it was as if something propelled him or thrust him upwards.

We spun round or so it must have been, and when I opened my eyes we stood in a familiar room. Long golden curtains settled around us. It was warm here. In the shadows I saw the glinting outline of a golden swan.

It was Bianca's room, her private sanctuary, her very own room.

"Master!" I said in fear and revulsion, that we should come like this, into her chamber, without so much as a word.

From the closed doors a tiny seam of light laid itself out upon her parqueted floor and its thick Persian carpet. It laid itself upon the deep-carved feathers of her swan bed.

Then came her footsteps hastily, emerging from an airy cloud of voices, so that she might investigate alone the noise she heard.

The cold wind swept into the room from the open window as she opened her doors. Against the draught she slammed them shut, such a fearless creature, and she reached out with unerring accuracy and raised the wick of her nearby lamp. The flame rose and I saw her staring at my Master, though she had seen me as well, for sure.

She was herself, as I had left her a world of hours ago, in gold velvet and silk tissue, her braid coiled about the back of her head to weigh down her voluminous tresses which fell in their rippled splendor over her shoulders and down her back.

Her small face was quick with questioning and alarm.

"Marius," she said. "How now, my Lord, do you come here like this, into my private room? How now, you come by the window, and with Amadeo? What is this, jealousy of me?"

"No, only I would have a confession," my Master said. His very voice trembled. He held me tight by my hand as if I were a mere child as he approached her, his long finger flying out to accuse her . . . "Tell him, my darling angel, tell him what lies behind your fabulous face."

"I don't know what you mean, Marius. But you anger me. And I order you out of my house. Amadeo, what do you say to this abuse?"

"I don't know, Bianca," I murmured. I was totally in fear. Never had I heard my Master's voice tremble, and never had I heard anyone address him so familiarly by name.

"Get out of my house, Marius. Go now. I speak to the honorable man in you."

"Ah, and how then did your friend Marcellus go, the Florentine, the one you were told to lure here with your clever words, the one whose drink you laced with enough poison to kill twenty men?"

My damsel's face grew brittle but never really hard. She seemed a porcelain princess as she appraised my angry, trembling Master.

"What is this to you, my Lord?" she asked. "Have you become the Grand Council or the Council of Ten? Take me up before the courts on charges, if you will, you stealthy sorcerer! Prove your words."

There was a great high-strung dignity to her. She craned her neck and raised her chin.

"Murderess," my Master said. "I see it now within

the solitary cell of your mind, a dozen confessions, a dozen cruel and importunate acts, a dozen crimes—."

"No, you cannot judge me! A magician you might be, but you are no angel, Marius. Not you with your boys."

He dragged her forward, and once again I saw his mouth open. I saw his deadly teeth.

"No, Master, no!" I ripped loose of his slack neglected hand and flew at him with my fists, crashing my body between hers and his and pounding on him with all my might. "You can't do it, Master. I don't care what she's done. You seek these reasons for what. Call her importunate? Her! And what is it with you?"

She fell backwards against her bed and struggled up onto it, her legs bent. She drew back into the shadows.

"You are the Fiend from Hell himself," she whispered. "You are a monster, and I have seen it. Amadeo, he'll never let me live."

"Let her live, my Lord, or I die with her!" I said. "She's no more than a lesson here, and I will not see her die."

My Master was wretched. He was dazed. He pushed me away from him, steadying me so that I didn't fall. He moved towards the bed, but not in pursuit of her. He sat down beside her. She recoiled ever deeper against the headboard, her hand reaching out vainly for the sheer gold drapery as if it could save her.

She was wan and small, and her fierce blue eyes remained fixed and wide.

"We are killers together, Bianca," he whispered to her. He reached out.

I rushed forward, but only to be stopped casually by his right hand, and with his left he smoothed her few tiny loose curls back from her forehead. He rested his hand on her as if he were a priest giving a blessing.

"Of rude necessity, Sir, all of it," she said. "What choice after all did I have?" How brave she was, how strong like fine silver suffused with steel. "Once given the commissions, what am I to do, for I know what is to be done and for whom? How clever they were. It was a brew which took days to kill its victim far from my warm rooms."

"Call your oppressor here, child, and poison him, instead of those he points out."

"Yes, that ought to do it," I said hastily. "Kill the man who put you up to it."

She seemed in truth to think on this and then to smile. "And what of his guards, his kinsmen? They would strangle me for the grand betrayal."

"I'll kill him for you, sweet," said Marius. "And for that, you'll owe me no high crimes, only your gentle forgetfulness of the appetite you have seen tonight in me."

For the first time, her courage seemed to waver. Her eyes filled with clear pretty tears. A tiny weariness showed itself in her. She hung her head for a moment. "You know who he is, you know where he lodges, you know that he is in Venice now."

"He's a dead man, my beautiful lady," my Master said.

I slipped my arm around his neck. I kissed his forehead. He kept his eyes on her.

"Come, then, cherub," he said to me while he still looked at her. "We'll go to rid the world of this Florentine, this banker, who uses Bianca to dispatch those who have given him accounts in secret."

This intelligence amazed Bianca, but once again she made a soft, knowing smile. How graceful she was, how devoid of pride and bitterness. How these horrors were cast aside.

My Master held me fast to him with his right arm. He reached inside his jacket with his left and took out of it a large beautiful pear-shaped pearl. It seemed a priceless thing. He gave it to Bianca, who took it only with hesitation, watching it drop into her lazy, open hand.

"Let me kiss you, darling princess," he said.

To my astonishment, she allowed it, and he covered her now with feathery kisses, and I watched her pretty golden eyebrows pucker, and I saw her eyes become dazzled, and her body go limp. She lay back on her pillows and then fell into a fast sleep.

We withdrew. I thought I heard the shutters close behind us. The night was wet and dark. My head was pressed to my Master's shoulder. I couldn't have looked up or moved if I wanted to.

"Thank you, my beloved Lord, that you didn't kill her," I whispered.

"She is more than a practical woman," he said. "She is unbroken still. She has the innocence and cunning of a duchess or a queen."

"But where do we go now?"

"We are there, Amadeo. We are on the roof. Look about you. Do you hear the din below?"

It was tambourines and drums and flutes playing.

"Ah, so, they will die at their banquet," my Master said thoughtfully. He stood at the edge of the roof, holding to the stone railing. The wind blew his cloak back, and he turned his eyes up to the stars.

"I want to see it all," I said.

He shut his eyes as if I'd struck him a blow.

"Don't think me cold, Sir," I said. "Don't think me tired and used to things brutal and cruel. I am only the fool, Sir, the fool for God. We don't question, if memory serves me right. We laugh and we accept and we turn all life into joy."

"Come down with me, then. There are a crowd of them, these crafty Florentines. Oh, but I am so hungry. I have starved myself for a night such as this."

5

PERHAPS mortals feel this way when they hunt the big beasts of the forest and of the jungle.

For me, as we went down the stairs from the ceiling into the banquet room of this new and highly decorated palazzo, I felt a rabid excitement. Men were going to die. Men would be murdered. Men who were bad, men who had wronged the beautiful Bianca, were going to be killed without risk to my all-powerful Master, and without risk to anyone whom I knew or loved.

An army of mercenaries could not have felt less compassion for these individuals. The Venetians in attacking the Turks perhaps had more feeling for their enemy than I.

I was spellbound; the scent of blood was already in

me insofar as it was symbolic. I wanted to see blood flow. I didn't like Florentines anyway, and I certainly didn't understand bankers, and I most definitely wanted swift vengeance, not only for those who had bent Bianca to their will but on those who had put her in the path of my Master's thirst.

So be it.

We entered a spacious and impressive banquet hall where a party of some seven men was gorging itself on a splendid supper of roast pork. Flemish tapestries, all very new and with splendid hunting scenes of lords and ladies with their horses and hounds, were hung from great iron rods all through the room, covering even the windows and falling heavily to the very floor.

The floor itself was a fine inlay of multicolored marble, fashioned in pictures of peacocks, complete with jewels in their great fanlike tails.

The table was very broad, and three men sat behind the table all on one side, virtually slobbering over heaps of gold plates littered with the sticky bones of fish and fowl, and the roasted pig himself, poor swollen creature, whose head remained, ignominiously grasping the inevitable apple as though it were the ultimate expression of his final wish.

The other three men—all young and somewhat pretty and most athletic, by the look of their beautifully muscled legs—were busy dancing in an artful circle, hands meeting in the center, as a small gathering of boys played the instruments whose pounding march we had heard on the roof.

All appeared somewhat greasy and stained from the feast. But not a member of the company lacked long thick fashionable hair, and ornate, heavily worked silk tunics and hose. There was no fire for heat, and indeed none of these men needed any such, and all were tricked out in velvet jackets with trimmings of powdered ermine or miniver or silver fox.

The wine was being slopped from the pitcher into the goblets by one who seemed quite unable to manage such a gesture. And the three who danced, though they had a courtly design to enact, were also roughhousing and shoving one another in some sort of deliberate mockery of the dance steps that all knew.

I saw at once that the servants had been dismissed. Several goblets had spilled. Tiny gnats, despite the winter, had congregated over the shiny half-eaten carcasses and the heaps of moist fruit.

A golden haze hung over the room which was the smoke from the tobacco of the men which they smoked in a variety of different pipes. The background of the tapestries was invariably a dark blue, and this gave the whole scene a warmth against which the rich vari-colored clothes of the boy musicians and the dinner guests shone brilliantly.

Indeed, as we entered the smoky warmth of the room, I felt intoxicated by the atmosphere, and when my Master bid me sit down at one end of the table, I did so out of weakness, though I shrank from touching even the top of the table, let alone the edge of the various plates.

The red-faced, bawling merrymakers took no notice of us. The thumping din of the musicians was sufficient to render us invisible, because it overpowered the senses. But the men were far too drunk to have seen us in perfect silence. Indeed, my Master, after planting a kiss on my cheek, went to the very center of the table, to a space left there, presumably by one of those cavorting to the music, and he stepped over the padded bench and sat down.

Only then did the two men on either side of him, who had been shouting at one another adamantly about some point or other, take notice of this resplendent scarlet-clad guest.

My Master had let the hood of his cape fall, and his hair was wondrously shaped in its prodigious length. He looked the Christ again at the Last Supper with his lean nose and mild full mouth, and the blond hair parted so cleanly in the middle, and the whole mass of it alive from the damp of the night.

He looked from one to the other of these guests, and to my astonishment as I looked down the table at him, he plunged into their conversation, discussing with them the atrocities visited upon those Venetians left in Constantinople when the twenty-one-year-old Turk, Sultan Mehmet II, had conquered the city.

It seemed there was some argument as to how the Turks actually breached the sacred capital, and one man was saying that had not the Venetian ships sailed away from Constantinople, deserting her before the final days, the city might have been saved.

No chance at all, said the other, a robust red-haired man with seemingly golden eyes. What a beauty! If this was the rogue who misled Bianca, I could see why. Between red beard and mustache, his lips were a lush Cupid's bow, and his jaw had the strength of Michelangelo's superhuman marble figure.

"For forty-eight days, the cannons of the Turk had

bombarded the walls of the city," he declared to his consort, "and eventually they broke through. What could be expected? Have you ever seen such guns?"

The other man, a very pretty dark-haired olive-skinned fellow with rounded cheeks very close to his small nose and large velvet black eyes, became furious and said that the Venetians had acted like cowards, and that their supported fleet could have stopped even the cannons if they had ever come. With his fist he rattled the plate in front of him. "Constantinople was abandoned!" he declared. "Venice and Genoa did not help her. The greatest empire on Earth was allowed on that horrible day to collapse."

"Not so," said my Master somewhat quietly, raising his eyebrows and tilting his head slightly to one side. His eyes swept slowly from one man to the other. "There were in fact many brave Venetians who came to the rescue of Constantinople. I think, and with reason, that even if the entire Venetian fleet had come, the Turks would have continued. It was the dream of the young Sultan Mehmet II to have Constantinople and he would never have stopped."

Oh, this was most interesting. I was ready for such a lesson in history. I had to hear and see this more clearly, so I jumped up and went round the table, pulling up a light cross-legged chair with a comfortable red leather sling seat, so that I might have a good vantage point on all of them. I put it at an angle so that I might better see the dancers, who even in their clumsiness made quite a picture, if only because of their long ornate sleeves flapping about and the slap of their jeweled slippers on the tile floor.

The red-haired one at table, tossing back his long richly curling mane, was most encouraged by my Master, and gave him a wild adoring look.

"Yes, yes, here is a man who knows what happened, and you lie, you fool," he said to the other man. "And you know the Genoese fought bravely, right to the end. Three ships were sent by the Pope; they broke through the blockade of the harbor, slipping right by the Sultan's evil castle of Rumeli Hisar. It was Giovanni Longo, and can you imagine the bravery?"

"Frankly, no!" said the black-haired one, leaning forward in front of my Master as if my Master were a statue.

"It was brave," said my Master casually. "Why do you say nonsense you don't believe? You know what had happened to the Venetian ships caught by the Sultan, come now."

"Yes, speak up on that. Would you have gone into that harbor?" demanded the red-haired Florentine. "You know what they did to the Venetian ships they caught six months before? They behcaded every man on board."

"Except the man in charge!" cried out a dancer who had turned to join the conversation, but went on so as not to lose his step. "They impaled him on a stake. This was Antonio Rizzo, one of the finest men there ever was." He went on dancing with an offhand contemptuous gesture over his shoulder. Then he slipped as he pivoted and almost fell. His dancing companions caught him.

The black-haired man at the table shook his head.

"If it had been a full Venetian fleet—," cried the black-haired man. "But you Florentines and you Venetians are all the same, treacherous, hedging your bets."

My Master laughed as he watched the man.

"Don't you laugh at me," declared the black-haired man. "You're a Venetian; I've seen you a thousand times, you and that boy!"

He gestured to me. I looked at my Master. My Master only smiled. Then I heard him whisper distinctly to me, so that it struck my ear as if he were next to me rather than so many feet away. "Testimony of the dead, Amadeo."

The black-haired man picked up his goblet, slopped some wine down his throat and spilt as much down his pointed beard. "A whole city of conniving bastards!" he declared. "Good for one thing, and that's borrowing money at high interest when they spend everything they've got on fancy clothes."

"You should talk," said the red-haired one. "You look like a goddamned peacock. I ought to cut off your tail. Let's get back to Constantinople since you're so damned sure it could have been saved!"

"You are a damned Venetian yourself now."

"I'm a banker; I'm a man of responsibility," said the redhead. "I admire those who do well by me." He picked up his own goblet, but instead of drinking the wine, he threw it in the face of the black-haired man.

My Master did not bother to lean back, so undoubtedly some of the wine spilled on him. He looked from one to the other of the ruddy sweating faces on either side of him.

"Giovanni Longo, one of the bravest Genoese ever to captain a ship, stayed in that city during the entire siege," cried the red-haired man. "That's courage. I'll put money on a man like that."

"I don't know why," cried the dancer again, the same one as before. He broke from the circle long enough to declare, "He lost the battle, and besides, your Father had plenty enough sense not to bank on any of them."

"Don't you dare!" said the red-haired man. "Here's to Giovanni Longo and the Genoese who fought with him." He grabbed the pitcher, all but knocking it over, showered wine on his goblet and the table, then took a deep gulp. "And here's to my Father. May God have mercy on his immortal soul. Father, I have slain your enemies, and I'll slay those who make of ignorance a pastime."

He turned, jammed his elbow into my Master's clothes and said, "That boy of yours is a beauty. Don't be hasty. Think this over. How much?"

My Master burst out laughing more sweetly and naturally than I'd ever heard him laugh.

"Offer me something, something I might want," said my Master as he looked at me, with a secretive, glittering shift of his eyes.

It seemed every man in the room was taking my measure, and understand, these were not lovers of boys; these were merely Italians of their time, who, fathering children as was required of them and debauching women any chance they got, nevertheless appreciated a plump and juicy young man, the way that men now might appreciate a slice of golden toast heaped with sour cream and the finest blackest caviar.

I couldn't help but smile. Kill them, I thought, slaughter them. I felt fetching and even beautiful. Come on, somebody, tell me I make you think of Mercury chasing away the clouds in Botticelli's *Primavera*, but the red-haired man, fixing me with an impish playful glance, said:

"Ah, he is Verrocchio's *David*, the very model for the bronze statue. Don't try to tell me he is not. And immortal, ah, yes, I can see it, immortal. He shall never die." Again he lifted his goblet. Then he felt of the breast of his tunic, and pulled up out of the powdered ermine trim of his jacket a rich gold medallion with a table diamond of immense size. He ripped the chain right off his neck and extended this proudly to my Master, who watched it spin on the dangle in front of him as if it were an orb with which he was to be spellbound.

"For all of us," said the black-haired man, turning and looking hard at me. There was laughter from the others. The dancers cried, "Yes, and for me," "Unless I go second with him, nothing" and "Here, to go first, even before you."

This last was said to the red-haired man, but the jewel the dancer tossed at my Master, a carbuncle ring of some glittering purple stone, I didn't know.

"A sapphire," said my Master in a whisper, with a teasing looking to me. "Amadeo, you approve?"

The third dancer, a blond-haired man, somewhat shorter than anyone present and with a small hump on his left shoulder, broke free of the circle and came towards me. He took off all his rings, as if shearing himself of gloves, and tossed them all clattering at my feet.

"Smile sweetly on me, young god," he said, though he panted from the dance and the velvet collar was drenched. He wobbled on his feet and almost turned over but managed to make fun of it, twirling heavily back into his dance.

The music thumped on and on, as if the dancers thought it meet to drown out the very drunkenness of their Masters.

"Does anybody care about the siege of Constantinople?" asked my Master.

"Tell me what became of Giovanni Longo," I asked in a small voice. All eyes were on me.

"It's the siege of . . . Amadeo, was it? . . . Yes, Amadeo, that I have in mind!" cried the blond-haired dancer.

"By and by, Sir," I said. "But teach me some history."

"You little imp," said the black-haired man. "You don't even pick up his rings."

"My fingers are covered with rings," I said politely, which was true.

The red-haired man immediately went back into the battle. "Giovanni Longo stayed for forty days of bombardment. He fought all night when the Turk breached the walls. Nothing frightened him. He was carried to safety only because he was shot."

"And the guns, Sir?" I asked. "Were they so very big?"

"And I suppose you were there!" cried the black-haired man to the redhead, before the redhead could answer me.

"My Father was there!" said the redhead man. "And lived to tell it. He was with the last ship that slipped out of the harbor with the Venetians, and before you speak,

Sir, mind you, you don't speak ill of my Father or those Venetians. They carried the citizenry to safety, Sir, the battle was lost . . ."

"They deserted, you mean," said the black-haired man.

"I mean slipped out carrying the helpless refugees after the Turks had won. You call my Father a coward? You know no more about manners than you know about war. You're too stupid to fight with, and too drunk."

"Amen," said my Master.

"Tell him," said the red-haired man to my Master. "You, Marius De Romanus, you tell him." He took another slobbering gulp. "Tell him about the massacre, what happened. Tell him how Giovanni Longo fought on the walls until he was hit in the chest. Listen, you crackbrained fool!" he shouted at his friend. "Nobody knows more about all of it than Marius De Romanus. Sorcerers are clever, so says my whore, and here is to Bianca Solderini." He drained his glass.

"Your whore, Sir?" I demanded. "You say that of such a woman and here in the presence of drunken disrespectful men?"

They paid no mind to me, not the red-haired man, who was again draining his goblet, or the others.

The blond-haired dancer staggered over to me. "They're too drunk to remember you, beautiful boy," he said. "But not I."

"Sir, you stumble at your dance," I said. "Don't stumble in your rounds with me."

"You miserable little whelp," said the man, and fell

towards me, losing his balance. I darted out of the chair to the right. He slipped over the chair and fell to the floor.

There was uproarious laughter from the others. The two remaining dancers gave up their patterned steps.

"Giovanni Longo was brave," my Master said calmly, surveying everything and then returning his cool glance to the red-haired man. "They were all brave. But nothing could save Byzantium. Her hour had come. Time had run out for the Emperors and chimney sweeps. And in the holocaust that followed, so much was irretrievably lost. Libraries by the hundreds were burnt. So many sacred texts with all their imponderable mysteries went up in smoke."

I backed away from the drunk attacker, who rolled over on the floor.

"You lousy little lapdog!" the sprawling man shouted at me. "Give me your hand, I tell you."

"Ah, but Sir," I said, "I think you want more than that."

"And I'll have it!" he said, but he only skidded and fell back down again with a miserable groan.

One of the other men at table—handsome but older, with long thick wavy gray hair and a beautifully lined face, a man who had been gorging himself in silence on a greasy joint of mutton—looked up at me over the joint and at the fallen, twisting man who struggled to get to his feet.

"Hmmm. So Goliath falls, little David," he said, smiling up at me. "Mind your tongue, little David, we are not all stupid giants, and your stones are not for throwing just yet."

I smiled back at him. "Your jest is as clumsy as your friend, Sir. As for my stones, as you put it, they'll stay right where they are in their pouch and wait for you to stumble in the way of your friend."

"Did you say the books, Sir," asked the red-haired man of Marius, completely oblivious to this little exchange. "The books were burnt in the fall of the greatest city in the world?"

"Yes, he cares about books, this fellow," said the black-haired man. "Sir, you better look to your little boy. He's a goner, the dance has changed. Tell him not to mock his elders."

The two dancers came towards me, both as drunk as the man who had fallen. They made to caress me, simultaneously becoming with great odoriferous and heavy breathing a beast with four arms.

"You smile at our friend rolling around on the ground?" one of them asked, sticking his knee between my legs.

I backed up, barely escaping the rude blow. "Seemed the kindest thing I could do," I answered. "Being that my worship was the cause of his fall. Don't plunge into such devotions, yourself, Sirs. I haven't the slightest inclination to answer your prayers."

My Master had risen.

"I tire of this," he said in a cold, clear voice that echoed through the tapestries off the walls. It had a chilling sound to it.

All looked at him, even the struggling man on the floor.

"Indeed!" said the black-haired man, looking up.

"Marius De Romanus, is it? I've heard of you. I don't fear you."

"How merciful for you," said my Master in a whisper with a smile. He placed his hand on the man's head and the man whipped himself back and away, almost falling off the bench, but now he was most definitely afraid.

The dancers took their measure of my Master, no doubt trying to gauge whether he would be easy to overwhelm.

One of them turned on me again. "Prayers, Hell!" he said.

"Sir, mind my Master. You weary him, and in weariness he is a perfect crank." I snatched back my arm as he meant to take it.

I backed away even further, into the very midst of the boy musicians so that the music rose about me like a protective cloud.

I could see panic in their faces, yet they played all the faster, ignoring the sweat on their brows.

"Sweet, sweet, gentlemen," I said. "I like it. But play a requiem, if you will."

They gave me desperate glances but no other regard. The drum beat on and the pipe made its snaky melody and the room throbbed with the strumming of the lutes.

The blond-haired man on the floor screamed for help, as he absolutely couldn't get up, and the two dancers went to his aid, though one shot his watchful darts at me.

My Master looked down at the black-haired challenger and then pulled him straight up from the bench with one hand and went to kiss his neck. The man hung in my Master's grip. He froze like a small tender mammal in the teeth of a great beast, and I almost heard the great draught of blood run out of him as my Master's hair shivered and fell down to cover the fatal repast.

Quickly, he let the man drop. Only the red-haired fellow observed all this. And he seemed in his intoxication not to know what to make of it. Indeed he raised one eye, wondering, and drank again from his filthy sloppy cup. He licked the fingers of his right hand, one by one, as if he were a cat, as my Master dropped his black-haired companion facedown on the table, indeed, right into a plate of fruit.

"Drunken idiot," said the red-haired man. "No one fights for valor, or honor, or decency."

"Not many in any event," said my Master looking down at him.

"They broke the world in half, those Turks," said the red-haired man, still staring at the dead one, who surely stared stupidly at him from the smashed plate. I couldn't see the dead man's face, but it excited me tremendously that he was dead.

"Come now, gentlemen," said my Master, "and you, Sir, come here, you who gave my child so many rings."

"Is he your son, Sir?" cried the blond humpback, who was finally on his feet. He pushed his friends away from him. He turned and went to the summons. "I'll father him better than you ever did."

My Master appeared suddenly and without a sound on our side of the table. His garments settled at once, as if he had only taken a step. The red-haired man did not even seem to see it.

"Skanderbeg, the great Skanderbeg, I raise a toast to him," said the red-haired man, to himself apparently. "He's been dead too long, and give me but five Skanderbegs and I'd raise a new Crusade to take back our city from the Turks."

"Indeed, who wouldn't with five Skanderbegs," said the elderly man further down the table, the one nibbling and tearing at the joint. He wiped his mouth with his naked wrist. "But there is no general like unto Skanderbeg, and there never was, save the man himself. What's the matter with Ludovico? You fool!" He stood up.

My Master had put his arm around the blond one, who pushed at him, quite dismayed that my Master was immovable. Now as the two dancers offered my Master pushes and shoves to free their companion, my Master again planted his fatal kiss. He lifted the chin of the blond one and went right for the big artery in the neck. He swung the man around and appeared to draw up the blood from him in one great draught. In a flash, he closed the man's eyes with two white fingers and let the body slip to the floor.

"It is your time to die, good Sirs," he said to the dancers who now backed away from him.

One of them pulled his sword.

"Don't be so stupid!" shouted his companion. "You're drunk. You'll never—."

"No, you won't," said my Master with a little sigh. His lips were more pink than I had ever seen them, and the blood he'd drunk paraded in his cheeks. Even his eyes had a greater gloss, and a greater gleam.

He closed his very hand over the man's sword and

with the press of his thumb snapped the metal, so that the man held only a fragment in his hand.

"How dare you!" cried the man.

"How did you is more to the point!" sang out the red-haired man at the table. "Cracked in half, is it? What kind of steel is that?"

The joint nibbler laughed very loud and threw back his head. He tore more meat from the bone.

My Master reached out and plucked from time and space the wielder of the broken sword, and now to bare the vein, broke the man's neck with a loud snap.

It seemed the other three had heard it—the one who ate the joint, the wary dancer and the man with the red hair.

It was the last of the dancers whom my Master embraced next. He caught the man's face in his hands as if it were love, and drank again, gasping the man's throat so that I saw the blood just for an instant, a veritable deluge of it, which my Master then covered with his mouth and his bent head.

I could see the blood pump into my Master's hand. I couldn't wait for him to raise his head, and this he did very soon, sooner even than he had left his last victim, and he looked at me dreamily and his countenance was all afire. He looked as human as any man in the room, even crazed with his special drink, as they were with their common wine.

His vagrant blond curls were plastered to his forehead by the sweat that rose in him, and I saw it was a fine sheen of blood.

The music abruptly stopped.

It was not the mayhem but the sight of my Master

which had stopped it, as he let this last victim slip, a loose sack of bones, to the floor.

"Requiem," I said again. "Their ghosts will thank you, kind Gentlemen."

"Either that," said Marius to the musicians as he drew close, "or fly the room."

"I say fly the room," whispered the lute player. At once they all turned and made for the doors. They pulled and pulled upon the latch in their haste, cursing and shouting.

My Master backed up and gathered the jeweled rings from around the chair where I'd been seated before.

"My boys, you go without payment," he said.

In their helpless whining fear, they turned and beheld the rings being tossed to them, and stupidly and eagerly and full of shame, they each caught a single treasure as my Master aimed it.

Then the doors flew open and cracked against the walls.

Out they went, all but scraping the doorframe, and the doors then shut.

"That's clever!" remarked the man with the joint which he laid aside at last, as all the meat was gone. "How you'd do it, Marius De Romanus? I hear tell you're a powerful magician. Don't know why the Great Council doesn't call you up on charges of witchcraft. Must be all the money you have, no?"

I stared at my Master. Never had I seen him so lovely as now when he was flushed with this new blood. I wanted to touch him. I wanted to go into his arms. His eyes were drunken and soft as he looked at me.

But he broke off his seductive stare and went back to the table, and around it properly, and stood beside the man who had feasted on the joint.

The gray-haired man looked up at him and then glanced at his red-haired companion. "Don't be a fool, Martino," he said to the redhead. "It's probably perfectly legal to be a witch in the Veneto as long as a man pays his tax. Put your money in Martino's bank, Marius De Romanus."

"Ah, but I do," said Marius De Romanus, my Master, "and it earns me quite a good return."

He sat down again between the dead man and the red-haired man, who seemed quite delighted and exhilarated to have him return.

"Martino," said my Master. "Let's talk some more of the fall of Empires. Your Father, why was he with the Genoese?"

The red-haired man, now quite aflame with the whole discussion, declared with pride that his Father had been the representative of the family bank in Constantinople, and that he had died afterwards due to the wounds he'd suffered on that last and awful day.

"He saw it," said the red-haired man, "he saw the women and children slaughtered. He saw the priests torn from the altars of Santa Sofia. He knows the secret."

"The secret!" scoffed the elderly man. He moved down the table and, with a big swipe of his left arm, shoved the dead man off over the bench so that he fell back on the floor.

"Good God, you heartless bastard," said the red-haired man. "Did you hear his skull crack? Don't treat my guest in that manner, not if you want to live."

I came closer to the table.

"Yes, do come on, pretty one," said the redhead. "Sit down." He turned on me his blazing golden eyes. "Sit here, opposite me. Good God, look at Francisco there. I swear I heard his skull crack."

"He's dead," said Marius softly. "It's all right for the moment, don't worry on it." His face was all the more bright from the blood he'd drunk. Indeed the color was even now, and radiant overall, and his hair seemed all the fairer against his blushing skin. A tiny spider's web of veins lived within each of his eyes, not detracting one jot from their awesome lustrous beauty.

"Oh, all right, fine, they're dead," said the redhead, with a shrug. "Yes, I was telling you, and you damned well better mark my words because I know. The priests, the priests picked up the sacred chalice and the Sacred Host and they went into a hiding place in Santa Sofia. My Father saw this with his own eyes. I know the secret."

"Eyes, eyes, eyes," said the elderly man. "Your Father must have been a peacock to have had so many eyes!"

"Shut up or I'll slit your throat," said the red-haired man. "Look what you did to Francisco, knocking him over like that. Good God!" He made the Sign of the Cross rather lazily. "There's blood coming from the back of his head."

My Master turned and, leaning down, swept up five fingerfuls of this blood. He turned to me slowly and then to the redhead. He sucked the blood off one finger. "Dead," he said with a little smile. "But it's plenty warm and thick." He smiled slowly.

The red-haired man was as fascinated as a child at a puppet show.

My Master extended his bloody fingers, palm up, and made a smile as if to say, "You want to taste it?"

The red-haired man grabbed Marius's wrist and licked the blood off his forefinger and thumb. "Hmmm, very good," he said. "All my companions are of the best blood."

"You're telling me," said my Master. I couldn't rip my eyes off him, off his changing face. It seemed now his cheeks did darken, or maybe it was only their curve as he smiled. His lips were rosy.

"And I'm not finished, Amadeo," he whispered. "I've only begun."

"He's not bad hurt!" insisted the elderly man. He studied the victim on the floor. He was worried. Had he killed him? "It's just a mere cut on the back of his head, that's all. Isn't it?"

"Yes, a tiny cut," said Marius. "What's this secret, my dear friend?" He had his back to the gray-haired man, speaking to the redhead with much more interest as he had been all along.

"Yes, please," I said. "What's the secret, Sir?" I asked. "Is that the secret, that the priests ran?"

"No, child, don't be dense!" said the red-haired man looking across the table at me. He was powerfully beautiful. Had Bianca loved him? She never said.

"The secret, the secret," he said. "If you don't believe in this secret, then you'll believe nothing, nothing sacred or otherwise."

He lifted his goblet. It was empty. I picked up the pitcher and filled it with the dark lovely-smelling red wine. I considered taking a taste of it, then a revulsion filled me.

"Nonsense," whispered my Master. "Drink to their passing. Go ahead. There's a clean goblet."

"Oh, yes, forgive me," said the redhead. "I haven't even offered you a cup. Good God, to think I threw a mere table diamond on the board for you, when I would have your love." He picked up the goblet, a rich fancy thing of inlaid silver with tiny stones. I saw now that all the goblets were a set, all carved with tiny delicate figures and set with these same bright little stones. He set down this goblet for me with a clonk. He took the pitcher from me and filled the goblet and then thrust it at me.

I thought I would become so sick I'd vomit on the floor. I looked up at him, at his near sweet face and his pretty blazing red hair. He gave a boyish smile, showing small but perfect white teeth, very pearly, and he seemed to dote on me and to drift, not uttering a word.

"Take it, drink," said my Master. "Yours is a dangerous road, Amadeo, drink for knowledge and drink for strength."

"You don't mock me now, Sir, do you?" I asked, staring at the red-haired man though I spoke to Marius.

"I love you, Sir, as I always have," said my Master, "but you do see something in what I say, for I'm coarsened by human blood. It's always the fact. Only in starvation do I find an ethereal purity."

"Ah, and you turn me from penance at every juncture," I said, "towards the senses, towards pleasure."

The red-haired man and I had locked eyes. Yet I heard Marius answer me.

"It's a penance to kill, Amadeo, that's the rub. It's a

penance to slay for nothing, nothing, not 'honor, not valor, not decency,' as our friend says here."

"Yes!" said "our friend," who turned to Marius and then back to me. "Drink!" He thrust the goblet at me.

"And when it's all done, Amadeo, gather up these goblets for me and bring them home so I might have a trophy of my failure and my defeat, for they will be one and the same, and a lesson for you as well. Seldom is it all so rich and clear as it is to me now."

The red-haired man leaned forward, deep into the flirt, and put the goblet right against my lip. "Little David, you'll grow up to be the King, remember? Oh, I would worship you now, tender-cheeked little man that you are, and beg for one psalm from your harp, just one, were it given with your own will."

My Master whispered low, "Can you grant a man's dying request?"

"I think he is dead!" said the gray-haired man with obnoxious loudness. "Look, Martino, I think I did kill him; his head's bleeding like a damned tomato. Look!"

"Oh, shut up about him!" said Martino, the redhead, without taking his eyes off mine. "Do grant a dying man's request, little David," he went on. "We are all dying, and I for you, and that you die with me, just a little, Sir, in my arms? Let us make a little game of it. It will amuse you, Marius De Romanus. You'll see I ride him and stroke him with one artful rhythm, and you'll behold a sculpture of flesh that becomes a fountain, as what I pump into him comes forth from him in my hand."

He cupped his hand as if he had my organ already in it. He kept his eyes on me. Then in a low whisper, he said,

"I'm too soft to make my sculpture. Let me drink it from you. Have mercy on the parched."

I snatched the goblet out of his wavering hand and drank down the wine. My body tightened. I thought the wine would come back up and spew. I made it go down. I looked at my Master.

"This is ugly, I hate it."

"Oh, nonsense," he said, barely moving his lips. "There's beauty all around!"

"Damned if he isn't dead," said the gray-haired man. He kicked the body of Francisco on the floor. "Martino, I'm out of here."

"Stay, Sir," said Marius. "I would kiss you good night." He clapped his hand over the gray-haired man's wrist and lunged at his throat, but what did it look like to the red-haired one, who gave it only a bleary glance before he continued his worship? He filled my goblet again.

A moan came from the gray-haired man, or was it from Marius?

I was petrified. When he turned from his victim, I would see even more blood teeming in him, and I would have given all the world to see him white again, my marble god, my graven Father in our private bed.

The red-haired man rose before me as he leant over the table and put his wet lips on mine. "I die for you, boy!" he said.

"No, you die for nothing," said Marius.

"Master, not him, please!" I cried.

I fell back, nearly losing my balance on the bench. My Master's arm had come between us, and his hand covered the red-haired man's shoulder.

"What's the secret, Sir?" I cried frantically, "the secret of Santa Sofia, the one we must believe?"

The red-haired man was utterly befuddled. He knew he was drunk. He knew things around him didn't make sense. But he thought it was because he was drunk. He looked at Marius's arm across his chest, and he even turned and looked at the fingers clutching his shoulder. Then he looked at Marius and so did I.

Marius was human, utterly human. There was no trace of the impermeable and indestructible god left. His eyes and his face simmered in the blood. He was flushed as a man from running, and his lips were bloody, and when he licked them now, his tongue was ruby red. He smiled at Martino, the last of them, the only one left alive.

Martino pulled his gaze away from Marius and looked at me. At once he softened and lost his alarm. He spoke with reverence.

"In the midst of the siege, as the Turks stormed the church, some of the priests left the altar of Santa Sofia," he said. "They took with them the chalice and the Blessed Sacrament, our Lord's Body and Blood. They are hidden this very day in the secret chambers of Santa Sofia, and on the very moment that we take back the city, on the very moment when we take back the great church of Santa Sofia, when we drive the Turks out of our capital, those priests, those very priests will return. They'll come out of their hiding place and go up the steps of the altar, and they will resume the Mass at the very point where they were forced to stop."

"Ah," I said, sighing and marveling at it. "Master," I said softly. "That's a good enough secret to save a man's life, isn't it?"

"No," said Marius. "I know the story, and he made our Bianca a whore."

The red-haired man strained to follow our words, to fathom the depth of our exchange.

"A whore? Bianca? A murderer ten times over, Sir, but not a whore. Nothing so simple as a whore." He studied Marius as though he thought this heated passionately florid man was beautiful, indeed. And well he was.

"Ah, but you taught her the art of murder," said Marius almost tenderly, his fingers massaging the man's shoulder, while with his left arm he reached around Martino's back, until his left hand might lock on the man's shoulder with his right. He bent his forehead to touch Martino's temple.

"Hmmm," Martino shook himself all over. "I've drunk too much. I never taught her any such thing."

"Ah, but you did, you taught her, and to kill for such paltry sums."

"Master, what is it to us?"

"My son forgets himself," said Marius, still looking at Martino. "He forgets that I am bound to kill you on behalf of our sweet lady, whom you so finagled into your dark, sticky plots."

"She rendered me a service," said Martino. "Let me have the boy!"

"Beg pardon?"

"You mean to kill me, so do it. But let me have the boy. A kiss, Sir, that's all I ask. A kiss, that is the world. I'm too drunk for anything else!"

"Please, Master, I can't endure this," I said.

"Then, how will you endure eternity, my child? Don't you know that's what I mean to give you? What power under God is there that can break me?" He threw a fierce angry glance at me, but it seemed more artifice than true emotion.

"I've learnt my lessons," I said. "I only hate to see him die."

"Ah, yes, then you have learnt. Martino, kiss my child if he'll allow it, and mark you, be gentle when you do."

It was I who leant across the table now and planted my kiss on the man's cheek. He turned and caught my mouth with his, hungry, sour with wine, but enticingly, electrically hot.

The tears sprang to my eyes. I opened my mouth to him and let his tongue come into me. And with my eyes shut, I felt it quiver, and his lips become tight, as if they had been turned to hard metal clamped to me and unable to close.

My Master had him, had his throat, and the kiss was frozen, and I, weeping, put out my hand blindly to find the very place in his neck where my Master's evil teeth had driven in. I felt my Master's silky lips, I felt the hard teeth beneath them, I felt the tender neck.

I opened my eyes and pulled myself away. My doomed Martino sighed and moaned and closed his lips, and sat back in my Master's grip with his eyes half-mast.

He turned his head slowly towards my Master. In a small raw drunken voice, he spoke. "For Bianca . . ."

"For Bianca," I said. I sobbed, muffling it with my hand.

My Master drew up. With his left hand, he smoothed back Martino's damp and tangled hair. "For Bianca," he said into his ear.

"Never . . . never should have let her live," came the last sighing words from Martino. His head fell forward over my Master's right arm.

My Master kissed the back of his head, and let him slip down onto the table.

"Charming to the last," said he. "Just a real poet to the bottom of your soul."

I stood up, pushing the bench away behind me, and I moved out into the center of the room. I cried and cried, and couldn't muffle it with my hand. I dug into my jacket for a handkerchief, and just as I went to wipe my tears, I stumbled backwards over the dead humpbacked man and almost fell. I cried out, a terrible weak and ignominious cry.

I moved back away from him and away from the bodies of his companions until I felt behind me the heavy, scratchy tapestry, and smelled its dust and threads.

"Ah, so this was what you wanted of me," I sobbed. I veritably sobbed. "That I should hate it, that I should weep for them, fight for them, beg for them."

He sat at the table still, Christ of the Last Supper, with his neatly parted hair, his shining face, his ruddy hands folded one on top of the other, looking with his hot and swimming eyes at me.

"Weep for one of them, at least one!" he said. His voice grew wrathful. "Is that too much to ask? That one death be regretted among so many?" He rose from the table. He seemed to quake with his rage.

I pushed the handkerchief over my face, sobbing into it.

"For a nameless beggar in a makeshift boat for a bed we have no tears, do we, and would not our pretty Bianca suffer because we've played the young Adonis in her bed! And of some of those, we weep for none but that one, the very most evil without question, because he flatters us, is it not so?"

"I knew him," I whispered. "I mean, in this short time I knew him, and . . ."

"And you would have them run from you, anonymous as foxes in the brush!" He pointed to the tapestries blazoned with the Courtly Hunt. "Behold with a man's eyes what I show you."

There was a sudden darkening of the room, a flutter of all the many candles. I gasped, but it was only he, come to stand right in front of me and look down at me, a feverish, blushing being whose very heat I could feel as if every pore of him gave forth warm breath.

"Master," I cried, swallowing my sobs. "Are you happy with what you've taught me or not? Are you happy with what I've learnt or not! Don't you play with me over this! I'm not your puppet, Sir, no, never that! What would you have me be, then? Why this anger?" I shuddered all over, the tears veritably flooding from my eyes. "I would be strong for you, but I . . . I knew him."

"Why? Because he kissed you?" He leant down and picked up my hair in his left hand. He yanked me towards him.

"Marius, for the love of God!"

He kissed me. He kissed me as Martino had, and his mouth was as human and as hot. He slipped his tongue into mine, and I felt not blood but manly passion. His finger burnt against my cheek.

I broke away. He let me break away. "Oh, come back to me, my cold white one, my god," I whispered. I lay my face on his chest. I could hear his heart. I could hear it beating. I had never before heard it, never heard a pulse within the stone chapel of his body. "Come back to me, most dispassionate teacher. I don't know what you want."

"Oh, my darling," he sighed. "Oh, my love." And there came the old demon shower of his kisses, not the mock of a passionate man, but his affection, petal soft, so many tributes laid upon my face and hair. "Oh, my beautiful Amadeo, oh, my child," he said.

"Love me, love me, love me," I whispered. "Love me and take me into it with you. I am yours."

In stillness, he held me. I drowsed on his shoulders.

A little breeze came, but it did not move the heavy tapestries in which the French lords and ladies drifted in their eternal and leafy green forest among hounds that would forever bay and birds that would always sing.

Finally, he released me and he stepped back.

He walked away from me, his shoulders hunched, his head down.

Then with a lazy gesture he beckoned for me to come, and yet he moved out of the room too fast.

I ran after him, down the stone stairs to the street. The doors were open when I got there. The cold wind washed away my tears. It washed away the evil heat of the room. I ran and ran along the stone quays, over the bridges, and after him towards the square.

I didn't catch him until I reached the Molo, and there he was walking, a tall man in a red hood and cape, past San Marco and towards the harbor. I ran after him. The wind from the sea was icy and very strong. It blasted me, and I felt doubly cleansed.

"Don't leave me, Master," I called out. My words were swallowed up, but he heard.

He came to a stop, as if it really were my doing. He turned and waited for me to catch up with him, and then he picked up my outstretched hand.

"Master, hear my lesson," I said. "Judge my work." I caught my breath in haste and went on. "I saw you drink from those who were evil, convicted in your heart of some gross crime. I saw you feast as it is your nature; I saw you take the blood with which you must live. And all about you lies this evil world, this wilderness of men no better than beasts who will yield up a blood as sweet and rich for you as innocent blood. I see it. That's what you meant for me to see, and it's done."

His face was impassive. He merely studied me. It seemed the burning fever in him was already dying away. The distant torches along the arcades shone on his face, and it was whitening and as ever hard. The ships creaked in the harbor. There came distant murmurs and cries from those, perhaps, who cannot or never sleep.

I glanced up at the sky, fearful I would see the fatal light. He'd be gone.

"If I drink such as that, Master, the blood of the wicked and those whom I overpower, will I become like you?"

He shook his head. "Many a man has drunk another's blood, Amadeo," he said in a low but calm voice. His reason had come back to him, his manners, his seeming soul. "Would you be with me, and be my pupil and my love?"

"Yes, Master, always and forever, or for so long as nature gives to you and me."

"Oh, it isn't fanciful the words I spoke. We are immortal. And only one enemy can destroy us—it's the fire that burns in that torch there, or in the rising sun. Sweet to think on it, that when we are at last weary of all this world there is the rising sun."

"I am yours, Master." I hugged him close and tried to vanquish him with kisses. He endured them, and even smiled, but he didn't move.

But when I broke off, and made a fist of my right hand as if to hit him, which I could never have done, to my amazement he began to yield.

He turned and took me in his powerful and ever careful embrace.

"Amadeo, I can't go on without you," he said. His voice was desperate and small. "I meant to show you evil, not sport. I meant to show you the wicked price of my immortality. And that I did. But in so doing, I saw it myself, and my eyes are dazzled and I am hurt and tired."

He laid his head against my head, and he held tight to me.

"Do what you will to me, Sir," I said. "Make me suffer and long for it, if that's what you want. I am your fool. I am yours."

He released me and kissed me formally.

"Four nights, my child," he said. He moved away. He kissed his fingers and planted that last kiss on my lips, and then he was gone. "I go now to an ancient duty. Four nights. Till then."

I stood alone in the earliest chill of the morning. I stood alone beneath a paling sky. I knew better than to look for him.

In the greatest dejection, I walked back through the alleys, cutting across little bridges to wander into the depth of the waking city, for what I didn't know.

I was half-surprised when I realized I had returned to the house of the murdered men. I was surprised when I saw their doorway still open, as if a servant would at any moment appear.

No one appeared.

Slowly the sky above ripened to a pale white and then to a faint blue. Mist crawled along the top of the canal. I went over the small bridge to the doorway, and again went up the stairs.

A powdery light came in from the loosely slatted windows. I found the banquet room where the candles still burnt. The smell of tobacco and wax and of pungent food was close and hanging in the air.

I walked inside, and I inspected the dead men, who lay as we had left them, disheveled, and now slightly yellowed and waxen and a prey to the gnats and the flies.

There was no sound but the humming of the flies.

The spilt wine had dried on the table in pools. The corpses were clean of all the rampant marks of death.

I was sick again, sick to trembling, and I took a deep breath that I shouldn't retch. Then I realized why I had come.

Men in those days wore short cloaks on their jackets, sometimes affixed, as you probably know. I needed one of these, and took it, ripping it loose from the humpback man, who lay almost on his face. It was a flaring coat of canary yellow with white fox for its border and a lining of heavy silk. I tied knots in it and made a thick deep sack of it, and then I went up and down the table, gathering up the goblets, dashing out the contents first, and then putting them in my sack.

Soon my sack was red with drops of wine and grease from where I'd rested it on the board.

I stood when finished, making certain that no goblet had escaped. I had them all. I studied the dead men—my sleeping red-haired Martino, his face on the bare marble in a puddle of the slopped wine, and Francisco, from whose head did leak a small bit of darkened blood.

The flies buzzed and droned over this blood as they did over the grease pooled around the remnants of the roasted pig. A battalion of little black beetles had come, most common in Venice, for they are carried by the water, and it made its way over the table, towards Martino's face.

A quiet warming light came in through the open doorway. The morning had come.

With one sweeping glance that imprinted on my mind the details of this scene for all time, I went out and home.

The boys were awake and busy when I arrived. An old carpenter was already there, fixing the door which I had shattered with the ax.

I gave to the maid my bulky sack of clanking cups, and she, sleepy and having just arrived, took it without a remark.

I felt a tightening inside me, a sickening, a sudden feeling that I would burst. My body seemed too small, too imperfect an enclosure for all I knew and felt. My head throbbed. I wanted to lie down, but before that I had to see Riccardo. I had to find him and the older boys.

I had to.

I went walking through the house until I came to them, all gathered for a lesson with the young lawyer who came from Padua only once or twice a month to begin our instructions in the law. Riccardo saw me in the door and motioned for me to be quiet. The teacher was speaking.

I had nothing to say. I only leant against the door and looked at my friends. I loved them. Yes, I did love them. I would die for them! I knew it, and with a terrible relief I began to cry.

Riccardo saw me turn away, and slipping out, he came to me.

"What is it, Amadeo?" he asked.

I was too delirious with my own torment. I saw again the slaughtered dinner party. I turned to Riccardo and wound him in my arms, so comforted by his warmth and his human softness compared to the Master, and then I told him that I would die for him, die for any of them, die for the Master too.

"But why, what is this, why vow this to me now?" he asked.

I couldn't tell him about the slaughter. I couldn't tell him of the coldness in me that had watched the men die.

I went off into my Master's bedchamber, and I lay down and tried to sleep.

In late afternoon, when I woke to find the doors had been closed, I climbed out of the bed and went to the Master's desk. To my astonishment I saw his book was there, the book that was always hidden when out of his sight.

Of course I could not turn a page of it, but it was open, and there lay a page covered in writing, in Latin, and though it seemed a strange Latin, and hard for me, there was no mistaking the final words:

How can so much beauty hide such a bruised and steely heart, and why must I love him, why must I lean in my weariness upon his irresistible yet indomitable strength? Is he not the wizened funereal spirit of a dead man in a child's clothes?

I felt a strange prickling over my scalp and over my arms.

Is this what I was? A bruised and steely heart! The wizened funereal spirit of a dead man in a child's clothes? Oh, but I couldn't deny it; I couldn't say it wasn't true. And yet how hurtful, how positively cruel it seemed. No, not cruel, merely merciless and accurate, and what right had I to expect anything else?

I started to cry.

I lay down in our bed, as was my custom, and plumped the softest pillows to make a nest for my crooked left arm and my head.

Four nights. How should I endure it? What did he want of me? That I go forth to all the things I knew and loved and take my leave of them as a mortal boy. That is what he would instruct. And that I should do.

Only a few hours were allowed to me by fate.

I was awakened by Riccardo, who shoved a sealed note in my face.

"Who's sent this?" I asked sleepily. I sat up, and I pushed my thumb beneath the folded paper and broke the wax seal.

"Read it and you tell me. Four men came to deliver

it, a company of four. Must be some damned important thing."

"Yes," I said unfolding it, "and to make you look so fearful too."

He stood there with his arms folded.

I read:

Dearest darling one,

Stay indoors. Do not on any account leave the house and bar any who seek to enter. Your wicked English lord, the Earl of Harlech, has discovered your identity through the most unscrupulous nosing about, and in his madness vows to take you back with him to England or leave you in fragments at your Master's door. Confess all to your Master. Only his strength can save you. And do send me something in writing, lest I too lose my wits over you, and over the tales of horror which are cried out this morning in every canal and piazza for every ear.

Your devoted Bianca

"Well, damn it," I said folding up the letter. "Four nights Marius will be gone, and now this. Am I to hide for these crucial four nights under this roof?"

"You had better," said Riccardo.

"Then you know the story."

"Bianca told me. The Englishman, having traced you there and heard tell of you being there all the time, would have torn her lodgings to pieces if her guests had not stopped him en masse."

"And why didn't they kill him, for the love of God," I said disgustedly.

He looked most worried and sympathetic.

"I think they count on our Master to do it," he said, "as it is you that the man wants. How can you be certain the Master means to stay away for four nights? When has he ever said such things? He comes, he goes, he warns no one."

"Hmmm, don't argue with me," I answered patiently. "Riccardo, he isn't coming home for four nights, and I will not stay cooped up in this house, and not while Lord Harlech stirs up dirt."

"You'd better stay here!" Riccardo answered. "Amadeo, this Englishman is famous with his sword. He practices with a fencing master. He's the terror of the taverns. You knew that when you picked up with him, Amadeo. Think on what you do! He's famous for everything bad and nothing good."

"So then come with me. You need only distract him and I'll take him."

"No, you're good with your sword, true enough, but you can't take a man who's been practicing with the blade since before you were born."

I lay back down on the pillow. What should I do? I was on fire to go out into the world, on fire to gaze at things with my great sense of the drama and significance of my last days among the living, and now this! And the man who had been worth a few nights' riotous roughhouse pleasure was no doubt advertising far and wide his discontent.

It was bitter, but it seemed I had to stay at home. There was nothing to do. I wanted very much to kill this man, kill him with my own dagger and sword, and even thought I had a good chance of it, but what was this petty adventure to what lay before me when my Master returned?

The fact was, I had already left the world of regular things, the world of regular scores to be settled, and could not be drawn now into a foolish blunder that might be my forfeit of the strange destiny towards which I moved.

"All right, and Bianca is safe from this man?" I asked Riccardo.

"Quite safe. She has more admirers than can fit in the door of her house, and she's marshaled all against this man and for you. Now write her something of gratitude and common sense, and swear to me as well that you'll remain indoors."

I got up and went to the Master's writing desk. I picked up the pen.

I was stopped by an awful clatter, and then a series of piercing irritating cries. They echoed through the stone rooms of the house. I heard people running. Riccardo leapt to attention and put his hand on the hilt of his sword.

I gathered up my own weapons, unsheathing my light rapier and my dagger, both.

"Good Lord Jesus, the man can't be in the house."

A horrid scream drowned out the others.

The smallest of us all, Giuseppe, appeared in the door, his face a luminous white, and his eyes big and round.

"What the hell's the matter," Riccardo demanded, catching hold of him.

"He's been stabbed. Look, he's bleeding!" I said.

"Amadeo, Amadeo!" It rang loudly from the stone stairwell. It was the Englishman's voice.

The boy doubled over in his pain. The wound was in the pit of his stomach, utterly cruel.

Riccardo was beside himself.

"Shut the doors!" he shouted.

"How can I," I cried, "when the other boys may blunder right into his path?"

I ran out and into the big salon and into the portego, the great room of the house.

Another boy, Jacope, lay crumpled on the floor, pushing at it with his knees. I saw the blood running on the stones.

"Oh, this is beyond all fairness; this is a slaughter of innocents!" I shouted. "Lord Harlech, show yourself. You're about to die."

I heard Riccardo cry out behind me. The little boy was obviously dead.

I ran towards the stairs. "Lord Harlech, I'm here!" I called out. "Come out, you brutish coward, you slayer of children! I have a millstone ready for your neck!"

Riccardo spun me around. "There, Amadeo," he whispered. "I'm with you." His blade sang out as he drew it. He was much better than me with the sword, but this battle was mine.

The man was at the far end of the portego. I had hoped he would be staggering drunk, but no such luck. I saw in a moment that any dream he might have had of taking me away by force was now gone; he had slain two boys, and he knew his lust had led him to a final stand. This was hardly an enemy crippled by love.

"Jesus in Heaven, help us!" whispered Riccardo.

"Lord Harlech," I cried. "You dare make a shambles of my Master's house!" I stepped aside from Riccardo to give us both room, as I motioned Riccardo to come forward, away from the head of the steps. I felt the weight of the rapier. Not heavy enough. I wished to God I had practiced with it more.

The Englishman came towards me, a taller man than I had ever noted, with a great reach to his arm that would be a powerful advantage, his cape flapping, his feet sheathed in heavy boots, his rapier raised and his long Italian dagger ready in the other hand. At least he didn't have a true and heavy sword.

Dwarfed by the great room, he was nevertheless big of stature and had a head of roaring British copper hair. His blue eyes were stewed in blood, but he was steady in his walk and in his murderous gaze. His face was wet with bitter tears.

"Amadeo," he called out over the vast room as he came on. "You cut my heart out of my chest while I lived and breathed, and you took it with you! We shall be together this night in Hell."

6

THE HIGH LONG PORTEGO of our house, the entrance hall, was a perfectly wonderful place to die. There was nothing in it to mar its gorgeous mosaic floors with their circles of colored marble stones, and their festive pattern of winding flowers and tiny wild birds.

We had the entire field upon which to fight, with not a chair in the way to stop us from killing each other.

I advanced on the Englishman before I had time to really admit that I wasn't very good with the sword yet, had never shown an instinct for it, and I had no inkling of just what my Master would have me do just now, that is, what he would advise if he were here.

I made several bold thrusts at Lord Harlech, which he parried so easily that I should have lost heart. But just when I thought I'd catch my breath and maybe even run, he swept in with his dagger and slashed my left arm. The cut stung me and infuriated me.

I went after him again, this time managing with considerable luck to get him across the throat. It was just a scratch, but it bled furiously down his tunic, and he was as angry as I was to be cut.

"You horrid damnable little devil," he said. "You made me adore you so you could draw and quarter me at your pleasure. You promised me you'd come back!"

In fact, he kept up this sort of verbal barrage the entire time we fought. He seemed to need it, rather like a goading battle drum and fife.

"Come on, you despicable little angel, I'll tear your wings off!" he said.

He drove me back with a fast volley of thrusts. I stumbled, lost my balance and fell but managed to scramble up again, using the low position to stab dangerously close to his scrotum as I did so, which gave him a start. I ran at him, knowing now there was nothing to be gained by drawing this out.

He dodged my blade, laughed at me and caught me with the dagger, this time on the face.

"Pig!" I growled before I could stop myself. I hadn't known I was so completely vain. My face, no less. He'd cut it. My face. I felt the blood gushing as it does from face wounds, and I rushed at him again, this time forgetting all the rules of the encounter and thrashing the air with my sword in a fierce crazy series of circles. Then as he parried frantically left and right, I ducked and caught him with the dagger in the belly and ripped upward, stopped by the thick gold-encrusted leather of his belt.

I backed up as he sought to slaughter me with both his weapons, and then he dropped them and grabbed, as men do, for the belching wound.

He fell down on his knees.

"Finish him!" shouted Riccardo. He stood back, a man of honor already. "Finish him now, Amadeo, or I do it. Think what he's done under this roof."

I lifted my sword.

The man suddenly grabbed up his own with his bloody hand and flashed it at me, even as he groaned and winced with his pain. He rose up and ran at me in one gesture. I jumped back. He fell to his knees. He was sick and shivering. He dropped the sword, feeling again for his wounded belly. He didn't die, but he couldn't fight on.

"Oh, God," said Riccardo. He clutched his dagger. But he obviously couldn't bring himself to hack away at the unarmed man.

The Englishman went over on his side. He drew his knees up. He grimaced and he laid his head down on the stone, his face formal as he took a deep breath. He fought terrible pain and the certainty that he would die.

Riccardo stepped forward and laid the tip of his sword on Lord Harlech's cheek.

"He's dying, let him die," I said. But the man continued to breathe.

I wanted to kill him, I really wanted to, but it was impossible to kill someone who lay there so placid and so brave.

His eyes took on a wise, poetical expression. "And so it ends here," he said in a small voice that perhaps Riccardo didn't even hear.

"Yes, it ends," I said. "End it nobly."

"Amadeo, he slew the two children!" said Riccardo.

"Pick up your dagger, Lord Harlech!" I said. I kicked the weapon at him. I pushed it right at his hand. "Pick it up, Lord Harlech," I said. The blood was running down my face and down my neck, tickling and sticky. I couldn't stand it. I wanted more to wipe my own wounds than to bother with him.

He turned over on his back. The blood came out of his mouth and out of his gut. His face was wet and shiny, and his breathing became very labored. He seemed young again, young as he had when he threatened me, an overgrown boy with a big mop of flaming curls.

"Think about me when you begin to sweat, Amadeo," he said, his voice still small, and now hoarse. "Think about me when you realize that your life, too, is finished."

"Run him through," said Riccardo in a whisper. "He could take two days to die with that wound."

"And you won't have two days," said Lord Harlech from the floor, panting, "with the poisoned cuts I gave you. Feel it in your eyes? Your eyes burn, don't they Amadeo? The poison goes into the blood, and it strikes the eyes first. Are you dizzy?"

"You bastard," said Riccardo. He stabbed the man with his rapier right through his tunic, once, twice, then three times. Lord Harlech grimaced. His eyelids fluttered, and out of his mouth came a final gout of blood. He was dead.

"Poison?" I whispered. "Poison on the blade?" Instinctively, I felt my arm where he had cut me. My face, however, bore the deeper wound. "Don't touch his sword or dagger. Poison!"

"He was lying, come, let me wash you," said Riccardo. "There's no time to waste."

He tried to pull me from the room.

"What are we going to do with him, Riccardo! What can we do! We're here alone without the Master. There are three dead in this house, maybe more."

As I spoke I heard steps at both ends of the great room. The little boys were coming out of their hiding places, and I saw one of the teachers with them, who had apparently been keeping them out of the way.

I had mixed feelings on this score. But these were all children, and the teacher an unarmed man, a helpless scholar. The older boys had all gone out, as was the custom in the morning. Or so I thought.

"Come on, we have to get them all to a decent place," I said. "Don't touch the weapons." I signaled for the little ones to come. "We'll carry him to the best bedchamber, come on. And the boys as well."

As the little ones struggled to obey, some of them began to cry.

"You, give us a hand!" I said to the teacher. "Watch out for the poisoned weapons." He stared at me wildly. "I mean it. It's poison."

"Amadeo, you're bleeding all over!" he cried shrilly

in a panic. "What poisoned weapons? Dear God save us all!"

"Oh, stop it!" I said. But I could stand this situation no longer, and as Riccardo took charge of the moving of the bodies, I rushed into my Master's bedroom to attend to my wounds.

I dumped the whole pitcherful of water into the basin in my haste, and grabbed up a napkin with which to catch the blood that was flowing down my neck and into my shirt. Sticky, sticky mess, I cursed. My head swam, and I almost fell. Grabbing the edge of the table, I told myself not to be Lord Harlech's fool. Riccardo had been right. Lord Harlech had made up that lie about the poison! Poison the blade, indeed!

But as I told myself this story, I looked down and saw for the first time a scratch, apparently made by his rapier on the back of my right hand. My hand was swelling as if this were an insect's venomous work.

I felt my arm and my face. The wounds there were swelling, great welts forming behind the cuts. Again, there came the dizziness. The sweat dripped off me right into the basin, which was now full of red water that looked like wine.

"Oh, my God, the Devil's done this to me," I said. I turned and the entire room began to tilt and then to float. I rocked on my feet.

Someone caught me. I didn't even see who it was. I tried to say Riccardo's name, but my tongue was thick in my mouth.

Sounds and colors mingled in a hot, pulsing blur. Then with astonishing clarity I saw the embroidered baldaquin of the Master's bed, over my head. Riccardo stood over me.

He spoke to me rapidly and somewhat desperately, but I couldn't make out what he said. Indeed, it seemed he spoke a foreign tongue, a pretty one, very melodious and sweet, but I couldn't understand a word of it.

"I'm hot," I said. "I'm burning, I'm so hot that I can't bear it. I have to have water. Put me in the Master's bath."

He didn't seem to have heard me at all. On and on he went with his obvious pleading. I felt his hand on my forehead and it burned me, positively burned me. I begged him not to touch me, but this he didn't hear, and neither did I! I wasn't even speaking. I wanted to speak, but my tongue was too heavy and too big. *You'll get the poison,* I wanted to cry. I could not.

I closed my eyes. Mercifully I drifted. I saw a great sparkling sea, the waters off the island of the Lido, crenelated and beautiful beneath the noonday sun. I floated on this sea, perhaps in a small bark, or maybe just on my back. I couldn't feel the water itself, but there seemed nothing between me and its gentle tossing waves that were big and slow and easy and carried me up and then down. Far off, a great city gleamed on the shore. At first I thought it was Torcello, or even Venice, and that I had been turned around somehow and was floating towards the land. Then I saw it was much bigger than Venice, with great piercing reflective towers, as if it had been made entirely of brilliant glass. Oh, it was so lovely.

"Am I going there?" I asked.

The waves seemed then to fold over me, not with a

suffocating wetness, but merely a quiet blanket of heavy light. I opened my eyes. I saw the red of the taffeta baldaquin above. I saw the golden fringe sewn on the velvet bed curtains, and then I saw Bianca Solderini there above me. She had a cloth in her hand.

"There wasn't enough poison on those blades to kill you," she said. "It's merely made you sick. Now, listen to me, Amadeo, you must take each breath with quiet force and resolve to fight this sickness and to get well. You must ask the very air itself to make you strong, and be confident of it, that's it, you must breathe deeply and slowly, yes, exactly, and you must realize that this poison is being sweated out of you, and you must not believe in this poison, and you must not fear."

"The Master will know," said Riccardo. He looked drawn and miserable, and his lips quivered. His eyes were flooded with his tears. Oh, ominous sign, certainly. "The Master will know somehow. He knows all things. The Master will break his journey and come home."

"Wash his face," said Bianca calmly. "Wash his face and be quiet." How brave she was.

I moved my tongue but I couldn't form words. I wanted to say that they must tell me when the sun sank, for then and only then might the Master come. There was surely a chance. Then and only then. He might appear.

I turned my head to the side, away from them. The cloth was burning me.

"Softly, quietly," said Bianca. "Take in the air, yes, and do not be afraid."

A long time passed as I lay there, hovering just below perfect consciousness, and thankful that their voices were not sharp, and their touch was not so terrible, but the sweating was awful, and I despaired utterly of being cool.

I tossed and tried to get up once, only to feel terribly sick, sick unto vomiting. With a great relief I realized they had laid me back down.

"Hold on to my hands," said Bianca, and I felt her fingers grasping mine, so small and too hot, hot like everything else, hot like Hell, I thought, but I was too sick to think of Hell, too sick to think of anything but vomiting up my insides into a basin, and getting to somewhere cool. Oh, just open the windows, open them on the winter; I don't care, open them!

It seemed quite a nuisance that I might die, and nothing more. Feeling better was of far greater importance, and nothing troubled me as to my soul or any world to come.

Then abruptly all things changed.

I felt myself rise upwards, as if someone had yanked me by my head out of the bed and sought to pull me up through the red cloth baldaquin and through the ceiling of the room. Indeed, I looked down, and to my utter amazement I saw myself lying on the bed. I saw myself as if there were no baldaquin above my body to block the view.

I looked far more beautiful than I ever imagined myself to be. Understand, it was utterly dispassionate. I did not feel an exultation in my own beauty. I only thought, What a beautiful young boy. How gifted he has been by God. Look at his long delicate hands, how they lie beside him, and look at the deep russet of his hair. And that was me all the time, and I didn't know it or think of it, or think what effect it had on those who saw me as I moved through life. I didn't believe their blandishments. I had only scorn for their passion. Indeed, even the Master had seemed before to be a weak and deluded being for ever desiring me. But I understood now why people had somewhat taken leave of their senses. The boy there, dying on the bed, the boy who was the cause of weeping all around in this large chamber, the boy seemed the very embodiment of purity and the very embodiment of youth on the verge of life.

What did not make sense to me was the commotion in the room. Why did everyone weep? I saw a priest in the doorway, a priest I knew from the nearby church, and I could see that the boys argued with him and feared to let him near me as I lay on the bed, lest I be afraid. It all seemed a pointless imbroglio. Riccardo should not wring his hands. Bianca should not work so hard, with her damp cloth and her soft but obviously desperate words.

Oh, poor child, I thought. You might have had a little more compassion for everyone if you had known how beautiful you were, and you might have thought yourself a little bit stronger and more able to gain something for yourself. As it was, you played sly games on those around you, because you did not have faith in your own self or even know what you were.

It seemed very clear, the error in all this. But I was leaving this place! The same draught that had pulled me up out of the pretty young body that lay on the bed was pulling me upwards into a tunnel of fierce, noisy wind.

The wind swirled around me, enclosing me completely and tightly in this tunnel, yet I could see in it other beings who looked on even as they were caught in it and moved by the incessant fury of this wind. I saw eyes looking on me; I saw mouths open as if in distress. I was pulled higher and higher through this tunnel. I didn't feel fear, but I felt a fatality. I could not help myself.

That was your error when you were that boy down there, I found myself thinking. But this is indeed hopeless. And just as I concluded, so I came to the end of this tunnel; it dissolved. I stood on the shore of that lovely sparkling sea.

I wasn't wet from the waves, but I knew them, and I said out loud, "Oh, I'm here, I've come to the shore! Look, there are the towers of glass."

As I looked up, I saw that the city was far away, over a series of deep green hills, and that a path led to it, and that flowers bloomed richly and gorgeously on either side of the path. I had never seen such flowers, never seen such shapes and petal formations, and never never beheld such colors in all my life. There were no names in the artistic canon for these colors. I couldn't call them by the few weak inadequate labels which I knew.

Oh, would the painters of Venice ever be astonished at these colors, I thought, and to think how they would transform our work, how they would set ablaze our paintings if only they could be discovered in some source that might be ground into pigment and blended with our oils. But what a pointless thing to do. No more painting was needed. All the glory that could be accomplished by color was here in this world revealed. I saw it in the flowers; I saw it in the variegated grass. I saw it in the boundless sky that rose up and over me and behind the distant blinding city, and it too flashed and glowed with this great harmony of colors, blending and twinkling and shimmering as if the towers of this city were made of a miraculous thriving energy rather than a dead or earthly matter or mass.

A great gratitude flowed out of me; my whole being gave itself up to this gratitude. "Lord, I see now," I said aloud. "I see and I understand." It did at that moment seem very clear to me, the implications of this varied and ever increasing beauty, this pulsing, radiant world. It was so very pregnant with meaning that all things were answered, all things were utterly resolved. I whispered the word "Yes" over and over. I nodded, I think, and then it seemed quite absurd to bother to say anything in words at all.

A great force emanated from the beauty. It surrounded me as if it were air or breeze or water, but it was none of these. It was far more rarefied and pervasive, and though it held me with a formidable strength it was nevertheless invisible and without pressure or palpable form. The force was love. Oh, yes, I thought, it is love, it is complete love, and in its completeness it makes all that I have ever known meaningful, for every disappointment, every hurt, every misstep, every embrace, every kiss was but a foreshadowing of this sublime acceptance and goodness, for the bad steps had told me what I lacked, and the good things, the embraces, had shown me a glimpse of what love could be.

All my life this love made meaningful, sparing nothing, and as I marveled at this, accepting it completely and without urgency or questioning, a miraculous process began. All my life came to me in the form of all those I had ever known.

I saw my life from the very first moments and up until the moment that had brought me here. It was not a terribly remarkable life; it contained no great secret or twist or pregnant matter that changed my heart. On the contrary, it was but a natural and common string of myriad tiny events, and these events involved all the other souls whom I had ever touched; I saw now the hurts I'd inflicted, and the words of mine which had brought solace, and I saw the result of the most casual and unimportant things I had done. I saw the banquet hall of the Florentines, and again in the midst of them, I saw the blundering loneliness with which they stumbled into death. I saw the isolation and the sadness of their souls as they had fought to stay alive.

What I could not see was my Master's face. I could not see who he was. I could not see into his soul. I could not see what my love meant to him, or what his love meant for me. But this was of no importance. In fact, I only realized it afterwards when I tried to recount the entire event. What mattered now was only that I understood what it meant to cherish others and to cherish life itself. I realized what it had meant when I painted pictures, not the ruby-red bleeding and vibrant pictures of Venice, but old pictures in the antique Byzantine style, which had once flowed so artlessly and perfectly from my brush. I knew then I had painted wondrous things, and I saw the effects of what I had painted . . . and it seemed then a great crowd of information inundated me. Indeed, there was such a wealth of it, and it was so easy to comprehend, that I felt a great light joy.

The knowledge was like the love and like the beauty; indeed, I realized with a great triumphant happiness that they were all—the knowledge, the love, and the beauty—they were all one.

"Oh, yes, how could one not see it. It's so simple!" I thought.

If I had had a body with eyes, I would have wept, but it would have been a sweet weeping. As it was, my soul was victorious over all small and enervating things. I stood still, and the knowledge, the facts, as it were, the hundreds upon hundreds of small details which were like transparent droplets of magical fluid passing through me and into me, filling me and vanishing to make way for more of this great shower of truth—all this seemed suddenly to fade.

There beyond stood the glass city, and beyond it a blue sky, blue as a sky at midday, only one which was now filled with every known star.

I started out for the city. Indeed, I started with such impetuosity and such conviction that it took three people to hold me back.

I stopped. I was quite amazed. But I knew these men. These were priests, old priests of my homeland, who had died long before I had even come to my calling, all of which was quite clear to me, and I knew their names and how they had died. They were in fact the saints of my city, and of the great house of catacombs where I had lived.

"Why do you hold me?" I asked. "Where's my Father? He's here now, is he not?" No sooner had I asked this than I saw my Father. He looked exactly as he had always looked. He was a big, shaggy man, dressed in leather for hunting, with a full grizzled beard and thick long auburn hair the same color as my own. His cheeks were rosy from the cold wind, and his lower lip, visible between his thick mustache and his gray-streaked beard, was moist and pink as I remembered. His eyes were the same bright china blue. He waved at me. He gave his usual, casual, hearty wave, and he smiled. He looked just like he was going off into the grasslands, in spite of everyone's advice, and everyone's caution to hunt, with no fear at all of the Mongols or the Tatars swooping down on him. After all, he had his great bow with him, the bow only he could string, as if he were a mythical hero of the great grassy fields, and he had his own sharpened arrows, and his big broadsword with which he could hack off a man's head with one blow.

"Father, why are they holding me?" I asked.

He looked blank. His smile simply faded and his face lost all expression, and then to my sadness, to my terrible shocking sadness, he faded in his entirety and he wasn't there.

The priests beside me, the men with their long gray beards and their black robes, spoke to me in soft sympathetic whispers and they said, "Andrei, it's not time for you to come."

I was deeply distressed, deeply. Indeed, I was so sad that I could form no words of protest. Indeed, I understood that no protest I might make mattered, and then one of the priests took my hand.

"No, this is always the way with you," he said. "Ask."

He didn't move his lips when he spoke, but it wasn't necessary. I heard him very clearly, and I knew that he meant no personal malice to me. He was incapable of such a thing.

"Why, then," I asked, "can't I stay? Why can't you let me stay when I want to, and when I've come this far."

"Think on all you've seen. You know the answer."

And I had to admit that in an instant I did know the answer. It was complex and yet profoundly simple, and it had to do with all the knowledge I had gained.

"You can't take this back with you," said the priest. "You'll forget all the particular things you learned here. But remember the overall lesson, that your love for others, and their love for you, that the increase of love in life itself around you, is what matters."

It seemed a marvelous and comprehensive thing! It seemed no simple small cliché. It seemed so immense, so subtle, yet so total that all mortal difficulties would collapse in the face of its truth.

I was at once returned to my body. I was at once the auburn-haired boy dying in the bed. I felt a tingling in my hands and feet. I twisted, and a wretched pain flamed down my back. I was all afire, sweating and writhing as before, only now my lips were badly cracked and my tongue was cut and blistered against my teeth.

"Water," I said, "please, water."

A soft sobbing came from those around me. It was mingled with laughter and expressions of awe.

I was alive, and they had thought me dead. I opened my eyes, and I looked at Bianca.

"I won't die now," I said.

"What is it, Amadeo?" she asked. She bent down and put her ear to my lips.

"It isn't time," I said.

They brought me cool white wine. It was mixed with honey and lemon. I sat up and I drank gulp after gulp of it. "It's not enough," I said softly, weakly, but I was falling asleep.

I went down into the pillows, and I felt Bianca's cloth wipe my forehead and my eyes. What a sweet mercy it was, and how very grand to give that small comfort, which was all the world to me. All the world. All the world.

I had forgotten what I had seen on the other side! My eyes snapped open. Recover it, I thought desperately. But I remembered the priest, vividly as though I had just talked to him in another room. He had said I couldn't remember. And there was so much more to it, infinitely more, such things as only my Master might understand.

I closed my eyes. I slept. Dreams couldn't come to me. I was too ill, too feverish, but in my own way, stretched thin upon a consciousness of the moist hot bed and the sluggish air beneath the baldaquin, upon the blurred words of the boys and Bianca's sweet insistence, I did sleep. The hours ticked. I knew them, and gradually some comfort came to me in that I got used to the sweat that smothered my skin, and the thirst that hurt my throat, and I lay without protest, drifting, waiting for my Master to come.

I have so many things to tell you, I thought. You will know about the glass city! I must explain that I was once . . . but I couldn't quite remember. A painter, yes, but what sort of painter, and how, and my name? Andrei? When had I been so called?

7

SLOWLY over my consciousness of the sickbed and the humid room there dropped the dark veil of Heaven. Spread out in all directions were the sentinel stars, splendid as they shone above the glinting towers of the glass city, and in this half-sleep, now aided by the most tranquil and blissful of illusions, the stars sang to me.

Each from its fixed position in constellation and in void gave forth a precious glimmering sound, as if great chords were struck inside each flaming orb and by means of its brilliant gyrations broadcast through all the universal world.

Such sounds I had never heard with my earthly ears. But no disclaimer can approximate this airy and translucent music, this harmony and symphony of cele-bration.

Oh, Lord, if Thou wert music, this then would be Thy voice, and no discord could ever prevail against Thee. Thou wouldst cleanse the ordinary world of every troubling noise with this, the fullest expres-sion of Thy most intricate and wondrous design, and all triviality would fade away, overwhelmed by this resounding perfection.

This was my prayer, my heartfelt prayer, coming in an ancient tongue, most intimate and effortless as I lay slumbering.

Stay with me, beauteous stars, I begged, and let me never seek to fathom this fusion of light and sound, but only give myself to it utterly and unquestionably.

The stars grew large and infinite in their cold majestic light, and slowly all the night was gone and there remained one great glorious and sourceless illumination.

I smiled. I felt my smile with blind fingers on my lips, and as the light grew brighter still and ever closer, as though it were an ocean of itself, I felt a great saving coolness over all my limbs.

"Don't fade, don't go away, don't leave me." My own whisper was a woeful small thing. I pressed my throbbing head into the pillow.

But it had spent its time, this grand and overriding light, and now must fade and let the common blink of candles move against my half-closed eyes, and I must see the burnished gloom around my bed, and simple things, such as a rosary laid across my right hand with ruby beads and golden cross, and there a prayer book open to my left, its pages gently folding in a small stir of breeze that moved as well the smooth taffeta in ripples overhead in its wood frame.

How lovely it all did seem, these plain and ordinary things that made up this silent and elastic moment. Where had they gone, my lovely swan-necked nurse and my weeping comrades? Had night worn them down to where they slept, so that I might cherish these quiet moments of unobserved wakefulness? My mind was gently crowded with a thousand lively recollections.

I opened my eyes. All were gone, save one who sat beside me on the bed, looking down at me with eyes both dreamy and remote and coldly blue, far paler than a summer sky and filled with a near faceted light as they fixed so idly and indifferently upon me.

My Master here, with hands folded in his lap, a seeming stranger viewing all as if it could not touch his chiseled grandeur. The smileless expression set upon his face seemed made there forever.

"Merciless!" I whispered.

"No, oh, no," he said. His lips did not move. "But tell me once again the whole tale. Describe this glassy city."

"Ah, yes, we've talked of it, have we not, of those priests who said I must come back, and those old paintings, so antique, which I thought so very beautiful. Not made by human hands, you see, but by the power invested in me, which passed through me, and I had only to take up the brush and there the Virgin and the Saints were mine to discover."

"Don't cast those old forms away," he said, and once again his lips showed no sign of the voice I heard so distinctly, a voice that pierced my very ears as any human voice might do, with his tone, his very timbre. "For forms change, and reason now is but tomorrow's superstition, and in that old restraint there lay a great sublime intent, an indefatigable purity. But tell me once again about the glassy city."

I sighed. "You've seen the molten glass, as I have," I said, "when taken from the furnace, a glowing blob of horrifying heat upon a spear of iron, a thing that melts and drips so that the artist's wand may pull and stretch it, or fill it full of breath to form the perfect rounded vessel.

Well, it was as if that glass came up out of the moist Mother Earth herself, a molten torrent spewing to the clouds, and out of these great liquid jets were born the crowded towers of the glassy city—not imitating any form built by men, but perfect as the heated force of Earth had naturally ordained, in colors unimaginable. Who lived in such a place? How far away it seemed, yet utterly attainable. But one short walk over hills sweet with willowing green grass and leafy fluttering flowers of the same fantastical hues and tints, a quiet thunderous and impossible apparition."

I looked at him, because I had been looking off and back into my vision.

"Tell me what these things mean," I asked. "Where is this place, and why was I allowed to see it?"

He gave a sad sigh and looked away himself and now back at me, his face as aloof and unbending as before, only now I saw the thick blood in it, that once again, as it had been the night before, was pumped full of human heat from human veins, which had no doubt been his late repast this same evening.

"Won't you even smile now as you say farewell?" I asked. "If this bitter coldness now is all you feel, and you would let me die of this rampant fever? I'm sick unto death, you know it. You know the nausea that I feel, you know the hurt inside my head, you know the ache in all my joints and how these cuts burn in my skin with their indisputable poison. Why are you so very far away, yet here, come home, to sit beside me and feel nothing?"

"I feel the love I've always felt when I look at you," he said, "my child, my son, my sweet enduring one. I feel it. It's walled up inside where it should stay, perhaps, and let you die, for yes, you will, and then perhaps your priests will take you, for how can they not when there is no returning?"

"Ah, but what if there are many lands? What if on the second fall, I find myself on yet another shore, and sulfur rises from the boiling earth and not the beauty first revealed to me? I hurt. These tears are scalding. So much is lost. I can't remember. It seems I say those same words so much. I can't remember!"

I reached out. He didn't move. My hand grew heavy and dropped on the forgotten prayer book. I felt the stiff vellum pages beneath my fingers.

"What's killed your love? Was it the things I did? That I brought the man here who slew my brothers? Or that I died and saw such wonders? Answer me."

"I love you still. I will all my nights and all my slumbering days, forever. Your face is as a jewel given me, which I can never forget, though I may foolishly lose it. Its glister will torture me forever. Amadeo, think on these things again, open your mind as if it were a shell, and let me see the pearl of all they taught you."

"Can you, Master? Can you understand how love and love alone could mean so very much, and all the world be made of it? The very blades of grass, the leaves of trees, the fingers of this hand that reaches for you? Love, Master. Love. And who will believe such simple and immense things when there are dexterous and labyrinthian creeds and philosophies of manmade and ever seductive complexity? Love. I heard the sound of it. I saw it. Were these the delusions of a feverish mind, a mind afraid of death?"

"Perhaps," he said, his face still feelingless and

motionless. His eyes were narrow, prisoners of their own shrinking from what they saw. "Ah, yes," he said. "You die and I let you, and I think there might be for you but one shore, and there you'll find again your priests, your city."

"It's not my time," I said. "I know it. And such a statement cannot be undone by a mere handful of hours. Smash the ticking clock. They meant, by a soul's incarnate life, it wasn't time. Some destiny carved in my infant hand will not be so soon fulfilled or easily defeated."

"I can tip the odds, my child," he said. This time his lips moved. The pale sweet coral brightened in his face, and his eyes grew wide and unguarded, the old self I knew and cherished. "I can so easily take the last strength left in you." He leant over me. I saw the tiny variegations in the pupils of his eyes, the bright deep-pointed stars behind the darkening irises. His lips, so wondrously decorated with all the tiny lines of human lips, were rosy as if a human kiss resided there. "I can so easily take one last fatal drink of your child's blood, one last quaff of all the freshness I so love, and in my arms I'll hold a corpse so rich in beauty that all who see it will weep, and that corpse will tell me nothing. You are gone, that much I'll know, and no more."

"Do you say these things to torture me? Master, if I cannot go there, I want to be with you!"

His lip worked in plain desperation. He seemed a man, and only that, the red blood of fatigue and sadness hovering on the borders of his eyes. His hand, out now to touch my hair, was trembling.

I caught it as if it were the high waving branch of a tree above me. I gathered his fingers to my lips like so many leaves and kissed them. Turning my head I laid them on my wounded cheek. I felt the throb of the venomous cut beneath them. But more keenly still, I felt a strong tremor within them.

I blinked my eyes. "How many died tonight to feed you?" I whispered. "And how can this be, and love be the very thing the world is made of? You are too beautiful to be overlooked. I'm lost. I cannot understand it. But could I, if I were to live from this moment on, a simple mortal boy, could I forget it?"

"You cannot live, Amadeo," he said sadly. "You cannot live!" His voice broke. "The poison's traveled in you too deep, too far and wide, and little draughts of my blood cannot overtake it." His face was filled with anguish. "Child, I can't save you. Close your eyes. Take my farewell kiss. There is no friendship between me and those on the far shore, but they must take what dies so naturally."

"Master, no! Master, I cannot try it alone. Master, they sent me back, and you are here, and were bound to be, and how could they not have known it?"

"Amadeo, they didn't care. The guardians of the dead are powerfully indifferent. They speak of love, but not of centuries of blundering ignorance. What stars are these that sing so beautifully when all the world is languishing in dissonance? I would you would force their hand, Amadeo." His voice all but broke in his pain. "Amadeo, what right have they to charge me with your fortune?"

I laughed a weak sad little laugh.

My fever shook me. A great wave of sickness overcame me. If I moved or spoke I would suffer a dread dry nausea that would shake me to no advantage. I'd rather die than feel this.

"Master, I knew you would give it some powerful analysis," I said. I tried not to make a bitter or sarcastic smile, but to seek the simple truth. My breath was now so hard for me. It seemed I could leave off breathing with no hardship at all. All Bianca's stern encouragements came back to me. "Master," I said, "there is no horror in this world that is without final redemption."

"Yes, but for some," he pressed, "what is the price of such salvation? Amadeo, how dare they requisition me to their obscure designs! I pray they were illusions. Don't speak anymore about their marvelous light. Don't think on it."

"No, Sir? And for whose comfort do I sweep my mind so clean? Who is dying here!"

He shook his head.

"Go ahead, wring the blood tears from your eyes," I said. "And for what death do you hope yourself, Sir, for you told me that it wasn't impossible for even you to die? Explain to me, that is, if there's time left before all the light I shall ever know winks out on me, and the Earth devours the incarnate jewel that you found wanting!"

"Never wanting," he whispered.

"Come now, where will you go, Sir? More comfort, please. How many minutes do I have?"

"I don't know," he whispered. He turned away from me and bowed his head. I had never seen him so forlorn.

"Let me see your hand," I said weakly. "There are closeted witches who in the shadows of the taverns of Venice have taught me how to read the lines in it. I'll tell you when you are like to die. Give it to me." I could scarcely see. A haze had come down over all things. But I meant my words.

"You come too late," he replied. "There are no lines left." He held up his palm for me to see. "Time has erased what men call fate. I have none."

"I am sorry that you come at all," I said. I turned away from him. I turned away against the clean cool linen of the pillow. "Would you leave me now, my beloved teacher? I would rather the company of a priest, and my old nurse if you haven't sent her home. I have loved you with my whole heart, but I don't want to die in your superior company."

Through a haze I saw the shape of him as he grew nearer to me. I felt his hands cup my face and turn it towards him. I saw the glimmer of his blue eyes, wintry flames, indistinct yet burning fiercely.

"Very well, beautiful one. This is the moment. Would you come with me, and be like me?" His voice was rich and soothing, though it was full of pain.

"Yes, always and forever yours."

"Forever to thrive in secret on the blood of the evil-doer, as I thrive, and to abide with these secrets until the end of the world, if need be."

"I shall. I want it."

"To learn from me all the lessons I can give."

"Yes, all of them."

He picked me up from the bed. I tumbled against him, my head spinning and the pain in it so sharp, I cried out softly.

"Only a little while, my love, my young and tender love," he said in my ear.

I was lowered into the warm water of the bath, my clothes softly stripped away, my head laid back against the tiled edge ever so carefully. I let my arms float in the water. I felt it lap around my shoulders.

He broke up handfuls of water to bathe me. He bathed first my face and then all of me. His hard satiny fingertips moved over my face.

"Not a vagrant hair yet of your beard, and yet you have the nether endowments of a man, and must now rise above the pleasures you have so loved."

"I do, I will," I whispered. A terrible burning lashed my cheek. The cut was spread wide. I struggled to touch it. But he held my hand. It was only his blood fallen into the festering wound. And as the flesh tingled and burnt I felt it closing. He did the same with the scratch on my arm, and then with the small scratch on the back of my hand. With my eyes closed, I surrendered to the eerie paralyzing pleasure of it.

His hand touched me again, running smoothly down my chest, past my private parts, examining first one leg and then the other, searching out the smallest break or flaw in the skin, perhaps. Again the rich throbbing chills of pleasure overcame me.

I felt myself lifted from the water, warmly wrapped, and then there came that shock of moving air that meant he carried me, that he moved more swiftly than any spying eye could see. I felt the marble floor before my bare feet, and in my fever, this jolting cold was very good to me.

We stood in the studio. We had our backs to the painting on which he'd worked only nights ago, and faced another masterly canvas of immense size, on which beneath a brilliant sun and cobalt sky a great copse of trees surrounded two rushing windblown figures.

The woman was Daphne, her upstretched arms changing into the branches of the laurel, already thick with leaves, her feet grown into roots that sought the deep brown earth beneath her. And behind her, the desperate and beautiful god Apollo, a champion of golden hair and finely muscled limbs, come too late to stop her frantic magical escape from his threatening arms, her fatal metamorphosis.

"See the indifferent clouds above," my Master whispered in my ear. He pointed to the great streaks of sun he had painted with more skill than the men who daily beheld them.

He spoke words I confided to Lestat so long ago when I told him my story, words that he salvaged so mercifully from the few images of these times which I was able to give him.

I hear Marius's voice when I repeat these words, the last I was ever to hear as a mortal child:

"This is the only sun that you will ever see again. But a millennium of nights will be yours to see light as no mortal has ever seen it, to snatch from the distant stars, as if you were Prometheus, an endless illumination by which to understand all things."

And I, who had beheld a far more wondrous celestial light in that realm from which I'd been turned away, longed only for him to eclipse it now forever.

8

THE MASTER'S PRIVATE SALONS: a string of rooms in which he had covered the walls with flawless copies of the works of those mortal painters he so admired— Giotto, Fra Angelico, Bellini.

We stood in the room of Benozzo Gozzoli's great work, from the Medici Chapel in Florence: *The Procession of the Magi*.

In the middle of the century, Gozzoli had created this vision, wrapping it around three walls of that small sacred chamber.

But my Master, with his supernatural memory and skill, had spread out the great work, rendering the whole flat from end to end on one great side of this immense and broad gallery.

Perfect as Gozzoli's original it loomed, with its hordes of beautifully dressed young Florentines, each pale face a study in thoughtful innocence, astride a cavalry of gorgeous horses following the exquisite figure of the young Lorenzo de' Medici himself, a youth with soft curling brownish-blond hair to his shoulders, and a carnal blush in his white cheeks. With a tranquil expression he appeared to gaze indifferently at the viewer of the painting as he sat, regal in his fur-trimmed gold jacket

with its long slashed sleeves, on a beautifully capari-
soned white horse. No detail of the painting was unworthy of another. Even the horse's bridle and fittings were
of beautifully worked gold and velvet, a match for the
tight sleeves of Lorenzo's tunic and his red velvet knee-
high boots.

But the enchantment of the painting arose most
powerfully from the faces of the youths, as well as the
few old men who made up the immense crowded procession, all with small quiet mouths and eyes drifting to
the sides as if a forward glance would have broken the
spell. On and on they came past castles and mountains,
winding their way to Bethlehem.

To illuminate this masterpiece, dozens of silver
branching candelabra had been lighted up and down
both sides of the room. The thick white candles of the
purest beeswax gave off a luxurious illumination. High
above a glorious wilderness of painted clouds surrounded an oval of floating saints who touched each
other's outstretched hands as they looked down benevo-
lently and contentedly upon us.

No furniture covered the rosy Carrara marble tiles of
the highly polished floor. A wandering border pattern of
green leafy vine marked off in great squares these tiles,
but the floor was otherwise plain and deeply lustrous,
and silken smooth to bare feet.

I found myself staring with the fascination of a
feverish brain into this hall of glorious surfaces. *The
Procession of the Magi,* rising as it did to fill the entire
wall to the right of me, seemed to give off a soft plethora
of real sounds . . . the muted crunch of the hoofs of the
horses, the shuffling steps of those who walked beside

them, the rustling of the red-flowered shrubbery beyond them and even the distant cries of the hunters who, with their lean hounds, streaked along the mountain paths beyond.

My Master stood in the very center of the hall. He had taken off his familiar red velvet. He wore only an open robe of gold tissue, with long bell sleeves down to his wrists, his hem just skirting his bare white feet.

His hair seemed to make for him a halo of yellow brilliance, hanging softly to his shoulders.

I wore a gown of the same sheerness and simplicity.

"Come, Amadeo," he said.

I was weak, thirsting for water, barely able to stand. He knew this however, and no excuse seemed appropriate. I took my faltering steps one after another until I reached his outstretched arms.

His hands slid about the back of my head.

He bent his lips. A sense of dreadful awesome finality swept over me.

"You will die now to be with me in life eternal," he whispered in my ear. "Never for a moment must you really fear. I will hold your heart safe in my hands."

His teeth cut into me, deeply, cruelly with the precision of twin daggers, and I heard my heart thud in my ears. My very bowels contracted, and my stomach was knotted in pain. Yet a savage pleasure swept through all my veins, a pleasure which coursed towards the wounds in my neck. I could feel my blood rush towards my Master, towards his thirst and my inevitable death.

Even my hands were transfixed with vibrant sensation. Indeed, I seemed suddenly to be but a puppet map of circuitry, all of it aglow, as with a low, obvious and deliberate sound, my Master drank my life's blood. The sound of his heart, slow, steady, a deep reverberating pounding, filled my ears.

The pain in my intestines was alchemized to a soft sheer rapture; my body lost all weight, all knowledge of itself in space. The throb of his heart was within me. My hands felt the long satin locks of his hair, but I did not hold to them. I floated, supported only by the insistent heartbeat and thrilling current of all my swiftly flowing blood.

"I die now," I whispered. This ecstasy could not endure.

Abruptly the world died.

I stood alone on the desolate and windy shore of the sea.

It was the land to which I'd journeyed before, but how different it was now, devoid of its shining sun and abundant flowers. The priests were there, but their robes were dusty and dark and reeked of the earth. I knew these priests, I knew them well. I knew their names. I knew their narrow bearded faces, their thin greasy hair and the black felt hats that they wore. I knew the dirt in their fingernails, and I knew the hungry hollow of their sunken gleaming eyes.

They beckoned for me to come.

Ah, yes, back to where I belonged. We climbed higher and higher until we stood on the bluff of the glass city, and it lay to the far left of us, and how forlorn and empty it was.

All the molten energy which had lighted its multitudinous and translucent towers was now dead and gone, turned off at the source. Nothing remained of the blazing colors except a deep dull residue of tints beneath the featureless span of hopeless gray sky. Oh, sad, sad, to see the glass city without its magic fire.

A chorus of sounds rose from it, a tinkling, as of glass dully striking glass. There was no music in it. There was only a bleary luminous despair.

"Walk on, Andrei," said one of the priests to me. His soiled hand with its thin bits of caked mud touched me and pulled at me, hurting my fingers. I looked down to see that my fingers were thin and luridly white. My knuckles shone as though the flesh had already been stripped away, but it had not.

All my skin merely cleaved to me, hungry and loose as their skin.

Before us came the water of the river, filled with ice sloughs and great tangles of blackened driftwood, covering the flatlands with a murky lake. We had to walk through it, and its coldness hurt us. Yet on we went, the four of us, the three priest guides and me. Above loomed the once golden domes of Kiev. It was our Santa Sofia, standing still after the horrid massacres and conflagrations of the Mongols who had laid waste our city and all her riches and all her wicked and worldly women and men.

"Come, Andrei."

I knew this doorway. It was to the Monastery of the Caves. Only candles illuminated these catacombs, and the smell of the earth overpowered all, even the stench of dried sweat on soiled and diseased flesh.

In my hands, I held the rough wooden handle of a small shovel. I dug into the heap of earth. I opened up the soft wall of rubble, until my eyes fell on a man not dead but dreaming as the dirt covered his face.

"Still alive, Brother?" I whispered, to this soul buried up to his neck.

"Still alive, Brother Andrei, give me only what will sustain me," said the cracked lips. The white eyelids were never lifted. "Give me only that much, so that our Lord and Savior, Christ Himself, will choose the time that I am to come home."

"Oh, Brother, how courageous you are," I said. I put a jug of water to his lips. The mud streaked them as he drank. His head rested back in soft rubble.

"And you, child," he said with labored breaths, turning ever so slightly from the proffered jug, "when will you have the strength to choose your earthen cell among us, your grave, and wait for Christ to come?"

"Soon, I pray, Brother," I answered. I stepped back. I lifted the shovel.

I dug into the next cell, and soon a dreadful unmistakable stench assailed me. The priest beside me stayed my hand.

"Our Good Brother Joseph is finally with the Lord," he said. "That's it, uncover his face so that we may see for ourselves that he died at peace."

The stench grew thicker. Only dead human beings reek this strongly. It's the smell of desolate graves and carts coming from those districts where the plague is at its worst. I feared I would be sick. But I continued to dig, until at last we uncovered the dead man's head. Bald, a skull encased in shrunken skin.

Prayers rose from the brothers behind me. "Close it up, Andrei."

"When will you have the courage, Brother? Only God can tell you when—."

"The courage to what!" I know this booming voice, this big-shouldered man who barrels his way down the catacomb. No mistaking his auburn hair and beard, his leather jerkin and his weapons hung on his leather belt.

"This is what you do with my son, the ikon painter!"

He grabbed me by the shoulder, as he'd done a thousand times, with the same huge paw of a hand that had beaten me senseless.

"Let go of me, please, you impossible and ignorant ox," I whispered. "We're in the house of God."

He dragged me so that I fell on my knees. My robe was tearing, black cloth ripping.

"Father, stop it and go away," I said.

"Deep in these pits to bury a boy who can paint with the skill of the angels!"

"Brother Ivan, stop your shouting. It's for God to decide what each of us will do."

The priests ran behind me. I was dragged into the workroom. Ikons in rows hung from the ceiling, covering all of the far wall. My Father flung me down in the chair at the large heavy table. He lifted the iron candlestick with its fluttering, protesting candle to light all the tapers around.

The illumination made a fire on his huge beard. Long gray hairs sprung from his thick eyebrows, combed upwards, diabolical.

"You behave like the village idiot, Father," I whispered. "It's a wonder I'm not a slobbering idiot beggar myself."

"Shut up, Andrei. Nobody's taught you any manners here, that's clear enough. You need me to beat you."

He slammed his fist into the side of my head. My ear went numb.

"I thought I'd beaten you enough before I brought you here, but not so," he said. He smacked me again.

"Desecration!" cried the priest, looming above me. "The boy's consecrated to God."

"Consecrated to a pack of lunatics," said my Father. He took a packet out of his coat. "Your eggs, Brothers!" he said with contempt. He lay back the soft leather and removed an egg. "Paint, Andrei. Paint to remind these lunatics that you have the gift from God Himself."

"And God Himself it is who paints the picture," cried the priest, the eldest of them, whose sticky gray hair was so soiled in time with oil that it was near black. He pushed his way between my chair and my Father.

My Father set down all but one egg. Leaning over a small earthen bowl on the table, he broke the shell of the egg, carefully gathering the yoke in one side, and letting all the rest spill into his leather cloth. "There, there, pure yoke, Andrei." He sighed, and then threw the broken shell on the floor.

He picked up the small pitcher and poured the water into the yoke.

"You mix it, mix your colors and work. Remind these—."

"He works when God calls him to work," declared the Elder, "and when God calls him to bury himself within the Earth, to live the life of the reclusive, the hermit, then will he do that."

"Like Hell," said my Father. "Prince Michael himself has asked for an Ikon of the Virgin. Andrei, paint!

Paint three for me that I may give the Prince the Ikon for which he asks, and take the others to the distant castle of his cousin, Prince Feodor, as he has asked."

"That castle's destroyed, Father," I said contemptuously. "Feodor and all his men were massacred by the wild tribes. You'll find nothing out there in the wild lands, nothing but stones. Father, you know this as well as I do. We've ridden plenty far enough to see for ourselves."

"We'll go if the Prince wants us to go," said my Father, "and we'll leave the ikon in the branches of the nearest tree to where his brother died."

"Vanity and madness," said the Elder. Other priests came into the room. There was much shouting.

"Speak clearly to me and stop the poetry!" cried my Father. "Let my boy paint. Andrei, mix your colors. Say your prayers, but begin."

"Father, you humiliate me. I despise you. I'm ashamed that I'm your son. I'm not your son. I won't be your son. Shut your filthy mouth or I'll paint nothing."

"Ah, that's my sweet boy, with the honey rolling off his tongue, and the bees that left it there left their sting too."

Again, he struck me. This time I became dizzy, but I refused to lift my hands to my head. My ear throbbed.

"Proud of yourself, Ivan the Idiot!" I said. "How can I paint when I can't see or even sit in the chair?"

The priests shouted. They argued amongst one another.

I tried to focus on the small row of earthen jars ready for the yoke and the water. Finally I began to mix the yoke and the water. Best to work and shut them all out. I could hear my Father laugh with satisfaction.

"Now, show them, show them what they mean to wall up alive in a lot of mud."

"For the love of God," said the Elder.

"For the love of stupid idiots," said my Father. "It isn't enough to have a great painter. You have to have a saint."

"You do not know what your son is. It was God who guided you to bring him here."

"It was money," said my Father. Gasps rose from the priests.

"Don't lie to them," I said under my breath. "You know damned good and well it was pride."

"Yes, pride," said my Father, "that my son could paint the Face of Christ or His Blessed Mother like a Master! And you, to whom I commit this genius, are too ignorant to see it."

I began to grind the pigments I needed, the soft brownish-red powder, and then to mix it over and over with the yoke and water until every tiny fragment of pigment was broken up and the paint was smooth and perfectly thin and clear. On to the yellow, and then to the red.

They fought over me. My Father lifted his fist to the Elder, but I didn't bother to look up. He wouldn't dare. He kicked my leg in his desperation, sending a cramp through my muscle, but I said nothing. I went on mixing the paint.

One of the priests had come round to my left, and he slipped a clean whitewashed panel of wood in front of me, primed and ready for the holy image.

At last I was ready. I bowed my head. I made the Sign of the Cross in our way, touching my right shoulder first, not my left.

"Dear God, give me the power, give me the vision, give my hands the tutelage which only your love can give!" At once I had the brush with no consciousness of having picked it up, and the brush began to race, tracing out the oval of the Virgin's face, and then the sloping lines of her shoulders and then the outline of her folded hands.

Now when their gasps came, they were tributes to the painting. My Father laughed in gloating satisfaction.

"Ah, my Andrei, my sharp-tongued, sarcastic, nasty ungrateful little genius of God."

"Thank you, Father," I whispered bitingly, right from the middle of my trancelike concentration, as I myself watched the work of the brush in awe. There her hair, cleaving close to the scalp and parted in the middle. I needed no instrument to make the outline of her halo perfectly round.

The priests held the clean brushes for me. One held a clean rag in his hands. I snatched up a brush for the red color which I then mixed with white paste, until it was the appropriate color of flesh.

"Isn't that a miracle!"

"That's just the point," said the Elder between clenched teeth. "It's a miracle, Brother Ivan, and he will do what God wills."

"He won't wall himself up in here, damn you, not as long as I'm alive. He's coming with me into the wild lands."

I burst out laughing. "Father," I said sneering at him. "My place is here."

"He's the best shot in the family, and he's coming with me into the wild lands," said my Father to the others, who had flown into a flurry of protests and negations all around.

"Why do you give Our Blessed Mother that tear in her eye, Brother Andrei?"

"It's God who gives her the tear," said one of the others.

"It is the Mother of All Sorrows. Ah, see the beautiful folds of her cloak."

"Ah, look, the Christ child!" said my Father, and even his face was reverent. "Ah, poor little baby God, soon to be crucified and die!" His voice was for once subdued and almost tender. "Ah, Andrei, what a gift. Oh, but look, look at the child's eyes and his little hand, at the flesh of his thumb, his little hand."

"Even you are touched with the light of Christ," said the Elder. "Even such a stupid violent man as you, Brother Ivan."

The priests pressed in close around me in a circle. My Father held out a palmful of small twinkling jewels. "For the halos, Andrei. Work fast, Prince Michael has ordained that we go."

"Madness, I tell you!" All voices were set to babbling at once. My Father turned and raised his fist.

I looked up, reached for a fresh, clean panel of wood. My forehead was wet with sweat. I worked on and on.

I had done three ikons.

I felt such happiness, such pure happiness. It was

sweet to be so warm in it, so aware of it, and I knew, though I said nothing, that my Father had made it possible, my Father, so cheerful and ruddy-cheeked and overpowering with his big shoulders and his glistening face, this man I was supposed to hate.

The Sorrowful Mother with her Child, and the napkin for her tears, and the Christ Himself. Weary, bleary-eyed, I sat back. The place was intolerably cold. Oh, if there were only a little fire. And my hand, my left hand was cramped from the cold. Only my right hand was all right because of the pace at which I had done my work. I wanted to suck the fingers of my left hand, but this would not do, not here at this moment, when all gathered to coo over the ikons.

"Masterly. The Work of God."

An awful sense of time came over me, that I had traveled far from this moment, far from this the Monastery of the Caves to which I had vowed my life, far from the priests who were my brethren, far from my cursing, stupid Father, who was in spite of his ignorance so very proud.

Tears flowed from his eyes. "My son," he said. He clutched my shoulder proudly. He was beautiful in his own way, such a fine strong man, afraid of nothing, a prince himself when among his horses and his dogs and his followers, of which I, his son, had been one.

"Let me alone, you thick-skulled oaf," I said. I smiled up at him to further outrage him. He laughed. He was too happy, too proud, to be provoked.

"Look what my son has done." His voice had a telltale thickness to it. He was going to cry. And he wasn't even drunk.

"Not by human hands," said the priest.

"No, naturally not!" boomed my Father's scornful voice. "Just by my son Andrei's hands, that's all."

A silken voice said in my ear, "Would you place the jewels into the halos yourself, Brother Andrei, or shall I perform this task?"

Behold, it was done, the paste applied, the stones set, five in the Ikon of Christ. The brush was in my hand again to stroke the brown hair of the Lord God, which was parted in the middle and brought back behind His ears, with only part of it to show on either side of His neck. The stylus appeared in my hand to thicken and darken the black letters on the open book which Christ held in His left hand. The Lord God stared, serious and severe, from the panel, His mouth red and straight beneath the horns of His brown mustache.

"Come now, the Prince is here, the Prince has come."

Outside the entrance of the Monastery, the snow fell in cruel gusts. The priests helped me with my leather vest, my jacket of shearling. They buckled my belt. It was good to smell this leather again, to breathe the fresh cold air. My Father had my sword. It was heavy, old, taken from his long-ago fighting against the Teutonic Knights in lands far to the east, the jewels long ago chipped out of its handle, but a fine, fine battle sword.

Through the snowy mist a figure appeared, on horseback. It was Prince Michael himself, in his fur hat and fur-lined cape and gloves, the great Lord who ruled Kiev for our Roman Catholic conquerors, whose faith we would not accept but who let us keep to our own. He was decked out in foreign velvet and gold, a fancy figure fit for royal Lithuanian courts, of which we heard fantastical tales. How did he endure Kiev, the ruined city?

The horse reared up on its hind legs. My Father ran to catch the reins, and threaten the animal as he threatened me.

The Ikon for Prince Feodor was wrapped thickly in wool for me to carry.

I placed my hand on the hilt of my sword.

"Ah, you will not take him on this Godless mission," cried the Elder. "Prince Michael, Your Excellency, our mighty ruler, tell this Godless man that he can not take our Andrei."

I saw the face of the Prince through the snow, square and strong, with gray eyebrows and beard and huge hard blue eyes. "Let him go, Father," he cried out to the priest. "The boy has hunted with Ivan since he was four years old. Never has anyone provided such bounty for my table, and for yours, Father. Let him go."

The horse danced backwards. My Father pulled down on the reins. Prince Michael blew the snow from off his lips.

Our horses were led to the fore, my Father's powerful stallion with the gracefully curved neck and the shorter gelding which had been mine before I had come to the Monastery of the Caves.

"I'll be back, Father," I said to the Elder. "Give me your blessing. What can I do against my gentle, sweet-tempered and infinitely pious Father when Prince Michael himself commands?"

"Oh, shut your lousy little mouth," said my Father. "You think I want to listen to this all the way to the Castle of Prince Feodor?"

"You'll hear it all the way to Hell!" declared the Elder. "You take my finest novice to his death."

"Novice, novice to a hole in the dirt! You take the hands that have painted these marvels—."

"God painted them," I said in a biting whisper, "and you know it, Father. Will you please stop making a display of your Godlessness and belligerence."

I was on the back of my horse. The Ikon was strapped in wool to my chest.

"I don't believe my brother Feodor is dead!" the Prince said, trying to control his mount, to bring it in line with that of my Father. "Perhaps these travelers saw some other ruin, some old—."

"Nothing survives in the grasslands now," pleaded the Elder. "Prince, don't take Andrei. Don't take him."

The priest ran alongside of my horse. "Andrei, you will find nothing; you will find only the wild blowing grass and the trees. Put the Ikon in the branches of a tree. Place it for the will of God, so that when it is found by the Tatars they will know His Divine power. Place it there for the pagans. And come home."

The snow came down so fierce and thick I couldn't see his face.

I looked up at the stripped and barren domes of our Cathedral, that remnant of Byzantine glory left to us by Mongol invaders, who now exacted their greedy tribute through our Catholic Prince. How bleak and desolate was this, my homeland. I closed my eyes and longed for the mud cubicle of the cave, for the smell of the earth close around me, for the dreams of God and His Goodness which would come to me, once I was half-entombed.

Come back to me, Amadeo. Come back. Do not let your heart stop!

I spun around. "Who calls to me?" The thick white veil of the snow broke to reveal the distant glass city, black and glimmering as if heated by hellish fires. Smoke rose to feed the ominous clouds of the darkening sky. I rode towards the glass city.

"Andrei!" This was my Father's voice behind me.

Come back to me, Amadeo. Don't let your heart stop!

The Ikon fell from my left arm as I struggled to bridle my mount. The wool had come undone. On and on we rode. The Ikon fell downhill beside us, turning over and over, corner bouncing upon corner, as it tumbled, the swaddling of wool falling loose. I saw the shimmering face of Christ.

Strong arms caught me, pulled me upwards as if from a whirlwind. "Let me go!" I protested. I looked back. Against the frozen earth lay the Ikon, and the staring, questioning eyes of the Christ.

Firm fingers pressed my face on either side. I blinked and opened my eyes. The room was filled with warmth and light. There loomed the familiar face of my Master right above me, his blue eyes shot with blood. "Drink, Amadeo," he said. "Drink from me."

My head fell forward against his throat. The blood fount had started; it bubbled out of his vein, flowing thickly down onto the neck of his golden tissue robe. I closed my mouth over it. I lapped at it.

I let out a cry as the blood inflamed me.

"Draw it from me, Amadeo. Draw it hard!"

My mouth filled with blood. My lips closed against

his silky white flesh so that not a drop would be lost. Deeply I swallowed. In a dim flash I saw my Father riding through the grasslands, a powerful leather-clad figure, his sword tied firmly to his belt, his leg crooked, his cracked and worn brown boot firmly in the stirrup. He turned to the left, rising and falling gracefully and perfectly with the huge strides of his white horse.

"All right, leave me, you coward, you impudent and miserable boy! Leave me!" He looked before him. "I prayed for it, Andrei, I prayed they wouldn't get you for their filthy catacombs, their dark earthen cells. Well, so my prayer is answered! Go with God, Andrei. Go with God. Go with God!"

My Master's face was rapt and beautiful, a white flame against the wavering golden light of countless candles. He stood over me.

I lay on the floor. My body sang with the blood. I climbed to my feet, my head swimming. "Master."

At the far end of the room he stood, his bare feet composed on the glowing rose-colored floor, his arms outstretched. "Come to me, Amadeo, walk towards me, come to me, to take the rest."

I struggled to obey him. The room raged with colors around me. I saw the Procession of the searching Magi. "Oh, that it's so vivid, so utterly alive!"

"Come to me, Amadeo."

"I'm too weak, Master, I'm fainting, I'm dying in this glorious light."

I took one step after another, though it seemed impossible. I placed one foot before the other, drawing ever closer to him. I stumbled.

"On your hands and knees, then, come. Come to me."

I clung to his robe. I had to climb this great height if I wanted it. I reached up and took hold of the crook of his right arm. I lifted myself, feeling the gold cloth against me. I straightened my legs until I stood. Once again, I embraced him; once again I found the fount. I drank, and drank, and drank.

In a gilded gush the blood went down into my bowels. It went through my legs and my arms. I was a Titan. I crushed him under me. "Give it to me," I whispered. "Give it to me." The blood hovered on my lips and then flooded down my throat.

It was as if his cold marble hands had seized my heart. I could hear it struggling, beating, the valves opening and closing, the wet sound of his blood invading it, the swoosh and flap of the valves as they welcomed it, utilizing it, my heart growing ever larger and more powerful, my veins becoming like so many invincible metallic conduits of this most potent fluid.

I lay on the floor. He stood above me, and his hands were open to me. "Get up, Amadeo. Come, come up, into my arms. Take it."

I cried. I sobbed. My tears were red, and my hand was stained with red. "Help me, Master."

"I do help you. Come, seek it out for yourself."

I was on my feet with this new strength, as if all human limitations had been loosened, as if they were bonds of rope or chain and had fallen away. I sprang at him, pulling back his robe, the better to find the wound.

"Make a new wound, Amadeo."

I bit into the flesh, puncturing it, and the blood

squirted over my lips. I clapped my mouth against it. "Flow into me."

My eyes closed. I saw the wild lands, the grass blowing, the sky blue. My Father rode on and on with the small band behind him. Was I one of them?

"I prayed you'd escape!" he called out to me, laughing, "and so you have. Damn you, Andrei. Damn you and your sharp tongue and your magical painter's hands. Damn you, you foul-mouthed whelp, damn you." He laughed and laughed, and rode on, the grass bending and falling for him.

"Father, look!" I struggled to shout. I wanted him to see the stony ruins of the castle. But my mouth was full of blood. They had been right. Prince Feodor's fortress was destroyed, and he himself long gone. My Father's horse reared up suddenly as it came to the first heap of vine-covered stones.

With a shock, I felt the marble floor beneath me, so wondrously warm. I lay with both hands against it. I lifted myself. The swarming rosy pattern was so dense, so deep, so wondrous, it was like water frozen to make the finest stone. I could have looked into its depths forever.

"Rise up, Amadeo, once more."

Oh, it was easy to make this climb, to reach for his arm and then his shoulder. I broke the flesh of his neck. I drank. The blood washed through me, once again revealing my entire form with a shock against the blackness of my mind. I saw the boy's body that was mine, of arms and legs, as with this form I breathed in the warmth and light around me, as if all of me had become one great multipored organ for seeing, for hearing, for breathing.

I breathed with millions of minute and strong tiny mouths.

The blood filled me so that I could take no more.

I stood before my Master. In his face I saw but the hint of weariness, but the smallest pain in his eyes. I saw for the first time the true lines of his old humanity in his face, the soft inevitable crinkles at the corners of his serenely folded eyes.

The drapery of his robe glistened, the light traveling on it as the cloth moved with his small gesture. He pointed. He pointed to the painting of *The Procession of the Magi*.

"Your soul and your physical body are now locked together forever," he said. "And through your vampiric senses, the sense of sight, and of touch, and of smell, and of taste, you'll know all the world. Not from turning away from it to the dark cells of the Earth, but through opening your arms to endless glory will you perceive the absolute splendor of God's creation and the miracles wrought, in His Divine Indulgence, by the hands of men."

The silk-clad multitudes of *The Procession of the Magi* appeared to move. Once more I heard the horses' hooves on the soft earth, and the shuffle of booted feet. Once more I thought I saw the distant hounds leap on the mountainside. I saw the masses of flowered shrubbery wobble with the press of the gilded procession against them; I saw petals fly from the flowers. Marvelous animals frolicked in the thick wood. I saw the proud Prince Lorenzo, astride his mount, turn his youthful head, just as my Father had done, and look at me. On and on went the world beyond him, the world with its white rocky cliffs, its hunters on their brown steeds and its leaping prancing dogs.

"It's gone forever, Master," I said, and how rounded and resonant was my voice, responding to all that I beheld.

"What is that, my child?"

"Russia, the world of the wild lands, the world of those dark terrible cells within the moist Mother Earth."

I turned around and around. Smoke rose from the wilderness of burning candles. Wax crawled and dripped over the chased silver that held them, dripping even to the spotless and shimmering floor. The floor was as the sea, so transparent suddenly, so silken, and high above the painted clouds in illimitable sweetest blue. It seemed a mist emanated from these clouds, a warm summer mist made up of mingling land and sea.

Once again, I looked at the painting. I moved towards it and threw out my hands against it, and stared upwards at the white castles atop the hills, at the delicate groomed trees, at the fierce sublime wilderness that waited so patiently for the sluggish journey of my crystal-clear gaze.

"So much!" I whispered. No words could describe the deep colors of brown and gold in the beard of the exotic magus, or the shadows at play in the painted head of the white horse, or in the face of the balding man who led him, or the grace of the arch-necked camels or the crush of rich flowers beneath soundless feet.

"I see it with all of me," I sighed. I closed my eyes and lay against it, recalling perfectly all aspects as the dome of my mind became this room itself, and the wall was there colored and painted by me. "I see it without any omission. I see it," I whispered.

I felt my Master's arms around my chest. I felt his kiss on my hair.

"Can you see again the glassy city?" he asked.

"I can make it!" I cried. I let my head roll back against his chest. I opened my eyes, and drew out of the riot of painting before me the very colors I wanted, and made this metropolis of bubbling, leaping glass rise in my imagination, until its towers pierced the sky. "It's there, do you see it?"

In a torrent of tumbling, laughing words I described it, the glittering green and yellow and blue spires that sparkled and wavered in the Heavenly light. "Do you see it?" I cried out.

"No. But you do," said my Master. "And that is more than enough."

In the dim chamber, we dressed in the black morn.

Nothing was difficult, nothing had its old weight and resistance. It seemed I only needed to run my fingers up the doublet to have it buttoned.

We hurried down the steps, which seemed to disappear beneath my feet, and out into the night.

To climb the slimy walls of a palazzo was nothing, to anchor my feet over and over in the chinks of the stone, to poise on a tuft of fern and vine as I reached for the bars of a window and finally pulled open the grate, it was nothing, and how easily I let the heavy metal grid drop into the glistening green water below. How sweet to see it sink, to see the water splash around the descending weight, to see the glimmer of the torches in the water.

"I fall into it."

"Come."

Inside the chamber, the man rose from his desk. Against the cold, he had wrapped his neck in wool. His dark blue robe was banded in pearly gold. Rich man, banker. Friend of the Florentine, not mourning his loss over these many pages of vellum, smelling of black ink but calculating the inevitable gains, all partners murdered by the blade and by poison, it seemed, in a private banquet room.

Did he guess now that we had done it, the red-cloaked man and the auburn-haired boy who came through his high fourth-story window in this frozen winter night?

I caught him as if he were the love of my young life, and unwound the wool from around the artery where I would feed.

He begged me to stop, to name my price. How still my Master looked, watching only me, as the man begged and I ignored him, merely feeling for this large pulsing, irresistible vein.

"Your life, Sir, I must have it," I whispered. "The blood of thieves is strong, isn't it, Sir?"

"Oh, child," he cried, all resolve shattering, "does God send His justice in such an unlikely form?"

It was sharp, pungent and strangely rank this human blood, spiked with the wine he'd drunk and the herbs of the foods he'd eaten, and almost purple in the light of his lamps as it flowed over my fingers before I could lap them with my tongue.

At the first draught I felt his heart stop.

"Ease up, Amadeo," whispered my Master.

I let go and the heart recovered.

"That's it, feed on it slowly, slowly, letting the heart pump the blood to you, yes, yes, and gently with your fingers that he not suffer unduly, for he suffers the worst fate he can know and that is to know that he dies."

We walked along the narrow quay together. No need anymore to keep my balance, though my gaze was lost in the depths of the singing, lapping water, gaining its movement through its many stonewalled connections from the faraway sea. I wanted to feel the wet green moss on the stones.

We stood in a small piazza, deserted, before the angled doors of a high stone church. They were bolted now. All windows were blinded, all doors locked. Curfew. Quiet.

"Once more, lovely one, for the strength it will give you," said my Master, and his lethal fangs pierced me, as his hands held me captive.

"Would you trick me? Would you kill me?" I whispered, as I felt myself again helpless, no preternatural effort that I could summon strong enough to escape his grasp.

The blood was pulled out of me in a tidal wave that left my arms dangling and shaking, my feet dancing as if I were a hanged man. I struggled to remain conscious. I pushed against him. But the flow continued, out of me, out of all my fibers and into him.

"Now, once again, Amadeo, take it back from me."

He dealt one fine blow to my chest. I almost toppled off my feet. I was so weak, I fell forward, only at the last grasping for his cloak. I pulled myself up and locked my

left arm around his neck. He stepped back, straighten-
ing, making it hard for me. But I was too determined, too
challenged and too determined to make a mockery of his
lessons.

"Very well, sweet Master," I said as I tore at his skin
once again. "I have you, and will have every drop of you,
Sir, unless you are quick, most quick." Only then did I
realize! I too had tiny fangs!

He started to laugh softly, and it heightened my pleasure, that this which I fed upon should laugh beneath
these new fangs.

With all my might I sought to tug his heart out of his
chest. I heard him cry out and then laugh in amazement.
I drew and drew on his blood, swallowing with a hoarse
disgraceful sound.

"Come on, let me hear you cry out again!" I whispered, sucking the blood greedily, widening the gash
with my teeth, my sharpened, lengthened teeth, these
fang teeth that were now mine and made for this slaughter. "Come on, beg for mercy, Sir!"

His laughter was sweet.

I took his blood swallow after swallow, glad and
proud at his helpless laughing, at the fact that he had
fallen down on his knees in the square and that I had him
still, and he must now raise his arm to push me away.

"I can't drink anymore!" I declared. I lay back on the
stones.

The frozen sky was black and studded with the white
blazing stars. I stared at it, deliciously aware of the stone
beneath me, of the hardness under my back and my
head. No care now about the soil, the damp, the threat of

disease. No care now whether the crawling things of the night came near. No care now what men might think who peeped from their windows. No care now for the lateness of the hour. Look at me, stars. Look at me, as I look at you.

Silent and glistering, these tiny eyes of Heaven.

I began to die. A withering pain commenced in my stomach, then moved to my bowels.

"Now, all that's left of a mortal boy will leave you," my Master said. "Don't be afraid."

"No more music?" I whispered. I rolled over and put my arms around my Master, who lay beside me, his head resting on his elbow. He gathered me to him.

"Shall I sing to you a lullaby?" he said softly.

I moved away from him. Foul fluid had begun to flow from me. I felt an instinctive shame, but this quite slowly vanished. He picked me up, easily as always, and pushed my face into his neck. The wind rushed around us.

Then I felt the cold water of the Adriatic, and I found myself tumbling on the unmistakable swell of the sea. The sea was salty and delicious and held no menace. I turned over and over, and finding myself alone, tried to get my bearings. I was far out, near to the island of the Lido. I looked back to the main island, and I could see through the great congregation of ships at anchor the blazing torches of the Palazzo Ducale, with a vision that was awesomely clear.

The mingled voices of the dark port rose, as if I were secretly swimming amongst the ships, though I was not.

What a remarkable power, to hear these voices, to be

able to hone in on one particular voice and hear its early-morning mumblings, and then to pitch my hearing to yet another and let other words sink in.

I floated under the sky for a while, until all the pain was gone from me. I felt cleansed, and I didn't want to be alone. I turned over and effortlessly swam towards the harbor, moving under the surface of the water when I neared the ships.

What astonished me now was that I could see beneath the water! There was enough life for my vampiric eyes to see the huge anchors lodged in the mushy bottom of the lagoon, and to see the curved bottoms of the galleys. It was an entire underwater universe. I wanted to explore it further, but I heard my Master's voice—not a telepathic voice, as we would call it now, but his audible voice—calling me very softly to return to the piazza where he waited for me.

I peeled off my rank clothes and climbed out of the water naked, hurrying to him in the cold darkness, delighted that the chill itself meant little. When I saw him I spread out my arms and smiled.

He held a fur cloak in his arms, which he opened now to receive me, rubbing my hair dry with it and winding it around me.

"You feel your new freedom. Your bare feet are not hurt by the deep cold of the stones. If you're cut, your resilient skin will heal instantly, and no small crawling creature of the dark will produce revulsion in you. They can't hurt you. Disease can't hurt you." He covered me with kisses. "The most pestilential blood will only feed you, as your preternatural body cleanses it and absorbs it. You are a powerful creature, and deep in here? In your chest, which I touch now with my hand, there is your heart, your human heart."

"Is it really so, Master?" I asked. I was exhilarated, I was playful. "Why so human still?"

"Amadeo, have you found me inhuman? Have you found me cruel?"

My hair had shaken off the water, drying almost instantly. We walked now, arm in arm, the heavy fur cloak covering me, out of the square.

When I didn't answer, he stopped and embraced me again and began his hungry kisses.

"You love me," I said, "as I am now, even more than before."

"Oh, yes," he said. He hugged me roughly and kissed my throat all over, and my shoulders, and began to kiss my chest. "I can't hurt you now, I can't snuff out your life with an accidental embrace. You're mine, of my flesh and of my blood."

He stopped. He was crying. He didn't want me to see. He turned away when I tried to catch his face with my impertinent hands.

"Master, I love you," I said.

"Pay attention," he said brushing me off, obviously impatient with his tears. He pointed to the sky. "You'll always know when morning's coming, if you pay attention. Do you feel it? Do you hear the birds? There are in all parts of the world those birds who sing right before dawn."

A thought came to me, dark and horrid, that one of the things I had missed in the deep Monastery of the Caves under Kiev was the sound of birds. Out in the wild grasses, hunting with my Father, riding from copse to copse of trees, I had loved the song of the birds. We had never been too long in the miserable riverside hovels of Kiev without those forbidden journeys into the wild lands from which so many didn't return.

But that was gone. I had all of sweet Italy around me, the sweet Serenissima. I had my Master, and the great voluptuous magic of this transformation.

"For this I rode into the wild lands," I whispered. "For this he took me out of the Monastery on that last day."

My Master looked at me sadly. "I hope so," he said. "What I know of your past, I learnt from your mind when it was open to me, but it's closed now, closed because I've made you a vampire, the same as I am, and we can never know each other's minds. We're too close, the blood we share makes a deafening roar in our ears when we try to talk in silence to one another, and so I let go forever of those awful images of that underground Monastery which flashed so brilliantly in your thoughts, but always with agony, always with near despair."

"Yes, despair, and all that is gone like the pages of a book torn loose and thrown into the wind. Just like that, gone."

He hurried me along. We were not going home. It was another way through the back alleys.

"We go now to our cradle," he said, "which is our crypt, our bed which is our grave."

We entered an old dilapidated palazzo, tenanted only with a few sleeping poor. I didn't like it. I had been brought up by him on luxury. But we soon entered a cellar, a seeming impossibility in rank and watery Venice, but a cellar it was, indeed. We made our way down stone stairs, past thick bronze doors, which men alone could not open, until in the inky blackness we had found the final room.

"Here's a trick," my Master whispered, "which some night you yourself will be strong enough to work."

I heard a riot of crackling and a small blast, and a great flaring torch blazed in his hand. He had lighted it with no more than his mind.

"With each decade you'll grow stronger, and then with each century, and you will discover many times in your long life that your powers have made a magical leap. Test them carefully, and protect what you discover. Use cleverly all that you discover. Never shun any power, for that's as foolish as a man shunning his strength."

I nodded, staring spellbound at the flames. I had never seen such colors in simple fire before, and I felt no aversion to it, though I knew that it was the one thing that could destroy me. He had said so, had he not?

He made a gesture. I should regard the room.

What a splendid chamber it was. It was paved in gold! Even its ceiling was of gold. Two stone sarcophagi stood in the middle of it, each graced with a carved figure in the old style, that is, severe and more solemn than natural; and as I drew closer, I saw that these figures were helmeted knights, in long tunics, with heavy broadswords carved close to their flanks, their gloved hands clasped in prayer, their eyes closed in eternal sleep. Each had been gilded, and plated with silver, and set with countless tiny gems. The belts of the knights were set with amethyst. Sapphires adorned the necks of their tunics. Topaz gleamed in the scabbards of their swords.

"Is this not a fortune to tempt a thief?" I asked. "Lying as it does here beneath this ruined house?"

He laughed outright.

"You're teaching me to be cautious already?" he asked, smiling. "What back talk! No thief can gain access here. You didn't measure your own strength when you opened the doors. Look at the bolt I've closed behind us, since you are so concerned. Now see if you can lift the lid of that coffin. Go ahead. See if your strength meets your nerve."

"I didn't mean it to be back talk," I protested. "Thank God you're smiling." I lifted the lid and then moved the lower part of it to one side. It was nothing to me, yet I knew this was heavy stone. "Ah, I see," I said meekly. I gave him a radiant and innocent smile. The inside was cushioned in damask of royal purple.

"Get into this crib, my child," he said. "Don't be afraid as you wait for the rise of the sun. When it comes you'll sleep soundly enough."

"Can I not sleep with you?"

"No, here in this bed which I have long ago prepared for you, this is where you belong. I have my own narrow place there next to you, which is not big enough for two. But you are mine now, mine, Amadeo. Vouchsafe me one last bevy of kisses, ah, sweet, yes, sweet—."

"Master, don't let me ever make you angry. Don't let me ever—."

"No, Amadeo, be my challenger, be my questioner,

be my bold and ungrateful pupil." He looked faintly sad. He pushed me gently. He gestured to the coffin. The purple satin damask shimmered.

"And so I lie in it," I whispered, "so young."

I saw the shadow of pain in his face after I'd said this. I regretted it. I wanted to say something to undo it, but he gestured that I must go on.

Oh, how cold this was, cushions be damned, and how hard. I moved the lid into place above me and lay still, listening, listening to the sound of the torch snuffed, and to the grinding of stone on stone as he opened his own grave.

I heard his voice:

"Good night, my young love, my child love, my son," he said.

I let my body go limp. How delicious was this simple relaxation. How new were all things.

Far away in the land of my birth, the monks chanted in the Monastery of the Caves.

Sleepily, I reflected on all I'd remembered. I had gone home to Kiev. I had made of my memories a tableau to teach me all that I might know. And in the last moments of nighttime consciousness, I said farewell to them forever, farewell to their beliefs and their restraints.

I envisaged *The Procession of the Magi* splendidly glowing on the Master's wall, the procession which would be mine to study when the sun set again. It seemed to me in my wild and passionate soul, in my newborn vampiric heart, that the Magi had come not only for Christ's birth but for my rebirth as well.

9

IF I HAD THOUGHT my transformation into a vampire
meant the end of my tutelage or apprenticeship to Marius, I was quite wrong. I wasn't immediately set free to
wallow in the joys of my new powers.

The night after my metamorphosis, my education
began in earnest. I was to be prepared now not for a tem-
poral life but for eternity.

My Master gave me to know that he had been created a vampire almost fifteen hundred years ago, and
that there were members of our kind all over the world.
Secretive, suspicious and often miserably lonely, the
wanderers of the night, as my Master called them, were
often ill prepared for immortality and made nothing of
their existence but a string of dreary disasters until despair consumed them and they immolated themselves
through some ghastly bonfire, or by going into the light
of the sun.

As for the very old, those who like my Master had
managed to withstand the passage of empires and
epochs, they were for the most part misanthropes, seeking for themselves cities in which they could reign
supreme among mortals, driving off fledglings who attempted to share their territory, even if it meant destroying creatures of their own kind.

Venice was the undisputed territory of my Master,

his hunting preserve, and his own private arena in which he could preside over the games which he had chosen as significant for him in this time of life.

"There is nothing that will not pass," he said, "except you yourself. You must listen to what I say because my lessons are first and foremost lessons in survival; the garnishes will come later on."

The primary lesson was that we slay only "the evildoer." This had once been, in the foggiest centuries of ancient time, a solemn commission to blood drinkers, and indeed there had been a dim religion surrounding us in antique pagan days in which the vampires had been worshiped as bringers of justice to those who had done wrong.

"We shall never again let such superstition surround us and the mystery of our powers. We are not infallible. We have no commission from God. We wander the Earth like the giant felines of the great jungles, and have no more claim upon those we kill than any creature that seeks to live.

"But it is an infallible principle that the slaying of the innocent will drive you mad. Believe me when I tell you that for your peace of mind you must feed on the evil, you must learn to love them in all their filth and degeneracy, and you must thrive on the visions of their evil that will inevitably fill your heart and soul during the kill.

"Kill the innocent and you will sooner or later come to guilt, and with it you will come to impotence and finally despair. You may think you are too ruthless and too cold for such. You may feel superior to human beings and excuse your predatory excesses on the ground that you do but seek the necessary blood for your own life. But it won't work in the long run.

"In the long run, you will come to know that you are more human than monster, all that is noble in you derives from your humanity, and your enhanced nature can only lead you to value humans all the more. You'll come to pity those you slay, even the most unredeemable, and you will come to love humans so desperately that there will be nights when hunger will seem far preferable to you than the blood repast."

I accepted this wholeheartedly, and quickly plunged with my Master into the dark underbelly of Venice, the wild world of taverns and vice which I had never, as the mysterious velvet-clad "apprentice" of Marius De Romanus, really seen before. Of course I knew drinking places, I knew fashionable courtesans such as our beloved Bianca, but I really didn't know the thieves and murderers of Venice, and it was on these that I fed.

Very soon, I understood what my Master meant when he said that I must develop a taste for evil and maintain it. The visions from my victims became stronger for me with every kill. I began to see brilliant colors when I killed. In fact, I could sometimes see these colors dancing around my victims before I ever even closed in. Some men seem to walk in red-tinged shadows, and others to emanate a fiery orange light. The anger of my meanest and most tenacious victims was often a brilliant yellow which blinded me, searing me, as it were, both when I first attacked and while I drank the victim dry of all blood.

I was at the onset a dreadfully violent and impulsive killer. Having been set down by Marius in a nest of assassins, I went to work with a clumsy fury, drawing out my prey from the tavern or the flophouse, cornering him on the quay and then tearing open his throat as if I were a wild dog. I drank greedily often rupturing the victim's heart. Once the heart is gone, once the man is dead, there is nothing to pump the blood into you. And so it is not so good.

But my Master, for all his lofty speeches on the virtues of humans, and his adamant insistence on our own responsibilities, nevertheless taught me to kill with finesse.

"Take it slowly," he said. We walked along the narrow banks of the canals where such existed. We traveled by gondola listening with our preternatural ears for conversation that seemed meant for us. "And half the time, you needn't enter a house in order to draw out a victim. Stand outside of it, read the man's thoughts, throw him some silent bait. If you read his thoughts, it is almost a certainty that he can receive your message. You can lure without words. You can exert an irresistible pull. When he comes out to you, then take him.

"And there is never any need for him to suffer, or for blood actually to be spilt. Embrace your victim, love him if you will. Fondle him slowly and sink your teeth with caution. Then feast as slowly as you can. This way his heart will see you through.

"As for the visions, and these colors you speak of, seek to learn from them. Let the victim in his dying tell you what he can about life itself. If images of his long life trip before you, observe them, or rather savor them. Yes, savor them. Devour them slowly as you do his blood. As for the colors, let them pervade you. Let the entire experience inundate you. That is, be both active and utterly passive. Make love to your victim. And listen always for the actual moment when the heart ceases to beat. You will feel an undeniably orgiastic sensation at this moment, but it can be overlooked.

"Dispose of the body after, or make certain that you have licked away all sign of the puncture wounds in the victim's throat. Just a little bit of your blood on the tip of your tongue will accomplish this. In Venice dead bodies are common. You need not take such pains. But when we hunt in the outlying villages, then often you may have to bury the remains."

I was eager for all these lessons. That we hunted together was a magnificent pleasure. I came to realize quickly enough that Marius had been clumsy in the murders he had committed for me to witness before I'd been transformed. I knew then, as perhaps I've made plain in this story, that he wanted me to feel pity for these victims; he wanted me to experience horror. He wanted me to see death as an abomination. But due to my youth, my devotion to him and the violence done me in my short mortal life, I had not responded as he hoped.

Whatever the case, he was now a much more skilled killer. We often took the same victim, together, I drinking from the throat of our captive, while he fed from the man's wrist. Sometimes he delighted in holding the victim tightly for me while I drank all of the blood.

Being new, I was thirsty every night. I could have lived for three or more without killing, yes, and sometimes I did, but by the fifth night of denying myself—this was put to the test—I was too weak to rise from the sarcophagus. So what this meant was that, when and if I were ever on my own, I must kill at least every fourth night.

My first few months were an orgy. Each kill seemed more thrilling, more paralyzingly delicious than the one which had gone before. The mere sight of a bared throat could bring about in me such a state of arousal that I became like an animal, incapable of language or restraint. When I opened my eyes in the cold stony darkness, I envisioned human flesh. I could feel it in my naked hands and I wanted it, and the night could have no other events for me until I had laid my powerful hands on that one which would be the sacrifice to my need.

For long moments after the kill, sweet throbbing sensations passed through me as the warm fragrant blood found all the corners of my body, as it pumped its magnificent heat into my face.

This, and this alone, was enough to absorb me utterly, young as I was.

But Marius had no intention of letting me wallow in blood, the hasty young predator, with no other thought but to glut himself night after night.

"You must really begin to learn history and philosophy and the law in earnest," he told me. "You are not destined for the University of Padua now. You are destined to endure."

So after our stealthy missions were completed, and we returned to the warmth of the palazzo, he forced me to my books. He wanted some distance between me and Riccardo and the others anyway, lest they become suspicious of the change that had occurred.

In fact, he told me they "knew" about the change

whether they realized it or not. Their bodies knew that I was no longer human, though it might take their minds some time to accept the fact.

"Show them only courtesy and love, only complete indulgence, but keep your distance," Marius told me. "By the time they realize the unthinkable is the fact, you will have assured them that you are no enemy to them, that you are indeed Amadeo still, whom they love, and that though you have been changed, you yourself have not changed towards them."

I understood this. At once I felt a greater love for Riccardo. I felt it for all of the boys.

"But Master," I asked, "don't you ever become impatient with them, that they think more slowly, that they are so clumsy? I love them, yes, but surely you see them in a more pejorative light even than I do."

"Amadeo," he said softly, "they are all going to die." His face was charged with grief.

I felt it immediately and totally, which was always the way with feelings now. They came on in a torrent and taught their lessons at once.

They are all going to die. Yes, and I am immortal.

After that, I could only be patient with them, and indeed, I indulged myself in the manner in which I looked at them and studied them, never letting them know it, but glorying in all the details of them as if they were exotic because . . . they were going to die.

There is too much to describe, too much. I can't find a way to put down all that became clear to me in the first few months alone. And there was nothing made known to me in that time which was not deepened afterwards.

I saw process everywhere I looked; I smelled corruption, but I also beheld the mystery of growth, the magic of things blossoming and ripening, and in fact all process, whether towards maturity or towards the grave, delighted and enthralled me, except, that is, the disintegration of the human mind.

My study of government and law was more of a challenge. Though reading was accomplished with infinitely greater speed and near instantaneous comprehension of syntax, I had to force myself to be interested in such things as the history of Roman Law from ancient times, and the great code of the Emperor Justinian, called the *Corpus Juris Civilis*, which my Master thought to be one of the finest codes of law ever written.

"The world is only getting better," Marius instructed me. "With each century, civilization becomes more enamored of justice, ordinary men make greater strides towards sharing the wealth which was once the booty of the powerful, and art benefits by every increase in freedom, becoming ever more imaginative, ever more inventive and ever more beautiful."

I could understand this only theoretically. I had no faith or interest in law. In fact, I had a total contempt in the abstract for my Master's ideas. What I mean is, I didn't have contempt for him, but I had an underlying contempt for law and for legal institutions and governmental institutions that was so total that I did not even understand it myself.

My Master said that he understood it.

"You were born in a dark savage land," he said. "I wish I could take you back two hundred years in time to the years before Batu, the son of Genghis Khan, sacked the magnificent city of Kiev Rus, to the time when indeed the domes of its Santa Sofia were golden, and its people full of ingenuity and hope."

"I heard ad nauseam of that old glory," I said quietly, not wanting to anger him. "I was stuffed with tales of the olden times when I was a boy. In the miserable wooden house in which we lived, only yards from the frozen river, I listened to that rot as I shivered by the fire. Rats lived in our house. There was nothing beautiful in it but the ikons, and my Father's songs. There was nothing but depravity there, and we speak now, as you know, of an immense land. You cannot know how big Russia is unless you have been there, unless you have traveled as I did with my Father into the bitter-cold northern forests to Moscow, or to Novgorod, or east to Cracow." I broke off. "I don't want to think of those times or that place," I said. "In Italy one cannot dream of enduring such a place."

"Amadeo, the evolution of law, of government, is different in each land and with each people. I chose Venice, as I told you long ago, because it is a great Republic, and because its people are firmly connected to the Mother Earth by the simple fact that they are all merchants and engaged in trade. I love the city of Florence because its great family, the Medici, are bankers, not idle titled aristocrats who scorn all effort in the name of what they believe has been given them by God. The great cities of Italy are made by men who work, men who create, men who do, and on account of this, there is a greater compassion to all systems, and infinitely greater opportunity for men and women in all walks of life."

I was discouraged by all this talk. What did it matter?

"Amadeo, the world now is yours," my Master said. "You must look at the larger movements of history. The state of the world will begin in time to oppress you, and you will find, as all immortals do, that you cannot simply shut your heart on it, especially not you."

"Why so?" I asked a little crossly. "I think I can shut my eyes. What do I care if a man is a banker or a merchant? What do I care whether I live in a city which builds its own merchant fleet? I can look forever on the paintings in this palazzo, Master. I have not yet begun to see all the details in *The Procession of the Magi*, and there are so many others. And what of all the paintings in this city?"

He shook his head. "The study of painting will lead you to the study of man, and the study of man will lead you to lament or celebrate the state of the world of men."

I didn't believe it, but I was not allowed to change the curriculum. I studied as I was told.

Now, my Master had many gifts which I did not possess, but which he told me I would develop in time. He could make fire with his mind, but only if conditions were optimum—that is, he could ignite a torch already prepared with pitch. He could scale a building effortlessly with only a few quick handholds on its windowsills, propelling himself upwards with graceful darting motions, and he could swim to any depth of the sea.

Of course his vampiric vision and his hearing were far more acute and powerful than my own, and while voices intruded upon me, he knew how to emphatically shut them out. I had to learn this, and indeed I worked at it desperately, for there were times when all Venice seemed nothing but a cacophony of voices and prayers.

But the one great power he possessed which I did not possess was that he could take to the air and cover immense distances with great speed. This had been demonstrated to me many times, but almost always, when he had lifted me and carried me, he had made me cover my face, or he had forced my head down so that I couldn't see where we went and how.

Why he was so reticent about it, I couldn't understand. Finally, one night when he refused to transport us as if by magic to the Island of the Lido so that we could watch one of the nighttime ceremonies of fireworks and torch-lit ships on the water, I pressed the question.

"It's a frightening power," he said coolly. "It's frightening to be unanchored from the Earth. In the early stages, it is not without its blunders and disasters. As one acquires skill, rising smoothly into the highest atmosphere, it becomes chilling not only to the body but to the soul. It seems not preternatural, but supernatural." I could see he suffered over this. He shook his head. "It is the one talent which seems genuinely inhuman. I cannot learn from humans how best to use it. With every other talent, humans are my teacher. The human heart is my school. Not so with this. I become the magician; I become the witch or the warlock. It's seductive, and one could become its slave."

"But how so?" I asked him.

He was at a loss. He didn't even want to talk about it. Finally he became just a little impatient.

"Sometimes, Amadeo, you grill me with your questions. You ask if I owe you this tutelage. Believe me, I do not."

"Master you made me, and you insist on my obedience. Why would I read Abelard's *History of My Calamities* and the writings of Duns Scotus of Oxford University if you didn't make me do it?" I stopped. I remembered my Father and how I never stopped throwing acidic words at him, fast answers and slurs.

I became discouraged. "Master," I said. "Just explain it to me."

He made a gesture as if to say "Oh, so simple, eh?"

"All right," he went on. "It's this way. I can go very high in the air, and I can move very fast. I cannot often penetrate the clouds. They're frequently above me. But I can travel so fast that the world itself becomes a blur. I find myself in strange lands when I descend. And I tell you, for all its magic, this is a deeply jarring and disturbing thing. I am lost sometimes, dizzy, unsure of my goals or my will to live, after I make use of this power. Transitions come too quickly; that's it, perhaps. I never spoke of this to anyone, and now I speak to you, and you're a boy, and you can't begin to understand."

I didn't.

But within a very short time, it was his wish that we undertake a longer journey than any we'd made before. It was only a matter of hours, but to my utter astonishment, we traveled between sundown and early evening to the far city of Florence itself.

There, set down in a wholly different world than that of the Veneto, walking quietly amongst an entirely different breed of Italian, into churches and palaces of a different style, I understood for the first time what he meant.

Understand, I'd seen Florence before, traveling as Marius's mortal apprentice, with a group of the others. But my brief glimpse was nothing to what I saw as a vampire. I had the measuring instruments now of a minor god.

But it was night. The city lay under the usual curfew. And the stones of Florence seemed darker, more drab, suggestive of a fortress, the streets narrow and gloomy, as they were not brightened by luminescent ribbons of water as were our own. The palaces of Florence lacked the extravagant Moorish ornament of Venice's showplaces, the high-gloss fantastical stone facades. They enclosed their splendor, as is more common to Italian cities. Yet the city was rich, dense and full of delights for the eye.

It was after all Florence—the capital of the man called Lorenzo the Magnificent, the compelling figure who dominated Marius's copy of the great mural which I had seen on the night of my dark rebirth, a man who had died only a few years before.

We found the city unlawfully busy, though it was quite dark, with groups of men and women lingering about in the hard paved streets, and a sinister quality of restlessness hung about the Piazza della Signoria, which was one of the most important of all the many squares of the town.

An execution had taken place that day, hardly an uncommon occurrence in Florence, or Venice for that matter. It had been a burning. I smelled wood and charred flesh though all the evidence had been cleared before night.

I had a natural distaste for such things, which not everyone has, by the way, and I edged towards the scene cautiously, not wishing with these heightened senses to be jarred by some horrible remnant of cruelty.

Marius had always cautioned us as boys not to "enjoy" these spectacles, but to place ourselves mentally in the position of the victim if we were to learn the maximum from what we saw.

As you know from history, the crowds at executions were often merciless and unruly, taunting the victim sometimes, I think, out of fear. We, the boys of Marius, had always found it terribly difficult to cast our mental lot with the man being hanged or burnt. In sum, he'd taken all the fun out of it for us.

Of course, as these rituals happened almost always by day, Marius himself had never been present.

Now, as we moved into the great Piazza della Signoria, I could see that he was displeased by the thin ash that still hung in the air, and the vile smells.

I also noticed that we slipped past others easily, two dark-draped swiftly moving figures. Our feet scarce made a sound. It was the vampiric gift that we could move so stealthily, shifting quickly out of sudden and occasional mortal observation with an instinctive grace.

"It's as though we're invisible," I said to Marius, "as if nothing can hurt us, because we don't really belong here and will soon take our leave." I looked up at the grim battlements that fronted on the Square.

"Yes, but we are not invisible, remember it," he whispered.

"But who died here today? People are full of torment and fear. Listen. There is satisfaction, and there is weeping."

He didn't answer.

I grew uneasy.

"What is it? It can't be any common thing," I said. "The city is too vigilant and unquiet."

"It's their great reformer, Savonarola," Marius said. "He died on this day, hanged, and then burnt here. Thank God, he was already dead before the flames rose."

"You wish mercy for Savonarola?" I asked. I was puzzled. This man, a great reformer in the eyes of some perhaps, had always been damned by all I knew. He had condemned all pleasures of the senses, denying any validity to the very school in which my Master thought all things were to be learnt.

"I wish mercy for any man," said Marius. He beckoned for me to follow, and we moved towards the nearby street.

We headed away from the grisly place.

"Even this one, who persuaded Botticelli to heap his own paintings on the Bonfires of the Vanities?" I asked. "How many times have you pointed to the details of your own copies of Botticelli's work to show me some graceful beauty you wanted me to never forget?"

"Are you going to argue with me until the end of the world!" said Marius. "I'm pleased that my blood has given you new strength in every aspect, but must you question every word that falls from my lips?" He threw me a furious glance, letting the light of nearby torches fully illuminate his half-mocking smile. "There are some students who believe in this method, and that greater truths rise out of the continued strife between teacher and pupil. But not me! I believe you need to let my lessons settle in quiet at least for the space of five minutes in your mind before you begin your counterattack."

"You try to be angry with me but you can't."

"Oh, what a muddle!" he said as if he were cursing. He walked fast ahead of me.

The small Florentine street was dreary, like a passageway in a great house rather than a city street. I longed for the breezes of Venice, or rather, my body did, out of habit. I was quite fascinated to be here.

"Don't be so provoked," I said. "Why did they turn on Savonarola?"

"Give men enough time and they'll turn on anyone. He claimed to have been a prophet, divinely inspired by God, and that these were the Last Days, and this is the oldest most tiresome Christian complaint in the world, believe you me. The Last Days! Christianity is a religion based on the notion that we are living in the Last Days! It's a religion fueled by the ability of men to forget all the blunders of the past, and get dressed once more for the Last Days."

I smiled, but bitterly. I wanted to articulate a strong presentiment, that we were always in the Last Days, and it was inscribed in our hearts, because we were mortals, when quite suddenly and totally I realized that I was no longer mortal, except insofar as the world itself was mortal.

And it seemed I understood more viscerally than

ever the atmosphere of purposeful gloom which had overhung my childhood in far-off Kiev. I saw again the muddy catacombs, and the half-buried monks who had cheered me on to become one of them.

I shook it off, and now how bright Florence seemed as we came into the broad torch-lighted Piazza del Duomo—before the great Cathedral of Santa Maria del Fiore.

"Ah, my pupil does listen now and then," Marius was saying to me in an ironic voice. "Yes, I am more than glad that Savonarola is no more. But to rejoice at the end of something is not to approve the endless parade of cruelty that is human history. I wish it were otherwise. Public sacrifice becomes grotesque in every respect. It dulls the senses of the populace. In this city, above all others, it's a spectacle. The Florentines enjoy it, as we do our Regattas and Processions. So Savonarola is dead. Well, if any mortal man asked for it, it was Savonarola, predicting as he did the end of the world, damning princes from his pulpit, leading great painters to immolate their works. The hell with him."

"Master, look, the Baptistery, let's go, let's look at the doors. The piazza's almost empty. Come on. It's our chance to look at the bronzes." I tugged on his sleeve.

He followed me, and he stopped his muttering, but he was not himself.

What I wanted so to see is work that you can see in Florence now, and in fact, almost every treasure of this city and of Venice which I've described here you can see now. You have only to go there. The panels in the door which were done by Lorenzo Ghiberti were my delight, but there was also older work done by Andrea Pisano, portraying the life of St. John the Baptist, and this, I didn't intend to overlook.

So keen was the vampiric vision that as I studied these various detailed bronze pictures, I could hardly keep from sighing with pleasure.

This moment is so clear. I think that I believed, then, that nothing ever could hurt me or make me sad again, that I had discovered the balm of salvation in the vampiric blood, and the strange thing is, that as I dictate this story now, I think the same thing once more.

Though unhappy now, and possibly forever, I believe again in the paramount importance of the flesh. My mind wanders to the words of D. H. Lawrence, the twentieth-century writer, who in his writings on Italy, recalled Blake's image of the "Tyger, Tyger, burning bright / In the forests of the night." Lawrence's words are:

> This is the supremacy of the flesh, which devours all, and becomes transfigured into a magnificent brindled flame, a burning bush indeed.
>
> This is one way of transfiguration into the eternal flame, the transfiguration through ecstasy in the flesh.

But I have done a risky thing here for a storyteller. I have left my plot, as I'm sure The Vampire Lestat (who is more skilled perhaps than I am, and so in love with the image of William Blake's tiger in the night, and who has, whether he cares to admit it or not, used the tiger in his work in the very same way) would point out to me, and I must speedily return to this moment in the Piazza del Duomo, where I left myself of long ago standing, side by side with Marius, looking at the burnished genius of Ghiberti, as he sings in bronze of Sybils and saints.

We took our time with these things. Marius said softly that next to Venice, Florence was the city of his choice, for here so much had magnificently flowered.

"But I can't be without the sea, not even here," he confided. "And as you see all around you, this city hugs her treasures close with shadowy vigilance, whereas in Venice, the very facades of our palaces are offered up in gleaming stone beneath the moon to Almighty God."

"Master, do we serve Him?" I pressed. "I know you condemn the monks who brought me up, you condemn the ravings of Savonarola, but do you mean to guide me by another route back to the Very Same God?"

"That's just it, Amadeo, I do," said Marius, "and I don't mean as the pagan I am to admit it so easily, lest its complexity be misunderstood. But I do. I find God in the blood. I find God in the flesh. I find it no accident that the mysterious Christ should reside forever for His followers in the Flesh and Blood within the Bread of the Transubtantiation."

I was so moved by these words! It seemed the very sun I had forever forsworn had come again to brighten the night.

We slipped into the side door of the darkened Cathedral called the Duomo. I stood gazing over the long vista of its stone floor, towards the altar.

Was it possible that I could have the Christ in a new way? Perhaps I had not after all renounced Him forever.

I tried to speak these troubled thoughts to my Master. Christ . . . in a new way. I couldn't explain it, and said finally:

"I stumble with my words."

"Amadeo, we all stumble, and so do all those who enter history. The concept of a Great Being stumbles down the centuries; His words and those principles attributed to Him do tumble after Him; and so the Christ is snatched up in His wandering by the preaching puritan on one side, the muddy starving hermit on the other, the gilded Lorenzo de' Medici here who would celebrate his Lord in gold and paint and mosaic stone."

"But is Christ the Living Lord?" I whispered.

No answer.

My soul hit a pitch of agony. Marius took my hand, and said that we go now, stealthily to the Monastery of San Marco.

"This is the sacred house that gave up Savonarola," he said. "We'll slip into it unbeknownst to its pious inhabitants."

We again traveled as if by magic. I felt only the Master's strong arms, and did not even see the frame of the doors as we exited and made our way to this other place.

I knew he meant to show me the work of the artist called Fra Angelico, long dead, who had labored all his life in this very Monastery, a painter monk, as I perhaps had been destined to be, far away in the lightless Monastery of the Caves.

Within seconds, we set down soundlessly on the moist grass of the square cloister of San Marco, the serene garden enclosed by Michelozzo's loggias, secure within its walls.

At once I heard many prayers reach my inner vampiric hearing, desperate agitated prayers of the brothers
who had been loyal or sympathetic to Savonarola. I put
my hands to my head as if this foolish human gesture
could signal to the Divine that I had had more than I
could bear.

My Master broke the current of thought reception
with his soothing voice.

"Come," he said, grasping my hand. "We'll slip into
the cells one by one. There is enough light for you to see
the works of this monk."

"You mean that Fra Angelico painted the very cells
where monks go to sleep?" I had thought his works
would be in the chapel, and in the other public or com-
munal rooms.

"That's why I want you to see this," said my Master.
He led me up a stairs and into a wide stone corridor. He
made the first door spring open, and gently we moved
inside, fleet and silent, not disturbing the monk who lay
curled on his hard bed, his head sweating against the
pillow.

"Don't look at his face," said my Master gently. "If
you do you'll see the troubled dreams he suffers. I want
you to look at the wall. What do you see, now, look!"

I understood at once. This art of Fra Giovanni, called
Angelico in honor of his sublime talent, was a strange
mixture of the sensuous art of our time with the pious
and forswearing art of the past.

I gazed on the bright, elegant rendering of the arrest
of Christ in the Garden of Gethsemane. The slender flattened figures resembled very much the elongated and
elastic images of the Russian ikon, and yet the faces

were softened and plastic with genuine and touching emotion. It seemed a kindness infused all beings here, not merely Our Lord Himself, condemned to be betrayed by one of His own, but the Apostles, who looked on, and even the unfortunate soldier, in his tunic of mail, who reached out to take the Lord away, and the soldiers watched.

I was transfixed by this unmistakable kindness, this seeming innocence that infected everyone, this sublime compassion on the part of the artist for all players in this tragic drama which had prefaced the salvation of the world.

Into another cell I was taken immediately. Once again the door gave way at Marius's command, and the sleeping occupant of the cell never knew that we were there.

This painting showed again the Garden of Agony, and Christ, before the arrest, alone among His sleeping Apostles, left to beg His Heavenly Father for strength. Once again I saw the comparison to the old styles in which I, as a Russian boy, had felt so sure. The folds in the cloth, the use of arches, the halo for each head, the discipline of the whole—all was connected to the past, and yet there shone again the new Italian warmth, the undeniable Italian love of the humanity of all included, even Our Lord Himself.

We went from cell to cell. Backwards and forwards through the Life of Christ we traveled, visiting the scene of the First Holy Communion, in which, so touchingly, Christ gave out the bread containing His Body and Blood as if it were the Host at Mass, and then the Sermon on the Mount, in which the smooth pleated rocks around

Our Lord and His listeners seemed made of cloth as surely as his graceful gown.

When we came to the Crucifixion, in which Our Lord gave over to St. John His Blessed Mother, I was heart-struck by the anguish in the Lord's face. How thoughtful in her distress was the face of the Virgin, and how resigned was the saint beside her, with his soft fair Florentine face, so like that of a thousand other painted figures in this city, barely fringed with a light brown beard.

Just when I thought I understood my Master's lessons perfectly, we happened upon another painting, and I would feel yet a stronger connection with the long-ago treasures of my boyhood and the quiet incandescent splendor of the Dominican monk who had graced these walls. Finally we left this clean, lovely place of tears and whispered prayers.

We went out into the night and back to Venice, traveling in cold and noisy darkness, and arriving at home in time to sit a while in the warm light of the sumptuous bedchamber and talk.

"Do you see?" Marius pressed me. He was at his desk with his pen in hand. He dipped it and wrote even as he talked, turning back the large vellum page of his diary. "In far off Kiev, the cells were the earth itself, moist and pure, but dark and omnivorous, the mouth that eats all life finally, that would bring to ruin all art."

I shivered. I sat rubbing the backs of my arms, looking at him.

"But there in Florence, what did this subtle teacher Fra Angelico bequeath to his brothers? Magnificent pictures to put them in mind of the Suffering of Our Lord?"

He wrote several lines before he resumed.

"Fra Angelico never scorned to delight your eye, to fill your vision with all the colors God has given you the power to see, for you were given by him two eyes, Amadeo, and not to be . . . not to be shut up in the dark earth."

I reflected for a long time. To know these things theoretically had been one thing. To have passed through the hushed and sleeping rooms of the Monastery, to have seen my Master's principles there emblazoned by a monk himself—this was something else.

"It is a glorious time, this," Marius said softly. "That which was good among the ancients is now rediscovered, and given a new form. You ask me, is Christ the Lord? I say, Amadeo, that He can be, for He never taught anything Himself but love, or so His Apostles, whether they know it or not, have led us to believe . . ."

I waited on him, as I knew he wasn't finished. The room was so sweetly warm and clean and bright. I have near my heart forever a picture of him at this moment, the tall fair-haired Marius, his red cloak thrown back to free his arm for the pen he held, his face smooth and reflecting, his blue eyes looking, beyond that time and any other in which he had lived, for the truth. The heavy book was propped on a low portable lectern for him, to give it a comfortable angle. The little ink pot was set inside a richly embellished silver holder. And the heavy candelabra behind him, with its eight thick melting candles, was made up of numberless engraved cherubs half-embedded in the deeply worked silver, with wings struggling, perhaps, to fly loose, and tiny round-cheeked faces turned this way and that with large contented eyes beneath loose serpentine curls.

It seemed an audience of little angels to watch and listen as Marius spoke, so many, many tiny faces peering indifferently forth from the silver, quite immune to the falling rivulets of pure, melted wax.

"I cannot live without this beauty," I said suddenly, though I had meant to wait. "I cannot endure without it. Oh, God, you have shown me Hell and it lies behind me, surely in the land where I was born."

He heard my little prayer, my little confession, my desperate plea.

"If Christ is the Lord," he said, returning to his point, returning us both to the lesson, "if Christ is the Lord, then what a beautiful miracle it is, this Christian mystery—." His eyes filmed with tears. "That the Lord Himself should come to Earth and clothe Himself in flesh the better to know us and to comprehend us. Oh, what God, ever made in the image of Man by His fancy, was ever better than one who would become Flesh? Yes, I would say to you, yes, your Christ, their Christ, the Christ even of the Monks of Kiev, He is the Lord! Only mark forever the lies they tell in His Name, and the deeds they do. For Savonarola called on His Name when he praised a foreign enemy bearing down on Florence, and those who burnt Savonarola as a false prophet, they too, as they lit the faggots beneath his dangling body, they too called on Christ the Lord."

I was overcome with tears.

He sat in silence, respecting me perhaps, or only collecting his thoughts. Then he dipped his pen again and wrote for a long time, much faster than men do, but deftly and gracefully, and never marking out a word.

At last, he set down the pen. He looked at me and he smiled.

"I set out to show you things, and it's never as I plan. I wanted you tonight to see the dangers in this power of flight, that we can too easily transport ourselves to other places, and that this feeling of slipping in and out so easily is a deception of which we must beware. But look, how differently it has all gone."

I didn't answer him.

"I wanted you," he said, "to be a little afraid."

"Master," I said, wiping my nose with the back of my hand, "count on me to be properly frightened when the time comes. I'll have this power, I know it. I can feel it now. And for now, I think it's splendid, and because of it, this power, one dark thought falls over my heart."

"What is that?" he asked in the kindest way. "You know, I think your angelic face is no more fit for sad things than those faces painted by Fra Angelico. What's this shadow I see? What is this dark thought?"

"Take me back there, Master," I said. I trembled, yet I said it. "Let us use your power to cover miles and miles of Europe. Let us go north. Take me back to see that cruel land that has become a Purgatorio in my imagination. Take me back to Kiev."

He was slow in giving his answer.

The morning was coming. He gathered up his cloak and robe, rose from the chair and took me with him up the stairs to the roof.

We could see the distant already paling waters of the Adriatic, twinkling under the moon and stars, beyond the familiar forest of the masts of the ships. Tiny lights flickered on the distant islands. The wind was mild and full of salt and sea freshness, and a particular deliciousness that comes only when one has lost all fear of the sea.

"Yours is a brave request, Amadeo. If you really wish it, tomorrow night we'll begin the journey."

"Have you ever traveled so far before?"

"In miles, in space, yes, many times," he said. "But in another's quest for understanding? No, never so very far."

He embraced me and took me to the palazzo where our tomb lay hidden. I was cold all over by the time we reached the soiled stone stairway, where so many of the poor slept. We picked our way among them, until we reached the entrance to the cellar.

"Light the torch for me, Sir," I said. "I am shivering. I want to see the gold around us, if I may."

"There, you have it," he said. We stood in our crypt with the two ornate sarcophagi before us. I lay my hand on the lid of the one which was mine, and quite suddenly there came over me another presentiment, that all I loved would endure for a very brief time.

Marius must have seen this hesitation. He passed his right hand through the very fire of the torch, and touched his warmed fingers to my cheek. Then he kissed me where this warmth hovered, and his kiss was warm.

10

IT TOOK US four nights to reach Kiev.

Only in the early hours before dawn did we hunt.

We made our graves in actual burial places, the dungeon vaults of old neglected castles and in the sepulchers beneath forlorn and ruined churches where the profane were wont now to stash their livestock and their hay.

There are tales I could tell of this journey, of those brave fortresses we roamed near morning, of those wild mountain villages where we found the evildoer in his rude den.

Naturally, Marius saw lessons in all this, teaching me how easy it was to find hiding places and approving the speed with which I moved through the dense forest, and had no fear of the scattered primitive settlements which we visited on account of my thirst. He praised me that I didn't shrink from the dark dusty nests of bones in which we lay down by day, reminding me that these burial places, having already been pillaged, were the least likely for men to trouble even in the light of the sun.

Our fancy Venetian clothes were soon streaked with dirt, but we were provided with thick fur-lined cloaks for the journey, and these covered all. Even in this Marius saw a lesson, that we must remember what fragile and meaningless protection our garments provide. Mortal men forget how to wear their garments lightly and that they are a mere covering for the body and no more. Vampires must never forget it, for we are far less dependent upon our raiment than men.

By the last morning before our arrival in Kiev, I knew the rocky northern woods only too well. The dread winter of the north was all around us. We had come upon one of the most intriguing of all my memories: the presence of snow.

"It no longer hurts me to hold it," I said, gathering the soft delicious cold snow in my hands and pressing it to my face. "It no longer chills me to see it, and indeed how beautiful it is, covering the poorest of towns and hovels with its blanket. Master, look, look how it throws back the light even of the weakest stars."

We were on the edge of the land that men call the Golden Horde—the southern steppes of Russia, which for two hundred years, since the conquest of Genghis Khan, had been too dangerous for the farmer, and often the death of the army or the knight.

Kiev Rus had once included this fertile and beautiful prairie, stretching far to the East, almost to Europe, as well as south of the city of Kiev, where I had been born.

"The final stretch will be nothing," my Master told me. "We make it tomorrow night so that you will be rested and fresh when you catch the first sight of home."

As we stood on a rocky crag looking out at the wild grass, flowing in the winter wind beneath us, for the first time in the nights since I'd become a vampire, I felt a terrible longing for the sun. I wanted to see this land by the light of the sun. I didn't dare confess it to my Master. After all, how many blessings can a being want?

On the final night, I awoke just after sunset. We had found a hiding place beneath the floor of a church in a village where no one lived now at all. The horrid Mongol hordes, which had destroyed my homeland over and over again, had long ago burnt this town to nothing, or so Marius had told me, and this church did not even possess a roof. There had been no one left here to pull the stones of the floor away for profit or building, and so we had gone down a forgotten stairway to lie with monks buried here some thousand years ago.

Rising from the grave, I saw high above a rectangle of sky where my Master had removed a marble paving block, an inscribed tombstone no doubt, for me to make my ascent. I propelled myself upwards. That is, I bent my knees and, using all my strength, shot upwards, as if I could fly, and passed through this opening to land on my feet.

Marius, who invariably rose before me, was sitting nearby. He immediately gave out the expected appreciative laugh.

"Have you been saving that little trick for such a moment?" he said.

I was dazed by the snow, as I looked around me. How afraid I was, merely looking at the frozen pines that had everywhere sprung up on the ruins of the village. I could scarce speak.

"No," I managed to say. "I didn't know I could do it. I don't know how high I can leap, or how much strength I have. You're pleased, however?"

"Yes, why shouldn't I be? I want you to be so strong that no one can ever hurt you."

"And who would, Master? We travel the world, but who even knows when we go and when we come?"

"There are others, Amadeo. And there are others here. I can hear them if I want to, but there is a good reason for not hearing them."

I understood. "You open your mind to hear them, and they know you are there?"

"Yes, clever one. Are you ready now to go home?"

I closed my eyes. I made the Sign of the Cross in our old way, touching the right shoulder before the left. I thought of my Father. We were in the wild fields and he stood high in his stirrups with his giant bow, the bow only he could bend, like unto the mythical Ulysses, shooting arrow after arrow at the raiders who thundered down on us, riding as if he were one of the Turks or Tatars himself, so great was his skill. Arrow after arrow, drawn out with a swift snap from the pouch on his back, went into the bow and was shot across the high blowing grass even as his horse galloped at full speed. His red beard was blowing in the fierce wind, and the sky was so blue, so richly blue that—.

I broke off this prayer and almost lost my balance. My Master held me.

"Pray, you'll be finished with all this very quickly," he said.

"Give me your kisses," I said, "give me your love, give me your arms as you always have, I need them. Give me your guidance. But give me your arms, yes. Let me rest my head against you. I need you, yes. Yes, I want it to be quick and done, and all its lessons in here, in my mind, to be taken back home."

He smiled. "Home is Venice now? You've made the decision so soon?"

"Yes, I know it even at this moment. What lies beyond is the birth land, and that's not always home. Shall we go?"

Gathering me in his arms, he took to the air. I shut my eyes, even forfeiting my last glimpse of the motionless stars. I seemed to sleep against him, dreamlessly and fearlessly.

Then he set me down on my feet.

At once I knew this great dark hill, and the leafless oak forest with its frozen black trunks and skeletal branches. I could see the gleaming strip of the Dnieper River far below. My heart scudded inside me. I looked about for the bleak towers of the high city, the city we called Vladimir's City, which was old Kiev.

Piles of rubble which had once been city walls were only yards from where I stood.

I led the way, easily climbing over them and wandering among the ruined churches, churches which had been of legendary splendor when Batu Khan had burnt the city in the year 1240.

I had grown up among this jungle of ancient churches and broken monasteries, often hurrying to hear Mass in our Cathedral of Santa Sofia, one of the few monuments which the Mongols had spared. In its day, it had been a spectacle of golden domes, dominating all those of the other churches, and was rumored to be more grand than its namesake in faraway Constantinople, being larger and packed with treasures.

What I had known was a stately remnant, a wounded shell.

I didn't want to enter the church now. It was enough to see it from the outside, because I knew now, from my happy years in Venice, just what the glory of this church had once been. I understood from the splendid Byzantine mosaics and paintings of San Marco, and from the old Byzantine church on the Venetian island of Torcello what glory had once been here for all to see. When I thought of the lively crowds of Venice, her students, scholars, lawyers, merchants, I could paint a dense vitality on this bleak and wasted scene.

The snow was deep and thick, and few Russians were out in it this frigid early evening. So we had it to ourselves, walking through it with ease, not having to pick our way as mortals would.

We came to a long stretch of ruined battlement, a shapeless guardrail now beneath the snow, and standing there, I looked down on the lower city, the city we called Podil, the only real city of Kiev that remained, the city where in a rough timber and clay house only a few yards from the river, I had grown up. I looked down on deep-pitched roofs, their thatch covered in cleansing snow, their chimneys smoking, and on narrow crooked snow-filled streets. A great grid of such houses and other buildings had long ago formed against the river and managed to survive fire after fire and even the worst Tatar raids.

It was a town made up of traders and merchants and craftsmen, all bound to the river and the treasures she brought from the Orient, and the money some would pay for the goods she took south into the European world.

My Father, the indomitable hunter, had traded bear skins which he himself had brought back singlehanded from the interior of the great forest which spread towards the north. Fox, martin, beaver, sheep, all these skins he had dealt in, so great was his strength and luck, that no man or woman of our household ever sold their handiwork or wanted for food. If we starved, and we had starved, it was because the winter ate the food, and the meat was gone, and there was nothing for my Father's gold to buy.

I caught the stench of Podil as I stood on the battlements of Vladimir's City. I caught the stench of rotting fish, and livestock, of soiled flesh, and river mud.

I pulled my fur cloak around me, blowing the snow off the fur when it came up to my lips, and I looked back up at the dark domes of the Cathedral against the sky.

"Let's walk on, let's go past the castle of the Voievoda," I said. "You see that wooden building, you would never call it a palace or a castle in fair Italy. That is a castle here."

Marius nodded. He made a little soothing gesture. I owed him no explanation of this alien place from which I'd come.

The Voievoda was our ruler, and in my time it had been Prince Michael of Lithuania. I didn't know who it would be now.

I surprised myself that I used the proper word for him. In my deathly dream vision, I had no consciousness of language, and the strange word for ruler, "voievoda," had never passed my lips. But I had seen him clearly then in his round black fur hat, his dark thick velvet tunic and his felt boots.

I led the way.

We approached the squat building, which seemed more a fortress than anything else, built as it was out of such enormous logs. Its walls had a graceful slope as they ascended; its many towers had four-tiered roofs. I could see its central roof, a great five-sided wooden dome of sorts, in stark outline against the starry sky. Torches blazed at its huge doorways and along the outer walls of its enclosures. All its windows were sealed against the winter and the night.

Time was when I thought it was the grandest building yet standing in Christendom.

It was no task at all to dazzle the guards with a few swift soft words and darting movements, to pass them and to enter the castle itself.

We found our way in by means of a rear storage room, and quietly made our way to a vantage point where we could spy upon the small crowd of fur-trimmed nobles or lords who clustered in the Great Room, beneath the bare beams of a wooden ceiling around the roaring fire.

On a great sprawling mass of brilliant Turkey rugs they sat, in huge Russian chairs whose geometrical carvings were no mystery to my eye. They drank from gold goblets, the wine being provided by two leather-clad serving boys, and their long belted robes were the colors of blue and red and gold as bright as the many designs in the rugs.

European tapestries covered the rudely stuccoed walls. Same old scenes of the hunt in the never-ending woodlands of France or England or Tuscany. On a long board set with blazing candles sat a simple meal of joints and fowl.

So cold was the room that these lords wore their Russian fur hats.

How exotic it had looked to me in boyhood when I'd been brought with my Father to stand before Prince Michael, who was eternally grateful for my Father's feats of bravery in bringing down delicious game in the wild fields, or delivering bundles of valuables to the allies of Prince Michael in the Lithuanian forts to the west.

But these were Europeans. I had never respected them.

My Father had taught me too well that they were but lackeys of the Khan, paying for the right to rule us.

"No one goes up against those thieves," my Father had said. "So let them sing their songs of honor and valor. It means nothing. You listen to the songs that I sing."

And my Father could sing some songs.

For all his stamina in the saddle, for all his dexterity with the bow and arrow, and his blunt brute force with the broadsword, he had the ability with his long fingers to pluck out music on the strings of an old harp and sing with cleverness the narrative songs of the ancient times when Kiev had been a great capital, her churches rivaling those of Byzantium, her riches the wonder of all the world.

Within a moment, I was ready to go. I took one last memorial glance at these men, huddled as they were over their golden wine cups, their big fur-trimmed boots resting on fancy Turkish foot rests, their shoulders hunkered, their shadows crowding the walls. And then, without their ever having known we were there, we slipped away.

It was time now to go to the other hilltop city, the

Pechersk, under which lay the many catacombs of the Monastery of the Caves.

I trembled at the mere thought of it. It seemed the mouth of the Monastery would swallow me and I should burrow through the moist Mother Earth, forever seeking the light of the stars, never to find my way out.

But I went there, trudging through the mud and snow, and again with a vampire's silky ease, I gained access, this time leading the way, snapping the locks silently with my superior strength and lifting the doors as I opened them so no weight would fall upon their creaky hinges, and dashing swiftly across rooms so that mortal eyes perceived no more than cold shadows, if they perceived anything at all.

The air was warm and motionless here, a blessing, but memory told me it had not been so terribly warm for a mortal boy. In the Scriptorium, by the smoky light of cheap oil, several brothers were bent over their slanted desks, working on their copying, as if the printing press were of no concern to them, and surely it was not.

I could see the texts on which they worked and I knew them—the Paterikon of the Kievan Caves Monastery, with its marvelous tales of the Monastery's founders and its many colorful saints.

In this room, laboring over that text, I had learned fully to read and write. I crept now along the wall until my eyes could fall on the page which one monk copied, his left hand steadying the crumbling model from which he worked.

I knew this part of the Paterikon by heart. It was the Tale of Isaac. Demons had fooled Isaac; they had come to him as beautiful angels, and even pretending to be Christ Himself. When Isaac had fallen for their tricks, they had danced with glee and taunted him. But after much meditation and penance, Isaac stood up to these demons.

The monk had just dipped his pen and he wrote now the words with which Isaac spoke:

When you deceived me in the form of Jesus Christ and the angels, you were unworthy of that rank. But now you appear in your true colors—

I looked away. I didn't read the rest. Cleaving there so well to the wall I might have gone on unseen forever. Slowly I looked at the other pages which the monk had copied, which were being let to dry. I found an earlier passage which I'd never forgotten, describing Isaac as he lay, withdrawn from all the world, motionless, and without food for two years:

For Isaac was weakened in mind and body and could not turn over on his side, stand up, or sit down; he just lay there on one side, and often worms collected under his thighs from his excrement and urine.

The demons had driven Isaac to this, with their deception. Such temptations, such visions, such confusion and such penance I myself had hoped to experience for the rest of my life when I entered here as a child.

I listened to the pen scratch on the paper. I withdrew, unseen, as if I'd never come.

I looked back at my scholarly brethren.

All were emaciated, dressed in cheap black wool, reeking of old sweat and dirt, and their heads were all but shaved. Their long beards were thin and uncombed.

I thought I knew one of them, had loved him somewhat even, but this seemed remote and not worth considering anymore.

To Marius, who stood beside me as faithfully as a shadow, I confided that I could not have endured it, but we both knew this was a lie. In all likelihood I would have endured it, and I would have died without ever knowing any other world.

I moved into the first of the long tunnels where the monks were buried, and, closing my eyes and cleaving to the mud wall, I listened for the dreams and prayers of those who lay entombed alive for the love of God.

It was nothing but what I could imagine, and exactly as I recalled. I heard the familiar, no longer mysterious words whispered in the Church Slavonic. I saw the prescribed images. I felt the sputtering flame of true devotion and true mysticism, kindled from the weak fire of lives of utter denial.

I stood with my head bowed. I let my temple rest against the mud. I wished to find the boy, so pure of soul, who had opened these cells to bring the hermits just enough food and drink to keep them alive. But I couldn't find the boy. I couldn't. And I felt only a raging pity for him that he had ever suffered here, thin and miserable, and desperate, and ignorant, oh, so terribly ignorant, having but one sensuous joy in life and that was to see the colors of the ikon catch fire.

I gasped. I turned my head and fell stupidly into Marius's arms.

"Don't cry, Amadeo," he said tenderly in my ear.

He brushed my hair from my eyes, and with his soft thumb he even wiped away my tears.

"Tell it all farewell now, son," he said.

I nodded.

In a twinkling we stood outside. I didn't speak to him. He followed me. I headed down the slope towards the waterfront city.

The smell of the river grew stronger, the stench of humans grew stronger, and finally I came to the house that I knew had been my own. What madness this seemed suddenly! What was I seeking? To measure all this by new standards? To confirm for myself that as a mortal child I had never had the slightest chance?

Dear God, there was no justification for what I was, an impious blood drinker, feeding off the luxurious stews of the wicked Venetian world, I knew it. Was this all a vain exercise in self-justification? No, something else pulled me towards the long rectangular house, like so many others, its thick clay walls divided by rough timbers, its four-tiered roof dripping with icicles, this large and crude house that was my home.

As soon as we reached it, I crept around the sides. The slush of the snow had here turned to water, and indeed, the water of the river leaked down the street and into everywhere as it had when I was a child. The water leaked into my fine-stitched Venetian boots. But it could not paralyze my feet as it had once done, because I drew my strength now from gods unknown here, and creatures for whom these filthy peasants, of which I had been one, had no name.

I lay my head against the rough wall, just as I had

done in the Monastery, cleaving to the mortar as if the solidity would protect me and transmit to me all that I wanted to know. I could see through a tiny hole in the broken clumps of clay that were forever crumbling, and I beheld in the familiar blaze of candles, and the brighter light of lamps, a family gathered around the warmth of the large brick stove.

I knew them all, these people, though some of their names were gone from my mind. I knew that they were kindred, and I knew the atmosphere that they shared.

But I had to see beyond this little gathering. I had to know if these people were well. I had to know if after that fateful day, when I'd been kidnapped, and my Father no doubt murdered in the wild lands, they had managed to go on with their usual vigor. I had to know, perhaps, what they prayed when they thought of Andrei, the boy with the gift to make ikons so perfectly, ikons not made by human hands.

I heard the harp inside, I heard singing. The voice was that of one of my uncles, one so young he might have been my brother. His name was Borys, and he had since early childhood been good with singing, memorizing easily the old dumys, or sagas, of the knights and heroes, and it was one of them, very rhythmical and tragic, which he was singing now. The harp was small and old, my Father's harp, and Borys strummed the strings in time with his phrases as he all but spoke the story of a lusty and fatal battle for ancient and great Kiev.

I heard the familiar cadences that had been passed down by our people from singer to singer for hundreds of years. I put my fingers up and broke loose a bit of mortar. I saw through the tiny opening the Ikon corner—

directly opposite the family gathering around the shimmering fire in the open stove.

Ah, what a spectacle! Amid dozens of little candle stubs and earthen lamps full of burning fat, there stood propped some twenty or more ikons, some very old and darkened in their gold frames, and some radiant, as though only yesterday they'd come alive through the power of God. There were painted eggs stuffed amongst the pictures, eggs beautifully decorated and colored with patterns I could well recall, though even with my vampire eyes I was too far away to see them now. Many times I had watched the women decorating these sacred eggs for Easter, applying the hot melting wax to them with their wooden pens to mark the ribbons or the stars or the crosses or the lines which meant the ram's horns, or the symbol which meant the butterfly or the stork. Once the wax had been applied, the egg would be dipped in cold dye of amazingly deep color. It had seemed there was an endless variety, and endless possibility for meaning, in these simple patterns and signs.

These fragile and beautiful eggs were kept for curing the sick, or for protection against the storm. I had hidden such eggs in an orchard for good luck with the coming harvest. I had placed one once over the door of the house in which my sister went to live as a young bride.

There was a beautiful story about these decorated eggs, that as long as the custom was followed, as long as such eggs existed, then the world would be safe from the monster of Evil who wanted always to come and devour all that was.

It was sweet to see these eggs placed there in the proud corner of the Ikons, as always, among the Holy Faces. That I had forgotten this custom seemed a shame and a warning of tragedy to come.

But the Holy Faces caught me suddenly and I forgot all else. I saw the Face of Christ blazing in the firelight, my brilliant scowling Christ, as I had so often painted Him. I had done so many of these pictures, and yet how like the one lost that day in the high grasses of the wild lands was this very one!

But that was impossible. How could anyone have recovered the ikon I had dropped when the raiders took me prisoner? No, it must surely be another, for as I said, I had done so many before my parents had ever gotten up the courage to take me to the monks. Why, all through this town were my ikons. My Father had even brought them to Prince Michael as proud gifts, and it was the Prince who had said that the monks must see my skill.

How stern Our Lord looked now compared to the recollection of the tender musing Christs of Fra Angelico or the noble sorrowful Lord of Bellini. And yet He was warm with my love! He was the Christ in our style, the old style, loving in severe lines, loving in somber color, loving in the manner of my land. And He was warm with the love that I believed He gave to me!

A sickness rose up in me. I felt my Master's hands on my shoulders. He didn't pull me back as I feared. He merely held me and put his cheek against my hair.

I was about to go. It was enough, was it now? But the music broke off. A woman there, my Mother, was she? No, younger, my sister Anya, grown into a woman, talked wearily of how my Father could sing again if somehow they could hide all the liquor from him and make him come back to himself.

My Uncle Borys sneered. Ivan was hopeless, said Borys. Ivan would never see another sober night or day, and would soon die. Ivan was poisoned with liquor, both with the fine spirits he got from the traders by selling off what he stole from this very house, and from the peasant brew he got from those he battered and bullied, still being the terror of the town.

I bristled all over. Ivan, my Father, alive? Ivan, alive to die again in such dishonor? Ivan not slain in the wild fields?

But in their thick skulls, the thoughts of him and the words of him stopped together. My uncle sang another song, a dancing song. No one would dance in this house, where all were tired from their labor, and the women half-blind as they continued to mend the clothes that lay piled in their laps. But the music cheered them and one of them, a boy younger than I had been when I died, yes, my little brother, whispered a soft prayer for my Father, that my Father would not freeze to death tonight, as he had almost done so many times, falling down drunk as he did in the snow.

"Please bring him home," came the little boy's whisper.

Then behind me, I heard Marius say, seeking to put it in order and to calm me:

"Yes, it seems it is true, beyond doubt. Your Father is alive."

Before he could caution me, I went around and opened the door. It was a fierce thing to do, a reckless thing to do, and I ought to have asked Marius's permission, but I was, as I've told you, an unruly pupil. I had to do this.

The wind gusted through the house. The huddled figures shivered and pushed their thick furs up around their shoulders. The fire deep in the mouth of the brick stove flared beautifully.

I knew that I should remove my hat, which in this case was my hood, and that I should face the Ikon corner and cross myself, but I couldn't do this.

In fact, to conceal myself, I pulled my hood up over my head as I shut the door. I stood alone against it. I held the fur cloak up against my mouth, so that nothing was visible of my face except my eyes, and perhaps a shock of reddish hair.

"Why has the drink gotten Ivan?" I whispered, the old Russian tongue coming back to me. "Ivan was the strongest man in this city. Where is he now?"

They were wary and angry at my intrusion. The fire in the stove crackled and danced from its feast of fresh air. The Ikon corner seemed a group of perfect radiant flames unto itself, with its brilliant images and random candles, another fire of a different and eternal sort. The Face of Christ was clear to me in the fluttering light, the eyes seeming to fix me as I stood against the door.

My uncle rose and shoved the harp into the arms of a younger boy I didn't know. I saw in the shadows the children sitting up in their heavily draped beds. I saw their shining eyes looking at me in the dark. The others in the firelight clumped together and faced me.

I saw my Mother, wizened and sad as if centuries had passed since I left her, a veritable crone in the corner, clinging to the rug that covered her lap. I studied her, trying to fathom the cause of her decay. Toothless, decrepit, her knuckles big and chafed and shiny from work, perhaps she was merely a woman being worked too rapidly towards her grave.

A great collection of thoughts and words struck me, as if I were being pelted with blows. Angel, devil, night visitor, terror from the dark, what are you? I saw hands raised, hastily making the Sign of the Cross. But the thoughts came clear in answer to my query.

Who does not know that Ivan the Hunter had become Ivan the Penitent, Ivan the Drunkard, Ivan the Mad, on account of the day in the wild lands when he couldn't stop the Tatars from kidnapping his beloved son, Andrei?

I shut my eyes. It was worse than death what had happened to him! And I had never so much as wondered, never so much as dared to think of him alive, or cared enough to hope that he was, or thought what his fate might be had he lived? All over Venice were the shops in which I might have penned a letter to him, a letter that the great Venetian traders could have carried to some port where it might have been delivered over the famous post roads of the Khan.

I knew all this. Selfish little Andrei knew all this, the details that might have sealed the past for him neatly so that he could have forgotten it. I might have written:

Family, I live and am happy, though I can never come home. Take this money I send to you for my brothers and sisters and my Mother—.

But then I hadn't really ever known. The past had been misery and chaos.

Whenever the most trivial picture had become vivid, then torment had reigned.

My uncle stood before me. He was as big as my Father, and was well dressed in a belted leather tunic and felt boots. He looked down at me calmly but severely.

"Who are you that comes into our house in this manner?" he asked. "What is this Prince that stands before us? You carry a message for us? Then speak, and we will forgive you that you broke the lock on our door."

I drew in my breath. I had no more questions. I knew that I could find Ivan the Drunkard. That he was in the tavern with the fishermen and the fur traders, for that was the only enclosed place he'd ever loved other than his home.

With my left hand, I reached over and found the purse that I always carried, tied, as it should be, to my belt. I ripped it loose, and I handed it to this man. He merely looked at it. Then he drew himself up, offended, and he stepped back.

He seemed then to become part of a deliberate picture with the house. I saw the house. I saw the hand-carved furniture, the pride of the family which had done it, the hand-carved wooden crosses and candlesticks which held the many candles. I saw the painted symbols decorating the wood frames of the windows, and the shelves on which fine homemade pots, kettles and bowls were displayed.

I saw them all in their pride, then, the entire family, the women with the embroidery, as well as those with mending, and I remembered with a lulling comfort the stability and the warmth of their daily life.

Yet it was sad, oh, woefully sad, compared to the world I knew!

I stepped forward and I held out the purse again to him, and I said in a muffled voice, still veiling my face:

"I beg you to take this as a kindness to me and that I might save my soul. It's from your nephew, Andrei. He is far, far away in the land to which the slave traders took him, and he will never come home. But he is well and must share some of what he has with his family. He bids me to tell him which of you lives and which of you is dead. If I do not give you this money, and if you don't take it, I will be damned to Hell."

There came no response from them verbally. But I had what I wanted from their minds. I had all of it. Yes, Ivan was alive, and now I, this strange man, was saying that Andrei lived too. Ivan mourned for a son who not only lived but prospered. Life is a tragedy, one way or another. What is certain is that you die.

"I beg you," I said.

My uncle took the proffered purse but with misgivings. It was full of gold ducats, which would buy anywhere.

I let my cloak drop and I pulled off my left glove, and then the rings that covered every finger of my left hand. Opal, onyx, amethyst, topaz, turquoise. I moved past the man and the boys, to the far side of the fire, and laid these respectfully in the lap of the old woman who had been my Mother as she looked up.

I could see that, in a moment, she would know who I was. I covered my face again, but with my left hand, I took my dagger from my belt. It was only a short Misericorde, that little dagger which a warrior takes into battle to dispatch his victims if they are too far gone for salvation and yet not dead. It was a decorative thing, an ornament more than a weapon, and its gold-plated scabbard was thickly lined with perfect pearls.

"For you," I said. "For Andrei's Mother, who always loved her necklace of river pearls. Take this for Andrei's soul." I laid the dagger at my Mother's feet.

And then I made a deep, deep bow with my head almost touching the floor, and I went out, without looking back, closing the door behind me, and hovering near, to hear them as they jumped up and crowded about to see the rings and the dagger, and some to see to the lock.

For a moment, I was weak with emotion. But nothing was going to stop me from what I meant to do. I didn't turn to Marius, because it would have been craven to ask his support in this, or assent to it. I went on down the muddy snowy street, through the sludge, towards the tavern nearest to the river, where I thought my Father might be.

I had rarely entered this place as a child, and then only to summon my Father home. I had no real memory of it, except as a place where foreign people drank and cursed.

It was a long building, made of the same rude unfinished logs as my house, with the same mud for mortar, and the same inevitable seams and cracks to let in the dreadful cold. Its roof was very high, with some six tiers to shed the weight of the snow, and its eaves too dripped with icicles, as had those of my house.

It marveled me that men could live like this, that the

cold itself did not push them to make something more permanent and more sheltering, but it had always been the way of this place, it seemed to me, of the poor and the sick and overburdened and the hungry, that the brutal winter took too much from them, and that the short spring and summer gave them too little, and that resignation became their greatest virtue in the end.

But I might have been wrong then about all of it, and I might be wrong now. What is important is this—it was a place of hopelessness, and though it was not ugly, for wood and mud and snow and sadness are not ugly, it was a place without beauty except for the ikons, and perhaps for the distant outline of the graceful domes of Santa Sofia, high on the hill, against the star-studded sky. And that was not enough.

When I entered the tavern, I counted some twenty men at a glance, all of them drinking and talking to one another with a conviviality that surprised me, given the Spartan nature of this place, which was no more than a shelter against the night which kept them safely ranged round the big fire. There were no ikons here to comfort them. But some of them were singing, and there was the inevitable harp player strumming his little stringed instrument, and another blowing on a small pipe.

There were many tables, some covered with linen, and others bare at which these fellows gathered, and some of the men were foreigners, as I had recalled. Three were Italian, I heard this instantly, and figured them to be Genoese. There were more foreigners indeed than I had expected. But these were men drawn by the trade of the river, and perhaps Kiev did not do so poorly just now.

There were plenty of kegs of beer and wine behind the counter, where the bartender sold his stock by the cup. I saw too many bottles of Italian wine, quite expensive no doubt, and crates of Spanish sack.

Lest I attract notice, I moved forward and far off to the left, into the depth of the shadows, where perhaps a European traveler clad in rich fur might not be noticed, for, after all, fine fur was one thing they did indeed seem to have.

These people were much too drunk to care who I was. The bartender tried to get excited about the idea of a new customer, but then went back to snoozing on the palm of his upturned hand. The music continued, another one of the dumy, and this one much less cheerful than the one my uncle had been singing at home, because I think the musician was very tired.

I saw my Father.

He lay on his back, full length, on a broad crude greasy bench, dressed in his leather jerkin and with his biggest heaviest fur cloak folded neatly over him, as though the others had done the honors with it after he had passed out. This was bearskin, his cloak, which marked him as a pretty rich man.

He snored in his drunken sleep, and the fumes of the drink rose from him, and he didn't stir when I knelt right beside him and looked down into his face.

His cheeks though thinner were still rosy, but there were hollows beneath the bones, and there were streaks of gray, most prominent in his mustache and long beard. It seemed to me that some of the hair of his temples was gone, and that his fine smooth brow was steeper, but this may have been an illusion. The flesh all around his eyes

was tender-looking and dark. His hands, clutched together beneath the cloak, were not visible to me, but I
could see that he was still strong, of powerful build, and
his love of drink had not destroyed him yet.

I had a disturbing sense of his vitality suddenly; I
could smell the blood of him and the life of him, as
though of a possible victim stumbling across my path. I
put all this away from my mind and stared at him, loving
him and thinking only that I was so glad that he was
alive! He had come out of the wild grasses. He had escaped that party of raiders, who had seemed then the
very heralds of death itself.

I pulled up a stool so that I might sit quietly beside
my Father, studying his face.

I had not put on my left glove.

I laid my cold hand now on his forehead, lightly, not
wanting to take liberties, and slowly he opened his eyes.
They were murky yet still beautifully bright, despite the
broken blood vessels and the wetness, and he looked at
me softly and wordlessly for a while, as if he had no
cause to move, as if I were a vision near to his dreams.

I felt the hood fall back from my head and I did nothing to stop it. I couldn't see what he saw, but I knew what
it was—his son, with a clean-shaven face, such as his
son had had when this man knew him, and long loose
auburn hair in snow-dusted waves.

Beyond, their bodies mere bulky outlines against
the huge blaze of the fire, the others sang or talked. And
the wine flowed.

Nothing came between me and this moment, between me and this man who had tried hard to bring down
the Tatars, who had sent one arrow after another sailing

at his enemies, even as their arrows rained down upon him in vain.

"They never wounded you," I whispered. "I love you and only now do I know how strong you were." Was my voice even audible?

He blinked as he looked at me, and then I saw his tongue roll out along his lips. His lips were bright, like coral, shining through the heavy red fringe of mustache and beard.

"They wounded me," he said in a low voice, small but not weak. "They got me, twice they got me, in the shoulder and in the arm. But they didn't kill me, and they didn't let go of Andrei. I fell off my horse. I got up. They never got me in the legs. I ran after them. I ran and ran and I kept shooting. I had a cursed arrow sticking right out of my right shoulder here."

His hand appeared from beneath the fur and he placed it up on the dark curve of his right shoulder.

"I kept shooting. I didn't even feel it. I saw them ride away. They took him. I don't even know if he was alive. I don't know. Would they have bothered to take him if they had shot him? There were arrows everywhere. The sky rained arrows! There must have been fifty of them. They killed every other man! I told the others, You have to keep shooting, don't stop even for an instant, don't cower, shoot and shoot and shoot, and when you have no more arrows, bring up your sword and go for them, ride straight into them, get down, get down close to your horse's head and ride into them. Well, maybe they did. I don't know."

He lowered his lids. He glanced around. He wanted to get up, and then he looked at me.

"Give me something to drink. Buy me something decent. The man has Spanish sack. Get me some of that, a bottle of sack. Hell, in the old days, I laid in wait for the traders out there in the river, and I never had to buy anything from any man. Get me a bottle of sack. I can see you're rich."

"Do you know who I am?" I asked.

He looked at me in plain confusion. This hadn't even occurred to him, this question.

"You come from the castle. You speak with the accent of the Lithuanians. I don't care who you are. Buy me some wine."

"With the accent of the Lithuanians?" I asked softly. "What a dreadful thing. I think it's the accent of a Venetian, and I'm ashamed."

"Venetian? Well, don't be. God knows they tried to save Constantinople, they tried. Everything's gone to Hell. The world will end in flame. Get me some sack before it ends, all right?"

I stood up. Did I have some more money? I was puzzling over it when the dark silent figure of my Master loomed over me and he handed me the bottle of Spanish sack, uncorked and ready for my Father to drink.

I sighed. The smell of it meant nothing to me now, but I knew that it was fine good stuff, and besides it was what he wanted.

He had meantime sat up on the bench, staring straight at the bottle as it hung from my hand. He reached out for it, and took it and drank it as thirstily as I drink blood.

"Take a good look at me," I said.

"It's too dark in here, idiot," he said. "How can I take a good look at anything? Hmmm, but this is good. Thank you."

Suddenly, he paused with the bottle just beneath his lips. It was a strange thing the way in which he paused. It was as if he were in the forest, and he'd just sensed a bear coming up on him, or some other lethal beast. He froze, as it were, with the bottle in hand, and only his eyes moved as he looked up at me.

"Andrei," he whispered.

"I'm alive, Father," I said gently. "They didn't kill me. They took me for booty and sold me for profit. And I was taken by ship south and north again and up to the city of Venice, and that is where I live now."

His eyes were calm. Indeed, a beautiful serenity settled over him. He was far too drunk for his reason to revolt or for cheap surprise to delight him. On the contrary, the truth stole in and over him in a wave, subduing him, and he understood all of its ramifications, that I had not suffered, that I was rich, I was well.

"I was lost, Sir," I said in the same gentle whisper, which surely was only audible to him. "I was lost, yes, but found by another, a kindly man, and was restored, and have never suffered since. I've journeyed a long time to tell you this, Father. I never knew you were alive. I never dreamed. I mean, I thought you'd died that day when all the world died for me. And now I'm come here to tell you that you must never, never grieve for me."

"Andrei," he whispered, but there was no change in his face. There was only the sedate wonder. He sat still, both hands on the bottle which he had lowered to his lap, his huge shoulders very straight, and his flowing red and gray hair as long as I'd ever seen it, melting into the fur of his cloak.

He was a beautiful, beautiful man. I needed a monster's eyes to know it. I needed a demon's vision to see the strength in his eyes coupled with the power in his giant frame. Only the bloodshot eyes gave him away in his weakness.

"Forget me now, Father," I said. "Forget me, as if the monks had sent me away. But remember this, on account of you, I shall never be buried in the muddy graves of the Monastery. No, other things may befall me. But that, I won't suffer. Because of you, that you wouldn't have it, that you came that day and demanded I ride out with you, that I be your son."

I turned to go. He shot forward, clasping the bottle by the neck in his left hand and clamping his powerful right hand over my wrist. He pulled me down to him, as if I were a mere mortal, with his old strength and he pressed his lips against my bowed head.

Oh, God, don't let him know! Don't let him sense any change in me! I was desperate. I closed my eyes.

But I was young, and not so hard and cold as my Master, no, not even by half or a half of that half. And he felt only the softness of my hair, and perhaps a cold icy softness, redolent of winter, to my skin.

"Andrei, my angel child, my gifted and golden son!"

I turned around and clasped him firmly with my left arm. I kissed him all over his head in a way I would never, never have done as a child. I held him to my heart.

"Father, don't drink anymore," I said in his ear. "Get up and be the hunter again. Be what you are, Father."

"Andrei, no one will ever believe me."

"And who are they to say that to you if you are your-self again, man?" I asked.

We looked into each other's eyes. I kept my lips sealed that he should never, never see the sharp teeth in my mouth that the vampiric blood had given me, the tiny evil vampire's teeth as a man as keen as himself, the natural hunter, might very definitely see.

But he was looking for no such disqualification here. He wanted only love, and love we gave one another.

"I have to go, I have no choice," I said. "I stole this time to come to you. Father, tell my Mother that it was I who came to the house earlier, and that it was I who gave her the rings and gave your brother the purse."

I drew back. I sat down on the bench beside him, for he had placed his feet on the floor. I pulled off my right glove and I looked at the seven or eight rings I wore, all of them made of gold or silver and rich with jewels, and then I slipped them off one by one, over his loud groan of protest, and I deposited the handful of them into his hand. How soft and hot was his hand, how flushed and alive.

"You take them because I have a world of them. And I will write to you and send you more, more so that you will never need to do anything but what you want to do—ride and hunt, and tell the tales of old times by the fire. Buy a fine harp with this, buy books if you will for the little ones, buy what you will."

"I don't want this; I want you, my son."

"Yes, and I want you, my Father, but this little power is all we may have."

I took his head in both my hands, displaying my strength, perhaps unwisely, but making him stay still while I gave him my kisses, and then with one long warm embrace, I rose to go.

I was out of the room so fast, he couldn't have seen anything but the door swinging shut.

The snow was coming down. I saw my Master several yards away, and I went to meet him and together we started up the hill. I didn't want for my Father to come out. I wanted to get away as fast as I could.

I was about to ask that we take to vampire speed and get clear of Kiev when I saw that a figure was hurrying towards us. It was a small woman, her long heavy furs trailing in the wet snow. She had something bright in her arms.

I stood fixed, my Master waiting on me. It was my Mother who had come to see me. It was my Mother who was making her way to the tavern, and in her arms, facing me, was an ikon of the scowling Christ, the one I looked at so long through the chink in the wall of the house.

I drew in my breath. She lifted the ikon by either side and she presented it to me.

"Andrei," she whispered.

"Mother," I said. "Keep it for the little ones, please." I embraced her and kissed her. How much older, how miserably older she seemed. But childbearing had done that to her, pulling the strength out of her, if only for babies to be buried in small plots in the ground. I thought of how many babies she had lost during my youth, and how many were still counted before I was born. She had called them her angels, her little babies, not big enough to live.

"Keep it," I said to her. "Keep it for the family here."

"All right, Andrei," she said. She looked at me with pale, suffering eyes. I could see that she was dying. I understood suddenly that it wasn't mere age that worked on her, nor the hardship of children. She was diseased from within, and would soon truly die. I felt such a terror, looking at her, such a terror for the whole mortal world. It was just a tiresome, common and inevitable disease.

"Goodbye, darling angel," I said.

"And goodbye to you, my darling angel," she answered. "My heart and soul are happy that you are a proud Prince. But show me, do you make the Sign of the Cross in the right way?"

How desperate she sounded. She meant these words. She meant simply, Had I gotten all this apparent wealth by converting to the church of the West? That is what she meant.

"Mother, you put a simple test to me." I made the Sign of the Cross for her, in our way, the Eastern Way, from right shoulder to left, and I smiled.

She nodded. Then she took something carefully from inside her heavy wool shift coat and she gave it to me, only releasing it when I had made a cradle for it with my hand. It was a dark ruby-red painted Easter egg.

Such a perfect and exquisitely decorated egg. It was banded with long lengthwise ribbons of yellow, and in a center created by them was painted a perfect rose or eight-pointed star.

I looked down at it and then I nodded to her.

I took out a handkerchief of fine Flemish linen and wrapped the egg in this, padding it over and over, and I slipped the little burden faithfully into the folds of my tunic beneath my jacket and cloak.

I bent over and kissed her again on her soft dry cheek. "Mother," I said, "the Joy of All Sorrows, that is what you are to me!"

"My sweet Andrei," she answered. "Go with God if you must go."

She looked at the ikon. She wanted me to see it. She turned the ikon around so that I could look at the gleaming golden Face of God, as waxen and fine as the day I'd painted it for her. Only I hadn't painted it for her. No, it was the very ikon which I had taken that day on our march into the wild lands.

Oh, what a marvel, that my Father had brought it back with him, all the way from the scene of such loss. And yet why not? Why not would such a man as he have done such a thing?

The snow fell onto the painted ikon. It fell on the stern Face of Our Savior, which had come ablaze under my racing brush as if by magic, a face which with its stern and smooth lips and slightly furrowed brow meant love. Christ, my Lord, could look even more stern peering out from the mosaics of San Marco. Christ, my Lord, could look as stern in many an old painting. But Christ, my Lord, in any manner and in any style, was full of unstinting love.

The snow came in flurries and seemed to melt when it touched His Face.

I feared for it, this fragile panel of wood, and this glistering lacquered image, meant to shine for all time. But she thought of this too, and she quickly shielded the ikon from the wetness of the melting snow with her cloak.

I never saw it again.

But is there anyone who needs now to ask me what an ikon means to me? Is there anyone who needs now to know why, when I saw the Face of Christ before me on the Veil of Veronica, when Dora held it high, this Veil, brought back from Jerusalem and the hour of Christ's passion, by Lestat himself, through Hell and into the world, that I fell down on my knees, and cried, "It is the Lord"?

11

THE JOURNEY from Kiev seemed a journey forwards in time, towards the place where I truly belonged.

All of Venice, upon my return, seemed to share the shimmer of the gold-plated chamber in which I made my grave. In a daze, I spent my nights roaming, with or without Marius, drinking up the fresh air of the Adriatic and perusing the splendid houses and government palaces to which I'd grown accustomed over the last few years.

Evening church services drew me like honey draws flies. I drank up the music of the choirs, the chanting of the priests and above all the joyous sensual attitude of the worshipers, as if all this would be a healing balm to those parts of me that were skinned and raw from my return to the Monastery of the Caves.

But in my heart of hearts I reserved a tenacious and heated flame of reverence for the Russian monks of the Monastery of the Caves. Having glimpsed a few words of the sainted Brother Isaac, I walked in the living memory of his teachings—Brother Isaac, who had been a Fool for God, and a hermit, and a seer of spirits, the victim of the Devil and then his Conqueror in the name of Christ.

I had a religious soul, there was no doubt of it, and I had been given two great modes of religious thought, and now in surrendering to a war between these modes, I made war on myself, for though I had no intention of giving up the luxuries and glories of Venice, the ever-shining beauty of Fra Angelico's lessons and the stunning and gilded accomplishments of all those who followed him, making Beauty for Christ, I secretly beatified the loser in my battle, the blessed Isaac, whom I imagined, in my childish mind, to have taken the true path to the Lord.

Marius knew of my struggle, he knew of the hold which Kiev had upon me, and he knew of the crucial importance of all this to me. He understood better than anyone I've ever known that each being wars with his own angels and devils, each being succumbs to an essential set of values, a theme, as it were, which is inseparable from living a proper life.

For us, life was the vampiric life. But it was in every sense life, and sensuous life, and fleshly life. I could not escape into it from the compulsions and obsessions I'd felt as a mortal boy. On the contrary, they were now magnified.

Within the month after my return, I knew I had set the tone for my approach to the world around me. I should wallow in the luscious beauty of Italian painting and music and architecture, yes, but I would do it with the fervor of a Russian saint. I would turn all sensuous experiences to goodness and purity. I would learn, I would increase understanding, I would increase in compassion for the mortals around me, and I would never cease to put a pressure upon my soul to be that which I believed was good.

Good was above all kind; it was to be gentle. It was to waste nothing. It was to paint, to read, to study, to listen, even to pray, though to whom I prayed I wasn't sure, and it was to take every opportunity to be generous to those mortals whom I did not kill.

As for those I killed, they were to be dispatched mercifully, and I was to become the absolute master of mercy, never causing pain and confusion, indeed snaring my victims as much as I could by spells induced by my soft voice or the depths of my eyes offered for soulful looks, or by some other power I seemed to possess and seemed able to develop, a power to thrust my mind into that of the poor helpless mortal and to assist him in the manufacture of his own comforting images so that the death became the flicker of a flame in a rapture, and then silence most sweet.

I also concentrated on enjoying the blood, on moving deeper, beneath the turbulent necessity of my own thirst, to taste this vital fluid of which I robbed my victim, and to feel most fully that which it carried with it to ultimate doom, the destiny of a mortal soul.

My lessons with Marius were broken off for a while. But at last he came to me gently and told me it was time to study again in earnest, that there were things that we must do.

"I make my own study," I said. "You know it well enough. You know I haven't been idle in my wanderings, and you know my mind is as hungry as my body. You know it. So leave me alone."

"That's all well and good, little Master," he said to me kindly, "but you must come back into the school I keep for you. I have things which you must know."

For five nights I put him off. Then, as I was dozing on his bed sometime after midnight, having spent the earlier evening in the Piazza San Marco at a great festival, listening to musicians and watching the jugglers, I was startled to feel his switch come crashing down on the back of my legs.

"Wake up, child," he said.

I turned over and looked up. I was startled. He stood, holding the long switch, with his arms folded. He wore a long belted tunic of purple velvet and his hair was tied back at the base of his neck.

I turned away from him. I figured he was being dramatic and that he would go away. The switch came crashing down again and this time there followed a volley of blows.

I felt the blows in a way I'd never felt them when mortal. I was stronger, more resistant to them, but for a split second each blow broke through my preternatural guard and caused a tiny exquisite explosion of pain.

I was furious. I tried to climb up off the bed, and probably would have struck him, so angry was I to be treated in this manner. But he placed his knee on my back and whipped me over and over with the switch, until I cried out.

Then he stood up and dragged me up by the collar. I was shaking with rage and with confusion.

"Want some more?" he asked.

"I don't know," I said, throwing off his arm, which he allowed with a little smile. "Perhaps so! One minute my heart is of the greatest concern to you, and the next I'm a schoolboy. Is that it?"

"You've had enough time to grieve and to weep," he said, "and to reevaluate all you've been given. Now it's back to work. Go to the desk and prepare to write. Or I'll whip you some more."

I flew into a tirade. "I'm not going to be treated this way; there's absolutely no necessity for this. What should I write? I've written volumes in my soul. You think you can force me into the dreary little mold of an obedient pupil, you think this is appropriate to the cataclysmic thoughts that I have to ponder, you think—."

He smacked me across the face. I was dizzy. As my eyes cleared, I looked into his.

"I want your attention again. I want you to come out of your meditation. Go to the desk and write for me a summary of what your journey to Russia meant to you, and what you see now here that you could not see before. Make it concise, use your finest similes and metaphors and write it cleanly and quickly for me."

"Such crude tactics," I muttered. But my body was throbbing from the blows. It was altogether different from the pain of a mortal body, but it was bad, and I hated it.

I sat down at the desk. I was going to write something really churlish such as "I've learned that I'm the slave of a tyrant." But when I looked up and saw him standing there with the switch in his hand, I changed my mind.

He knew it was the perfect moment to come to me and kiss me. And he did this, and I realized I had lifted my face for his kiss before he bent his head. This didn't stop him.

I felt the overwhelming happiness of giving in to him. I put my arm up and around his shoulders.

He let me go after a long sweet moment, and then I did write out many sentences, pretty much describing what I've explained above. I wrote about the battle in me between the fleshly and the ascetic; I wrote of my Russian soul as seeking after the highest level of exaltation. In the painting of the ikon I had found it, but the ikon had satisfied the need for the sensual because the ikon was beautiful. And as I wrote, I realized for the first time that the old Russian style, the antique Byzantine style, embodied a struggle in itself between the sensual and the ascetic, the figures suppressed, flattened, disciplined, in the very midst of rich color, the whole giving forth pure delight to the eyes while representing denial.

While I wrote, my Master went away. I was aware of it, but it didn't matter. I was deep into my writing, and gradually I slipped out of my analysis of things, and began to tell an old tale.

In the old days, when the Russians didn't know Jesus Christ, the great Prince Vladimir of Kiev—and in those days Kiev was a magnificent city—sent his emissaries to study the three religions of the Lord: the Moslem religion, which these men found to be frantic and foul-smelling; the religion of Papal Rome, in which these men did not find any glory; and finally the Christianity of Byzantium. In the city of Constantinople, the Russians were led to see the magnificent churches in which the Greek Catholics worshiped their God, and they found these buildings so beautiful that they didn't know whether they were in Heaven or still on Earth. Never had the Russians seen anything so splendid; they were certain then that God dwelt among men in the religion of Constantinople, and so it was this Christianity which Russia embraced. It was beauty therefore that gave birth to our Russian Church.

In Kiev once men could find what Vladimir sought to recreate, but now that Kiev is a ruin and the Turks have taken Santa Sofia of Constantinople, one must come to Venice to see the great Theotokos, the Virgin who is the God-Bearer, and her Son when He becomes the Pantokrator, the Divine Creator of All. In Venice, I have found in sparkling gold mosaics and in the muscular images of a new age the very miracle which brought the Light of Christ Our Lord to the land where I was born, the Light of Christ Our

Lord which burns still in the lamps of the Monastery of the Caves.

I put down the pen. I pushed the page aside, and I laid my head down on my arms and cried softly to myself in the quiet of the shadowy bedroom. I didn't care if I was beaten, kicked or ignored.

Finally, Marius came for me to take me to our crypt, and I realize now, centuries later, as I look back, that his forcing me to write on this night caused me to remember always the lessons of those times.

The next night, after he'd read what I had written, he was contrite about having hit me, and he said that it was difficult for him to treat me as anything but a child, but that I was not a child. Rather I was some spirit like unto a child—naive and maniacal in my pursuit of certain themes. He had never expected to love me so much.

I wanted to be aloof and distant, on account of the whipping, but I couldn't be. I marveled that his touch, his kisses, his embraces meant more to me than they had when I was human.

12

I WISH I could slip away now from the happy picture of Marius and me in Venice and take up this tale in New York City, in modern times. I want to go to the moment in the room in New York City when Dora held up Veronica's Veil, the relic brought back by Lestat from his journey into the Inferno, for then I would have a tale told in two perfect halves—of the child I had been and of the worshiper I became, and of the creature I am now.

But I cannot fool myself so easily. I know that what happened to Marius and to me in the months that followed my journey to Russia is part and parcel of my life.

There is nothing to do but cross The Bridge of Sighs in my life, the long dark bridge spanning centuries of my tortured existence which connects me to modern times. That my time in this passage has been described so well already by Lestat doesn't mean that I can escape without adding my own words, and above all my own acknowledgment of the Fool for God that I was to be for three hundred years.

I wish I had escaped this fate. I wish that Marius had escaped what happened to us. It is plain now that he survived our separation with far greater insight and strength than I survived it. But then he was already centuries old and a wise being, and I was still a child.

Our last months in Venice were unmarred by any premonition of what was to come. Vigorously, he taught me the essential lessons.

One of the most important of these was how to pass for human in the midst of human beings. In all the time since my transformation, I had not kept good company with the other apprentices, and I had avoided altogether my beloved Bianca, to whom I owed a vast debt of gratitude not merely for past friendship but for nursing me when I was so ill.

Now, I had to face Bianca, or so Marius decreed. I

was the one who had to write a polite letter to her explaining that on account of my illness I had not been able to come to her before.

Then, one evening early, after a brief hunt in which I drank the blood of two victims, we set out to visit her, laden with gifts for her, and found her surrounded by her English and Italian friends.

Marius had dressed for the occasion in smart dark blue velvet, with a cloak of the same color for once, which was unusual for him, and he had urged me to dress in sky blue, his favorite color for me. I carried the wine figs and sweet tarts in a basket for her.

We found her door open as always, and we entered unobtrusively, but she saw us at once.

The moment I saw her I felt a heartbreaking desire for a certain kind of intimacy, that is, I wanted to tell her everything that had happened! Of course this was forbidden, and that I could love her without confiding in her—this was something that Marius insisted I learn.

She got up and came to me, and put her arms around me, accepting the usual ardent kisses. I realized at once why Marius had insisted on two victims for this evening. I was warm and flushed with blood.

Bianca felt nothing that frightened her. She slipped her silken arms around my neck. She was radiant in a dress of yellow silk tissue and dark-green velvet, the underdress of yellow, powdered with embroidered roses, and her white breasts were barely covered as only a courtesan would have them.

When I began to kiss her, careful to conceal my tiny fanged teeth from her, I felt no hunger because the blood of my victims had been more than enough. I kissed her with love and love only, my mind quickly plunging into heated erotic memories, my body surely demonstrating the urgency that it had had with her in the past. I wanted to touch her all over, as a blind man might touch a sculpture, the better to see each curve of her with his hands.

"Oh, you're not only well, you're splendid," Bianca said. "You and Marius, come in, come, let's go into the next room." She made a careless gesture to her guests, who were all busy anyway, talking, arguing, playing cards in small groups. She drew us with her into her more intimate parlor adjacent to the bedroom, a room cluttered with frightfully expensive damask chairs and couches, and told me to sit down.

I remembered the candles, that I must never get too close to them, but must use the shadows so no mortal would have an optimum opportunity to study my changed and more perfect skin.

This wasn't so hard as, in spite of her love of light and her penchant for luxury, she had the candelabra scattered for the mood.

The lack of light would also make the sparkle of my eyes less noticeable; I knew this too. And the more I spoke, the more animated I became, the more human I would appear.

Stillness was dangerous for us when we were among mortals, Marius had taught me, for in stillness we appear flawless and unearthly and finally even faintly horrible to mortals, who sense that we are not what we seem.

I followed all these rules. But I was overcome with anxiety that I could never tell her what had been done to me. I started to talk. I explained that the illness had abated entirely, but that Marius, wiser by far than any physician, had ordered solitude and rest. When I had not been in bed, I had been alone, struggling to regain my strength.

"Make it as near to the truth as you can, the better to make it a lie," Marius had taught. Now I followed these words.

"Oh, but I thought I'd lost you," she said. "When you sent word, Marius, that he was recovering, I didn't at first believe you. I thought you meant to soften the inevitable truth."

How lovely she was, a perfect flower. Her blond hair was parted in the middle, and a thick lock on either side was wound with pearls and bound back with a clasp encrusted with them. The rest of her hair fell down à la Botticelli, in rivulets of shining yellow over her shoulders.

"You had cured him as completely as any human being could," Marius told her. "My task was to give him some old remedies of which only I know. And then to let the remedies do their work." He spoke simply, but to me he seemed sad.

A terrible sadness gripped me. I couldn't tell her what I was, or how different she seemed now, how richly opaque with human blood she seemed compared to us, and how her voice had taken on for me a new timbre that was purely human, and which gently nudged my senses if she but said one word.

"Well, you are both here, and you must both come often," she said. "Don't ever let such a separation occur again. Marius, I would have come to you, but Riccardo told me you wanted peace and quiet. I would have nursed Amadeo in any state."

"I know you would have, my darling," Marius said.

"But as I said, it was solitude he needed, and your beauty is an intoxicant, and your words a stimulus more intense perhaps than you realize." It had no tone of flattery but sounded like a sincere confession.

She shook her head a little sadly. "I've discovered that Venice is not my home unless you're here." She looked cautiously towards the front parlor, and then she lapsed into a low voice. "Marius, you freed me from those who had a hold on me."

"That was simple enough," he said. "It was a pleasure, in fact. How rank those men were, cousins of yours, if I'm not mistaken, and eager to use you and your great reputation for beauty in their twisted financial affairs."

She blushed, and I lifted my hand to beg him to go easy with what he said. I knew now that during the slaughter of the Florentine banquet chamber, he had read from the victims' minds all kinds of things which were unknown to me.

"Cousins? Perhaps," she said. "I have conveniently forgotten that. That they were a terror to those whom they lured into expensive loans and dangerous opportunities, that I can say without a doubt. Marius, the strangest things have happened, things upon which I never counted."

I loved the look of seriousness on her delicate features. She seemed too beautiful to have a brain.

"I find myself richer," she said, "as I can keep the larger portion of my own income, and others—this is the strange part—others, in gratitude that our banker and our extortionist is gone, have lavished on me countless gifts of gold and jewels, yes, even this necklace, look, and you know these are all sea pearls and matched in size, and this is a veritable rope of them, see, and all this is given me, though I have averred a hundred times that I never had the deed done."

"But what of blame?" I asked. "What of the danger of a public accusation?"

"They have no defenders or mourners," she said quickly. She planted another little bouquet of kisses on my cheek. "And earlier today, my friends among the Great Council were here as always, to read a few new poems to me and settle in quiet where they could know peace from clients and the endless demands of their families. No, I don't think anyone is going to accuse me of anything, and as everyone knows, on the night of the murders, I was here in company with that awful Englishman, Amadeo, the very one who tried to kill you, who has of course . . ."

"Yes, what?" I asked.

Marius narrowed his eyes as he looked at me. He made a light gesture of tapping the side of his head with his gloved finger. Read her mind, he meant. But I couldn't think of such a thing. Her face was too pretty.

"The Englishman," she said, "who has disappeared. I suspect he's drowned somewhere, that, staggering drunk about the town, he fell into one of the canals or, worse yet, into the lagoon."

Of course my Master had told me that he had taken care of all our difficulties on account of the Englishman, but I had never asked in what particular way.

"So they think you hired killers to dispatch the Florentines?" Marius asked her.

"Seems so," she said. "And there are even those who

think that I had the Englishman dispatched as well. I've become a rather powerful woman, Marius."

Both of them laughed, his laugh the deep but metallic laugh of a preternatural being, and her laugh higher yet thicker with the sound of her human blood.

I wanted to go into her mind. I tried but cast away the idea at once. I was inhibited, just as I was with Riccardo and the boys closest to me. In fact, it seemed such a terrible invasion of the privacy of the person that I used this power only in hunting to find those who were evil and whom I might kill.

"Amadeo, you blush, what is it?" Bianca asked. "Your cheeks are scarlet. Let me kiss them. Oh, you are hot as if the fever has come back."

"Look into his eyes, angel," said Marius. "They are clear."

"You're right," she said, peering into my eyes with such a sweet frank curiosity that she became irresistible to me.

I pushed back the yellow cloth of her underdress and the heavy velvet of her dark-green sleeveless overgarment and kissed her bare shoulder.

"Yes, you're well," she cooed into my ear, her lips moist against it.

I was blushing still as I drew back.

I looked at her, and I went into her mind; it seemed I had loosened the gold clasp beneath her breasts and parted her voluminous dark-green velvet skirts. I stared at the well between her half-exposed breasts. Blood or no blood, I could remember hot passion for her, and I felt it now in a strange overall manner, not localized in the forgotten organ as it had been before. I wanted to take her breasts in my hands and suckle them slowly, arousing her, making her moist and fragrant for me and making her head fall back. Yes, I blushed. A dim sweet swoon came over me.

I want you, I want you now, you and Marius both in my bed, together, a man and a boy, a god and a cherub. This is what her mind was saying to me, and she was remembering me. I saw myself as if in a smoky mirror, a boy naked except for a full-sleeved open shirt, seated on the pillows beside her, displaying the half-erect organ, ever ready to be completely aroused by her tender lips or her long graceful white hands.

I banished all this. I focused my gaze only on her beautiful tapering eyes. She studied me, not suspiciously but in fascination. Her lips were not rouged in any vulgar manner but deeply pink by nature, and her long lashes, darkened and curled only with a clear pomade, looked like the points of stars around her radiant eyes.

I want you, I want you now. These were her thoughts. They struck my ears. I bowed my head and put my hands up.

"Angel darling," she said. "Both of you!" she whispered to Marius. She took my hands. "Come in with me."

I was certain he would put a stop to it. He had cautioned me to avoid close scrutiny. But he only rose from his chair and moved towards her bedchamber, pushing back the two painted doors.

From the distant parlors came the steady sound of conversation and laughter. Singing had been added. Someone played the Virginal. All this went on.

We slipped into her bed. I was shaking all over. I saw that my Master had adorned himself in a thick tunic and beautiful dark blue doublet which I'd hardly noticed before. He wore soft sleek dark blue gloves over his hands, gloves which perfectly cleaved to his fingers, and his legs were covered by thick soft cashmere stockings all the way to his beautiful pointed shoes. He has covered all the hardness, I thought.

Having settled against the headboard of the bed, he had no compunction about helping Bianca to sit directly next to him. I looked across from him as I took my place beside her. As she turned to me, putting her hands on my face and kissing me eagerly again, I saw him perform a small act which I hadn't seen before.

Lifting her hair, he appeared to kiss her on the back of the neck. This she neither felt nor acknowledged. When he drew back, however, his lips were bloody. And lifting the finger of his gloved hand, he smoothed this blood, her blood, but a few droplets of it from a shallow scratch, undoubtedly, all over his face. It appeared to me as a living sheen, and to her it would look very different.

It quickened the pores in his skin, which had become all but invisible, and it deepened a few lines around his eyes and his mouth which otherwise were lost. It gave him a more human look, overall, and served as a barrier to her gaze, which was now so close.

"I have my two, as I always dreamed," she said softly.

Marius came round in front of her, tucking his arm behind her and began to kiss her as greedily as I had ever done. I was astonished for a moment, and jealous, but then her free hand found me and pulled me down close to her, and she turned from Marius, dazed with desire, and kissed me as well.

Marius reached over and brought me close to her, so that I was against her soft curves, feeling all the warmth rising from her voluptuous thighs.

He lay on top of her, but lightly, not letting his weight hurt her, and with his right hand he drew up her skirt and moved his fingers between her legs.

It was so bold. I lay against her shoulder, looking at the swell of her breasts, and beyond that the tiny, down-covered mound of her sex which he clasped in his entire hand.

She was past all decorum. He laid kisses on her neck and on her breasts as he embraced her lower down with his fingers, and she began to writhe with undisguised longing, her mouth open, her eyelids fluttering, her body suddenly moist all over and fragrant with this new heat.

That was the miracle, I realized, that a human could be brought to this higher temperature, and thereby give forth all of her sweet scents and even a strong invisible shimmer of emotions; it was rather like stoking a fire until it became a blaze.

The blood of my victims teemed in my face as I kissed her. It seemed to become living blood again, heated by my passion, and yet my passion had no demonic focus. I pressed my open mouth to the skin of her throat, covering the place where the artery showed like a blue river moving down from her head. But I didn't want to hurt her. I felt no need to hurt her. Indeed, I felt only pleasure as I embraced her, as I slipped my arm between her and Marius, so that I could cradle her tightly as he continued to toy with her, his fingers lifting and falling on the tender little mound of her sex.

"You tease me, Marius," she whispered, her head tossing. The pillow was damp beneath her and drenched with the perfume of her hair. I kissed her lips. They locked to my mouth. To keep her tongue from discovering my vampiric teeth, I drove my tongue into her. Her nether mouth couldn't have been sweeter, tighter, more moist.

"Ah, then this, my sweet," said Marius tenderly, his fingers sliding inside her.

She lifted her hips, as though the fingers were lifting her as she would have them do.

"Oh, Heaven help me," she whispered, and then came the fullness of her passion, her face darkening with blood, and the rosy fire spreading down her breasts. I pushed back the cloth and saw the redness consume her bosom, her nipples standing rigid in tiny raisinlike points.

I closed my eyes and lay beside her. I let myself feel the passion rock her, and then the heat was lessened in her, and she seemed to become sleepy. She turned her head away. Her face was still. Her eyelids were beautifully molded over her closed eyes. She sighed and her pretty lips parted in a natural way.

Marius brushed her hair back from her face, smoothing the tiny unruly ringlets that were caught in the moisture, and then he kissed her forehead.

"Sleep now, knowing you're safe," he said to her. "I'll take care of you forever. You saved Amadeo," he whispered. "You kept him alive until I could come."

Dreamily she turned to look up at him, her eyes glossy and slow.

"Am I not beautiful enough for you to love me for that alone?" she asked.

I realized suddenly that what she said was bitter, and that she was bestowing a confidence on him. I could feel her thoughts!

"I love you whether or not you dress in gold or wear pearls, whether or not you speak wittily and quickly, whether or not you make a well-lighted and elegant place in which I can rest, I love you for the heart here inside you, which came to Amadeo when you knew there was danger that those who knew or loved the Englishman might hurt you, I love you for courage and for what you know of being alone."

Her eyes widened for a moment. "For what I know of being alone? Oh, I know very well what it means to be utterly alone."

"Yes, brave one, and now you know I love you," he whispered. "You always knew that Amadeo loved you."

"Yes, I do love you," I whispered, lying next to her, holding her.

"Well, now you know I love you as well."

She studied him as best she could in her languor. "There are so many questions on the tip of my tongue," she said.

"They don't matter," Marius said. He kissed her and I think he let his teeth touch her tongue. "I take all your questions and I cast them away. Sleep now, virginal heart," he said. "Love whom you will, quite safe in the love we feel for you."

It was the signal to withdraw.

As I stood at the foot of the bed, he placed the embroidered covers over her, careful to fold the fine Flemish linen sheet over the edge of the rougher white wool blanket, and then he kissed her again, but she was like a little girl, soft and safe, and fast asleep.

Outside, as we stood on the edge of the canal, he lifted his gloved hand to his nostrils, and he savored the fragrance of her on it.

"You've learnt much today, haven't you? You cannot tell her anything of who you are. But do you see now how close you might come?"

"Yes," I said. "But only if I want nothing in return."

"Nothing?" he asked. He looked at me reprovingly. "She gave you loyalty, affection, intimacy; what more could you want in return?"

"Nothing now," I said. "You've taught me well. But what I had before was her understanding, that she was a mirror in which I could study my reflection and thereby judge my own growth. She can't be that mirror now, can she?"

"Yes, in many ways she can. Show her by gestures and simple words what you are. You needn't tell her tales of blood drinkers that would only drive her mad. She can comfort you marvelously well without ever knowing what hurts you. And you, you must remember that to tell her everything would be to destroy her. Imagine it."

I was silent for a long moment.

"Something's occurred to you," he said. "You have that solemn look. Speak."

"Can she be made into what we—."

"Amadeo, you bring me to another lesson. The answer is no."

"But she'll grow old and die, and—."

"Of course she will, as she is meant to do. Amadeo, how many of us can there be? And on what grounds would we bring her over to us? And would we want her as our companion forever? Would we want her as our pupil? Would we want to hear her cries if the magic blood were to drive her mad? It is not for any soul, this blood, Amadeo. It demands a great strength and a great preparation, all of which I found in you. But I do not see it in her."

I nodded. I knew what he meant. I didn't have to think over all that had befallen me, or even think back to the rude cradle of Russia where I'd been nursed. He was right.

"You will want to share this power with them all," he said. "Learn that you cannot. Learn that with each one you make there comes a terrible obligation, and a terrible danger. Children rise against their parents, and with each blood drinker made by you you make a child that will live forever in love for you or hate. Yes, hate."

"You needn't say any more," I whispered. "I know. I understand."

We went home together, to the brightly lighted rooms of the palazzo.

I knew then what he wanted of me, that I mingle with my old friends among the boys, that I show kindness in particular to Riccardo, who blamed himself, I soon realized, for the death of those few undefended ones whom the Englishman had murdered on that fateful day.

"Pretend, and grow strong with each pretense," he

whispered in my ear. "Rather, draw close and be loving and love, without the luxury of complete honesty. For love can bridge all."

13

IN THE FOLLOWING MONTHS, I learned more than I can ever recount here. I studied vigorously, and paid attention even to the government of the city, which I thought basically as tiresome as any government, and read voraciously the great Christian scholars, completing my time with Abelard, Duns Scotus and other thinkers whom Marius prized.

Marius also found for me a heap of Russian literature so that for the first time I could study in writing what I had only known from the songs of my uncles and my Father in the past. At first I deemed this too painful for a serious inquiry, but Marius laid down the law and wisely. The inherent value of the subject matter soon absorbed my painful recollections and a greater knowledge and understanding was the result.

All of these documents were in Church Slavonic, the written language of my childhood, and I soon fell into reading this with extraordinary ease. *The Lay of Igor's Campaigns* delighted me, but I also loved the writings, translated from the Greek, of St. John Chrysostom. I also reveled in the fantastical tales of King Solomon and of the Descent of the Virgin into Hell, works which were not part of the approved New Testament but which were very evocative of the Russian soul. I read also our great chronicle, *The Tale of Bygone Years*. I read also *Orison on the Downfall of Russia* and the *Tale of the Destruction of Riasan*.

This exercise, the reading of my native stories, helped me to put them in perspective alongside the other learning which I acquired. In sum, it lifted them from the realm of personal dreams.

Gradually, I saw the wisdom of this. I made my reports to Marius with more enthusiasm. I asked for more of the manuscripts in Church Slavonic, and I soon had for reading the *Narrative of the Pious Prince Dovmont and His Courage* and *The Heroic Deeds of Mercurius of Smolensk*. Finally, I came to regard the works in Church Slavonic to be a pure pleasure, and I kept them for the hours after official study when I might pore over the old tales and even make up from them my own mournful songs.

I sang these sometimes to the other apprentices when they went to sleep. They thought the language very exotic, and sometimes the pure music and my sad inflection could make them cry.

Riccardo and I, meantime, became close friends again. He never asked why I was now a creature of night like the Master. I never sounded the depths of his mind. Of course I would do it if I had to for my safety and for Marius's safety, but I used my vampiric wits to gloss him in another way, and I always found him devoted, unquestioning and loyal.

Once I asked Marius what Riccardo thought of us.

"Riccardo owes me too great a debt to question anything I do," Marius answered, but without any haughtiness or pride.

"Then he is far better bred than I am, isn't he? For I owe you the same debt and I question everything you say."

"You're a smart, devil-tongued little imp, yes," Marius conceded with a small smile. "Riccardo was won in a card game from his drunken Father by a beastly merchant who worked him night and day. Riccardo detested his Father, which you never have. Riccardo was eight years old when I bought him for the price of a gold necklace. He'd seen the worst of men whom children don't move to natural pity. You saw what men will do with the flesh of children for pleasure. It's not as bad. Riccardo, unable to believe that a tender little one could move anyone to compassion, believed in nothing until I wrapped him in safety and filled him with learning, and told him in terms on which he could count that he was my prince.

"But to answer you more in the way you ask the question, Riccardo thinks that I am a magician, and that with you I've chosen to share my spells. He knows that you were on death's door when I bestowed on you my secrets, and that I do not tease him or the others with this honor, but regard it rather as something of dire consequence. He doesn't seek after our knowledge. And will defend us with his life."

I accepted this. I didn't have the need in me to confide in Riccardo as I had with Bianca.

"I feel the need to protect him," I said to my Master. "Pray he should never have to protect me."

"So I feel also," said Marius. "I feel this for them all. God granted your Englishman a great mercy that he was not alive when I came home to find my little ones slain by him. I don't know what I would have done. That he had injured you was bad enough. That he had laid out two child sacrifices at my door to his pride and bitterness, this was even more despicable. You had made love to him, and you could fight him. But they were innocents who stood in his path."

I nodded. "What did happen to his remains?" I asked.

"Such a simple thing," he said with a shrug. "Why do you want to know? I can be superstitious too. I broke him into fragments and scattered those fragments to the wind. If the old tales are true that his shade will pine for the restoration of his body, then his soul wanders the winds."

"Master, what will become of our shades if our bodies are destroyed?"

"God only knows, Amadeo. I despair of knowing. I have lived too long to think of destroying myself. My fate is perhaps the same fate of the whole physical world. That we could have come from nothing and return to nothing, this is entirely possible. But let us enjoy our illusions of immortality, as mortals enjoy theirs."

Good enough.

My Master was absent from the palazzo twice, when he went on those mysterious journeys which he wouldn't explain to me any more now than he had before.

I hated these absences, but I knew that they were tests of my new powers. I had to rule within the house gently and unobtrusively, and I had to hunt on my own and make some account, upon Marius's return, of what I had done with my leisure time.

After the second journey, he came home weary and uncommonly sad. He said, as he had said once before, that "Those Who Must Be Kept" seemed to be at peace.

"I hate it what these creatures are!" I said.

"No, never say such a thing to me, Amadeo!" he burst out. In a flash I'd seen him more angry and uncomposed than ever in our lives. I'm not sure I'd ever seen him really angry in our lives.

He approached me and I shrank back, actually afraid. But by the time he struck me, hard across the face, he'd recovered himself, and it was just the usual brain-jarring blow.

I accepted it, and then threw him one exasperated searing glance. "You act like a child," I said, "a child playing Master, and so I must master my feelings and put up with this."

Of course it took all my reserves to say this, especially when my head was swimming, and I made my face such an obdurate mask of contempt that suddenly he burst out laughing.

I started to laugh too.

"But really, Marius," I said, feeling very cheeky, "what are these creatures you speak of?" I made my wisdom nice and reverent. My question was, after all, sincere. "You come home miserable, Sir. You know you do. So what are they, and why must they be kept?"

"Amadeo, don't ask me anymore. Sometimes just before morning, when my fears are at their worst, I imagine that we have enemies among the blood drinkers, and they're close."

"Others? As strong as you?"

"No, those who have come in past years are never as strong as me, and that is why they're gone."

I was enthralled. He had hinted at this before, that he kept our territory clean of others, but he wouldn't elaborate, and now he seemed softened up with unhappiness and willing to talk.

"But I imagine that there are others, and that they'll come to disturb our peace. They won't have a good reason. They never do. They'll want to hunt the Veneto, or they will have formed some willful little battalion, and they'll try to destroy us out of sheer sport. I imagine . . . but the point is, my child—and you are my child, smart one!—I don't tell you any more about the ancient mysteries than you need to know. That way, no one can pick your apprentice mind for its deepest secrets, either with your cooperation or without your knowledge, or against your will."

"If we have a history worth knowing, Sir, then you should tell me. What ancient mysteries? You wall me up with books on human history. You've made me learn Greek, and even this miserable Egyptian script which no one else knows, and you question me all the time on the fate of ancient Rome and ancient Athens, and the battles of every Crusade ever sent from our shores to the Holy Land. But what of us?"

"Always here," he said, "I told you. Ancient as mankind itself. Always here, and always a few, and always warring and best when alone and needing the love only of one other or two at most. That's the history, plain and simple. I will expect you to write it out for me in all five languages you now know."

He sat down on the bed, disgruntled, letting his muddy boot dig into the satin. He fell back on the pillows. He was really raw and strange and seemingly young.

"Marius, come on now," I coaxed. I was at the desk. "What ancient mysteries? What are Those Who Must Be Kept?"

"Go dig into our dungeons, child," he said, lacing his voice with sarcasm. "Find the statues there I have from so-called pagan days. You'll find things as useful as Those Who Must Be Kept. Leave me alone. I'll tell you some night, but for now, I give you what counts. In my absence you were supposed to study. Tell me now what you learnt."

He had in fact demanded that I learn all of Aristotle, not from the manuscripts which were common currency in the piazza, but from an old text of his own which he said was purer Greek. I'd read it all.

"Aristotle," I said. "And St. Thomas Aquinas. Ah, well, great systems give comfort, and when we feel ourselves slipping into despair, we should devise great schemes of the nothing around us, and then we will not slip but hang on a scaffold of our making, as meaningless as nothing, but too detailed to be so easily dismissed."

"Well done," he said with an eloquent sigh. "Maybe some night in the far distant future, you'll take a more hopeful approach, but as you seem as animated and full of happiness as you can be, why should I complain?"

"We must come from somewhere," I said, pushing the other point.

He was too crestfallen to answer.

Finally, he rallied, climbing up off the pillows and coming towards me. "Let's go out. Let's find Bianca, and dress her up as a man for a while. Bring your finest. She needs to be freed of those rooms for a spell."

"Sir, this may come as a rude shock to you, but Bianca, like many women, already has that habit. In the guise of a boy, she slips out all the time to make the rounds of the city."

"Yes, but not in our company," he said. "We shall show her the worst places!" He made a dramatic comical face. "Come on."

I was excited.

As soon as we told the little plan to her, she was excited too.

We came bursting in with an armful of fine clothes, and she immediately slipped away with us to get dressed.

"What have you brought me? Oh, I'm to be Amadeo tonight, splendid," she said. She shut the doors on her company, who as usual carried on without her, several men singing around the Virginal and others arguing heatedly over their dice.

She stripped off her clothes and stepped out of them, naked as Venus from the sea. We both dressed her in blue leggings and tunic and doublet. I pulled her belt tight, and Marius caught her hair up in a soft velvet hat.

"You're the prettiest boy in the Veneto," he said stepping back. "Something tells me I'll have to protect you with our life."

"Are you really going to take me to the worst haunts? I want to see dangerous places!" She threw up her arms. "Give me my stiletto. You don't expect me to go unarmed."

"I have all the proper weapons for you," Marius said. He had brought a sword with a beautiful diamond-studded diagonal belt which he clasped at her hip. "Try to draw this. It's no dancing rapier. It's a war sword. Come on."

She took the handle with both hands and brought it forth in a wide sure sweep. "I wish I had an enemy," she cried out, "who was ready to die."

I looked at Marius. He looked at me. No, she couldn't be one of us.

"That would be too selfish," he whispered in my ear.

I couldn't help but wonder, if I had not been dying after my fight with the Englishman, if the sweating sickness had not taken me over, would he have ever made me a vampire?

The three of us hurried down the stone steps to the quay. There was our canopied gondola waiting. Marius gave the address.

"Are you sure you want to go there, Master?" asked the gondolier, shocked because he knew the district where the worst of the foreign seamen congregated and drank and fought.

"Most sure of it," he said.

As we moved off in the black waters, I put my arm around tender Bianca. Leaning back on the cushions, I felt invulnerable, immortal, certain that nothing would ever defeat me or Marius, and in our care Bianca would always be safe.

How very wrong I was.

Nine months perhaps we had together after our trip

to Kiev. Nine or maybe ten, I cannot mark the climax by any exterior event. Let me say only, before I proceed to bloody disaster, that Bianca was always with us in those last months. When we were not spying upon the carousers, we were in our house, where Marius painted her portraits, devising her as this or that goddess, as the Biblical Judith with the head of the Florentine for her Holofernes, or as the Virgin Mary staring rapt at a tiny Christ child, as perfectly rendered by Marius as any image he ever made.

Those pictures—perhaps some of them endure to this very day.

One night, when all slept except for the three of us, Bianca, about to give up on a couch as Marius painted, sighed and said, "I like your company too much. I don't ever want to go home."

Would that she had loved us less. Would that she had not been there on the fatal evening in 1499, just before the turn of the century, when the High Renaissance was in its glory, ever to be celebrated by artists and historians, would that she had been safe when our world went up in flames.

14

IF YOU'VE READ *The Vampire Lestat* you know what happened, for I showed it all to Lestat in visions two hundred years ago. Lestat set down in writing the images I made known to him, the pain I shared with him. And though I now propose to relive these horrors, to flesh out the tale in my own words, there are points where I cannot improve on his words, and may from time to time freely call them up.

It began suddenly. I awoke to find that Marius had lifted back the gilded cover of the sarcophagus. A torch blazed behind him on the wall.

"Hurry, Amadeo, they're here. They mean to burn our house."

"Who, Master? And why?"

He snatched me from the shining coffin box, and I rushed after him up the decaying stairs to the first floor of the ruined dwelling.

He wore his red cape and hood, and he moved so fast it took all my power to keep up with him.

"Is it Those Who Must Be Kept?" I asked. He slung his arm around me, and off we went to the rooftop of our own palazzo.

"No, child, it's a pack of foolish blood drinkers, bent on destroying all the work I've done. Bianca is there, at their mercy, and the boys too."

We entered by the roof doors and went down the marble steps. Smoke rose from the lower floors.

"Master, the boys, they're screaming!" I shouted.

Bianca came running to the foot of the stairs far below.

"Marius! Marius, they are demons. Use your magic!" she cried out, her hair streaming from the couch, her garments undone. "Marius!" Her wail echoed up the three floors of the palazzo.

"Dear God, the rooms are everywhere on fire!" I cried out. "We must have water to put this out. Master, the paintings!"

Marius dropped down over the railing and appeared, suddenly below, at her side. As I ran to join him, I saw a crowd of black-robed figures close in on him, and to my horror, try to set his clothes afire with the torches they brandished, as they gave forth horrid shrieks and hissed curses from beneath their hoods.

From everywhere these demons came. The cries of the mortal apprentices were terrible.

Marius knocked his assailants away, turning his arm in a great arc, the torches rolling on the marble floor. He closed his cloak about Bianca.

"They mean to kill us!" she screamed. "They mean to burn us, Marius, they've slaughtered the boys, and others they've taken prisoner!"

Suddenly more of the black figures came running before the first attackers could climb to their feet. I saw what they were. All had the same white faces and hands as we had; all possessed the magic blood.

They were creatures such as we!

Again, Marius was attacked, only to fling off all of them. The tapestries of the great hall were ignited. Dark odoriferous smoke belched forth from the adjacent rooms. Smoke filled the stairwell above. An infernal flickering light suddenly made the place as bright as day.

I pitched myself into battle with the demons, finding them amazingly weak. And picking up one of their torches I rushed at them, driving them back, away from me, just as the Master did.

"Blasphemer, heretic!" came a hiss from one. "Demon idolator, pagan!" cursed another. They came on, and I fought them again, setting their robes afire so that they screamed and fled to the safety of the waters of the canal.

But there were too many of them. More poured into the hall even as we fought.

Suddenly, to my horror, Marius shoved Bianca away from him towards the open front doors of the palazzo.

"Run, darling, run. Get clear of the house."

Savagely he fought those who would follow her, running after her, to bring them down one by one as they tried to stop her, until I saw her vanish through the open doors.

There was no time to make certain she had reached safety. More of them had closed in on me. The flaming tapestries fell from their rods. Statues were overturned and smashed on the marble. I was nearly dragged down by two of the little demons who clutched at my left arm, until I drove my torch into the face of one, and set the other completely alight.

"To the roof, Amadeo, come!" Marius shouted.

"Master, the paintings, the paintings in the storage rooms!" I cried.

"Forget the paintings. It's too late. Boys, run from here, get out now, save yourselves from the fire."

Knocking the attackers back, he shot up the stairwell and called down to me from the uppermost railing. "Come, Amadeo, fight them off, believe in your strength, child, fight."

Reaching the second floor, I was everywhere surrounded, and no sooner did I set one ablaze than another was on me, and not seeking to burn me they grabbed my arms and my legs. All my limbs were caught by them, until finally the torch was wrenched from my hand.

"Master, leave me, get away!" I called. I turned, kicking and writhing, and looked up to see him high above, and again surrounded, and this time a hundred torches were plunged into his ballooning red cloak, a hundred fiery brands were beating against his golden hair and his furious white face. It was as a swarm of blazing insects, and so by such numbers and such tactics the swarm rendered him first motionless; and then, with a great loud gust, his entire body went up in flames.

"Marius!" I screamed and screamed, unable to take my eyes off him, warring still with my captors, jerking loose my legs only to have them caught again by cold, hurting fingers, shoving with my arms, only to be pinioned once more. "Marius!" This cry came out of me with all my worst anguish and terror.

It seemed that nothing I had ever feared could be so unspeakable, so unendurable as the sight of him, high above, at the stone banister, completely engulfed in flame. His long slender form became a black outline but for one second, and it seemed I saw his profile, head thrown back, as his hair exploded and his fingers were like black spiders clawing up out of the fire for air.

"Marius!" I cried. All comfort, all goodness, all hope was burning in this black figure which my eyes would not let go, even as it dwindled, and lost all perceptible form.

Marius! My will died.

What remained was a remnant of it, and the remnant,

as if commanded by a secondary soul made up of magic blood and power, fought mindlessly on.

A net was thrown over me, a net of steel mesh so heavy and so fine that I could see nothing suddenly, only feel myself bound up in it, rolled over and over in it, by enemy hands. I was being carried out of the house. I could hear screams all around me. I could hear the running feet of those who carried me, and when the wind howled past us, I knew we had come to the shore.

Down into the bowels of a ship I was carried, my ears still full of mortal wails. The apprentices had been taken prisoner with me. I was thrown down among them, their soft frantic bodies heaped on me and beside me, and I, tightly bound in the net, could not even speak to utter words of comfort, and had no words to give them besides.

I felt the oars rise and fall, heard the inevitable splash in the water, and the great wooden galley shivered and moved out towards the open sea. It gained speed as if there were no night to fight its passage, and on and on plowed the oarsmen with a force and strength that mortal men could not have commanded, driving the ship south.

"Blasphemer," came a whisper near my ear.

The boys sobbed and prayed.

"Stop your impious prayers," said a cold preternatural voice, "you servants of the pagan Marius. You will die for your Master's sins, all of you."

I heard a sinister laughter, rumbling like low thunder over the moist soft sounds of their anguish and suffering. I heard a long, dry cruel laugh.

I closed my eyes, I went deep deep inside myself. I lay in the dirt of the Monastery of the Caves, a wraith of myself, tumbled back into safest and most terrible memories.

"Dear God," I whispered without moving my lips, "save them, and I swear to You I shall bury myself alive among the monks forever, I shall give up all pleasures, I shall do nothing hour by hour but praise Your Holy Name. Lord, God, deliver me. Lord, God—." But as the madness of panic took over, as I lost all sense of time and place, I called out for Marius. "Marius, for the love of God, Marius!"

Someone struck me. A leather-clad foot struck my head. Another struck my ribs, and yet another crushed my hand. All around me were these wicked feet, kicking me and bruising me. I went soft. I saw the shocks of the blows as so many colors, and I thought to myself bitterly, ah, what beautiful colors, yes, colors. Then came the increased wails of my brothers. They too must suffer this, and what mental refuge did they have, these fragile young students, each so well loved and so well taught and groomed for the great world, to find themselves now at the mercy of these demons whose purpose was unknown to me, whose purpose lay beyond anything of which I could conceive.

"Why do this to us?" I whispered.

"To punish you!" came a gentle whisper. "To punish you for all your vain and blasphemous deeds, for the worldly and Godless life you've lived. What is Hell to this, young one?"

Ah, so the executioners of the mortal world said a thousand times when they led heretics to the stake.

"What are the fires of Hell to this brief suffering?" Oh, such self-serving and arrogant lies.

"Do you think so?" came the whisper. "Lay a caution on your thoughts, young one, for there are those who can pick your mind barren of all its thoughts. There may be no Hell for you, child, but there will be suffering eternal. Your nights of luxury and lasciviousness are over. The truth awaits you now."

Once again, I retreated into my deepest mental hiding place. I had no body anymore. I lay in the Monastery, in the earth, unfeeling of my body. I put my mind at work on the tone of the voices near me, such sweet and pitiable voices. I picked out the boys by name and slowly made a count of them. Over half our little company, our splendid cherubic company, was in this abominable prison.

I did not hear Riccardo. But then, when our captors had finished their abuse for a while, I did hear Riccardo.

He intoned a litany in Latin, in a raw and desperate whisper. "Blessed be God." The others were quick to answer. "Blessed be His Holy Name." And so on it went, the prayers, the voice gradually becoming weak in the silence until Riccardo alone prayed.

I did not give the responses.

Yet on he went, now that his charges mercifully slept, praying to comfort himself, or perhaps merely for the glory of God. He moved from the litany into the *Pater Noster*, and from then into the comforting age-old words of the *Ave* which he said over and over, as if making a rosary, all alone, as he lay imprisoned in the bottom of the ship.

I spoke no words to him. I did not even let him know that I was there. I couldn't save him. I couldn't comfort him. I couldn't even explain this terrible fate which had befallen us. I couldn't above all reveal what I had seen: the Master perishing, the great one gone into the simple and eternal agony of fire.

I had slipped into a shock near to despair. I let my mind recover the sight of Marius burning, Marius a living torch, turning and twisting in the fire, his fine fingers reaching heavenward like spiders in the orange flame. Marius was dead; Marius was burned. There had been too many of them for Marius. I knew what he would have said if he had come to me a comforting specter. "There were simply too many of them, Amadeo, too many. I couldn't stop them, though I tried."

I slipped into tormented dreams. The ship bore on through the night, carrying me away from Venice, away from the ruin of all that I believed in, all that I held dear.

I awoke to the sounds of singing and to the smell of the earth, but it was not Russian earth.

We were no longer at sea. We were imprisoned on land.

Still bound in the net, I listened to hollow preternatural voices chanting with a villainous gusto the awful hymn, *Dies Irae,* or Day of Wrath.

A low drum carried on the zesty rhythm as if it were a song for dancing rather than a terrible lament of the Final Days. On and on went the Latin words speaking of the day when all the world would be turned to ashes, when the great trumpets of the Lord would blast to signal the opening of all graves. Death itself and nature would both shudder. All souls would be brought together, no soul able anymore to hide anything from the

Lord. Out of His book, every sin would be read aloud. Vengeance would fall upon everyone. Who was there to defend us, but the Judge Himself, Our Majestic Lord? Our only hope was the pity of Our God, the God who had suffered the Cross for us, who would not let His sacrifice be in vain.

Yes, beautiful old words, but they issued from an evil mouth, the mouth of one who did not even know their meaning, who tapped at his eager drum as if ready for a feast.

A night had passed. We were entombed and now being released from our prison, as the dreaded little voice sang on to its spirited little drum.

I heard the whispers of the older boys, seeking to give the young ones comfort, and the steady voice of Riccardo assuring all of them that surely they would soon discover what these creatures wanted, and perhaps be allowed to go free.

Only I heard the rustling, impish laughter everywhere. Only I knew how many preternatural monsters lurked about us, as we were brought into a light of a monstrous fire.

The net was torn from me. I rolled over, clutching at the grass. I looked up and saw that we were in a great clearing beneath high and indifferent bright stars. It was the summery air, and great towering green trees surrounded us. But the blast of the raging bonfire distorted everything. The boys, chained together, their clothes torn, their faces scratched and streaked with blood, cried out frantically when they saw me, yet I was snatched away from them and held, a bevy of little hooded demons fastened to both my hands.

"I can't help you!" I cried. It was selfish and terrible. It came from my pride. It made only panic among them.

I saw Riccardo, as badly beaten as the rest, turn from right to left, trying to quiet them, his hands bound before him, his doublet almost torn off his back.

He turned his glance to me, and then together we looked around us at the great wreath of dark-dressed figures that enclosed us. Could he see the whiteness of their faces and hands? Did he, on an instinctive level, know what they were?

"Be quick if you mean to kill us!" he called out. "We've done nothing. We don't know who you are or why you've taken us. We are innocent, to a one."

I was touched by his bravery, and I pulled my thoughts together. I must stop shrinking in horror from my last memory of the Master, but imagine him living, and think what he would tell me to do.

We were outnumbered, that was obvious, and I could now detect smiles on the faces of the hooded figures, who though they draped their eyes in shadow, revealed their long twisted mouths.

"Where is the leader here?" I demanded, raising my voice above the level of human power. "Surely you see these boys are nothing but mortals! Your argument must be with me!"

The long string of surrounding black-robed figures caved in to whispering and murmuring amongst themselves at this. Those clustered about the band of enchained boys tightened their ranks. And as others whom I could scarce see threw more and more wood and pitch onto the great fire, it seemed the enemy prepared for action.

Two couples placed themselves before the apprentices who seemed not in their wailing and crying to realize what this meant.

I realized it at once.

"No, you must speak with me, reason with me!" I shouted, straining against those who held me. To my horror, they only laughed.

Suddenly drums began again, some one-hundred-fold louder than before, as if an entire circle of drummers surrounded us and the hissing, spitting fire.

They took up that steady beat of the *Dies Irae* hymn, and suddenly the wreath of figures all to a one straightened and locked hands. They began to sing the words in Latin of the terrible day of woe. Each figure began to rock playfully, lifting knees in playful march as a hundred voices spit out the words to the obvious rhythm of a dance. It made an ugly mockery of the piteous words.

The drums were joined by the shrill squeal of pipes, and the repeated slam of tambourines, and suddenly the entire wreath of dancers, still hand in hand, was moving, bodies swaying side to side from the waist up, heads bobbing, mouths grinning. "Dee-eees- - -a- - -ray, dee-ees- -eee- - -raw!" they sang.

I panicked. But I couldn't shake loose of my captors. I screamed.

The first pair of robed beings before the boys had broken out the first of them who was to suffer and tossed his struggling body high in the air. The second pair of figures caught it, and, with great preternatural thrusts, hurled the helpless child in an arc into the great fire.

With piteous shrieks, the boy fell into the flames and vanished, and the other apprentices, now certain of their fate, went wild with crying and sobbing and screaming, but to no avail.

One after another, boys were disentangled from the others and hurled into the flames.

I thrashed back and forth, kicking at the ground and at my opponents. Once I broke one arm loose only to have it imprisoned by three other figures with hard pinching fingers. I sobbed:

"Don't do this, they're innocent. Don't kill them. Don't."

No matter how loud I cried out I could hear the dying cries of the boys who burned, *Amadeo, save us,* whether there were words to the final terror or no. Finally all the living took up this chant. *"Amadeo, save us!"* but their band was not halved and soon only a fourth remained, squirming and struggling, as they were finally heaved up to the unspeakable death.

The drums played on, with the mocking chink, chink, chink of the tambourines and the whining melody of the horns. The voices made a fearful chorus, each syllable sharpened with venom as the hymn was sung out.

"So much for your cohorts!" hissed the figure nearest me. "So you sob for them, do you? When you should have made a meal of them each and every one for the love of God!"

"The love of God!" I cried. "How dare you speak of the love of God! You slaughter children!" I managed to turn and kick at him, wounding him far worse than he expected, but as ever, three more guards took his place.

Finally in the lurid blast of the fire, only three white-faced children were left, the very youngest of our household, and none of them made a sound. It was eerie their silence, their little faces wet and quivering, as they were given up, their eyes dull and unbelieving, into the flames.

I called their names. At the top of my lungs, I called out: "In Heaven, my brothers, in Heaven, you go into the arms of God!"

But how could their mortal ears hear over the deafening song of the chanters.

Suddenly, I realized Riccardo had not been among them. Riccardo had either escaped or been spared, or been saved for something worse. I knotted my brows in a tight frown to help me lock these thoughts in my mind, lest these preternatural beasts remember Riccardo.

But I was yanked from my thoughts and dragged towards the pyre.

"Now you, brave one, little Ganymede of the blasphemers, you, you willful, brazen cherub."

"No!" I dug in my heels. It was unthinkable. I couldn't die like this; I couldn't go into the flames. Frantically I reasoned with myself, "But you have just seen your brothers die, why not you?" and yet I couldn't accept this as possible, no, not me, I was immortal, no!

"Yes, you, and fire will make a roast of you as it has of them. Do you smell their flesh roasting? Do you smell their burnt bones?"

I was thrown high in the air, high enough by their powerful hands to feel the very breeze catch hold of my hair, and then to peer down into the fire, as its annihilating blast struck my face, my chest, my outstretched arms.

Down, down, down into the heat I went, sprawled out, in the thunder of crackling wood and dancing orange flames. *So I die!* I thought if I thought anything, but

I think that all I knew was panic, and surrender, surrender to what would be unspeakable pain.

Hands clutched me, burning wood tumbled and roared beneath me. I was being dragged off the fire. I was being dragged across the ground. Feet stomped on my burning clothes. My burning tunic was ripped off me. I gasped for air. I felt pain all over my body, the dread pain of burnt flesh, and I deliberately rolled my eyes up into my head to seek oblivion. *Come, Master, come if there is a paradise for us, come to me.* I pictured him, burnt, a black skeleton, but he put out his arms to receive me.

A figure stood over me. I lay on the moist Mother Earth, thank God, the smoke still rising from my scorched hands and face and my hair. The figure was big-shouldered, tall, black-haired.

He lifted two strong thick-knuckled white hands and drew his hood back off his head, revealing a huge mass of shining black hair. His eyes were large with pearly whites and pupils of jet, and his eyebrows, though very thick, were beautifully arched and curved over his eyes. He was a vampire, as were the others, but he was one of unique beauty and immense presence, looking down at me as though he were more interested in me than himself, though he expected to be the center of all eyes.

A tiny shiver of thanks passed through me, that he seemed by virtue of these eyes and his smooth Cupid's bow mouth to be possessed of the semblance of human reason.

"Will you serve God?" he asked. His voice was cultured and gentle, and his eyes held no mockery. "Answer me, Will you serve God, for if you will not, you will be thrown back into the fire."

I felt pain in all my frame. No thought came to me except that the words he spoke were impossible, they made no sense, and I could therefore make no response.

At once, his vicious helpers lifted me again, laughing, and chanting in time with the loud singing of the hymn which had never ceased, "Into the fire, into the fire!"

"No!" the leader cried out. "I see in him the pure love of our Savior." He lifted his hand. The others released their grip, though they held me suspended, my legs and arms spread out, in the air.

"You are good?" I whispered desperately to the figure. "How can this be?" I wept.

He drew nearer. He leant over me. What beauty he possessed! His thick mouth was the perfect Cupid's bow, as I have said, but only now did I see its rich dark color, natural to it, and the even shadow of beard, shaven away for the last time in mortal life no doubt, that covered all his lower face, giving it the strong mask of a man. His high broad forehead seemed made of pure white bone only by comparison, with full rounded temples and a peaked hairline, from which his dark curls fell back gracefully to make a striking frame for his face.

But it was the eyes, yes, as always with me, the eyes that held me, the large oval and shimmering eyes.

"Child," he whispered. "Would I suffer such horrors if it were not for God?"

I wept all the more.

I was no longer afraid. I didn't care that I was in pain. The pain was red and golden as the flames had been and ran through me as if it were fluid, but though I felt it, it didn't hurt me, and I didn't care.

Without protest, I was carried, my eyes closed, into a passage, where the shuffling feet of those who carried me made a soft, crumbling echo against low ceiling and walls.

Let loose to roll over on the ground, I turned my face to it, sad that I lay on a nest of old rags because I couldn't feel the moist Mother Earth when I needed her, and then this too was of no import whatsoever, and I laid my cheek on the soiled linen and drifted, as if I had put there to sleep.

My scalded skin was a part from me, and not a part of me. And I let a long sigh come out of me, knowing, though I didn't form words in my mind, that all my poor boys were safely dead. The fire could not have tortured them for long, no. Its heat was too great, and surely their souls had fled Heavenward like nightingales that had drifted into the smoky blast.

My boys were of the Earth no more and no one could do them harm. All the fine things which Marius had done for them, the teachers, the skills they'd been taught, the lessons they'd learned, their dancing, their laughter, their singing, the works they had painted—all of this was gone, and the souls went Heavenward on soft white wings.

Would I have followed? Would God have received the soul of a blood drinker into his golden cloudy Heaven? Would I have left the awful sound of these demons chanting Latin for the realm of angels' song?

Why did those near me allow these thoughts in me, for surely they read them from my mind. I could feel the presence of the leader, the black-eyed one, the powerful one. Perhaps I was here with him alone. If he could make sense of this, if he could lend it meaning and thereby contain its monstrousness, then he would be some saint of God. I saw soiled and starving monks in caves.

I rolled over on my back, luxuriating in the splashy red and yellow pain that bathed me, and I opened my eyes.

15

A MELLOW and comforting voice spoke to me, directly to me:

"Your Master's vain works are all burnt; nothing but ashes remain now of his paintings. God forgive him, that he used his sublime powers not in the service of God but in the service of the World, the Flesh and the Devil, yes, I say the Devil, though the Devil is our standard bearer, for the Evil One is proud of us and satisfied with our pain; but Marius served the Devil with no regard to the wishes of God, and the mercies granted us by God, that rather than burn in the flames of Hell, we rule in the shadows of the Earth."

"Ah," I whispered. "I see your twisted philosophy."

There came no admonition.

Gradually, though I had rather hear only the voice, my eyes began to focus. There were human skulls, bleached and covered with dust, pressed in the domed earth over my head. Skulls pressed into the earth with mortar so that they formed the entire ceiling, like clean white shells from the sea. Shells for the brain, I thought, for what is left of them, as they protrude from the mortared soil behind them, but the dome that covers the brain and the round black holes where once the jellied eyes were poised, acute as dancers, ever vigilant to report the splendors of the world to the carapaced mind.

All skulls, a dome of skulls, and where the dome came down to meet the walls, a lacing of thigh bones all around it, and below that the random bones of the mortal form, making no pattern, any more than random stones do when they are similarly pressed in mortar to make a wall.

All bones, this place, and lighted with candles. Yes, I smelled the candles, purest beeswax, as for the rich.

"No," said the voice, thoughtfully, "rather for the church, for this is God's church, though the Devil is our Superior General, the founding saint of our Order, so why not beeswax? Leave it to you, a vain and a worldly Venetian, to think it luxury, to confuse it with the wealth in which you wallowed rather like the pig in his slops."

I laughed softly. "Give me more of your generous and idiotic logic," I said. "Be the Aquinas of the Devil. Speak on."

"Don't mock me," he said imploringly and sincerely. "I saved you from the fire."

"I would be dead now if you had not."

"You want to burn?"

"No, not to suffer so, no, I can't bear the thought of it, that I or anyone should suffer so. But to die, yes."

"And what do you think will be your destination if

you do die? Are the fires of Hell not fifty times as hot as the fires we lighted for you and your friends? You are Hell's child; you were from the first moment that the blasphemer Marius infused you with our blood. No one can reverse this judgment. You are kept alive by blood that is cursed and unnatural and pleasing to Satan, and pleasing to God only because He must have Satan to show forth His goodness, and to give mankind a choice to be good or bad."

I laughed again, but as respectfully as I could. "There are so many of you," I said. I turned my head. The numerous candles blinded me, but it wasn't unpleasant. It was as if a different species of flame danced on the wicks, than the species that had consumed my brothers.

"Were they your brothers, these spoilt and pampered mortals?" he asked. His voice was unwavering.

"Do you believe all the rot you're talking to me?" I asked, imitating his tone.

He laughed now, and it was a decently churchly laugh as though we were whispering together about the absurdity of a sermon. But the Blessed Sacrament was not here as it would be in a consecrated church, so why whisper?

"Dear one," he said. "It would be so simple to torture you, to turn your arrogant little mind inside out, and make you nothing but an instrument for raucous screams. It would be nothing to wall you up so that your screams would not be too loud for us, but merely a pleasing accompaniment to our nightly meditation. But I have no taste for such things. That is why I serve the Devil so well; I have never come to like cruelty or evil. I despise them, and would that I could look upon a Crucifix, I would do so and weep as I did when I was a mortal man."

I let my eyes close, forsaking all the dancing flames that besprinkled the gloom. I sent my strongest most stealthy power into his mind, but came upon a locked door.

"Yes, that is my image for shutting you out. Painfully literal for such an educated infidel. But then your dedication to Christ the Lord was nourished among the literal and the naive, was it not? But here, someone comes with a gift for you which will greatly hasten our agreement."

"Agreement, Sir, and what agreement will that be?" I asked.

I too heard the other. A strong and terrible odor penetrated my nostrils. I did not move or open my eyes. I heard the other one laughing in that low rumbling fashion so perfected by the others who had sung the *Dies Irae* with such lewd polish. The smell was noxious, the smell was that of human flesh burnt or something thereof. I hated it. I began to turn my head and tried to stop myself. Sound and pain I could endure, but not this terrible, terrible odor.

"A gift for you, Amadeo," said the other.

I looked up. I stared into the eyes of a vampire formed like a young man with whitish-blond hair and the long lean frame of a Norseman. He held up a great urn with both hands. And then he turned it.

"Ah, no, stop!" I threw up my hands. I knew what it was. But it was too late.

The ashes came down in a torrent on me. I choked

and cried, and turned over. I couldn't get them out of my eyes and my mouth.

"The ashes of your brothers, Amadeo," said the Norse vampire. He gave way to a wild peal of laughter.

Helpless, lying on my face, my hands up to the sides of my face, I shook myself all over, feeling the hot weight of the ashes. At last I turned over and over, and then sprang up to my knees, and to my feet. I backed into the wall. A great iron rack of candles went over, the little flames arcing in my blurred vision, the tapers themselves thudding in the mud. I heard the clatter of bones. I flung my arms up in front of my face.

"What's happened to our pretty composure?" asked the Norse vampire. "We are a weeping cherub, aren't we? That is what your Master called you, cherub, no? Here!" He pulled at my arm, and with the other hand tried to smear the ashes on me.

"You damnable fiend!" I cried. I went mad with fury and indignation. I grabbed his head with both my hands, and using all my strength turned it around on his neck, snapping all the bones, and then I kicked him hard with my right foot. He sank down on his knees, moaning, living still with his broken neck, but not in one piece would he live, I vowed, and kicking at him with the full weight of my right foot, I tore his head from him, the skin ripping and snapping, and the blood pouring out of the gaping trunk, I yanked the head free.

"Ah, look at you now, Sir!" I said, staring down into his frantic eyes. The pupils still danced. "Oh, die, will you, for your own sake." I buried my left fingers tight in his hair, and turning this way and that, I found a candle with my right hand, ripped it from the iron nail that held it and jammed it into his eye sockets one after the other, until he saw no more.

"Ah, then it can be done this way as well," I said looking up and blinking in the dazzle of the candles.

Slowly, I made out his figure. His thick curly black hair was free and tangled, and he sat at an angle, black robes flowing down around his stool, facing slightly away from me, but regarding me so that I could trace the lineaments of his face easily in the light. A noble and beautiful face, with the curling lips as strong as the huge eyes.

"I never liked him," he said softly, raising his eyebrows, "though I must say, you do impress me, and I did not expect to see him gone so soon."

I shuddered. A horrible coldness seized me, a soulless ugly anger, routing sorrow, routing madness, routing hope.

I hated the head I held and wanted to drop it, but the thing still lived. The bleeding sockets quivered, and the tongue darted from side to side out of the mouth. "Oh, this is a revolting thing!" I cried.

"He always said such unusual things," said the black-haired one. "He was a pagan, you see. That you never were. I mean he believed in the gods of the north forest, and in Thor ever circling the world with his hammer . . ."

"Are you going to talk forever?" I asked. "I must burn this thing even after this, mustn't I?" I asked.

He threw me the most charming innocent smile.

"You are a fool to be in this place," I whispered. My hands shook uncontrollably.

Not waiting for a response, I turned and snatched up

another candle, having so thoroughly snuffed the other, and set fire to the dead being's hair. The stench sickened me. I made a sound like a boy crying.

I dropped the flaming head into the robed and headless body. I threw the candle down into the flames, so that the wax might feed it. Gathering up the other candles I had knocked down, I fed them to the fire and stepped back as a great heat rose from the dead one.

The head appeared to roll about in the flames, more than was likely, so I grabbed up the iron candelabra I had knocked over, and using this like a rake, I plunged it into the burning mass to flatten and crush what lay beneath the fire.

At the very last his outstretched hands curled, fingers digging into the palms. Ah, to have life in this state, I thought wearily, and with the rake I knocked the arms against the torso. The fire reeked of rags and human blood, blood he'd drunk no doubt, but there was no other human scent to it, and with despair I saw that I had made a fire of him right in the middle of the ashes of my friends.

Well, it seemed appropriate. "You are revenged in one of them," I said with a defeated sigh. I threw down the crude candleholder rake. I left him there. The room was large. I walked dejectedly, my feet bare from the fire having burned off my felt slippers, to another broad place among iron candelabra, where the moist good earth was black and seemingly clean, and there I lay down again, as I had before, not caring that the black-haired one had a very good view of me there, as I was more in front of him than even before.

"Do you know that Northern worship?" he asked, as

if nothing dreadful had happened. "Oh, that Thor is forever circling with his hammer, and the circle grows smaller and smaller, and beyond lies chaos, and we are here, doomed within the dwindling circle of warmth. Have you ever heard it? He was a pagan, made by renegade magicians who used him to murder their enemies. I am glad to be rid of him, but why do you cry?"

I didn't answer. This was beyond all hope, this horrid domed chamber of skulls, the myriad candles illuminating only remnants of death, and this being, this beautiful powerfully built black-haired being ruling amid all this horror and feeling nothing on the death of one who had served him, who was now a pile of smoldering stinking bones.

I imagined I was home. I was safe within my Master's bedchamber. We sat together. He read from a Latin text. It did not matter what the words were. All around us were the accouterments of civilization, sweet and pretty things, and the fabrics of the room had all been worked by human hands.

"Vain things," said the black-haired one. "Vain and foolish, but you'll come to see it. You are stronger than I reckoned. But then he was centuries old, your Maker, nobody even tells of a time when there wasn't Marius, the lone wolf, who abides no one in his territory, Marius, the destroyer of the young."

"I never knew him to destroy any but those who were evil," I said in a whisper.

"We are evil, aren't we? All of us are evil. So he destroyed us without compunction. He thought he was safe from us. He turned his back on us! He considered us not worthy of his attentions, and look, how he has lavished all his strength on a boy. But I must say you are a most beautiful boy."

There was a noise, an evil rustling, not unfamiliar. I smelled rats.

"Oh, yes, my children, the rats," he said. "They come to me. Do you want to see? Turn over and look up at me, if you will? Think no more on St. Francis, with his birds and squirrels and the wolf at his side. Think on Santino, with his rats."

I did look. I drew in my breath. I sat up in the dirt and stared at him. A great gray rat sat on his shoulder, its tiny whiskered snout just kissing his ear, its tail curling behind his head. Another rat had come to sit sedately, as if spellbound, in his lap. There were others gathered at his feet.

Seeming loath to move lest they startle, he carefully dipped his right hand into a bowl of dried bread crumbs. I caught the scent only now, mingled with that of the rats. He offered a handful of crumbs to the rat on his shoulder, who ate from it gratefully and with strange delicacy, and then he dropped some of the bread in his lap, where three rats came to feast at once.

"Do you think I love such things?" he said. He looked intently at me, his eyes widening with the emphasis on his words. His black hair was a dense tangled veil on his shoulders, his forehead very smooth and shining white in the candlelight.

"Do you think I love to live here in the bowels of the world," he asked sadly, "under the great city of Rome, where the earth seeps waste from the foul throng above, and have these, the vermin, as my familiars? Do you think I was never flesh and blood, or that, having undergone this change for the sake of Almighty God and His Divine Plan, I don't long for the life you lived with your greedy Master? Have I not eyes to see the brilliant colors which your Master spread over his canvases? Do I not like the sounds of ungodly music?" He gave a soft agonizing sigh.

"What has God made or ever suffered to be made that is distasteful in itself?" he continued. "Sin is not repulsive in itself; how absurd to think so. No one comes to love pain. We can only hope to endure it."

"Why all this?" I asked. I was sick unto vomiting, but I held it back. I breathed as deeply as I could to let all the smells of this horror chamber flood my lungs and cease to torment me.

I sat back, crossing my legs so that I could study him. I wiped the ashes out of my eye. "Why? Your themes are entirely familiar, but what is this realm of vampires in black monkly robes?"

"We are the Defenders of Truth," he said sincerely.

"Oh, who is not the defender of truth, for the love of Heaven," I said bitterly. "Look, the blood of your brother in Christ is stuck all over my hands! And you sit, the freakish blood-stuffed replicant of a human being staring on all this as if it were so much chitchat among the candles!"

"Ah, but you have a fiery tongue for one with such a sweet face," he said in cool wonder. "So pliant you seem with your soft brown eyes and dark autumnal red hair, but you are clever."

"Clever? You burnt my Master! You destroyed him. You burnt up his children! I am your prisoner here, am I not? What for? And you talk of the Lord Jesus Christ to me? You? You? Answer me, what is this morass of filth and fancy, molded out of clay and blessed candles!"

He laughed. His eyes crinkled at the edges, and his face was cheerful and sweet. His hair, for all its filth and tangles, kept its preternatural luster. How fine he would have been if freed from the dictates of this nightmare.

"Amadeo," he said. "We are the Children of Darkness," he explained patiently. "We vampires are made to be the scourge of man, as is pestilence. We are part of the trials and tribulations of this world; we drink blood, and we kill for the glory of God who would test his human creatures."

"Don't speak horrors." I put my hands over my ears. I cringed.

"Oh, but you know it's true," he insisted without raising his voice. "You know it as you see me in my robes and you look about my chamber. I am restrained for The Living Lord as were the monks of old before they learned to paint their walls with erotic paintings."

"You talk madness, and I don't know why you do it." I would not remember the Monastery of the Caves!

"I do it because I have found my purpose here and the purpose of God, and there is nothing Higher. Would you be damned and alone, and selfish and without purpose? Would you turn your back on a design so magnificent that not one tiny child is forgotten! Did you think you could live forever without the splendor of that great scheme, struggling to deny the handiwork of God in every beautiful thing which you coveted and made your own?"

I fell silent. Don't think on the old Russian saints. Wisely, he did not press. On the contrary, very softly, without the devilish lilt, he began to sing the Latin hymn . . .

Dies irae, dies illa
Solvet saeclum in favilla
Teste David cum Sibylla
Quantus tremor est futurus . . .

That day of wrath, that day will turn the earth to
  ashes.
As both David and Sybelle have foretold
How great a tremor there will be . . .

"And on that Day, that Final Day, we shall have duties for Him, we His Dark Angels shall take the Evil souls down into the inferno as is His Divine Will."

I looked up at him again. "And then the final plea of this hymn, that He have mercy on us, was His Passion not for us?"

I sang it softly in Latin:

Recordare, Jesu pie,
Quod sum causa tuae viae . . .

Remember, merciful Jesus,
That I was the cause of your way . . .

I pressed on, scarcely having the spirit for it, to fully acknowledge the horror. "What monk was there in the Monastery of my childhood who didn't hope one day to be with God? What do you say to me now, that we, the

Children of Darkness, serve Him with *no hope of ever being with Him*?"

He looked broken suddenly.

"Pray there is some secret that we don't know," he whispered. He looked off as if he were in fact praying. "How can He not love Satan when Satan has done so well? How can He not love us? I don't understand, but I am what I am, which is this, and you are the same." He looked at me, eyebrows rising gently again to under-score his wonder. "And we must serve Him. Otherwise we are lost."

He slipped from the stool and came down towards me, settling on the floor opposite me, cross-legged, and putting his long arm out to place his hand on my shoulder.

"Splendid being," I said, "and to think God made you as he made the boys you destroyed tonight, the per-fect bodies you rendered to the fire."

He was in deep distress. "Amadeo, take another name and come with us, be with us. We need you. And what will you do alone?"

"Tell me why you killed my Master."

He let go of me and let his hand fall in the lap made by his black robe stretched across his knees.

"It's forbidden to us to use our talents to dazzle mortals. It is forbidden us to trick them with our skills. It is forbidden us to seek the solace of their company. It is forbidden us to walk in the places of light."

Nothing in this surprised me.

"We are monks as pure at heart as those of Cluny," he said. "We make our Monasteries strict and holy, and we hunt and we kill to perfect the Garden of Our Lord as a Vale of Tears." He paused, and then making his voice all the more soft and wondering, he continued. "We are as the bees that sting, and the rats that steal the grain; we are as the Black Death come to take young or old, beautiful or ugly, that men and women shall tremble at the power of God."

He looked at me, imploring me for understanding.

"Cathedrals rise from dust," he said, "to show man wonder. And in the stones men carve the Danse Macabre to show that life is brief. We carry scythes in the army of the robed skeleton who is carved on a thousand doorways, a thousand walls. We are the followers of Death, whose cruel visage is drawn in a million tiny prayer books which the rich and the poor alike hold in their hands." His eyes were huge and dreamy. He looked about us at the grim domed cell in which we sat. I could see the candles in the black pupils of his eyes. His eyes closed for a moment, and then opened, clearer, more bright.

"Your Master knew these things," he said regretfully. "He knew. But he was of a pagan time, obdurate and angry, and refusing ever the grace of God. In you, he saw God's grace, because your soul is pure. You are young and tender and open like the moonflower to take the light of the night. You hate us now, but you will come to see."

"I don't know that I will ever see anything again," I said. "I'm cold and small and have no understanding now of feeling, of longing, even of hate. I don't hate you, when I should. I'm empty. I want to die."

"But it's God will when you die, Amadeo," he said. "Not your own." He stared hard at me, and I knew I couldn't hide from him any longer my recollection—the monks of Kiev, starving slowly in their earthen cells, saying they must take sustenance for it was God's will when they should die.

I tried to hide these things, I drew these tiny pictures to myself and locked them up. I thought of nothing. One word came to my tongue: horror. And then the thought that before this time I had been a fool.

Another came into the room. It was a female vampire. She entered through a wooden door, letting it close carefully behind her as a good nun might do, in order that no unnecessary noise be made. She came up to him and stood behind him.

Her full gray hair was tangled and filthy, as was his, and it too had formed a shapely veil of beauteous weight and density behind her shoulders. Her clothes were antique rags. She wore the low hip belt of women of olden times adorning a shapely dress that revealed her small waist and gently flaring hips, the courtly costume one sees graven on the stone figures of rich sarcophagi. Her eyes, like his, were huge as if to summon every precious particle of light in gloom. Her mouth was strong and full, and the fine bones of her cheeks and jaw shone well for the thin layer of silvery dust that covered her. Her neck and bosom were almost bare.

"Will he be one of us?" she asked. Her voice was so lovely, so comforting, that I felt I'd been touched by it. "I have prayed for him. I have heard him weeping inside though he makes no sound."

I looked away from her, bound to be disgusted by her, my enemy, who had slain those I loved.

"Yes," said Santino, the dark-haired one. "He'll be one of us, and he can be a leader. He has such strength. He slew Alfredo there, you see? Oh, it was wonderful to behold how he did it, with such rage and with such a baby's scowl on his face."

She looked beyond me, at the ruin of what that vampire had been, and I didn't know myself what was left. I didn't turn to look at it.

A deep bitter sorrow softened her expression. How beautiful she must have been in life; how beautiful still if the dust were taken away from her.

Her eyes shot to me suddenly, accusingly, and then became mild.

"Vain thoughts, my child," she said. "I don't live for looking glasses, as your Master did. I need no velvet or silks to serve my Lord. Ah, Santino, such a newborn thing he is, look at him." She spoke of me. "In centuries gone by I might have penned verses in honor of such beauty, that it should come to us to grace God's sooted fold, a lily in the dark he is, a fairy's child planted by moonlight in a milkmaid's cradle to thrall the world with his girlish gaze and manly whisper."

Her flattery enraged me, but I could not bear in this Hell to lose the sheer beauty of her voice, its deep sweetness. I didn't care what she said. And as I looked at her white face in which many a vein had become a ridge in stone, I knew she was far too old for my impetuous violence. Yet kill, yes, yank head from body, yes, and stab with candles, yes. I thought of these things with clenched teeth, and him, how I would dispatch him for he was not so old, not nearly by half with his olive skin, but these compulsions died like weeds sprung from my mind stung by a northern wind, the deep frozen wind of my will dying inside of me.

Ah, but they were beautiful.

"You will not renounce all beauty," she said kindly, having drunk up my thoughts perhaps, despite all my devices for concealing them. "You will see another variant of beauty—a harsh and variegated beauty—when you take life and see that marvelous corporeal design become a blazing web as you do suck it dry, and dying thoughts do fall on you like wailing veils to dim your eyes and make you but the school of those poor souls you hasten to glory or perdition—yes, beauty. You will see beauty in the stars that can forever be your comfort. And in the earth, yes, the earth itself, you will find a thousand shades of darkness. This will be your beauty. You do but forswear the brash colors of mankind and the defiant light of the rich and the vain."

"I forswear nothing," I said.

She smiled, her face filling with a warm and irresistible warmth, her huge long mat of white hair curling here and there in the ardent flicker of the candles.

She looked to Santino. "How well he understands the things we say," she said. "And yet he seems the naughty boy who mocks all things in ignorance."

"He knows, he knows," the other answered with surprising bitterness. He fed his rats. He looked at her and me. He seemed to muse and even to hum the old Gregorian chant again.

I heard others in the dark. And far away the drums still beat, but that was unendurable. I looked to the ceiling of this place, the blinded mouthless skulls that looked on all with limitless patience.

I looked at them, the seated figure of Santino brooding or lost in thought, and behind him and above him, her statuesque form in its ragged raiment, her gray hair parted in the middle, her face ornamented by the dust.

"Those Who Must Be Kept, child, who were they?" she asked suddenly.

Santino raised his right hand and made a weary gesture.

"Allesandra, of that he does not know. Be sure of it. Marius was too clever to tell him. And what of it, this old legend we've chased for countless years? Those Who Must Be Kept. If They are such that They must be kept, then They are no more, for Marius is no more to keep Them."

A tremor ran through me, a terror that I would break into uncontrollable weeping, that I should let them see this, no, an abomination. Marius no more . . .

Santino hastened to go on, as if in fear for me.

"God willed it. God has willed that all edifices should crumble, all texts be stolen or burnt, all eyewitnesses to mystery be destroyed. Think on it, Allesandra. Think. Time has plowed under all those words written in the hand of Matthew, Mark, Luke and John and Paul. Where is there one parchment scroll left which bears the signature of Aristotle? And Plato, would that we had one scrap he threw into the fire when feverishly working—?"

"What are those things to us, Santino?" she asked reprovingly, but her hand touched his head as she looked down. She smoothed his hair as though she were his Mother.

"I meant to say that it is the way of God," Santino said, "the way of His creation. Even what is writ in stone is washed away by time, and cities lie beneath the fire and ash of roaring mountains. I meant to say the Earth eats all, and now it's taken him, this legend, this Marius, this one so much older than any we ever knew by name, and with him go his precious secrets. So be it."

I locked my hands together to stop their trembling. I said nothing.

"There was a town in which I lived," he went on, murmuring. He held a fat black rat now in his arms, stroking its fur as if it were the prettiest of cats, and it with its tiny eye seemed unable to move, its tail a great curved scythe turned downward. "A lovely town it was, with high thick walls, and such a Fair each year; words can't describe where all the merchants showed their wares and all the villages both far and near sent young and old to buy, to sell, to dance, to feast . . . it seemed a perfect place! And yet the plague took it. The plague came, respecting no gate or wall or tower, invisible to the Lord's men, and to the Father in the field and the Mother in her kitchen garden. The plague took all, all it seemed except the most wicked. In my house they walled me up, with bloating corpses of my brothers and sisters. It was a vampire found me out, for foraging there he found no other blood to drink but mine. And there had been so many!"

"Do we not give up our mortal history for the love of God?" Allesandra asked but most carefully. Her hand worked on his hair and brushed it back from his forehead.

His eyes were huge with thought and memory, yet as he spoke again he looked at me, perhaps not even seeing me.

"There are no walls there now. It's gone to trees and blowing grass and piles of rubble. And in castles far away one finds the stones which once made up our lord's keep, our finest hard-paved street, our proudest houses. It is the very nature of this world that all things are devoured and time is a mouth as bloody as any other."

A silence fell. I could not stop my shivering. My body quaked. A moan broke from my lips. I looked from right to left and bowed my head, my hands tight to my neck to stop from screaming.

When I looked up again, I spoke.

"I won't serve you!" I whispered. "I see your game. I know your scriptures, your piety, your love of resignation! You're spiders with your dark and intricate webs, no more than that, and breed for blood is all you know, all you know round which to weave your tiresome snares, as wretched as the birds that make their nests in filth on marble casements. So spin your lies. I hate you. I will not serve you!"

How lovingly they both looked at me.

"Oh, poor child," Allesandra said with a sigh. "You have only just begun to suffer. Why must it be for pride's sake and not for God?"

"I curse you!"

Santino snapped his fingers. It was such a small gesture. But out of the shadows, through doorways like secretive dumb mouths in the mud walls, there came his servants, hooded, robed, as before. They gathered me up, securing my limbs, but I didn't struggle.

365

They dragged me to a cell of iron bars and earthen walls. And when I sought to dig my way out of it, my clawing fingers came upon iron-bound stone, and I could dig no more.

I lay down. I wept. I wept for my Master. I didn't care if anyone heard or mocked. I didn't care. I knew only loss and in that loss the very size of my love, and in knowing the size of love could somehow feel its splendor. I cried and cried. I turned and groveled in the earth. I clutched at it, and tore at it, and then lay still with only silent tears flowing.

Allesandra stood with her hands on the bars. "Poor child," she whispered. "I will be with you, always with you. You have only to call my name."

"And why is that? Why?" I called out, my voice echoing off the stony walls. "Answer me."

"In the very depths of Hell," she said, "do not demons love one another?"

An hour passed. The night was old.

I thirsted.

I burned with it. She knew it. I curled up on the floor, my head bowed, sitting back on my heels. I would die before I would drink blood again. But it was all that I could see, all that I could think of, all that I could want. Blood.

After the first night, I thought I would die of this thirst.

After the second, I thought I would perish screaming.

After the third, I only dreamed of it in weeping and in desperation, licking at my own blood tears on my fingertips.

After six nights of this when I could bear the thirst no longer, they brought a struggling victim to me.

Down the long black passage I smelled the blood. I smelled it before I saw their torchlight.

A great stinking muscular youth who was dragged towards my cell, who kicked at them and cursed them, growling and drooling like a madman, screaming at the very sight of the torch with which they bullied him, forcing him towards me.

I climbed to my feet, too weak almost for this effort, and I fell on him, fell on his succulent hot flesh and tore open his throat, laughing and weeping as I did it, as my mouth was choked with blood.

Roaring and stammering, he fell beneath me. The blood bubbled up out of the artery over lips and my thin fingers. How like bones they looked, my fingers. I drank and drank and drank until I could contain no more, and all the pain was gone from me, and all the despair was gone in the pure satisfaction of hunger, the pure greedy hateful selfish devouring of the blessed blood.

To this gluttonous, mindless, mannerless feast they left me.

Then falling aside, I felt my vision clear again in the dark. The walls around me sparkled once more with tiny bits of ore like a starry firmament. I looked and saw that the victim I had taken was Riccardo, my beloved Riccardo, my brilliant and goodhearted Riccardo—naked, wretchedly soiled, a fattened prisoner, kept all this while in some stinking earthen cell just for this.

I screamed.

I beat at the bars and bashed my head against them. My white-faced warders rushed to the bars and then backed away in fear and peered at me across the dark corridor. I fell down on my knees crying.

I grabbed up the corpse. "Riccardo, drink!" I bit into my tongue and spit the blood on his greasy staring face. "Riccardo!" But he was dead and empty, and they had gone, leaving him there to rot in this place with me, to rot beside me.

I began to sing *"Dies irae, dies illa"* and to laugh as I sang it.

Three nights later, screaming and cursing, I tore the reeking corpse of Riccardo limb from limb so I could hurl the pieces out of the cell. I could not endure it! I flung the bloated trunk at the bars again and again and fell down, sobbing, unable to drive my fist or foot into it to break its bulk. I crawled into the farthest corner to get away from it.

Allesandra came. "Child, what can I say to comfort you?" A bodiless whisper in the darkness.

But there was another figure there, Santino. Turning I saw by some errant light which only a vampire's eyes could gather that he put his finger to his lip and he shook his head, gently correcting her. "He must be alone now," Santino said.

"Blood!" I screamed. I flew at the bars, my arm stretched out so that both were affrighted and rushed away from me.

At the end of seven more nights, when I was starved to the point where even the scent of the blood didn't rouse me, they laid the victim—a small boy child of the streets crying for pity—directly in my arms.

"Oh, don't be afraid, don't," I whispered, sinking my teeth quickly into his neck. "Hmmmmm, trust in me," I whispered, savoring the blood, drinking it slowly, trying not to laugh with delight, my blood tears of relief falling down on his little face. "Oh, dream, dream sweet and pretty things. There are saints who will come; do you see them?"

Afterwards I lay back, satiated, and picking from the muddy ceiling over my head those infinitesimal stars of hard bright stone or flinty iron that lay embedded in the earth. I let my head roll to the side, away from the corpse of the poor child which I had arranged carefully, as for the shroud, against the wall behind me.

I saw a figure in my cell, a small figure. I saw its gauzy outline against the wall as it stood gazing at me. Another child? I rose up, aghast. No scent came from it. I turned and stared at the corpse. It lay as before. Yet there, against the far wall, was the very boy himself, small and wan and lost, looking at me.

"How is this?" I whispered.

But the wretched little thing couldn't speak. It could only stare. It was clothed in the very same white shift that its corpse wore, and its eyes were large and colorless and soft with musing.

A distant sound came into my hearing. It was of a shuffling step in the long catacomb that led to my little prison. This was no vampire's step. I drew up, my nostrils flaring ever so slightly as I tried to catch the scent of this being. Nothing changed in the damp musty air. Only the scent of death was the aroma of my cell, of the poor broken little body.

I fixed my eyes on the tenacious little spirit.

"Why do you linger here?" I asked it desperately in a whisper. "Why can I see you?"

It moved its little mouth as if it meant to speak, but it

only shook its head ever so slightly, piteously eloquent of its confusion.

The steps came on. And once again I struggled to catch the scent. But there was nothing, not even the dusty reek of a vampire's robes, only this, the approach of this shuffling sound. And finally there came to the bars the tall shadowy figure of a haggard woman.

I knew that she was dead. I knew. I knew she was as dead as the little one who hovered by the wall.

"Speak to me, please, oh, please, I beg you, I pray you, speak to me!" I cried out.

But neither phantom could look away from the other. The child with a quick soft tread hurried into the woman's arms, and she, turning, with her babe restored, began to fade even as her feet once again made the dry scraping sound on the hard mud floor which had first announced her.

"Look at me!" I begged in a low voice. "Just one glance."

She paused. There was almost nothing left of her. But she turned her head and the dim light of her eye fixed on me. Then soundlessly, totally, she vanished.

I lay back, and flung out my arm in careless despair and felt the child's corpse, still faintly warm beside me.

I did not always see their ghosts.

I did not seek to master the means of doing so.

They were no friends to me—it was a new curse— these spirits that would now and then collect about the scene of my bloody destruction. I saw no hope in their faces when they did pass through those moments of my wretchedness when the blood was warmest in me. No bright light of hope surrounded them. Was it starvation that had brought about this power?

I told no one about them. In that damned cell, that cursed place where my soul was broken week after week without so much as the comfort of an enclosing coffin, I feared them and then grew to hate them.

Only the great future would reveal to me that other vampires, in the main, never see them. Was it a mercy? I didn't know. But I get ahead of myself.

Let me return to that intolerable time, that crucible.

Some twenty weeks were passed in this misery.

I didn't even believe anymore that the bright and fantastical world of Venice had ever existed. And I knew my Master was dead. I knew it. I knew that all I loved was dead.

I was dead. Sometimes I dreamt I was home in Kiev in the Monastery of the Caves, a saint. Then I awoke to anguish.

When Santino and the gray-haired Allesandra came to me, they were gentle as ever, and Santino shed tears to see me as I was, and said:

"Come to me, come now, come study with me in earnest, come. Not even those as wretched as we should suffer as you suffer. Come to me."

I entrusted myself to his arms, I opened my lips to his, I bowed my head to press my face to his chest, and as I listened to his beating heart, I breathed deep, as if the very air had been denied me until that moment.

Allesandra laid her cool, soft hands so gently on me.

"Poor orphan child," she said. "Wandering child, oh, such a long road you've traveled to come to us."

And what a wonder it was that all they had done to me should seem but a thing we shared, a common and inevitable catastrophe.

SANTINO'S CELL.

I lay on the floor in the arms of Allesandra, who rocked me and stroked my hair.

"I want you to hunt with us tonight," said Santino. "You come with us, with Allesandra and with me. We won't let the others torment you. You are hungry. You are so very hungry, are you not?"

And so my tenure with the Children of Darkness began.

Night after night I did hunt in silence with my new companions, my new loved ones, my new Master and my new Mistress, and then I was ready to begin my new apprenticeship in earnest, and Santino, my teacher, with Allesandra to help him now and then, made me his own pupil, a great honor in the coven, or so the others were quick to tell me when they had the chance.

I learnt what Lestat has already written from what I revealed to him, the great laws.

One, that we were formed in Covens throughout the world, and each Coven would have its leader, and I was destined to be such a one, like unto the Superior of a convent, and that all matters of authority would be in my hands. I and I alone should determine when a new vampire should be made to join us; I and I alone would see to it that the transformation was made in the proper way.

Two, the Dark Gift, for that is what we called it, must

never be given to those who were not beautiful, for the enslaving of the beautiful with the Dark Blood was more pleasing to a Just God.

Three, that never should an ancient vampire make the new fledgling, for our powers increase with time and the power of the old ones is too great for the young. Witness the tragedy of myself, made by the last of the known Children of the Millennia, the great and terrible Marius. I had the strength of a demon in the body of a child.

Four, that no one among us can destroy another among us, save the coven leader, who must at any time be prepared to destroy the disobedient of his flock. That all vagabond vampires, belonging to no coven, must be destroyed by that leader on sight.

Five, no vampire must ever reveal his identity or his magical strengths to a mortal and thereafter be let to live. No vampire must ever write any words that reveal these secrets. Indeed no vampire's name was ever to be known in the mortal world, and any evidence of our existence which ever escaped into that realm must at all costs be eradicated, along with those who allowed such a terrible violation of God's will.

There were other things. There were rituals, there were incantations, there was a folklore of sorts.

"We do not enter churches, for God should strike us dead if we do," declared Santino. "We do not look upon the crucifix, and its mere presence on a chain about the neck of a victim is sufficient to save that mortal's life. We turn our eyes and fingers from the medals of the Virgin. We cower before the images of the saints.

"But we strike with a holy fire those who go unprotected. We feast when and where we will and with cruelty, and upon the innocent and upon those most blessed with beauty and riches. But we make no boast to the world of what we do, nor boast to one another.

"The great castles and courtrooms of the world are shut to us, for we must never, never, meddle in the destiny which Christ Our Lord had ordained for those made in His Image, any more than do the vermin, or the blazing fire, or the Black Death.

"We are a curse of the shadows; we are a secret. We are eternal.

"And when our work is done for Him, we gather without the comfort of riches or luxuries, in those places blessed by us underground for our slumber, and there with only fire and candles for light, we come together to say the prayers and sing the songs and dance, yes, dance about the fire, thereby to strengthen our will, thereby to share with our sisters and brothers our strength."

Six long months passed during which I studied these things, during which I ventured forth into the back alleys of Rome to hunt with the others, to gorge myself upon the abandoned of fate who fell so easily into my hands.

No more did I search the mind for a crime that justified my predatory feasting. No more did I practice the fine art of drinking without pain to the victim, no more did I shield the wretched mortal from the horror of my face, my desperate hands, my fangs.

One night, I awoke to find myself surrounded by my brothers. The gray-haired woman helped me from my coffin of lead and told me that I should come with them.

Out under the stars we went together. The bonfire had been built high, as it had been on the night my mortal brothers had died.

The air was cool and full of the scent of spring flowers. I could hear the nightingale singing. And far off the whisperings and murmurings of the great crowded city of Rome. I turned my eyes towards the city. I saw her seven hills covered over with soft flickering lights. I saw the clouds above, tinged with gold, as they bore down on these scattered and beautiful beacons, as if the darkness of the sky were full with child.

I saw the circle had formed around the fire. Two and three deep were the Children of Darkness. Santino, in a costly new robe of black velvet, ah, such a violation of our strict rubrics, came forward to kiss me on either cheek.

"We are sending you far away, to the north of Europe," he said, "to the city of Paris, where the Coven leader has gone, as we all go sooner or later, into the fire. His children wait for you. They have heard tales of you, of your gentleness and your piety and your beauty. You will be their leader and their saint."

My brothers one by one came to kiss me. My sisters, who were few in number, planted their kisses on my cheeks as well.

I said nothing. I stood quiet, listening still for the song of the birds in the nearby pines, my eyes drifting now and then to the lowering Heavens and wondering if the rain would come, the rain which I could smell, so clean and pure, the only cleansing water allowed to me now, the sweet Roman rain, gentle and warm.

"Do you take the solemn vow to lead the Coven in the Ways of Darkness as Satan would have it and his Lord and Creator, God, would have it?"

"I do."

"Do you vow to obey all orders sent to you from the Roman Coven?"

"I do . . ."

Words and words and words.

Wood was heaped on the fire. The drums had begun. The solemn tones.

I began to cry.

Then came the soft arms of Allesandra, the soft mass of her gray hair against my neck.

"I will go with you north, my child," she said.

I was overwhelmed with gratitude. I threw my arms around her, I held her hard cold body close to me, and I shook with sobs.

"Yes, dear, dear little one," she said. "I will stay with you. I am old and I will stay with you until it is time for me to go to God's Justice, as we all must."

"Then we dance in jubilation!" cried Santino. "Satan and Christ, brothers in the House of the Lord, we give you this perfected soul!"

He threw up his arms.

Allesandra stepped back from me, her eyes bright with tears. I could think of nothing but only my gratitude that she would be with me, that I would not make this awful terrible journey alone. With me, Allesandra, with me. Oh, Fool for Satan and the God Who made him!

She stood beside Santino, tall as he was, majestic as she too threw up her arms and swung her hair from side to side.

"Let the dancing begin!" she cried.

The drums became a thunder, the horns wailed, and the thump of the tambourines filled my ears.

A long low cry rose from the huge thick circle of

vampires, and all at once, locking hands, they began to dance.

I was pulled back into the chain they made about the raging bonfire. I was jerked from left to right as the figures turned this way, then that, then broke free and leapt spinning into the air.

I felt the wind on the back of my neck as I turned, as I leapt. I reached out with perfect accuracy to receive the hands on either side of me, then to sway to the right and to the left again.

Above, the silent clouds thickened, curled and sailed across the darkling sky. The rain came, its soft roar lost in the cries of the mad dancing figures, in the crackle of fire and the torrent of drums.

I heard it. I turned and leapt high into the air and received it, the silvery rain floating down to me like the blessing of the dark Heavens, the baptismal waters of the damned.

The music surged. A barbarous rhythm broke loose everywhere, the orderly chain of dancers forgotten. In rain and in the unquenchable blaze of the giant fire, the vampires threw out their arms, howling, writhing, their limbs constricting so that they stomped with backs bent, heels pounded into the earth, and then sprang free, arms outstretched, mouths open, hips churning as they whirled and leapt, and caught in raucous open-throated volume the hymn came again, *Dies irae, dies illa.* Oh, yes, oh, yes, day of woe, oh, day of fire!

Afterwards, when the rain came down solemnly and steadily, when the bonfire was no more but a black wreckage, when they all had gone off to hunt, when only a few milled the dark ground of the Sabbat, chanting their prayers in anguished delirium, I lay still, the rain washing me, as I put my face against the ground.

It seemed the monks were there from the old Monastery in Kiev. They laughed at me, but gently. They said, "Andrei, what made you think you could escape? Didn't you know that God had called you?"

"Get away from me, you are not here, and I am nowhere; I am lost in the dark wastes of a winter without end."

I tried to picture Him, His Holy Face. But there was only Allesandra, come to help me to my feet. Allesandra, who promised to tell me of dark times, long before Santino was made, when she had been given the Dark Gift in the forests of France to which we now would be going together.

"Oh Lord, Lord hear my prayer," I whispered. If I could but see the Holy Face.

But we were forbidden such things. We could never, never look upon His Image! Until the end of the world, we would work without that comfort. Hell is the absence of God.

What can I say in defense of myself now?

What can I say?

Others have told the tale, how for centuries I was the stalwart leader of the Paris Coven, how I lived out those years in ignorance and shadow, obeying old laws until there was no more any Santino or Roman Coven to send them to me, how in rags and quiet despair, I clung to the Old Faith and the Old Ways as others went into the fire to destroy themselves, or simply wandered away.

What can I say in defense of the convert and the saint that I became?

For three hundred years I was the vagabond angel child of Satan, I was his baby-faced killer, his lieutenant, his fool. Allesandra was always with me. When others perished or deserted, there was Allesandra who kept the faith. But it was my sin, it was my journey, it was my terrible folly, and I alone must carry the burden of it for as long as I exist.

THAT LAST MORNING in Rome, before I was to leave for the north, it was decided that my name must be changed.

Amadeo, containing the very word for God, was most unseemly for a Child of Darkness, especially one meant to lead the Paris Coven.

From various choices given me, Allesandra chose the name Armand.

So I became Armand.

PART II

The BRIDGE
of SIGHS

16

I REFUSE to discuss the past another moment. I don't like it. I don't care about it. How can I tell you about something that doesn't interest me? Is it supposed to interest you?

The problem is that too much has been written about my past already. But what if you haven't read those books? What if you haven't wallowed in The Vampire Lestat's florid descriptions of me and my alleged delusions and errors?

All right, all right. A little bit more, but only to bring me to New York, to the moment when I saw Veronica's Veil, so that you don't have to go back and read his books, so that my book will be enough.

All right. We must continue to cross this Bridge of Sighs.

For three hundred years, I was faithful to the Old Ways of Santino, even after Santino himself had disappeared. Understand, this vampire was by no means dead. He turned up in the modern era, quite healthy, strong, silent and without apology for the credos he had stuffed down my throat in the year 1500 before I was sent north to Paris.

I was mad during those times. Lead the Coven I did, and of its ceremonies, his fanciful dark litanies and bloody baptisms, I became the architect and the master.

My physical strength increased with each year, as is the case with all vampires, and drinking greedily from my victims, for it was the only pleasure of which I could dream, I fed my vampiric powers.

Spells I could make around those I killed, and choosing the beautiful, the promising, the most audacious and splendid for my feast, I nevertheless conveyed upon them fantastical visions to blunt their fear or suffering.

I was mad. Denied the places of light, the comfort of entering the smallest church, bent on perfection in the Dark Ways, I wandered as a dusty wraith through the blackest alleyways of Paris, turning her noblest poetry and music into a din by the wax of piety and bigotry by which I stopped my ears, blind to the soaring majesty of her cathedrals or palaces.

The Coven took all my love, with chatter in the dark of how we might best be Satan's saints, or whether a beautiful and bold poisoner should be offered our demonic pact and made one of us.

But sometimes I went from an acceptable madness to a state of which I alone knew the dangers. In my earthen cell in the secret catacombs beneath the great Paris Cemetery of Les Innocents where we made our lair, I dreamt night after night of one strange and meaningless thing: What had become of that fine little treasure my mortal Mother had given me? What had become of that strange artifact of Podil which she'd taken from the Ikon corner and put in my hands, that painted egg, that crimson painted egg with the star so beautifully painted on it? Now, where could it be? What had become of it? Had I not left it, wrapped thickly in fur in a golden coffin in which I'd once lodged, ah, had all that really ever taken place, that life I thought I recalled from a city of brilliant white-tiled palaces and glittering canals and a great sweet gray sea full of swift and graceful ships, plying their long oars in perfect unison as if they were living things, those ships, those beautifully painted ships, so often decked with flowers, and with the whitest sails, oh, that could not have been real, and to think, a golden chamber with a golden coffin in it, and this special treasure, this fragile and lovely thing, this painted egg, this brittle and perfect egg, whose painted covering locked inside to utter perfection a moist, mysterious concoction of living fluids—oh, what strange imaginings. But what had happened to it! Who had found it!

Somebody had.

Either that or it was still there, hidden far below a palazzo in that floating city, hidden in a waterproof dungeon built deep into the oozing earth beneath the waters of the lagoon. No, never. Not so, not there. Don't think of it. Don't think of profane hands getting that thing. And you know, you lying treacherous little soul, you never, never went back to any such place as the low city with the icy water in its streets, where your Father, a thing of myth and nonsense to be sure, drank wine from your hands and forgave you that you had gone to become a dark and strong winged bird, a bird of the night soaring higher even than the domes of Vladimir's City, as if someone had broken that egg, that meticulously and wondrously painted egg which your Mother so cherished as she gave it you, broken that egg with a vicious thumb, cracked right into it, and out of that rotten fluid, that stinking fluid, you had been born, the night bird, flying high over the smoking chimneys of Podil, over the domes of Vladimir's Town, higher and farther and farther away over the wild lands and over the world and into this dark wood, this deep and dark and endless forest from which you will never escape, this cold and comfortless wilderness of the hungry wolf and the chomping rat and the crawling worm and the screaming victim.

Allesandra would come. "Wake, Armand. Wake. You dream the sad dreams, the dreams that precede madness, you cannot leave me, my child, you cannot, I fear death more than I fear this and will not be alone, you cannot go into the fire, you cannot go and leave me here."

No. I couldn't. I did not have the passion for such a step. I did not have the hope for anything, even though no word of the Roman Coven had come in decades.

But there came an end to my long centuries of Satan's service.

Clad in red velvet it came, the very covering my old Master had so loved, the dream king, Marius. It came swaggering and camping through the lighted streets of Paris as though God had made it.

But it was a vampire child, the same as I, son of the seventeen hundreds, as they reckoned the time to be then, a blazing, brash, bumbling, laughing and teasing blood drinker in the guise of a young man, come to stomp out whatever sacred fire yet burnt in the cleft scar tissue of my soul and scatter the ashes.

It was The Vampire Lestat. It wasn't his fault. Had one of us been able to strike him down one night, break him apart with his own fancy sword and set him ablaze, we might have had a few more decades of our wretched delusions.

But nobody could. He was too damned strong for us.

Created by a powerful and ancient renegade, a legendary vampire by the name of Magnus, this Lestat, aged twenty in mortal years, an errant and penniless country aristocrat from the wild lands of Auvergne, who had thrown over custom and respectability and any hope of court ambitions, of which he had none anyway since he couldn't even read or write, and was too insulting to wait on any King or Queen, who became a wild blond-haired celebrity of the boulevard gutter theatricals, a lover of men and women, a laughing happy-go-lucky blindly ambitious self-loving genius of sorts, this Lestat, this blue-eyed and infinitely confident Lestat, was orphaned on the very night of his creation by the ancient monster who made him, bequeathed to him a fortune in a secret room in a crumbling medieval tower, and then went into the eternal comfort of the ever devouring flames.

This Lestat, knowing nothing of Old Covens and Old Ways, of soot covered gangsters who thrived under cemeteries and believed they had a right to brand him a heretic, a maverick and a bastard of the Dark Blood, went strutting about fashionable Paris, isolated and tormented by his supernatural endowments yet glorying in his new powers, dancing at the Tuileries with the most magnificently clad women, reveling in the joys of the ballet and the high court theater and roaming not only in the Places of Light, as we called them, but meandering mournfully in Notre Dame de Paris itself, right before the High Altar, without the lightning of God striking him where he stood.

He destroyed us. He destroyed me.

Allesandra, mad by then as most of the old ones were in those times, had one merry argument with him after I dutifully arrested him and dragged him to our underground Court to stand trial, and then she too went into the flames, leaving me with the obvious absurdity: that Our Ways were finished, our superstitions obviously laughable, our dusty black robes ludicrous, our penance and self-denial pointless, our beliefs that we served God and the Devil self-serving, naive and stupid, our organization as preposterous in the gay atheistic Parisian world of the Age of Reason as it might have seemed to my beloved Venetian Marius centuries before.

Lestat was the smasher, the laughing one, the pirate who, worshiping nothing and no one, soon left Europe to find his own safe and agreeable territory in the colony of New Orleans in the New World.

He had no comforting philosophy for me, the baby-faced deacon who had come forth out of the darkest prison, shorn of all belief, to put on the fashionable clothes of the age and walk once again on its high streets as I had done over three hundred years ago in Venice.

And my followers, those few whom I could not overpower and bitterly consign to the flames, how helplessly they blundered in their new freedom—free to pick the gold from the pockets of their victims and don their silks and their white-powdered wigs, and sit in marvelous astonishment before the glories of the painted stage, the lustrous harmony of a hundred violins, the antics of versifying actors.

What was to be our fate, as with dazzled eyes we made our way through crowded early evening boulevards, fancy mansions and grandly decorated ball-rooms?

In satin-lined boudoirs we fed, and against the damask cushions of gilded carriages. We bought fine coffins for ourselves, full of fancy carvings and pad-ded velvet, and were closeted for the night in gilded mahogany-paneled cellars.

What would have become of us, scattered, my chil-dren fearful of me, and I uncertain of when the fopperies and frenzy of the French City of Light might drive them to rash or hideously destructive antics?

It was Lestat who gave me the key, Lestat who gave me the place where I could lodge my crazed and pound-ing heart, where I could bring my followers together for some semblance of newfangled sanity.

Before leaving me stranded in the waste of my old ways, he bequeathed to me the very boulevard theater in which he had once been the young swain of the Com-media dell'Arte. All its human players were gone. Nothing remained but the elegant and inviting husk, with its stage of gaily painted backdrops and gilded proscenium arch, its velvet curtains and empty benches just waiting for a clamoring audience again. In it we found our safest refuge, so eager to hide behind the mask of greasepaint and glamour that flawlessly disguised our polished white skin and fantastical grace and dexterity.

Actors we became, a regular company of immortals bound together to perform cheerfully decadent pan-tomimes for mortal audiences who never suspected that we white-faced mummers were more monstrous than any monster we ever presented in our little farces or tragedies.

The Théâtre des Vampires was born.

And worthless shell that I was, dressed up like a human with less claim to that title than ever in all my years of failure, I became its mentor.

It was the least I could do for my orphans of the Old Faith, giddy and happy as they were in a gaudy and God-less world on the verge of political revolution.

Why I governed this palladian theater so long, why I remained year after long year with this Coven of sorts, I know not except that I needed it, needed it as surely as I'd ever needed Marius and our household in Venice, or Allesandra and the Coven beneath the Paris Cemetery of Les Innocents. I needed a place to turn my steps before sunrise where I knew others of my kind were safely at rest.

And I can say truthfully that my vampire followers needed me.

They needed to believe in my leadership, and when worst came to worst I did not fail them, exercising some restraint upon those careless immortals who now and then endangered us by public displays of supernatural power or extreme cruelty, and by managing with the arithmetical skill of an idiot savant our business affairs with the world.

Taxes, tickets, handbills, heating fuel, foot lamps, the fostering of ferocious fabulists, I managed it all.

And now and then, I took exquisite pride and plea-sure in it.

With the seasons we grew, as did our audiences,

crude benches giving way to velvet seats, and penny pantomimes to more poetical productions.

Many a night as I took my place alone in my velvet-curtained box, a gentleman of obvious means in the narrow trousers of the age, with fitted waistcoat of printed silk and close-cut coat of bright wool, my hair combed back beneath a black ribbon or finally trimmed above my high stiff white collar, I thought upon those lost centuries of rancid ritual and demonic dreams as one might think back on a long painful illness in a lightless room amid bitter medicines and pointless incantations. It could not have been real, all that, the ragged plague of predatory paupers that we were, singing of Satan in the rimy gloom.

And all the lives I'd lived, and worlds I'd known, seemed even less substantial.

What lurked beneath my fancy frills, behind my quiet unquestioning eyes? Who was I? Had I no remembrance of a warmer flame than that which gave its silvery glow to my faint smile at those who asked it of me? I remembered no one who had ever lived and breathed within my quietly moving form. A crucifix with painted blood, a saccharine Virgin on a prayer book page or made of pastel-painted bisque, what were these things but vulgar remnants of a coarse, unfathomable time when powers now dismissed had hovered in the chalice of gold, or blazed most fearfully inside a face above a glowing altar.

I knew nothing of such things. The crosses snatched from virgin necks were melted down to make my golden rings. And rosaries cast aside with other paste as thieving fingers, mine, tore off a victim's diamond buttons.

I developed in those eight decades of the Théâtre des Vampires—we weathered the Revolution with amazing resiliency, the public clamoring to our seemingly frivolous and morbid entertainments—and maintained, long after the theatre was gone, into the late twentieth century a silent, concealed nature, letting my childlike face deceive my adversaries, my would-be enemies (I rarely took them seriously) and my vampire slaves.

I was the worst of leaders, that is, the indifferent cold leader who strikes fear in the hearts of everyone but bothers to love no one, and I maintained the Théâtre des Vampires, as we called it well into the 1870s, when Lestat's child Louis came wandering into it, seeking the answers which his cocky insolent maker had never given him to the age-old questions: Where do we vampires come from? Who made us and for what?

Ah, but before I discourse on the coming of the famous and irresistible vampire Louis, and his small exquisite paramour, the vampire Claudia, let me relate one tiny incident that happened to me in the earlier years of the nineteenth century.

It may mean nothing; or perhaps it is the betrayal of another's secret existence. I don't know. I relate it only because it touches fancifully, if not certainly, upon one who has played a dramatic role in my tale.

I cannot mark the year of this little event. Let me say only that Chopin's lovely, dreamy piano music was well revered in Paris, that the novels of George Sand were the rage, and that women had already given up the slender lascivious gowns of the Empire to wear the huge heavy-skirted, small-waisted taffeta dresses in which they appear so often in old shining daguerreotypes.

The theatre was booming as one would say in modern parlance, and I, the manager, having grown tired of its performances, was wandering alone one night in the wooded land just beyond the glow of Paris, not far from a country house full of merry voices and blazing chandeliers.

It was there that I came upon another vampire.

I knew her immediately by her silence, lack of scent and the near divine grace with which she made her way through the wild brush, managing a full flowing cape and abundant skirt with small pale hands, her goal the nearby brilliantly lighted and beckoning windows.

She realized my presence almost as quickly as I sensed hers; quite alarming to me at my age and with my powers. She froze without turning her head.

Though the vicious vampire players of the theatre maintained their right to do away with mavericks or intruders among the Undead, I, the leader, after my years as deluded saint, did not give a damn for such things.

I meant the creature no harm, and, carelessly, I tossed out in a soft casual voice, speaking in French, a warning.

"Ravaged territory, my dear. No game unbespoken here. Make for a safer city before sunup."

No human ear could have heard this.

The creature made no reply, her taffeta hood drooping as she had obviously bowed her head. Then, turning, she revealed herself to me in the long shafts of golden light falling from the multipaned glass windows beyond her.

I knew this creature. I knew her face. I knew it.

And in a dreadful second—a fateful second—I perceived that she might not know me, not with my hair nightly clipped short for these times, not in these sombre trousers and dull coat, not in this tragic moment when I posed as a man, so utterly transformed from the lushly adorned child she'd known, she couldn't.

Why didn't I cry out? Bianca!

But I couldn't grasp it, couldn't believe in it, couldn't rouse my dulled heart to triumph in what my eyes told me to be true, that the exquisite oval face surrounded by its golden hair and taffeta hood was hers, most definitely, framed exactly as it might have been in those days, and it was she, she whose face had been etched into my fevered soul before and after any Dark Gift had ever been given me.

Bianca.

She was gone! For less than a second I saw her wide wary eyes, full of vampiric alarm, more urgent and menacing than any human could ever evince, and then the figure was vanished, disappeared from the wood, gone from the environs, gone from all the large rambling gardens that I searched, sluggishly, shaking my head, mumbling to myself, saying, No, couldn't be, no, of course, not. No.

I never saw her again.

I do not know at this very moment whether or not this creature was Bianca. But I believe in my soul now, now as I dictate this tale, I believe in a soul that is healed and no stranger to hope, that it was Bianca! I can picture her too perfectly as she turned on me in the wooded garden, and in that picture lies one last detail which confirms it for me—because on that night outside of Paris, she had in her blond hair pearls interwoven. Oh, how Bianca had loved pearls, and how she had loved to weave them in her hair. And I had seen them in the light of the country house, beneath the shadow of her hood, ropes of tiny pearls wound in her blond hair, and within that frame was the Florentine beauty I could never forget—as delicate in vampiric whiteness as it had been when filled with Fra Filippo Lippi's colors.

It did not hurt me then. It did not shake me. I was too pale of soul, too numbed, too used to seeing all things as figments in a series of unconnected dreams. Very likely, I could not allow myself to believe such a thing.

Only now do I pray it was she, my Bianca, and that someone, and you can guess very well who that might be, someone might tell me whether or not it was my darling courtesan.

Did some member of the hateful murderous Roman Coven, chasing her out into the Venetian night, fall under her spell so that he deserted his Dark Ways, and made her his lover forever? Or did my Master, surviving the horrid fire, as we know he did, seek her out for sustaining blood and bring her over into immortality to assist him in his recovery?

I cannot bring myself to ask Marius this question. Perhaps you will. And perhaps I prefer to hope that it was she, and not to hear denials that render it less likely.

I had to tell you this. I had to tell you. I think it was Bianca.

Let me return now to the Paris of the 1870s—some decades after—to the moment when the young New World vampire, Louis, came through my door, seeking so sadly the answers to the terrible questions of why we are here, and for what purpose.

How sad for Louis that he should put those questions to me. How sad for me.

Who could have scoffed more coldly than I at the whole idea of a redemptive framework for the creatures of the night who, once having been human, could never be absolved of fratricide, their feasting on human blood? I had known the dazzling, clever humanism of the Renaissance, the dark recrudescence of asceticism in the Roman Coven and the bleak cynicism of the Romantic era.

What did I have to tell this sweet-faced vampire, Louis, this all too human creation of the stronger and brasher Lestat, except that in the world Louis would find enough beauty to sustain him, and that in his soul he must find the courage to exist, if indeed it was his choice to go on living, without looking to images of God or the Devil to give him an artificial or short-lived peace.

I never imparted to Louis my own bitter history; I confessed to him the awful anguishing secret, however, that as of the year 1870, having existed for some four hundred years among the Undead, I knew of no blood drinker older than myself.

The very avowal brought me a crushing sense of loneliness, and when I looked into Louis's tortured face, when I followed his slim, delicate figure as it picked its way through the clutter and nineteenth-century Paris, I knew that this black-clad dark-haired gentleman, so lean, so finely sculpted, so sensitive in all his lineaments, was the alluring embodiment of the misery I felt.

He mourned the loss of grace of one human lifetime.

I mourned the loss of the grace of centuries. Amenable to the styles of the age which had shaped him—given him his flaring black frock coat, and fine waistcoat of white silk, his high priestly-looking collar and frills of immaculate linen—I fell in love with him hopelessly, and leaving the Théâtre des Vampires in ruins (he burnt it to the ground in a rage for a very good reason), I wandered the world with him until very late in this modern age.

Time eventually destroyed our love for one another. Time withered our gentle intimacy. Time devoured whatever conversation or pleasures we once agreeably shared.

One other horrible inescapable and unforgettable ingredient went into our destruction. Ah, I don't want to speak of it, but who among us is going to let me be silent on the matter of Claudia, the child vampire whom I am accused for all time by all of having destroyed?

Claudia. Who among us today for whom I dictate this narrative, who among the modern audience who reads these tales as palatable fiction does not have in mind a vibrant picture of her, the golden-curled child vampire made by Louis and Lestat one wicked and foolish night in New Orleans, the child vampire whose mind and soul became as immense as that of an immortal woman while her body remained that of a precious all too perfect painted bisque French bébé doll?

For the record, she was slain by my Coven of mad demon actors and actresses, for, when she surfaced at the Théâtre des Vampires with Louis as her mournful, guilt-ridden protector and lover, it became all too clear to too many that she had tried to murder her principal Maker, The Vampire Lestat. It was a crime punishable by death, the murdering of one's creator or the attempt at it, but she herself stood among the condemned the moment she became known to the Paris Coven, for she was a forbidden thing, a child immortal, too small, too fragile for all her charm and cunning to survive on her own. Ah, poor blasphemous and beauteous creature. Her soft monotone voice, issuing from diminutive and ever kissable lips, will haunt me forever.

But I did not bring about her execution. She died more horribly than anyone has ever imagined, and I have not the strength now to tell the tale. Let me say only that before she was shoved out into a brick-lined air well to await the death sentence of the god Phoebus, I tried to grant her fondest wish, that she should have the body of a woman, a fit shape for the tragic dimension of her soul.

Well, in my clumsy alchemy, slicing heads from bodies and stumbling to transplant one to another, I failed. Some night when I am drunk on the blood of many victims, and more accustomed than I am now to confession, I will recount it, my crude and sinister operations, conducted with a sorcerer's willfulness and a boy's blundering, and describe in grim and grotesque detail the writhing jerking catastrophe that rose from beneath my scalpel and my surgical needle and thread.

Let me say here, she was herself again, hideously wounded, a botched reassemblage of the angelic child she'd been before my attempts, when she was locked out in the brutal morning to meet her death with a clear mind. The fire of Heaven destroyed the awful unhealed evidence of my Satanic surgery as it turned her to a monument in ash. No evidence remained of her last hours within the torture chamber of my makeshift laboratory. No one need ever have known what I say now.

For many a year, she haunted me. I could not strike from my mind the faltering image of her girlish head and tumbling curls fixed awkwardly with gross black stitching to the flailing, faltering and falling body of a female vampire whose discarded head I'd thrown into the fire.

Ah, what a grand disaster was that, the child-headed monster woman unable to speak, dancing in a frenetic circle, the blood gurgling from her shuddering mouth, her eyes rolling, arms flapping like the broken bones of invisible wings.

It was a truth I vowed to conceal forever from Louis de Pointe du Lac and all whoever questioned me. Better let them think that I had condemned her without trying to effect her escape, both from the vampires of the theatre and from the wretched dilemma of her small, enticing, flat-chested and silken-skinned angelic form.

She was not fit for deliverance after the failure of my butchery; she was as a prisoner subjected to the cruelty of the rack who can only smile bitterly and dreamily as she is led, torn and miserable, to the final horror of the stake. She was as a hopeless patient, in the reeking antiseptic death cubicle of a modern hospital, freed at last from the hands of youthful and overzealous doctors, to give up the ghost on a white pillow alone.

Enough. I won't relive it.

I will not.

I never loved her. I didn't know how.

I carried out my schemes in chilling detachment and with fiendish pragmatism. Being condemned and therefore being nothing and no one, she was a perfect specimen for my whim. That was the horror of it, the secret horror which eclipsed any faith I might have pleaded later in the high-blown courage of my experiments. And so the secret remained with me, with Armand, who had witnessed centuries of unspeakable and refined cruelties, a story unfit for the tender ears of a desperate Louis, who could never have borne such descriptions of her degradation or suffering, and who did not truly, in his soul, survive her death, cruel as it was.

As for the others, my stupid cynical flock, who listened so lasciviously at my door to the screaming, who maybe guessed the extent of my failed wizardry, those vampires died by Louis's hand.

Indeed the entire theatre paid for his grief and his rage, and justly so perhaps.

I can make no judgment.

I did not love those decadent and cynical French mummers. Those I had loved, and those who I could love, were, save for Louis de Pointe du Lac, utterly beyond my grasp.

I must have Louis, that was my injunction. I knew no other. So I did not interfere when Louis incinerated the Coven and the infamous theatre, striking, at the risk of his own life, with flame and scythe at the very hour of dawn.

Why did he come away with me afterwards?

Why did he not abhor the one whom he blamed for Claudia's death? "You were their leader; you could have stopped them." He did say those words to me.

Why did we wander for so many years together, drifting like elegant phantoms in our lace and velvet cerements into the garish electric lights and electronic noise of the modern age?

He remained with me because he had to do it. It was the only way that he could go on existing, and for death he has never had the courage, and never will.

And so he endured after the loss of Claudia, just as I had endured through the dungeon centuries, and through the years of tawdry boulevard spectacle, but in time he did learn to be alone.

Louis, my companion, dried up of his own free will, rather like a beautiful rose skillfully dehydrated in sand so that it retains its proportions, nay, even its fragrance and even its tint. For all the blood he drank, he himself became dry, heartless, a stranger to himself and to me.

Understanding all too well the limits of my warped spirit, he forgot me long before he dismissed me, but I too had learnt from him.

For a short time, in awe of the world and confused by it, I too went on alone—perhaps for the first time really and truly alone.

But how long can any of us endure without another? For me at my darkest hours there had been the ancient nun of the Old Ways, Allesandra, or at least the babble of those who thought I was a little saint.

Why in this final decade of the twentieth century do we seek each other out if only for occasional words and exchanges of concern? Why are we here gathered in this old and dusty convent of so many brick-walled empty rooms to weep for The Vampire Lestat? Why have the very ancient among us come here to witness the evidence of his most recent and terrifying defeat?

We can't stand it, to be alone. We cannot bear it, any

more than the monks of old could bear it, men who though they had renounced all else for Christ's sake, nevertheless came together in congregations to be with one another, even as they enforced upon themselves the harsh rules of single solitary cells and unbroken silence. They couldn't bear to be alone.

We are too much men and women; we are yet formed in the image of the Creator, and what can we say of Him with any certainty except that He, whoever He may be—Christ, Yahweh, Allah—He made us, did He not, because even He in His Infinite Perfection could not bear to be alone.

In time I conceived another love naturally, a love for a mortal boy Daniel, to whom Louis had poured out his story, published under the absurd title *Interview with the Vampire*, whom I later made into a vampire for the same reasons that Marius had made me so long ago: the boy, who had been my faithful mortal companion, and only sometimes an intolerable nuisance, was about to die.

That is no mystery unto itself, the making of Daniel. Loneliness will always inevitably press us to such things. But I was a firm believer that those we make our-selves will always despise us for it. I cannot claim that I have never despised Marius, both for making me and never returning to me to assure me that he had survived the horrible fire created by the Roman Coven. I had sought Louis rather than create others. And having cre-ated Daniel I saw at last my fear realized within a short time.

Daniel, though alive and wandering, though civil and gentle, can no more stand my company than I can stand his. Equipped with my powerful blood, he can contend with any who should be foolish enough to interrupt his plans for an evening, a month or a year, but he cannot contend with my continuous company, and I cannot contend with his.

I turned Daniel from a morbid romantic into a true killer; I made real in his natural blood cells the horror that he so fancied he understood in mine. I pushed his face into the flesh of the first young innocent he had to slaughter for his inevitable thirst, and thereby fell off the pedestal on which he'd placed me in his demented, overimaginative, feverishly poetical and ever exuberant mortal mind.

But I had others around me when I lost Daniel, or rather when gaining Daniel as a fledgling, I lost him as a mortal lover and gradually began to let him go.

I had others because I had again, for reasons that I cannot explain to myself or anyone, made yet another Coven—another successor to the Paris Coven of Les Innocents, and the Théâtre des Vampires, and this was a swank, modern hiding place for the most ancient, the most learned, the most enduring of our kind. It was a honeycomb of luxurious chambers hidden in that most concealing of edifices—a modern resort hotel and shopping palace on an island off the coast of Miami, Florida, an island on which the lights never went out and the music never ceased to play, an island where men and women came by the thousands in small boats from the mainland to browse the expensive boutiques, or to make love in opulent, decadent, magnificent and always fashionable hotel suites and rooms.

"The Night Island," that was my creation, with its own copter pad and marina, its secret illegal gambling casinos, its mirror-lined gymnasiums and overheated swimming pools, its crystal fountains, its silver escalators, its emporium of dazzling consumables, its bars, taverns, lounges and theaters where I myself, decked out in smart velvet jackets, tight denim pants and heavy black glasses, hair clipped each night (for it grows back to its Renaissance length each day), could roam in peace and anonymity, swimming in the soft caressing murmurs of the mortals around me, searching out when thirst prompted it that one individual who truly wanted me, that one individual who for reasons of health or poverty or sanity or insanity wanted to be taken into the tentative and never overpowering arms of death and sucked free of all blood and all life.

I didn't go hungry. I dropped my victims in the deep warm clean waters of the Caribbean. I opened my doors to any of the Undead who would wipe their boots before entering. It was like the old days of Venice, with Bianca's palazzo open to all ladies and gentlemen, indeed, to all artists, poets, dreamers and schemers who dared to present themselves, had come again.

Well, they had not come again.

It took no bunch of black-robed tramps to disperse the Coven of The Night Island. Indeed those who were couched there for a short while simply wandered off on their own. Vampires do not really want the company of other vampires. They want the love of other immortals, yes, always, and they need it, and they need the deep bonds of loyalty which inevitably grow amongst those who refuse to become enemies. But they don't want the company.

And my splendid glass-walled drawing rooms on

The Night Island were soon empty, and I myself had long before that started to wander for weeks, even months on my own.

It is there still, The Night Island. It is there, and now and then I do go back, and I find there some lone immortal who has checked in, as we say in the modern age, to see how it goes with the rest of us, or with some other who might be visiting as well. The great enterprise I sold for a mortal fortune—but I maintain my ownership of the four-story villa (a private club: name, Il Villagio), with its deep secret underground crypts to which all of our kind are welcome to come.

All of our kind.

There are not so many. But let me tell you now who they were. Let me tell you now who has survived the centuries, who has resurfaced after hundreds of years of mysterious absence, who has come forward to be counted in the unwritten census of the modern Living Dead.

There is Lestat, first and foremost, the author of four books of his life and his adventures comprising everything you could ever possibly want to know about him and some of us. Lestat, ever the maverick and the laughing trickster. Six feet tall, a young man of twenty when made, with huge warm blue eyes and thick flashy blond hair, square of jaw, with a generous beautifully shaped mouth and skin darkened by a sojourn in the sun which would have killed a weaker vampire, a ladies' man, an Oscar Wildean fantasy, the glass of fashion, the most bold and disregarding dusty vagabond on occasion, loner, wanderer, heartbreaker and wise guy, dubbed the "Brat Prince" by my old Master—yes, imagine it, my

Marius, yes, my Marius, who did indeed survive the torches of the Roman Coven—dubbed by Marius the "Brat Prince," though in whose Court and by whose Divine Right and whose Royal Blood I should like to know. Lestat, stuffed with the blood of the most ancient of our kind, indeed the very blood of the Eve of our species, some five to seven thousand years the survivor of her Eden, a perfect horror who, emerging from the deceptive poetical title of Queen Akasha of Those Who Must Be Kept, almost destroyed the world.

Lestat, not a bad friend to have, and one for whom I would lay down my immortal life, one for whose love and companionship I have ofttimes begged, one whom I find maddening and fascinating and intolerably annoying, one without whom I cannot exist.

So much for him.

Louis de Pointe du Lac, already described above but always fun to envisage: slender, slightly less tall than Lestat, his maker, black of hair, gaunt and white of skin, with amazingly long and delicate fingers, and feet that do not make a sound. Louis, whose green eyes are soulful, the very mirror of patient misery, soft-voiced, very human, weak, having lived only two hundred years, unable to read minds, or to levitate, or to spellbind others except inadvertently, which can be hilarious, an immortal with whom mortals fall in love. Louis, an indiscriminate killer, because he cannot satisfy his thirst without killing, though he is too weak to risk the death of the victim in his arms, and because he has no pride or vanity which would lead him to a hierarchy of intended victims, and therefore takes those who cross his path, regardless of age, physical endowments, or blessings bestowed by nature or fate. Louis, a deadly and romantic vampire, the kind of night creature who hovers in the deep shadows at the Opera House to listen to Mozart's Queen of the Night give forth her piercing and irresistible song.

Louis, who has never vanished, who has always been known to others, who is easy to track and easy to abandon, Louis who will not make others after his tragic blunders with vampiric children, Louis who is past questing for God, for the Devil, for Truth or even for love.

Sweet, dusty Louis, reading Keats by the light of one candle. Louis standing in the rain on a slick deserted downtown street watching through the store window the brilliant young actor Leonardo DiCaprio as Shakespeare's Romeo kissing his tender and lovely Juliet (Claire Danes) on a television screen.

Gabrielle. She's around now. She was around on The Night Island. Everyone hates her. She is Lestat's Mother, and abandons him for centuries, and somehow doesn't manage to heed Lestat's periodic and inevitable frantic cries for help, which though she could not receive them, being his fledgling, could certainly learn of them from other vampiric minds which are on fire with the news round the world when Lestat is in trouble. Gabrielle, she looks just like him, except she's a woman, totally a woman, that is, sharper of feature, small-waisted, big-breasted, sweet-eyed in the most unnerving and dishonest fashion, gorgeous in a black ball gown with her hair free, more often dusty, genderless, sheathed in supple leather or belted khaki, a steady walker, and a vampire so cunning and cold that she has forgotten what it ever meant to be human or in pain. Indeed, I think she forgot overnight, if she ever knew it. She was in mortal life one of those creatures who always wondered what the others were carrying on about. Gabrielle, low-voiced, unintentionally vicious, glacial, forbidding, ungiving, a wanderer through snowy forests of the far north, a slayer of giant white bears and white tigers, an indifferent legend to untamed tribes, something more akin to a prehistoric reptile than a human. Beautiful, naturally, blond hair in a braid down her back, almost regal in a chocolate-colored leather safari jacket and a small droopy brimmed rain hat, a stalker, a quick killer, a pitiless and seemingly thoughtful but eternally secretive thing. Gabrielle, virtually useless to anyone but herself. Some night she'll say something to someone, I suppose.

Pandora, child of two millennia, consort to my own beloved Marius a thousand years before I was ever born. A goddess, made of bleeding marble, a powerful beauty out of the deepest and most ancient soul of Roman Italy, fierce with the moral fiber of the old Senatorial class of the greatest Empire the Western world has ever known. I don't know her. Her oval face shimmers beneath a mantle of rippling brown hair. She seems too beautiful to hurt anyone. She is tender-voiced, with innocent, imploring eyes, her flawless face instantly vulnerable and warm with empathy, a mystery. I don't know how Marius could ever have left her. In a short shift of filmy silk, with a snake bracelet on her bare arm, she is too ravishing for mortal males and the envy of females. In her longer concealing gowns, she moves as a wraith through the rooms around her as if they are not real to her, and she, the ghost of a dancer, seeks for some perfect setting that she alone can find. Her powers certainly rival those of Marius. She has drunk from the Eden fount, that is, the blood of Queen Akasha. She can kindle crisp dry objects into fire with the power of her mind, levitate and vanish in the dark sky, slay the young blood drinkers if they menace her, and yet she seems harmless, forever feminine though indifferent to gender, a wan and plaintive woman whom I want to close in my arms.

Santino, the old saint of Rome. He has wandered into the disasters of the modern era with all his beauty unblemished, still the big-shouldered, strong-chested one, olive skin paler now with the workings of the fierce magical blood, huge head of black curling hair often clipped each night at sunset for the sake of anonymity perhaps, unvain, perfectly dressed in black. He says nothing to anyone. He looks at me silently as if we never talked together of theology and mysticism, as if he never broke my happiness, burnt my youth to cinders, drove my Maker into century-long convalescence, divided me from all comfort. Perhaps he fancies us as fellow victims of a powerful intellectual morality, an infatuation with the concept of purpose, two lost ones, veterans of the same war.

At times he looks shrewd and even hateful. He knows plenty. He doesn't underestimate the powers of the ancient ones, who, eschewing the social invisibility of centuries past, now walk among us with perfect ease. When he looks at me, his black eyes are unflinching and passive. The shadow of his beard, fixed forever into the tiny cut-off dark hairs embedded in his skin, is beautiful as it always was. He is all in all conventionally virile, crisp white shirt open at the throat to show the portion of the thick curly black hair that covers his chest, a similar enticing black fleece covering the visible flesh of his arms at the wrists. He favors sleek but sturdy black coats lapeled in leather or fur, low-slung black cars that move at two hundred miles an hour, a golden cigarette lighter reeking of combustible fluid, which he lights over and over again just to peer into the flame. Where he actually lives, and when he will surface, nobody knows.

Santino. I know no more about him than that. We keep a gentlemanly distance from one another. I suspect his own suffering has been terrible; I do not seek to break the shiny black fashionable carapace of his demeanor to discover some raw bloody tragedy beneath it. To know Santino, there is always time.

Now let me describe for the most virginal of readers my Master, Marius, as he is now. So much time and experience divide us now that it is like a glacier between us, and we stare at each other across the glowing whiteness of that impassable waste, able only to speak in lulled and polite voices, so mannerly, the young creature I appear to be, too sweet-faced for casual belief, and he, ever the worldly sophisticate, the scholar of the moment, the philosopher of the century, ethicist of the millennium, historian for all time.

He walks tall as he always did, imperial still in his subdued twentieth-century fashion, carving his coats out of old velvet that they may give some faint clue of the magnificence that was once his nightly dress. On occasions now he clips the long flowing yellow hair which he wore so proudly in old Venice. He is ever quick of wit and tongue and eager for reasonable solutions, possessed of infinite patience and unquenchable curiosity and a refusal to give up on the fate of himself, or of us, or of this world. No knowledge can defeat him; tempered by fire and time, he is too strong for the horrors of technology or the spells of science. Neither microscopes nor computers shake his faith in the infinite, though his once solemn charges—Those Who Must Be Kept, who held such promise of redemptive meaning—have long been toppled from their archaic thrones.

I fear him. I don't know why. Perhaps I fear him because I could love him again, and loving him, I would come to need him, and needing him, I would come to learn from him, and learning from him, I would be again his faithful pupil in all things, only to discover that his patience for me is no substitute for the passion which long ago blazed in his eyes.

I need that passion! I need it. But enough of him. Two thousand years he had survived, slipping in and out of the very mainstream of human life without compunction, a great practitioner of the art of being human, carrying with him forever the grace and quiet dignity of the Augustan Age of seemingly invincible Rome, in which he was born.

There are others who are not here now with me, though they have been on The Night Island, and I will see them again. There are the ancient twins, Mekare and Maharet, custodians of the primal blood fount from which our life flows, the roots of the vine, so to speak, upon which we so stubbornly and beautifully bloom. They are our Queens of the Damned.

Then there is Jesse Reeves, a twentieth-century fledgling made by Maharet, the very eldest and therefore

a dazzling monster, unknown to me, but greatly admired. Bringing with her into the world of the Undead
an incomparable education in history, the paranormal,
philosophy and languages, she is the unknown. Will the
fire consume her, as it has so many others who, weary of
life, cannot accept immortality? Or will her twentieth-
century wit give her some radical and indestructible
armor for the inconceivable changes that we now know
must lie ahead?

Ah, there are others. There are wanderers. I can hear
their voices from time to time in the night. There are
those far away who know nothing of our traditions and
have styled us, in hostility to our writings and in amusement at our antics, "The Coven of the Articulate,"
strange "unregistered" beings of various ages, strengths,
attitudes, who sometimes seeing on a paperback rack a
copy of *The Vampire Lestat* tear it loose and grind the
small book to powder within their powerful and scornful
hands.

They may lend their wisdom or their wit to our unfolding chronicle in some unpredictable future. Who
knows?

For now, there is but one more player who must be
described before my tale can be advanced.

That one is you, David Talbot, whom I scarcely
know, you, who write with furious speed all the words
that come slowly tumbling from me as I watch you, mes-
merized on some level by the mere fact that these senti-
ments so long allowed to burn inside of me are now
recorded on the seemingly eternal page.

What are you, David Talbot—over seven decades
old in mortal education, a scholar, a deep and loving

soul? How can one tell? That which you were in life, wise in years, strengthened by routine calamity and deepened by the full four seasons of a man's span upon the Earth, was transported with all memory and learning intact into the splendid body of a younger man. And then that body, a precious chalice for the Grail of your very self, who knew so well the value of both elements, was then assaulted by your closest of friends, the loving monster, the vampire who would have you as his fellow traveler in eternity whether or not you gave him leave, our beloved Lestat.

I cannot imagine such a rape. I stand too far from all humanity, never having been a full man. In your face I see the vigor and beauty of the dark golden-skinned Anglo-Hindi whose body you enjoy, and in your eyes the calm and dangerously well-tempered soul of the old man.

Your hair is black and soft and handily trimmed below your ears. You dress with high vanity submitted to a staunch British sense of style. You look at me as though your curiosity will put me off guard, when nothing of the sort is true.

Hurt me and I'll destroy you. I don't care how strong you are, or what blood Lestat gave you. I know more than you do. Because I show you my pain, I do not of necessity love you. I do this for myself and for others, for the very idea of others, for any who would know, and for my mortals, those two I've gathered to me so recently, those two precious ones who have become the ticking clock of my capacity to go on.

Symphony for Sybelle. That might as well be the

name of this confession. And having done my best for Sybelle, I do my best for you as well.

Is this not enough of the past? Is this not enough prologue to the moment in New York when I saw Christ's Face in the Veil? There begins the final chapter of my life of late. There is nothing more to it. You have all the rest, and what must needs come now is but the brief harrowing account of what has brought me here.

Be my friend, David. I didn't mean to say such terrible things to you. My heart aches. I need you just to tell me that I may rush on. Help me with your experience. Isn't this enough? May I go on? I want to hear Sybelle's music. I want to talk of beloved rescuers. I can't measure the proportions of this story. I only know I am ready . . . I have reached the far side of The Bridge of Sighs.

Ah, but it's my decision, yes, and you wait to write what I will say.

Well, let me go now to the Veil.

Let me go now to the Face of Christ, as if I were walking uphill in the long-ago snowy winter in Podil, beneath the broken towers of Vladimir's City, to seek within the Monastery of the Caves the paint and the wood on which to see it take form before me: His Face. Christ, yes, the Redeemer, the Living Lord once more.

PART III

APPASSIONATA

17

I DIDN'T WANT to go to him. It was winter, and I was contented in London, haunting the theatres to see the plays of Shakespeare, and reading the plays and the sonnets the whole night long. I had no other thoughts just now but Shakespeare. Lestat had given him to me. And when I'd had a bellyful of despair, I'd opened the books and begun to read.

But Lestat was calling. Lestat was, or so he claimed, afraid.

I had to go. The last time he'd been in trouble, I hadn't been free to rush to his rescue. There is a story to that, but nothing as important as this one which I tell now.

Now I knew that my hard-won peace of mind might be shattered by the mere contact with him, but he wanted me to come, so I went.

I found him first in New York, though he didn't know it and he couldn't have led me into a worse snowstorm if he'd tried. He slew a mortal that night, a victim with whom he'd fallen in love, as was his custom of late—to pick these celebrities of high crimes and horrid murders—and to stalk them before the night of the feast.

So what did he want of me, I wondered. You were there, David. You could help him. Or so it seemed. Being his fledgling you hadn't heard his call directly, but he'd reached you somehow, and the two of you, such proper

gentlemen, came together to discuss in low, sophisticated whispers Lestat's latest fears.

When next I caught up with him he was in New Orleans. And he put it to me plain and simple. You were
there. The Devil had come to him in the guise of a man.
The Devil could change shapes, being at one moment
horrific and ghastly with webbed wings and hoofed feet;
and then next, the Devil could be an ordinary man. Lestat was wild with these stories. The Devil had offered
him a dreadful proposition, that he, Lestat, become the
Devil's helper in the service of God.

Do you remember how calmly I responded to his
story, his questions, his pleading for our advice? Oh, I
told him firmly it was madness to follow this spirit, to believe that any discarnate thing was bound to tell him the
truth.

But only now do you know the wounds he opened
with this strange and marvelous fable. So the Devil
would make him a hellish helper and thereby a servant
of God? I might have laughed outright, or wept, throwing it in his face that I had once believed myself a saint of
evil, shivering in rags as I stalked my victims in the
Parisian winter, all for the honor and glory of God.

But he knew all this. There was no need to wound
him further, to shift from him the limelight of his own
tale, which Lestat, being the bright star, must always
have.

Under moss-hung oaks we talked in civilized voices.
You and I begged him to be cautious. Naturally, he ignored all we said.

It was all mixed up with the entrancing mortal Dora,
who was living then in this very building, this old brick

convent, the daughter of the man Lestat had stalked and slain.

When he bound us to look out for her, I was angry, but only mildly so. I have fallen in love with mortals. I have those tales to tell. I am in love now with Sybelle and Benjamin, whom I call my children, and I had been a secret troubadour to other mortals in the dim past.

All right, he was in love with Dora, he'd laid his head on a mortal breast, he wanted the womb blood of her that would be no loss to her, he was smitten, crazed, goaded by the ghost of her Father and courted by the Prince of Evil Himself.

And she, what shall I say of her? That she possessed the power of a Rasputin behind the face of a nunnery postulant, when in fact she is a practiced theologian and not a mystic, a ranting raving leader, not a visionary, whose ecclesiastical ambitions would have dwarfed those of Saints Peter and Paul put together, and that of course, she is like any flower Lestat ever gathered from the Savage Garden of this world: a most fine and fetching little creature, a glorious specimen of God's Creation—with raven hair, a pouty mouth, cheeks of porcelain and the dashing limbs of a nymph.

Of course I knew the very moment that hc lcft this world. I felt it. I was in New York already, very near to him and aware that you were there as well. Neither of us meant to let him out of our sight if at all possible. Then came the moment when he vanished in the blizzard, when he was sucked out of the earthly atmosphere as if he'd never been there.

Being his fledgling you couldn't hear the perfect silence that descended when he vanished. You couldn't know how completely he'd been withdrawn from all things minuscule yet material which had once echoed with the beating of his heart.

I knew, and I think it was to distract us both that I proposed we go to the wounded mortal who must have been shattered by her Father's death at the hands of a blond-haired handsome blood-swilling monster who'd made her his confidant and a friend.

It was not difficult to help her in the short event-filled nights that followed, when horror was heaped upon horror, her Father's murder discovered, his sordid life at once made by media magic the madcap conversation of the wide world.

It seems a century ago, not merely so short a time, that we moved south to these rooms, her father's legacy of crucifixes and statues, of ikons which I handled so coolly as if I'd never loved such treasures at all.

It seems a century ago that I dressed decently for her, finding in some fashionable Fifth Avenue shop a shapely coat of old red velvet, a poet's shirt, as they call it now, of starched cotton and ample flopping lace, and to set this off, pegged-leg trousers of black wool and shiny boots that buckled at the ankle, all this the better to accompany her to identify her Father's severed head under the leeching fluorescent lights of some immense and over-crowded morgue.

One good thing about this final decade of the twentieth century is that a man of any age can wear his hair at any length.

It seems a century ago that I combed out mine, full and curly and clean for once, just for her.

It seems a century ago we stood so staunchly beside

her, indeed even held her, this long-necked, short-haired, spellbinding witchlet, in our very arms as she wept over the death of her Father and pelted us with feverish and maniacally intelligent and dispassionate questions about our sinister nature, as if a great crash course in the anatomy of the vampire could somehow close the cycle of horror threatening her wholesomeness and her sanity and somehow bring her wicked con-scienceless Father back.

No, it wasn't the return of Roger, actually, that she prayed for; she believed too totally in the omniscience and mercy of God. Besides, seeing a man's severed head is a bit of a shock, even if the head is frozen, and a dog had chomped on Roger a bit before he'd been discovered, and what with the strict "no touch" rules of modern forensics, he was—for me even—quite a sight. (I remember the coroner's assistant saying soulfully to me that I was awfully young to have to see such a thing. She thought I was Dora's little brother. What a sweet woman she was. Perhaps it's worth it to make a foray into the official mortal world once in a while in order to be called "a real trouper" instead of a Botticelli angel, which has become my tag line among the Undead.)

It was the return of Lestat Dora dreamed of. What else would ever allow her to break free of our enchantment but some final blessing from the crowned prince himself?

I stood at the dark glass windows of the high-rise apartment, looking out over the deep snows of Fifth Avenue, waiting and praying with her, wishing the great Earth were not so empty of my old enemy and thinking in my foolish heart that in time this mystery of his disappearance would be resolved, as were all miracles, with sadness and small losses, with no more than little revelations that would leave me as I had always been left since that long-ago night in Venice when my Master and I were divided forever, simply a little more clever at pretending that I was still alive.

I didn't fear for Lestat, not really. I had no hopes for his adventure, except that he would appear sooner or later and tell us some fantastical yarn. It would be regular Lestat talk, for nobody aggrandizes as he does his preposterous adventures. This is not to say that he hasn't switched bodies with a human. I know that he has. This is not to say that he didn't wake our fearsome goddess Mother, Akasha; I know that he did. This is not to say that he didn't smash my old superstitious Coven to bits and pieces in the garish years before the French Revolution. I've already told you so.

But it's the way he describes things that happen to him that maddens me, the way that he connects one incident to another as though all these random and grisly occurrences were in fact links in some significant chain. They are not. They are capers. And he knows it. But he must make a gutter theatrical out of stubbing his toe.

The James Bond of the Vampires, the Sam Spade of his own pages! A rock singer wailing on a mortal stage for all of two hours and, on the strength of that, retiring with a slew of recordings that feed him filthy lucre still from human agencies to this very night.

He has a knack for making tragedy of tribulation, and forgiving himself for anything and everything in every confessional paragraph he pens.

I can't fault him, really. I cannot help but hate it that

he lies now in a coma on the floor of his chapel here, staring into a self-contained silence, despite the fledglings that circle him—for precisely the same reason as I did, to see for themselves if the blood of Christ has transformed him somehow and he does not represent some magnificent manifestation of the miracle of the Transubstantiation. But I'll come to that soon enough.

I've ranted myself into a little corner. I know why I resent him so, and find it so soothing to hammer at his reputation, to beat upon his immensity with both my fists.

He has taught me too much. He has brought me to this very moment, here, where I stand dictating to you my past with a coherence and calm that would have been impossible before I came to his assistance with his precious Memnoch the Devil and his vulnerable little Dora.

Two hundred years ago he stripped me of illusions, lies, excuses, and thrust me on the Paris pavements naked to find my way back to a glory in the starlight that I had once known and too painfully lost.

But as we waited finally in the handsome high-rise apartment above St. Patrick's Cathedral, I had no idea how much more he could strip from me, and I hate him only because I cannot imagine my soul without him now, and, owing him all that I am and know, I can do nothing to make him wake from his frigid sleep.

But let me take things one at a time. What good is it to go back down now to the chapel here and lay my hands on him again and beg him to listen to me, when he lies as though all sense has truly left him and will never return.

I can't accept this. I won't. I've lost all patience; I've

lost the numbness that was my consolation. I find this moment intolerable—.

But I have to tell you things.

I have to tell you what happened when I saw the Veil, and when the sun struck me and, more wretchedly for me, what I saw when finally I reached Lestat and drew so close to him that I could drink his blood.

Yes, stay on course. I know now why he makes the chain. It isn't pride, is it? It's the necessity. The tale can't be told without one link being connected to the other, and we poor orphans of ticking time know no other means of measure but those of sequence. Dropped into the snowy blackness, into a world worse than a void, I reached for a chain, did I not? Oh, God, what I would have given in that awful descent to grasp the firmness of a metal chain!

He came back so suddenly—to you and Dora and me.

It was the third morning, and not long enough before dawn. I heard the doors slam far below us in the glass tower, and then that sound, that sound which gains in eerie volume each year, the beating of his heart.

Who was first to rise from the table? I was still with fear. He came too fast, and there were those wild fragrances whirling about him, of woodland and raw earth. He crashed through all barriers as if he were pursued by those who'd stolen him away, and yet there was no one behind him. He came alone into the apartment, slamming the door in his wake and then standing before us, more horrible than I could ever have imagined, more ruined than I had ever seen him in any of his former little defeats.

With absolute love Dora ran to him, and in a desperate need that was all too human he clutched at her so fiercely that I thought he would destroy her.

"You're safe now, darling," she cried, struggling so as to make him understand.

But we had only to look at him to know it wasn't finished, though we murmured the same hollow words in the face of what we beheld.

18

HE HAD COME from the maelstrom. One shoe was left to him, the other foot bare, his coat torn, his hair wild and snagged with thorns and dried leaves and bits of errant flowers.

In his arms, to his chest he clutched a flat bundle of folded cloth as if it carried the whole fate of the world embroidered on it.

But the worst, the very worst horror of all, was that one eye had been torn from his beautiful face, and the socket of vampiric lids puckered and shuddered, seeking to close, refusing to acknowledge this horrid disfigurement to the body rendered perfect for all time when he'd been made immortal.

I wanted to take him in my arms. I wanted to comfort him, to tell him wherever he'd gone and whatever had taken place, he was now safe again with us, but nothing could quiet him.

A deep exhaustion saved us all from the inevitable tale. We had to seek our dark corners away from the prying sun, we had to wait until the following night when he would come out to us and tell us what had happened.

Still clutching the bundle, refusing all help, he closeted himself up with his wound. I had no choice but to leave him.

As I sank down that morning into my own resting place, secure in clean modern darkness, I cried and cried like a child on account of the sight of him. Oh, why had I come to his aid? Why must I see him brought low like this when it had taken so many painful decades to cement my love for him forever?

Once before, a hundred years ago, he'd come stumbling into the Théâtre des Vampires on the trail of his renegade fledglings, sweet gentle Louis and the doomed child, and I hadn't pitied him then, his skin scored with scars from Claudia's foolish and clumsy attempt to kill him.

Loved him then, yes, I had, but this had been a bodily disaster which his evil blood would heal, and I knew from our old lore that in the healing he would gain even greater strength than serene time itself would have given him.

But what I'd seen now was a devastation of the soul in his anguished face, and the vision of the one blue eye, shining so vividly in his streaked and wretched face, had been unbearable.

I don't remember that we spoke, David. I remember only that the morning hastened us away, and if you cried too, I never heard you, I never thought to listen. As for the bundle he had carried in his arms, what could it have possibly been? I do not even think I thought of it.

The next night:

He came quietly into the parlor of the apartment as the darkness clambered down, starry for a few precious moments before the dreary descent of snow. He was washed and dressed, his torn and bleeding foot no doubt healed. He wore new shoes.

But nothing could lessen the grotesque picture of his torn face where the cuts of a claw or fingernails surrounded the gaping, puckering lids. Quietly he sat down.

He looked at me, and a faint charming smile brightened his face. "Don't fear for me, little devil Armand," he said. "Fear for all of us. I am nothing now. I am nothing."

In a low voice I whispered to him my plan. "Let me go down into the streets, let me steal from some mortal, some evil being who has wasted every physical gift that God ever gave, an eye for you! Let me put it here in the empty socket. Your blood will rush into it and make it see. You know. You saw this miracle once with the ancient one, Maharet, indeed, with a pair of mortal eyes swimming in her special blood, eyes that could see! I'll do it. It won't take me but a moment, and then I'll have the eye in my hand and be the doctor myself and place it here. Please."

He only shook his head. He kissed me quickly on the cheek.

"Why do you love me after all I've done to you?" he asked. There was no denying the beauty of his smooth poreless sun-darkened skin, and even as the dark slit of the empty socket seemed to peer at me with some secret power to relay its vision to his heart. He was handsome and radiant, a darkish ruddy glow coming from his face as though he'd seen some powerful mystery.

"Yes, but I have," he said, and now began to cry. "I have, and I must tell you everything. Believe me, as you believe what you saw last night, the wildflowers clinging still to my hair, the cuts—look, my hands, they heal but not fast enough—believe me."

You intervened then, David. "Tell us, Lestat. We would have waited here forever for you. Tell us. Where did this demon Memnoch take you?" How comforting and reasonable your voice sounded, just as it does now. I think you were made for this, for reasoning, and given to us, if I may speculate, to force us to see our catastrophes in the new light of modern conscience. But we can talk of those things for many nights hereafter.

Let me return to the scene, the three of us gathered in the black-lacquered Chinese chairs around the thick glass table, and Dora coming in, at once struck by the presence of him, of which her mortal senses hadn't given her a clue, a pretty picture with her short gleaming knavish black hair, cut high to show the fragile nape of her swanlike neck, her long supple body clad in a loose ungirdled gown of purple red tissue that folded itself about her small breasts and slender thighs exquisitely. Ah, what an angel of the Lord, this, I thought musing, this heiress of the druglord Father's severed head. She teaches doctrines with every step that would make the pagan gods of lust canonize her with glee.

About her pale sweet throat she wore a crucifix so tiny it seemed a gilded gnat suspended from a weightless chain of minuscule links woven by fairies. What are such holy objects now, tumbling on milky bosoms with such ease, but trinkets of the marketplace? My thoughts were merciless, but I was but an indifferent cataloger of her beauty. Her swelling breasts, their shadowy cleft quite visible against the simple stitching of her dark low-cut dress, told more of God and Divinity.

But her greatest adornment in these moments was the tearful and eager love for him, her lack of fear of his mutilated face, the grace of her white arms as she enclosed him again, so sure of herself and so grateful for the gentle yielding of his body in towards her. I was so thankful that she loved him.

"So the Prince of Lies had a tale to tell, did he?" she asked. She could not kill the quaver in her voice. "So he's taken you to his Hell and sent you back?" She took Lestat's face in her hands and turned it towards her. "Then tell us what it was, this Hell, tell us why we must be afraid. Tell us why you are afraid, but I think it's something far worse than fear that I see now in you."

He nodded his head to say that it was. He pushed back the Chinese chair, and wringing his hands he began to pace, the inevitable prelude to his tale telling.

"Listen to all I say, before you judge," he declared, fixing us now, the three who crowded about the table, an anxious little audience willing to do whatever he asked of us. His eyes lingered on you, David, you, the English scholar in your manly tweed, who in spite of love abundantly clear beheld him with a critical eye, ready to evaluate his words with a wisdom natural to you.

He began to talk. Hour by hour he talked. Hour by hour the words streamed out of him, heated and rushing and sometimes tumbling over one another so that he had to stop and catch his breath, but he never really paused, as he poured it out over the long night, this tale of his adventure.

Yes, Memnoch the Devil had taken him to Hell, but it was a Hell of Memnoch's devising, a Purgatorial place in which the souls of all who had ever lived were welcome to come of their own accord from the whirlwind of death which had inherited them. And in that Purgatorial Hell, confronted with all the deeds they'd ever done, they learnt the most hideous lesson of all, the endless consequences of every action ever committed by them. Murderer and Mother alike, vagrant children slaughtered in seeming innocence and soldiers bathed in blood from battlefields, all were admitted to this awful place of smoke and sulfurous fire, but only to see the gaping wounds in others made by their wrathful or unwitting hands, to plumb the depths of other souls and hearts which they had injured!

All horror was an illusion in this place, but the worst horror of all was the person of God Incarnate, who had allowed this Final School for those who would be worthy to enter His Paradise. And this too Lestat had seen, the Heaven glimpsed a million times by saints and deathbed victims, of ever blooming trees and flowers eternally sweet and endless crystal towers of happy, happy beings, shorn of all flesh and one at last with countless choirs of singing angels.

It was an old tale. It was too old. It had been told too many times, this tale—of Heaven with her open gates, and God Our Maker sending forth His endless light to those who climbed the mythic stairs to join the celestial court forever.

How many mortals waking from a near death sleep have struggled to describe these same wonders!

How many saints have claimed to have glimpsed this indescribable and eternal Eden?

And how cleverly this Devil Memnoch had laid out his case to plead for mortal compassion for his sin, that he and he alone had opposed a merciless and indifferent God, to beg that Deity to look down with compassionate eyes on a fleshly race of beings who had by means of their own selfless love managed to engender souls worthy of His interest?

This, then, was the fall of Lucifer like the Star of Morning from the sky—an angel begging for the Sons and Daughters of Men that they had now the countenances and hearts of angels.

"Give them Paradise, Lord, give it to them when they have learnt in my school how to love all that you have created."

Oh, a book has been filled with this adventure. *Memnoch the Devil* cannot be condensed here in these few unjust paragraphs.

But this was the sum of what fell on my ears as I sat in this chilly New York room, gazing now and then past Lestat's frantic, pacing figure at the white sky of ever falling snow, shutting out beneath his roaring narrative the rumble of the city far below, and struggling with the awful fear in myself that I must at the climax of his tale disappoint him. That I must remind him that he had done no more than shape the mystic journey of a thousand saints in a new and palatable fashion.

So it is a school that replaces those rings of eternal

fire which the poet Dante described in such degree as to sicken the reader, and even the tender Fra Angelico felt compelled to paint, where naked mortals bathed in flame were meant to suffer for eternity.

A school, a place of hope, a promise of redemption great enough perhaps to welcome even us, the Children of the Night, who counted murders among their sins as numerous as those of ancient Huns or Mongols.

Oh, this was very sweet, this picture of the life here-after, the horrors of the natural world laid off upon a wise but distant God, and the Devil's folly rendered with such keen intelligence.

Would that it were true, would that all the poems and paintings of the world were but a mirror of such hopeful splendor.

It might have saddened me; it might have broken me down to where I hung my head and couldn't look at him.

But a single incident from his tale, one which to him had been a passing encounter, loomed large for me be-yond all the rest and locked itself to my thoughts, so that as he went on and on, I couldn't banish this from my mind: that he, Lestat, had drunk the very blood of Christ on the road to Calvary. That he, Lestat, had spoken to this God Incarnate, who by His own will had walked towards this horrible Death on Golgotha. That he, Le-stat, a fearful and trembling witness had been made to stand in the narrow dusty streets of ancient Jerusalem to see Our Lord pass, and that this Lord, Our Living Lord, had, with the crossbeam of the crucifix strapped to His shoulders, offered His throat to Lestat, the chosen pupil.

Ah, such fancy, this madness, such fancy. I had not expected to be so hurt by anything in this tale. I had not expected this to make a burning in my chest, a tightness in my throat from which no words could escape. I had not wanted this. The only salvation of my wounded heart was to think how quaint and foolish it was that such a tableau—Jerusalem, the dusty street, the angry crowds, the bleeding God, now scourged and limping beneath His wooden weight—should include a legend old and sweet of a woman with a Veil outstretched to wipe the bloody Face of Christ in comfort, and thereby to receive for all time His Image.

It does not take a scholar, David, to know such saints were made by other saints in centuries to come as actors and actresses chosen for a Passion Play in a country village. Veronica! Veronica, whose very name means True Ikon.

And our hero, our Lestat, our Prometheus, with that Veil given him by the very hand of God, had fled this great and ghastly realm of Heaven and Hell and the Stations of the Cross, crying No! and I will not! and come back, breathless, running like a madman through the snows of New York, seeking only to be with us, turning his back on all of it.

My head swam. There was a war inside of me. I couldn't look at him.

On and on he went, going over it, talking again of the sapphiric Heavens and the angels' song, arguing with himself and with you and with Dora, and the conversation seemed like so much shattered glass. I couldn't bear it.

The Blood of Christ inside him? The Blood of Christ passing his lips, his unclean lips, his Undead lips, the Blood of Christ making of him a monstrous Ciborium? The Blood of Christ?

"Let me drink!" I cried out suddenly. "Lestat, let me drink, from you, let me drink your blood that has His blood inside it!" I couldn't believe my own earnestness, my own wild desperation. "Lestat, let me drink. Let me look for the blood with my tongue and my heart. Let me drink, please; you can't deny me that one moment of intimacy. And if it was Christ . . . if it was . . ." I couldn't finish it.

"Oh, mad and foolish child," he said. "All you'll know if you sink your teeth into me is what we learn from the visions we see with all our victims. You'll learn what I think I saw. You'll learn what I think was made known to me. You'll learn that my blood runs in my veins, which you know now. You'll learn that I believe it was Christ, but no more than that."

He shook his head in disappointment as he glared at me.

"No, I'll know," I said. I rose from the table, my hands quivering. "Lestat, give me this one embrace and I'll never ask another thing of you for all eternity. Let me put my lips to your throat, Lestat, let me test the tale, let me do it!"

"You break my heart, you little fool," he said with tears welling. "You always did."

"Don't judge me!" I cried.

He went on, speaking to me alone, from his mind as much as with his voice. I couldn't tell if anyone else there could even hear him. But I heard him. I would not forget a single word.

"And what if it was the Blood of God, Armand," he asked, "and not part and parcel of some titanic lie, what would you find in me? Go out to the early morning Mass and snatch your victims from those just come from the Communion Rail! What a pretty game that would be, Armand, to feed forever only on Holy Communicants! You can have your Blood of Christ from any one of them. I tell you, I do not believe these spirits, God, Memnoch, these liars; I tell you, I refuse! I wouldn't stay, I fled their damned school, I lost my eye as I battled them, they snatched it from me, wicked angels clawing at me when I ran away from them! You want the Blood of Christ, then go down now in the dark church to the fisherman's Mass and knock the sleepy priest aside from the Altar, if you will, and grab the Chalice from his consecrated hands. Go ahead, do it!

"Blood of Christ!" he continued, his face one great eye fixing me in its merciless beam. "If it was ever in me, this sacred blood, then my body has dissolved it and burnt it up like candle wax devours the wick. You know this. What's left of Christ in the belly of His faithful when they leave the church?"

"No," I said. "No, but we are not humans!" I whispered, seeking somehow in softness to drown out his angry vehemence. "Lestat, I'll know! It was His blood, not transubstantiated bread and wine! His blood, Lestat, and I'll know if it's inside of you. Oh, let me drink, I beg you. Let me drink so I can forget every damned thing you've told us, let me drink!"

I could scarcely keep myself from laying hands on him, from forcing him to my will, never mind his legendary strength, his gruesome temper. I'd lay hold of him and make him submit. I'd take the blood—.

But these thoughts were foolish and vain. His whole tale was foolish and vain, and yet I turned around, and in a fury I spit the words at him:

"Why didn't you accept? Why didn't you go with Memnoch if he could have taken you from this awful living Hell we share, why didn't you?"

"They let you escape," you said to him, David. You broke in, quieting me with a small pleading gesture of your left hand.

But I had no patience for analysis or inevitable interpretation. I couldn't get the image out of my mind, Our Bloody Lord, Our Lord with the crossbeam bound to His shoulders, and she, Veronica, this sweet figment with the Veil in her hands. Oh, how is it such a fantasy could get its hook so deep?

"Back away from me, all of you," he cried. "I have the Veil. I told you. Christ gave it to me. Veronica gave it to me. I took it with me out of Memnoch's Hell, when all his imps tried to take it from me."

I scarcely heard. Veil, the actual Veil, what trick is this? My head ached. The fisherman's Mass. If there was such a thing in St. Patrick's below, I wanted to go there. I was weary of this glass-walled tower room, cut off from the taste of the wind and the wild refreshing wetness of the snow.

Why did Lestat back up against the wall? What did he take out of his coat? The Veil! Some gaudy trick to seal this whole masterpiece of mayhem?

I looked up, my eyes roaming over the snowy night beyond the glass and only slowly finding their mark: the opened cloth which he held up in his hands, his own head bowed, the cloth revealed as reverently as it might have been by Veronica.

"My Lord!" I whispered. All the world was gone in curls of weightless sound and light. I saw Him there. "My Lord." I saw His Face, not painted, printed or otherwise daintily tricked into the tiny fibers of the fine white cloth, but blazing with a flame that would not consume the vehicle that bore the heat of it. My Lord, my Lord the Man, my Lord, my Christ, the Man with black and sharpened crown of thorns, and long twisted brown hair so fearfully clotted with blood, and great wondering dark eyes that stared straight at me, the sweet and vivid portals of the Soul of God, so radiant their immeasurable love that all poetry dies before it, and a soft and silken mouth of unquestioning and unjudging simplicity, open to take a silent and agonizing breath at the very moment the Veil had come to soothe this hideous suffering.

I wept. I clamped my hand to my mouth, but I couldn't stop my words.

"Oh, Christ, my tragic Christ!" I whispered. "Not made by human hands!" I cried out. "Not made by human hands!" How wretched my words, how feeble, how filled with sorrow. "This Man's Face, this Face of God and Man. He bleeds. For the love of Almighty God, look at it!"

But not a sound had come from me. I couldn't move. I couldn't breathe. I'd fallen down on my knees in my shock and in my helplessness. I never wanted to take my eyes from it. I never wanted anything anymore again ever. I wanted only to look at it. I wanted only to look at Him, and I saw Him, and I saw back, back over the centuries, back to His Face in the light of the earthen lamp burning in the house in Podil, His Face gazing at me from the panel between my quivering fingers amid the candles of the Scriptorium of the Monastery of the Caves, His Face as I had never seen it on those glorious walls of Venice or Florence where I had for so long and so desperately sought it.

His Face, His manly Face infused with the Divine, my tragic Lord gazing at me from my Mother's arms in the frozen sludge of the long-ago street of Podil, my loving Lord in bloody Majesty.

I didn't care what Dora said.

I didn't care that she screamed His Holy Name. I didn't care. I knew.

And as she declared her faith, as she snatched the Veil from Lestat's very hands and ran with it out of this apartment, I followed, moving after her and after the Veil—though in the sanctuary of my heart I never moved.

I never stirred.

A great stillness had overtaken my mind, and my limbs no longer mattered.

It did not matter that Lestat fought with her, and cautioned her that she must not believe this thing, and that the three of us stood on the steps of the Cathedral and that the snow fell like some splendid blessing from the invisible and fathomless Heavens.

It did not matter that the sun was soon to rise, a fiery silver ball beyond the canopy of melting clouds.

I could die now.

I had seen Him, and all the rest—the words of Memnoch and his fanciful God, the pleas of Lestat that we come away, that we hide ourselves before the morning devoured us all—it did not matter.

I could die now.

"Not made by human hands," I whispered.

A crowd gathered around us at the doors. The warm air came out of the church in a deep delicious gust. It didn't matter.

"The Veil, the Veil," they cried. They saw! They saw His Face.

Lestat's desperate imploring cries were dying away.

The morning came down in its thunderous white-hot light, rolling over roofs and curdling the night in a thousand glassy walls and slowly unleashing its monstrous glory.

"Bear witness," I said. I held up my open arms to the blinding light, this molten silvery death. "This sinner dies for Him! This sinner goes to Him."

Cast me into Hell, Oh Lord, if that is Your will. You have given me Heaven. You have shown me Your Face.

And Your Face was human.

19

I SHOT UPWARDS. The pain I felt was total, scalding away all will or power to choose momentum. An explosion inside me sent me skyward, right into the pearly snowy light which had come in a sudden flood, as it always does, from a threatening eye one moment, sending its endless rays over the cityscape, to a tidal wave of weightless molten illumination, rolling over all things great and small.

Higher and higher I went, spinning as if the force of the interior explosion would not stop its intensity, and in my horror I saw that my clothes had been burnt away, and a smoke veered off my limbs into the whirling wind.

I caught one full glimpse of my limbs, my naked out-stretched arms and splayed legs, silhouetted against the obliterating light. My flesh was burnt black already, shiny, sealed to the sinews of my body, collapsed to the intricate tangle of muscles which encased my bones.

The pain reached the zenith of what I could bear, but how can I explain that it didn't matter to me; I was on the way to my own death, and this seemingly endless torture was nothing, nothing. I could endure all things, even the burning in the eyes, the knowledge that they would soon melt or explode in this furnace of sunlight, and that all that I was would pass out of flesh.

Abruptly the scene changed. The roar of the wind was gone, my eyes were quiet and focused, and all around there arose a great familiar chorus of hymns. I stood at an altar, and as I looked up I beheld a church before me thronged with people, its painted columns rising like so many ornate tree trunks out of the wilderness of singing mouths and wondering eyes. Everywhere, to right and to left, I saw this immense and endless congregation. The church had no walls to bind it, and even the rising domes, decorated in the purest and most glittering gold with the hammered saints and angels, gave way to the great ever thinning and never ending blue sky.

Incense filled my nostrils. Around me, the tiny golden bells rang in unison, and with one riff of delicate melody tumbling fast upon another. The smoke burnt my eyes but so sweetly, as the fragrance of the incense filled my nostrils and made my eyes water, and my vision become one with all I tasted and touched and heard.

I threw out my arms, and I saw long golden-trimmed white sleeves covering them, falling back from wrists which were covered with the soft fleecy down of a man's natural hair. These were my hands, yes, but my hands years past the mortal point where life had been fixed in me. They were the hands of a man.

Out of my mouth there came a song, echoing loudly and singly over the congregation, and then their voices rose in answer, and once again I intoned my conviction, the conviction that had overcome me to the marrow of my bones:

"Christ is come. The Incarnation is begun in all things and in all men and women, and will go on forever!" It seemed a song of such perfection that the tears flowed from me, and as I bowed my head and clasped my hands I looked down to see the bread and the wine in front of me, the rounded loaf waiting to be blessed and broken and the wine in the golden chalice there to be transformed.

"This is the Body of Christ, and this is Blood shed for us now and before and forever, and in every moment of which we are alive!" I sang out. I laid my hands on the loaf and lifted it, and a great stream of light poured forth out of it, and the congregation gave forth their sweetest loudest hymn of praise.

In my hands I held the chalice. I held it high as the bells pealed from the towers, towers and towers that crowded near the towers of this grand church, stretching for miles in all directions, the whole world having become this great and glorious wilderness of churches, and here beside me the little golden bells chimed.

Once again came the gusts of incense. Setting down the chalice I looked at the sea of faces stretching before me. I turned my head from left to right, and then I looked Heavenward at the disappearing mosaics which became one with the rising, roiling white clouds.

I saw gold domes beneath Heaven.

I saw the endless rooftops of Podil.

I knew it was Vladimir's City in all its glory, and that I stood in the great sanctuary of Santa Sofia, all screens having been taken away that would have divided me from the people, and all those other churches which had been but ruins in my long-ago dim childhood were now restored to magnificence, and the golden domes of Kiev drank the light of the sun and gave it back with the power of a million planets basking eternal in the fire of a million stars.

"My Lord, my God!" I cried out. I looked down at the embroidered splendor of my vestments, the green satin and its threads of pure metallic gold.

On either side of me stood my brothers in Christ, bearded, eyes glowing as they assisted me, as they sang the hymns which I sang, as our voices mingled, pressing on from anthem to anthem in notes that I could almost see rising before me to the airy firmament above.

"Give it to them! Give it to them because they are hungry," I cried. I broke the loaf of bread in my hands. I broke it into halves, and then into quarters, and tore these hastily into small morsels which crowded the shining golden plate.

En masse, the congregation mounted the steps, tender pink little hands reaching for the morsels, which I gave out as fast as I could, morsel after morsel, not a crumb spilling, the bread divided among dozens, and then scores, and then hundreds, as they pressed forward, the newcomers barely allowing those who had been fed to make their way back.

On and on they came. But the hymns did not cease. Voices, muted at the altar, silenced as the bread was devoured, soon burst forth loud and jubilant again.

The bread was eternal.

I tore its soft thick crust again and again and put it into the outstretched palms, the gracefully cupped fingers.

"Take it, take the Body of Christ!" I said.

Dark wavering shadowy forms rose around me, rising up out of the gleaming gold and silver floor. They were trunks of trees, and their limbs arched upward and then down towards me, and leaves and berries fell from these branches, down onto the altar, onto the golden plate and onto the sacred bread now in a great mass of fragments.

"Gather them up!" I cried. I picked up the soft green leaves and the fragrant acorns and I gave these too to the eager hands. I looked down and I saw grain pouring through my fingers, grain which I offered to opened lips, grain which I poured into open mouths.

The air was thick with the soundless falling of the green leaves, so much so that the soft brilliant shade of green tinted all around it, broken suddenly everywhere by the flight of tiny birds. A million sparrows flushed Heavenward. A million finches soared, the brilliant sun flitting on their tiny outstretched wings.

"Forever, ongoing, always in every cell and every atom," I prayed. "The Incarnation," I said. "And the Lord has dwelt among us." My words rang out again as if a roof covered us, a roof that could echo my song, though our roof was now the roofless sky alone.

The crowd pressed in. They surrounded the altar. My brothers had slipped away, thousands of hands tugging gently at their vestments, pulling them back from the table of God. All around me there pressed these hungry ones who took the bread as I gave it, who took the grain, who took the acorns by the handful, who took even the tender green leaves.

There stood my Mother beside me, my beautiful and sad-faced Mother, a fine embroidered headdress gracing her thick gray hair, with her wrinkled little eyes fastened on me, and in her trembling hands, her dried and fearful fingers, she held the most splendid of offerings, the painted eggs! Red and blue, and yellow and golden, and decorated with bands of diamonds and chains of the flowers of the field, the eggs shimmered in their lacquered splendor as if they were giant polished jewels.

And there in the very center of her offering, this offering which she held up with shivering wrinkled arms, there lay the very egg which she had once so long ago entrusted to me, the light, raw egg so gorgeously decorated in brilliant ruby red with the star of gold in the very center of the framed oval, this precious egg which had surely been her finest creation, the finest achievement of her hours with the burning wax and boiling dye.

It wasn't lost. It had never been lost. It was there. But something was happening. I could hear it. Even under the great swelling song of the multitudes I could hear it, the tiny sound inside the egg, the tiny fluttering sound, the tiny cry.

"Mother," I said. I took it. I held it in both hands and brought my thumbs down against the brittle shell.

"No, my son!" she cried. She wailed. "No, no, my son, no!"

But it was too late. The lacquered shell was smashed beneath my thumbs and out of its fragments had risen a bird, a beautiful and full-grown bird, a bird of snow-white wings and tiny yellow beak and brilliant black eyes like bits of jet.

A long full sigh came out of me.

Out of the egg, it rose, unfolding its perfectly feathered white wings, its tiny beak open in a sudden shrill cry. Up it flew, this bird, freed of the broken red shell, up and up, over the heads of the congregation, and up through the soft swirling rain of the green leaves and fluttering sparrows, up through the glorious clamour of the pealing bells, it flew.

The bells of the towers rang out so loud that they shook the swirling leaves in the atmosphere, so loud that the soaring columns quivered, that the crowd rocked and sang all the more heartily as if to be in perfect unison with the great resounding golden-throated peals.

The bird was gone. The bird was free.

"Christ is born," I whispered. "Christ is risen. Christ is in Heaven and on Earth. Christ is with us."

But no one could hear my voice, my private voice, and what did it matter, for all the world sung the same song?

A hand clutched me. Rudely, meanly, it tore at my white sleeve. I turned. I drew in my breath to scream and froze in terror.

A man, come out of nowhere, stood beside me, so close that our faces almost touched. He glared down at me. I knew his red hair and beard, his fierce and impious blue eyes. I knew he was my Father, but he was not my Father but some horrific and powerful presence infused into my Father's visage, and there, planted beside me, a colossus beside me, glaring down at me, mocking me by his power and his height.

He reached out and slammed the back of his hand against the golden chalice. It wobbled and fell, the consecrated wine staining the morsels of bread, staining the altar cloth of woven gold.

"But you can't!" I cried. "Look what you've done!" Could nobody hear me over the singing? Could no one hear me above the peal of the bells?

I was alone.

I stood in a modern room. I stood beneath a white plaster ceiling. I stood in a domestic room.

I was myself, a smallish man figure with my old tousled shoulder-length curls and the purple-red coat of velvet and the ruff of layered white lace. I leant against the wall. Stunned and still, I leant there, knowing only that every particle of this place, every particle of me, was as solid and real as it had been a split second before.

The carpet beneath my feet was as real as the leaves which had fallen like snowflakes throughout the immense Cathedral of Santa Sofia, and my hands, my hairless boyish hands, were as real as the hands of the priest I'd been a moment before, who had broken the bread.

A terrible sob rose in my throat, a terrible cry that I myself could not bear to hear. My breath would stop if I didn't release it, and this body, damned or sacred, mortal or immortal, pure or corrupt, would surely burst.

But a music comforted me. A music slowly articulated itself, clean and fine, and wholly unlike the great seamless and magnificent chorus which I had only just heard.

Out of the silence there leapt these perfectly formed and discrete notes, this multitude of cascading sounds that seemed to speak with crispness and directness, as if in beautiful defiance of the inundation of sound which I had so loved.

Oh, to think that ten fingers alone could draw these sounds from a wooden instrument in which the hammers, with a dogged rigid motion, would strike upon a bronze harp of tautly stretched strings.

I knew it, I knew this song, I knew the piano Sonata, and had loved it in passing, and now its fury paralyzed me. *Appassionata*. Up and down the notes rang in gorgeous throbbing arpeggios, thundering downward to rumble in a staccato drumming, only to rise and race again. On and on went the sprightly melody, eloquent, celebratory and utterly human, demanding to be felt as well as heard, demanding to be followed in every intricate twist and turn.

Appassionata.

In the furious torrent of notes, I heard the resounding echo of the wood of the piano; I heard the vibration of its giant taut bronze harp. I heard the sizzling throb of its multitudinous strings. Oh, yes, on, and on, and on, and on, and on, louder, harder, ever pure and ever perfect, ringing out and wrung back as if a note could be a whip. How can human hands make this enchantment, how can they pound out of these ivory keys this deluge, this thrashing, thundering beauty?

It stopped. So great was my agony I could only shut my eyes and moan, moan for the loss of those racing crystalline notes, moan for the loss of this pristine sharpness, this wordless sound that had nevertheless spoken to me, begged me to bear witness, begged me to share and understand another's intense and utterly demanding furor.

A scream jolted me. I opened my eyes. The room around me was large and jammed with rich and random contents, framed paintings to the ceiling, flowered carpets running rampant beneath the curly legs of modern chairs and tables, and there the piano, the great piano out of which had come this sound, shining in the very middle of this mayhem, with its long strip of grinning white keys, such a triumph of the heart, the soul, the mind.

Before me on the floor a boy knelt praying, an Arab boy of glossy close-cropped curls and a small perfectly fitted djellaba, that is, a cotton desert robe. His eyes were shut, his round little face pointed upwards, though he didn't see me, his black eyebrows knit and his lips moving frantically, the words tumbling in Arabic:

"Oh, come some demon, some angel and stop him, oh, come something out of the darkness I care not what, something of power and vengeance, I care not what, come, come out of the light and out of the will of the gods who won't stand to see the oppression of the wicked. Stop him before he kills my Sybelle. Stop him, this is Benjamin, son of Abdulla, who calls upon you, take my soul in forfeit, take my life, but come, come, that which is stronger than me and save my Sybelle."

"Silence!" I shouted. I was out of breath. My face was wet. My lips were shuddering uncontrollably. "What do you want, tell me?"

He looked at me. He saw me. His round little Byzantine face might have come wonder-struck from the church wall, but he was here and real and he saw me and I was what he wanted to see.

"Look, you angel!" he shouted, his youthful voice sharpened with its Arab accent. "Can't you see with your big beautiful eyes!"

I saw.

The whole reality of it came down at once. She, the young woman, Sybelle, was fighting to cling to the piano, not to be snatched off the bench, her hands out struggling to reach the keys, her mouth shut, and a terrible groan pushing up against her sealed lips, her yellow hair flying about her shoulders. And the man who shook her, who pulled at her, who screamed at her, suddenly dealing her one fine blow with his fist that sent her over backwards, falling off the piano bench so that a scream escaped from her and she fell over herself, an ungainly tangle of limbs on the carpeted floor.

"*Appassionata, Appassionata,*" he growled at her, a bear of a creature in his megalomaniacal temper. "I won't listen to it, I will not, I will not, you will not do this to me, to my life. It's my life!" He roared like a bull. "I won't let you go on!"

The boy leapt up and grabbed me. He clutched at my wrists and when I shook him off, staring at him in bafflement, he clutched my velvet cuffs.

"Stop him, angel. Stop him, devil! He cannot beat her anymore. He will kill her. Stop him, devil, stop him, she is good!"

She crawled to her knees, her hair a shredded veil concealing her face. A great smear of dried blood covered the side of her narrow waist, a stain sunk deep into the flowered fabric.

Incensed, I watched as the man withdrew. Tall, his head shaven, his eyes bulging, he put his hands to his ears, and he cursed her: "Mad stupid bitch, mad mad selfish bitch. Do I have no life? Do I have no justice? Do I have no dreams?"

But she had flung her hands on the keys again. She was racing right into the Second Movement of the *Appassionata* as though she had never been interrupted. Her hands beat on the keys. One furious volley of notes after another rose, as if written for no other purpose than to answer him, to defy him, as if to cry out, I will not stop, I will not stop—.

I saw what was to happen. He turned around and glared at her, but it was only to let the rage rise to its full power, his eyes wide, his mouth twisted in anguish. A lethal smile formed on his lips.

Back and forth she rocked on the piano bench, her hair flying, her face lifted, her mind having no need to see the keys she struck, to plot the course of her hands that raced from right to left, that never lost control of the torrent.

Out of her sealed lips there came a low humming, a grinding humming right in tune with the melodies that gushed from the keys. She arched her back and lowered her head, her hair falling down on the backs of her racing hands. On she went, on into thunder, on into certainty, on into refusal, on into defiance, on into affirmation, yes, yes, yes, yes, yes.

The man made his move for her.

The frantic boy, leaving me in desperation, darted to come between them, and the man slammed him aside with such fury that the boy was knocked flat and sprawling on the floor.

But before the man's hands could reach her shoulders, before he could so much as touch her—and she went now into the First Movement again, ah, ah aaaah! the *Appassionata* all over again in all its power—I had hold of him, and spun him round to face me.

"Kill her, will you?" I whispered. "Well, we shall see."

"Yes!" he cried out, face sweating, protuberant eyes glistening. "Kill her! She's vexed me to utter madness, that's what she's done, and she'll die!" Too incensed even to question my presence, he tried to push me aside, his sights fixed already once again on her. "Damn you, Sybelle, stop that music, stop it!"

Her melody and chords were in the mode of thunder again. Flinging her hair from side to side, she charged onward.

I forced him backwards, my left hand catching his shoulder, my right pushing his chin up out of my way as I nuzzled in against his throat, tore it open and let the blood come into my mouth. It was scalding and rich and full of his hatred, full of bitterness, full of his blasted dreams and vengeful fancies.

Oh, the heat of it. I took it in in deep draughts, seeing it all, how he had loved her, nourished her, she his talented sister, he the clever, vicious-tongued and tone-deaf brother, guiding her towards the pinnacle of his precious and refined universe, until a common tragedy had broken her ascent and left her mad, turning from him, from memory, from ambition, locked forever in mourning for the victims of that tragedy, their loving and applauding parents, struck down on a winding road through a dark and distant valley in the very nights before her greatest triumph, her debut as full-fledged genius of the piano for all the wide world.

I saw their car rattling and plummeting through the darkness. I heard the brother in the back seat chattering, his sister beside him fast asleep. I saw the car strike the other car. I saw the stars above in cruel and silent witness. I saw the bruised and lifeless bodies. I saw her stunned face as she stood unharmed, her clothes torn, by the side of the road. I heard him cry out in horror. I heard him curse in disbelief. I saw the broken glass. Broken glass everywhere glittering beautifully in the light of headlamps. I saw her eyes, her pale blue eyes. I saw her heart close.

My victim was dead. He slipped out of my grasp.

He was as lifeless as his parents had been in that hot desert place.

He was dead and crumpled and could never hurt her again, could never pull her long yellow hair, or beat her, or stop her as she played.

The room was sweetly still except for her playing. She had come again to the Third Movement, and she swayed gently with its quieter beginning, its polite and measured steps.

The boy danced for joy. In his fine little djellaba, his feet bare, his round head covered with thick black curls, he was the Arab angel leaping into the air, dancing, crying out, "He's dead, he's dead, he's dead." He clapped his hands, he rubbed them together, he clapped them again, he flung them up. "He's dead, he's dead, he's dead, he'll never hurt her, he'll never vex her, he's double-vexed forever, he's dead, he's dead."

But she didn't hear him. On she played, making her way through these slumberish low notes, humming softly and then parting her lips to make a monosyllabic song.

I was full with his blood. I felt it washing through me. I loved it, I loved every drop of it. I regained my breath from the effort of having so quickly consumed it, and then I walked slowly, quietly as I could, as if she could hear when she could not, and stood at the end of the piano looking at her.

What a small tender face she had, so girlish with deep-set, huge and pale blue eyes. But look at the bruises on her face. Look at the blood-red scratches on her cheek. Look at the field of tiny red bleeding pinpoint wounds on her temple where a shock of her hair had been ripped right out by the roots.

She didn't care. The greenish-black bruises on her bare arms meant nothing to her. She played on.

How delicate her neck was, even with the blackish swelling imprint of his fingers, and how graceful her small bony shoulders, barely holding up the sleeves of her thin flowered cotton dress. Her strong ashen eyebrows came together in the sweetest frown of concentration as she gazed before her at nothing but her lilting, peaking music, her long clean fingers alone envincing her titanic and indomitable strength.

She let her gaze drift to me, and she smiled as if she had seen something that momentarily pleased her; she bowed her head once, twice, three times in rapid time with the music, but as though she were nodding to me.

"Sybelle," I whispered. I put my fingers to my lips and kissed them and blew the kiss to her, as her fingers marched on.

But then her vision misted, and she was off again, the Movement demanding speed from her, her head jerked back with the effort of her assault on the keys. And the Sonata sprang once again into its most triumphant life.

Something more powerful than the light of the sun engulfed me. It was a power so total that it utterly surrounded me and sucked me up out of the room, out of the world, out of the sound of her playing, out of my senses.

"Noooo, don't take me now!" I screamed. But an immense and empty blackness swallowed the sound.

I was flying, weightless, with my burnt black limbs outstretched, and in a Hell of excrutiating pain. This cannot be my body, I sobbed, seeing the black flesh sealed to my muscles like leather, seeing every tendon of my arms, my fingernails bent and blackened like bits of burnt horn. No, not my body, I cried, Oh, Mother help me, help me! Benjamin, help me . . .

I began to fall. Oh, there was no one who could help me now but one Being.

"God, give me the courage," I cried. "God if it's begun, give me the courage, God, I can't give up my reason, God, let me know where I am, God, let me understand what is happening, God, where is the church, God, where is the bread and the wine, God, where is she, God help me, help me."

Down and down I fell, past spires of glass, past grids of blind windows. Past rooftops and pointed towers. I fell through the harsh and wild wailing of the wind. I fell through the stinging torrent of snow. I fell and I fell. I fell past the window where the unmistakable figure of Benjamin stood with his tiny hand on the drape, his black eyes fixed on me for one split second, his mouth open, tiny Arab angel. I fell down and down, the skin shriveling and tightening on my legs so that I couldn't bend them, tightening on my face so that I couldn't open my mouth, and with an agonizing explosion of raw pain, I struck hard-packed snow.

My eyes were open and fire flooded them.

The sun had fully risen.

"I shall die now. I shall die!" I whispered. "And in this last moment of burning paralysis, when all the world is gone and there is nothing left, I hear her music! I hear her playing the final notes of the *Appassionata*! I hear her. I hear her tumultuous song."

20

I DIDN'T DIE. Not by any means.

I awoke to hear her playing, but she and her piano were very far away. In the first few hours after twilight, when the pain was at its worst, I used the sound of her music, used the search for it, to keep myself from screaming in madness because nothing could make the pain stop.

Deeply encased in snow, I couldn't move and couldn't see, save what my mind could see if I chose to use it, and wishing to die, I used nothing. I only listened to her playing the *Appassionata*, and sometimes I sang along with her in my dreams.

All the first night and the second, I listened to her, that is, when she was disposed to play. She would stop for hours, to sleep perhaps. I couldn't know. Then she would begin again and I'd begin with her.

I followed her Three Movements until I knew them, as she must know them, by heart. I knew the variations she worked into her music; I knew how no two musical phrases she played were ever the same.

I listened to Benjamin calling for me, I heard his crisp little voice, speaking very rapidly and very much in New York style, saying, "Angel, you've not done with us, what are we to do with him? Angel, come back. Angel, I'll give you cigarettes. Angel, I have plenty of good cigarettes. Come back. Angel, that's just a joke. I know you can get your own cigarettes. But this is really vexing, you leaving this dead body, Angel. Come back."

There were hours when I heard nothing of either of them. My mind hadn't the strength to reach out telepathically to them, just to see them, one through the eyes of the other. No. That kind of strength was gone.

I lay in mute stillness, burnt as much by all that I'd seen and felt as by any sunlight, hurt and empty inside, and dead of mind and heart, save for my love for them. It was easy enough, wasn't it, in blackest misery to love two pretty strangers, a mad girl and a mischievous streetwise boy who cared for her? There was no history to it, my killing her brother. Bravo, and finished. There was five hundred years of history to the pain of everything else.

There were hours when only the city talked to me, the great clattering, rolling, rustling city of New York, with its traffic forever clanking, even in the thickest snow, with its layers upon layers of voices and lives rising up to the plateau on which I lay, and then beyond it, vastly beyond it in towers such as the world before this time has never beheld.

I knew things but I didn't know what to make of them. I knew that the snow covering me was growing ever deeper, and ever harder, and I didn't understand how such a thing as ice could keep away from me the rays of the sun.

Surely, I must die, I thought. If not this coming day, then the next. I thought of Lestat holding up the Veil. I thought of His Face. But the zeal had left me. All hope had left me.

I will die, I thought. Morning by morning, I will die. But I didn't.

In the city far below, I heard others of my kind. I didn't really try to hear them, and so it was not their thoughts that came to me, but now and then their words. Lestat and David were there, Lestat and David thought that I was dead. Lestat and David mourned for me. But far worse horrors plagued Lestat because Dora and the world had taken the Veil, and the city was now crowded with believers. The Cathedral could scarce control the multitudes.

Other immortals came, the young, the feeble and sometimes, most horribly, the very ancient, wanting to view this miracle, slipping into the nighttime Church among the mortal worshipers and looking with crazed eyes on the veil.

Sometimes they spoke of poor Armand or brave Armand or St. Armand, who in his devotion to the Crucified Christ had immolated himself at this very Church door!

Sometimes they did the same. And just before the sun was to rise again, I'd have to hear them, hear their last desperate prayers as they waited for the lethal light. Did they fare better than I? Did they find their refuge in the arms of God? Or were they screaming in agony, agony such as I felt, unendurably burnt and unable to break away from it, or were they lost as I was, remnants in alleyways or on distant roofs? No, they came and they went, whatever their fate.

How pale it all was, how far away. I felt so sad for Lestat that he had bothered to weep for me, but I was to die here. I was to die sooner or later. Whatever I had seen in that moment when I'd risen into the sun didn't matter. I was to die. That was all there was.

Piercing the snowy night, electronic voices spoke of the miracle, that Christ's Face upon a Veil of linen had cured the sick and left its imprint on other cloths pressed to it. Then came an argument of clergymen and skeptics, a perfect din.

I followed the sense of nothing. I suffered. I burned. I couldn't open my eyes, and when I tried, my eyelashes scratched my eyes and the agony was too much to bear. In darkness, I waited for her.

Sooner or later, without fail, there came her magnificent music, with all its new and wondrous variations, and nothing mattered to me then, not the mystery of where I was, or what I might have seen, or what it was that Lestat and David meant to do.

It was not until the seventh night perhaps that my senses were fully restored to me, and the full horror of my state was understood.

Lestat was gone. So was David. The Church had been shut up. From the murmurings of mortals I soon realized that the Veil had been taken away.

I could hear the minds of all the city, a din that was unsupportable. I shut myself off from it, fearing the vagrant immortal who'd home in on me if he caught but one spark from my telepathic mind. I couldn't endure the thought of some attempted rescue by immortal strangers. I couldn't endure the thought of their faces, their questions, their possible concern or merciless indifference. I hid myself from them, coiled up in my cracked and tightened flesh. Yet I heard them, as I heard the mortal voices around them, speaking of miracles and redemption and the love of Christ.

Besides, I had enough to think about to figure my present predicament and how it had come to be.

I was lying on a roof. That is where my fall had left me, but not under the open sky, as I might have hoped or supposed. On the contrary, my body had tumbled down a slope of metal sheeting, to lodge beneath a torn and rusted overhang, where it had been repeatedly buried in the wind-stirred snow.

How had I gotten here? I could only suppose.

By my own will, and with the first explosion of my blood in the light of the morning sun, I had been driven upwards, as high perhaps as I could go. For centuries I'd known how to climb to airy heights and how to move there, but I'd never pushed it to a conceivable limit, but with my zeal for death, I had strained with all my available strength to move Heavenward. My fall had been from the greatest height.

The building beneath me was empty, abandoned, dangerous, without heat or light.

Not a sound issued from its hollow metal stairwells or its battered, crumbling rooms. Indeed the wind played the structure now and then as if it were a great pipe organ, and when Sybelle was not at her piano it was to this music I listened, shutting out the rich cacophony of the city above, beyond and below.

Now and then mortals crept inside the lower floors of the building. I felt a sudden wrenching hope. Would one be fool enough to wander to this rooftop where I might lay hands on him and drink the blood I needed merely to crawl free of the overhang which protected me and thereby give myself unsheltered to the sun? As I lay now, the sun could scarce reach me. Only a dull white light scorched me through the snowy shroud in which I was wound, and with the lengthening of each night this newly inflicted pain would mellow into the rest.

But nobody ever came up here.

Death would be slow, very slow. It might have

to wait until the warm weather came and the snow melted.

And so each morning, as I longed for death, I came to accept that I would wake, more burnt perhaps then ever, but all the more concealed by the winter blizzard, as I had been concealed all along, from the hundreds of lighted windows that looked down upon this roof from above.

When it was deadly quiet, when Sybelle slept and Benji had ceased praying to me and talking to me at the window, the worst happened. I thought, in a cold listless broken way, of those strange things that had befallen me when I'd been tumbling through space, because I could think of nothing else.

How utterly real it had been, the altar of Santa Sofia and the bread I'd broken in my hands. I'd known things, so many things, things which I couldn't recall any longer or put into words, things which I could not articulate here in this narrative even as I sought to relive the tale.

Real. Tangible. I had felt the altar cloth and seen the wine spill, and before that the bird rise out of the egg. I could hear the sound of the cracking of the shell. I could hear my Mother's voice. And all the rest.

But my mind didn't want these things anymore. It didn't want them. The zeal had proved fragile. It was gone, gone like the nights with my Master in Venice, gone like the years of wandering with Louis, gone like the festive months on The Night Island, gone like those long shameful centuries with the Children of Darkness when I had been a fool, such a pure fool.

I could think of the Veil, I could think of Heaven, I

could think of my standing at the Altar and working the miracle with the Body of Christ in my hands. Yes, I could think of all of it. But the totality had been too terrible, and I was not dead, and there was no Memnoch pleading with me to become his helper, and no Christ with arms outstretched against the backdrop of God's unending light.

It was sweeter by far to think of Sybelle, to remember that her room of rich red and blue Turkey carpets and darkly varnished overblown paintings had been every bit as real as Santa Sofia of Kiev, to think of her oval white face when she'd turned to glance at me, to think of the sudden brightness of her moist, quick eyes.

One evening, as my eyes actually opened, as the lids truly drew back over the orbs of my eyes so that I could see through the white cake of ice above me, I realized I was healing.

I tried to flex my arms. I could raise them ever so slightly, and the encasing ice shattered; what an extraordinary electric sound.

The sun simply couldn't reach me here, or not enough to work against the preternatural fury of the powerful blood my body contained. Ah, God, to think of it, five hundred years of growing ever stronger and stronger, and born from the blood of Marius in the first place, a monster from the start who never knew his own strength.

It seemed for a moment that my rage and despair could grow no greater. It seemed the fiery pain in all my body could be no worse.

Then Sybelle started to play. She began to play the *Appassionata*, and nothing else mattered.

It wouldn't matter again until her music had stopped. The night was warmer than usual; the snow had melted slightly. There seemed no immortals anywhere near. I knew that the Veil had been spirited away to the Vatican in Rome. No cause now, was there, for immortals to come here?

Poor Dora. The nightly news said that her prize had been taken from her. Rome must examine this Veil. Her tales of strange blond-haired angels were the stuff of tabloids, and she herself was no longer here.

In a moment of daring, I fastened my heart upon Sybelle's music, and with an aching straining head, sent out my telepathic vision as if it were a fleshly part of me, a tongue requiring stamina, to see through Benjamin's eyes, the room where they were both lodged.

In a lovely golden haze, I saw it, saw the walls covered with the heavy framed paintings, saw my beautiful one herself, in a fleecy white gown with worn slippers, her fingers hard at work. How grand the sweep of the music. And Benjamin, the little worrier, frowning, puffing on a black cigarette, with hands folded behind his back, pacing in his bare feet and shaking his head as he mumbled to himself.

"Angel, I have told you to come back!"

I smiled. The creases in my cheeks hurt as if someone had made them with the point of a sharp knife. I shut my telepathic eye. I let myself slumber in the rushing crescendos of the piano. Besides, Benjamin had sensed something; his mind, unwarped by Western sophistication, had picked up some glimmer of my prying. Enough.

Then another vision came to me, very sharp, very

special and unusual, something that would not be ignored. I turned my head again and made the ice crackle.
I held my eyes open. I could see a blur of lighted towers
high above.

Some immortal down there in the city was thinking
of me, someone far away, many blocks from the closed-
up Cathedral. In fact, I sensed in an instant the distant
presence of two powerful vampires, vampires I knew,
and vampires who knew of my death and lamented it bitterly as they went about some important task.

Now there was a risk to this. Try to see them and they
might catch much more than the glimmer of me which
Benjamin had been so quick to catch. But the city was
empty of blood drinkers save for them, for all I could figure, and I had to know what it was that caused them to
move with such deliberation and such stealth.

An hour passed perhaps. Sybelle was silent. They,
the powerful vampires, were still at their work. I decided
to chance it.

I drew in close with my disincarnate vision, and
quickly realized that I could see one through the eyes of
the other, but that it did not work for me the other way
around.

The reason was plain. I sharpened my sight. I was
looking through the eyes of Santino, my old Roman
Coven Master, Santino, and the other whom I saw was
Marius, my Maker, whose mind was locked to me for all
time.

It was a vast official building in which they made
their careful progress, both dressed as gentlemen of the
moment in trim dark blue clothes, even to starched white
collars and thin silk ties. Both had trimmed their hair in

deference to corporate fashion. But this was no corporation in which they prowled, clearly putting into harmless thrall any mortal who tried to disturb them. It was a medical building. And I soon guessed what their errand must be.

It was the forensics laboratory of the city through which they wandered. And though they had taken their time in gathering up documents for their heavy briefcases, they were quick now with agitation as they pulled from refrigerated compartments the remains of those vampires who, following my example, had turned themselves over to the mercy of the sun.

Of course, they were confiscating what the world now had on us. They were scooping up the remains. Into simple glistening plastic sacks they put the residue, out of coffinlike drawers and off shining steel trays. Whole bones, ashes, teeth, ah, yes, even teeth, they swept into their little sacks. And now from a series of filing cabinets they withdrew the plastic-wrapped samples of clothing that remained.

My heart quickened. I stirred in the ice and the ice spoke back to me again. Oh, heart be still. Let me see. It was my lace, my very lace, the thick Venetian Rose Point, burnt at the edges, and with it a few shredded rags of purple-red velvet! Yes, my pitiful clothes which they took from the labeled compartment of the filing drawer and slipped into their bags.

Marius stopped. I turned my head and my mind elsewhere. Do not see me. See me and come here, and I swear to God I will . . . I will what? I have no strength even to move. I have no strength to escape. Oh, Sybelle, please, play for me, I have to escape this.

But then, remembering that he was my Master, remembering that he could trace me only through the weaker more muddled mind of his companion, Santino, I felt my heart go quiet.

From the bank of recent memory, I took her music, I framed it with numbers and figures and dates, all the little detritus I had brought with me over the centuries to her: that Beethoven had written her sweet masterpiece, that it was Sonata No. 23 in F Minor, Opus 57. Think on that. Think on Beethoven. Think on a make-believe night in cold Vienna, make-believe for I knew nothing really about it, think on him writing music with a noisy scratchy quill, which he himself perhaps could not hear. Think on him being paid in pittances. And think with a smile, yes, a painful cutting smile that makes your face bleed, of how they brought him piano after piano, so powerful was he, so demanding, so fiercely did he bang away.

And she, pretty Sybelle, what a fine daughter to him she was, her powerful fingers striking the keys with terrifying power that would surely have delighted him had he ever seen in the distant future, amid all his frenzied students and worshipers, just this particular maniacal girl.

It was warmer tonight. The ice was melting. There was no denying it. I pressed my lips together and again lifted my right hand. A cavity existed now in which I could move my right fingers.

But I couldn't forget about them, the unlikely pair, the one who'd made me and the one who'd tried to destroy him, Marius and Santino. I had to check back. Cautiously I sent out my weak and tentative beam of probing thought. And in an instant, I'd fixed them.

They stood before an incinerator in the bowels of the building and heaved into a fiery mouth all the evidence which they had brought together, sack after sack curling and crackling in the flames.

How odd. Didn't they themselves want to look at these fragments under microscopes? But then surely others of our kind had done this, and why look at the bones and teeth of those who have been baked in Hell when you can carve pale white tissue from your own hand, and place this on the glass slide while your hand heals itself miraculously, as I was healing even now?

I lingered on the vision. I saw the hazy basement round about them. I saw the low beams above their heads. Gathering all my power into my projected gaze, I saw Santino's face, so troubled, soft, the very one who had shattered the only youth I might have ever had. I saw my old Master gazing almost wistfully at the flames. "We're finished," Marius said in his quiet, commanding voice, speaking Italian perfectly to the other. "I cannot think of another thing that we should do."

"Break apart the Vatican, and steal the veil from them," answered Santino. "What right have they to claim such a thing?"

I could only see Marius's reaction, his sudden shock and then his polite and poised smile. "Why?" he asked, as if he held no secrets. "What's the Veil to us, my friend? You think it will bring him back to his senses? Forgive me, Santino, but you are so very young."

His senses, bring him back to his senses. This had to

mean Lestat. There was no other possible meaning. I pushed my luck. I scanned Santino's mind for all he knew, and found myself recoiling in horror, but holding fast to what I saw.

Lestat, my Lestat—for he was never theirs, was he?—my Lestat was crazed and railing as the result of his awful saga, and held prisoner by the very oldest of our kind on the final decree that if he did not cease to disturb the peace, which meant of course our secrecy, he would be destroyed, as only the oldest could accomplish, and no one could plead for him on any account.

No, that could not happen! I writhed and twisted. The pain sent its shocks through me, red and violet and pulsing with orange light. I hadn't seen such colors since I'd fallen. My mind was coming back, and coming back for what? Lestat to be destroyed! Lestat imprisoned, as I had once been centuries ago under Rome in Santino's catacombs. Oh, God, this is worse than the sun's fire, this is worse than seeing that bastard brother strike the little plum-cheeked face of Sybelle and knock her away from her piano, this is murderous rage I feel.

But the smaller damage was done. "Come, we have to get out of here," said Santino. "There's something wrong, something I sense that I can't explain. It's as if someone is right near us yet not near us; it's as if someone as powerful as myself has heard my footfall over miles and miles."

Marius looked kindly, curious, unalarmed. "New York is ours tonight," he said simply. And then with faint fear he looked into the mouth of the furnace one last time. "Unless something of spirit, so tenacious of life, clung still to his lace and to the velvet he wore."

I closed my eyes. Oh, God, let me close my mind. Let me shut it up tight.

His voice went on, piercing the little shell of my consciousness where I had so softened it.

"But I have never believed such things," he said. "We're like the Eucharist itself, in some measure, don't you think? Being Body and Blood of a mysterious god only so long as we hold to the chosen form. What's strands of reddish hair and scorched and tattered lace? He's gone."

"I don't understand you," Santino confessed gently. "But if you think I never loved him, you are very very wrong."

"Let's go then," Marius said. "Our work's done. Every trace of every one is now obliterated. But promise me in your old Roman Catholic soul, you won't go seeking the Veil. A million pairs of eyes have looked on it, Santino, and nothing's changed. The world is the world, and children die in every quadrant under Heaven, hungry and alone."

I could risk no more.

I veered away, searching the night like a high beam, casting about for the mortals who might see them leave the building in which they'd done their all-important work, but their retreat was too secret, too swift for that.

I felt them go. I felt the sudden absence of their breath, their pulse, and knew the winds had taken them away.

At last when another hour had ticked, I let my eye roam the same old rooms where they had wandered.

All was quiet with those poor muddled technicians and guards whom white-faced specters from another realm had gently spellbound as they went about their gruesome task.

By morning, the theft and all the missing work would be discovered, and Dora's miracle would suffer yet another dreary insult, receding ever more swiftly out of current time.

I was sore; I wept a dry, hoarse weeping, unable even to muster tears.

I think that once in the glimmering ice I saw my hand, a grotesque claw, more like a thing flayed than burnt, and shiny black as I had remembered it or seen it.

Then a mystery began to prey upon me. How could I have killed the evil brother of my poor love? How could it have been anything but an illusion, that swift horrible justice, when I had been rising and falling beneath the weight of the morning sun?

And if that had not happened, if I had not sucked dry that awful vengeful brother, then they too were a dream, my Sybelle and my little Bedouin. Oh, please, was that the final horror?

The night struck its worst hour. Dim clocks chimed in painted plastered rooms. Wheels churned the crunching snow. Again, I raised my hand. There came the inevitable crack and snap. Tumbling all around me was the broken ice like so much shattered glass!

I looked above on pure and sparkling stars. How lovely this, these guardian glassy spires with all their fast and golden squares of light cut in ranks run straight across and sharply down to score the airy blackness of the winter night, and here now comes the tyrant wind, whistling through crystalline canyons down across this small neglected bed where one forgotten demon lies, gazing with the larcenous vision of a great soul at the city's emboldened lights on clouds above. Oh, little stars, how much I've hated you, and envied you that in the ghastly void you can with such determination plot your dogged course.

But I hated nothing now. My pain was as a purgative for all unworthy things. I watched the sky cloud over, glisten, become a diamond for a still and gorgeous moment, and then again the white soft limitless haze took up the golden glow of city lamps and sent in answer the softest lightest fall of snow.

It touched my face. It touched my outstretched hand. It touched me all over as it melted in its tiny magical flakes.

"And now the sun will come," I whispered, as if some guardian angel held me close, "and even here beneath this twisted little awning of tin, it will find me through this broken canopy and take my soul to further depths of pain."

A voice cried out in protest. A voice begged that it not be so. My own, I thought, of course, why not this self-deception? I am mad to think that I can bear the burning that I've suffered and that I could willingly endure it once again.

But it wasn't my voice. It was Benjamin, Benjamin at his prayers. Flinging out my disembodied eyes, I saw him. He knelt in the room as she lay sleeping like a ripe and succulent peach amid her soft tangled bedcovers. "Oh, angel, Dybbuk, help us. Dybbuk, you came once. So come again. You vex me that you don't come!"

How many hours is it till sunrise, little man? I whispered this to his little seashell ear, as if I didn't know.

"Dybbuk," he cried out. "It's you, you speak to me. Sybelle, wake up, Sybelle."

Ah, but think before you wake her. It's a horrid errand. I'm not the resplendent being you saw who sucked your enemy dry of blood and doted on her beauty and your joy. It's a monster you come to collect if you mean to pay your debt to me, an insult to your innocent eyes. But be assured, little man, that I'll be yours forever if you do me this kindness, if you come to me, if you succor me, if you help me, because my will is leaving me, and I'm alone, and I would be restored now and cannot help myself, and my years mean nothing now, and I'm afraid.

He scrambled to his feet. He stood staring at the distant window, the window through which I had seen him in a dream glimpse me with his mortal eyes, but through which he could not possibly see me now, as I lay on a roof far far below the fine apartment which he shared with my angel. He squared his little shoulders, and now with black eyebrows in their perfect serious frown he was the very image off the Byzantine wall, a cherub smaller than myself.

"Name it, Dybbuk, I come for you!" he declared, and made his mighty little right hand into a fist. "Where are you, Dybbuk, what do you fear that we cannot conquer together! Sybelle, wake up, Sybelle! Our Divine Dybbuk has come back and he needs us!"

21

THEY WERE COMING for me. It was the building beside their own, a derelict heap. Benjamin knew it. In a few faint telepathic whispers I'd begged him to bring a hammer and a pick to break up the ice such as remained and to have big soft blankets with which to wrap me.

I knew I weighed nothing. Painfully twisting my arms, I broke up more of the transparent covering. I felt with my clawlike hand that my hair had come back, thick and red-brown as ever. I held up a lock to the light, and then my arm could stand the scalding pain no more and I let it drop, unable to close or move my dried and twisted fingers.

I had to throw a spell, at least when they first came. They could not see the thing that I was, this black leathery monster. No mortal could bear the sight of this, no matter what words came from my lips. I had to shield myself somehow.

And having no mirror, how could I know how I looked or what I must do precisely? I had to dream, dream of the old Venetian days when I had been a beauty well known to myself from the tailor's glass, and project that vision right into their minds even if it took all the strength I possessed; yes, that, and I must give them some instructions.

I lay still, gazing up into the soft warm snowfall of

tiny flakes, so unlike the terrible blizzards that had come earlier. I didn't dare to use my wits to track their progress.

Suddenly I heard the loud crash of breaking glass. A door slammed far below. I heard their uneven steps rushing up the metal stairs, clambering over the landings.

My heart beat hard, and with each little convulsion, the pain was pumped through me, as if my blood itself were scalding me.

Suddenly, the steel door on the roof was flung back. I heard them rushing towards me. In the faint dreamy light of the high towers all around, I saw their two small figures, she the fairy woman, and he the child of no more than twelve years perhaps, hurrying towards me.

Sybelle! Oh, she came out on the roof without a coat, hair streaming, the terrible pity of it, and Benjamin no better in his thin linen djellaba. But they had a big velvet comforter to cover me, and I had to make a vision.

Give me the boy I was, give the finest green satin and ruff upon ruff of fancy lace, give me stockings and braided boots, and let my hair be clean and shining.

Slowly I opened my eyes, looking from one to the other of their small pale and rapt faces. Like two vagrants of the night they stood in the drifting snow.

"Oh, but Dybbuk, you had us so very worried," said Benjamin, in his wildly excited voice, "and look at you, you are beautiful."

"No, don't think it's what you see, Benjamin," I said. "Hurry with your tools, chop at the ice, and lay the cover over me."

It was Sybelle who took up the wooden-handled iron hammer and with both hands slammed it down, fracturing the soft top layer of ice immediately. Benjamin chopped at it all with the pick as if he had become a small machine, thrusting to left and to right over and over, sending the shards flying.

The wind caught Sybelle's hair and whipped around into her eyes. The snow clung to her eyelids.

I held the image, a helpless satin-clad child, with soft pinkish hands upturned and unable to help them.

"Don't cry, Dybbuk," declared Benjamin, grabbing a giant thin slab of ice with both hands. "We'll get you out, don't cry, you're ours now. We have you."

He threw aside the shining jagged broken sheets, and then he himself appeared to freeze, more solid than any ice, staring at me, his mouth a perfect O of amazement.

"Dybbuk, you are changing colors!" he cried. He reached to touch my illusory face.

"Don't do it, Benji," said Sybelle.

It was the first time I'd heard her voice, and now I saw the deliberate brave calm of her blanched face, the wind making her eyes tear, though she herself remained staunch. She picked the ice from my hair.

A terrible chill came over me, quelling the heat, yes, but sending the tears down my face. Were they blood? "Don't look at me," I said. "Benji, Sybelle, look away. Just put the cover into my hands."

Her tender eyes squinted as she stared, disobediently, steadily, one hand up to close the collar of her flimsy cotton bed gown against the wind, the other poised above me.

"What's happened to you since you came to us?" she asked in the kindest voice. "Who's done this to you?"

I swallowed hard, and made the vision come again. I

pushed it up from all my pores, as if my body were one agency of breath.

"No, don't do it anymore," said Sybelle. "It weakens you and you suffer terribly."

"I can heal, my sweet," I said, "I promise I can. I won't be like this always, not even soon. Only take me off this roof. Take me out of this cold, and take me where the sun can't get to me again. It's the sun that did this. Only the sun. Take me, please. I can't walk. I can't crawl. I'm a night thing. Hide me in the darkness."

"Enough, don't say any more," cried Benji.

I opened my eyes to see a huge wave of brilliant blue settle over me as though a summer sky had come down to be my wrapping. I felt the soft pile of the velvet, and even this was pain, pain on the blazing skin, but it was pain that could be borne because their ministering hands were on me, and for this, for their touch, for their love, I would have endured anything.

I felt myself lifted. I knew that I was light, and yet how dreadful it was to be so helpless, as they wrapped me.

"Am I not light enough to carry?" I asked. My head had fallen back, and I could see the snow again, and I fancied that when I sharpened my gaze I could see the stars too, high above, biding their time beyond the haze of one tiny planet.

"Don't be afraid," whispered Sybelle, her lips close to the covers.

The smell of their blood was suddenly rich and thick as honey.

Both of them had me, hoisted in their arms, and they ran together over the roof. I was free of the hurtful snow and ice, almost free forever. I couldn't let myself think about their blood. I couldn't let this ravenous burnt body have its way. That was unthinkable.

Down through the metal stairwell we went, making turn after turn, their feet strumming the brittle steel treads, my body shocked and throbbing with agony. I could see the ceiling above, and then the smell of their blood, mingling together, overpowered me, and I shut my eyes and clenched my burnt fingers, hearing the leathery flesh crack as I did so. I dug my nails into my palms.

I heard Sybelle at my ear. "We have you, we're holding you tight, we won't let you go. It isn't far. Oh, God, but look at you, look what the sun's done to you."

"Don't look!" said Benji crossly. "Just hurry! Do you think such a powerful Dybbuk doesn't know what you think? Be wise, hurry up."

They had come to the lower floor and to the broken window. I felt the arms of Sybelle lift me beneath my head and beneath my crooked knees, and I heard Benji's voice from beyond, no longer echoing on enclosing walls.

"That's it, now give him to me, I can hold him!" How furious and excited he sounded, but she had come through the window with me, I could tell this much, though my clever Dybbuk's mind was utterly spent, and I knew nothing, nothing but pain and the blood and the pain again and the blood and that they were running through a long dark alleyway from which I could see nothing of Heaven.

But how sweet it was. The rocking motion, the swinging of my burnt legs and the soft touch of her soothing fingers through the blanket, all this was wickedly wondrous. It wasn't pain anymore, it was merely sensation. The cover fell over my face.

On they hurried, feet crunching in the snow, Benji sliding once with a loud cry, and Sybelle grabbing hold of him. He caught his breath.

What labor it was for them in this cold. They must get out of it.

We entered the hotel in which they lived. The pungent warm air rushed out to take hold of us even as the doors were pulled open and before they fell shut, the hallway echoing with the sharp steps of Sybelle's little shoes and the quick shuffle of Benji's sandals.

With a sudden burst of agony through my legs and back, I felt myself doubled, knees brought up and head tipped towards them, as we crowded into the elevator. I bit down on the scream in my throat. Nothing could matter less. The elevator, smelling of old motors and tried and true oil, began its swaying jerking progress upwards.

"We're home, Dybbuk," whispered Benji with his hot breath on my cheek, his little hand grasping for me through the cover and pushing painfully against my scalp. "We are safe now, we have captured you and we have you."

Click of locks, feet on hardwood floors, the scent of incense and candles, of a woman's rich perfume, of rich polish for fine things, of old canvases with cracked oil paint, of fresh and overpoweringly sweet white lilies.

My body was laid down gently into the bed of down, the blanket loosened so that I sank into layers of silk and velvet, the pillows seeming to melt beneath me.

It was the very disheveled nest in which I'd

glimpsed her with my mind's eye, golden and sleeping in her white gown, and she had given it over to such a horror.

"Don't pull away the cover," I said. I knew that my little friend wanted so to do it.

Undaunted, he gently pulled it away. I struggled with my one recovering hand to catch it, to bring it back, but I couldn't do any more than flex my burnt fingers.

They stood beside the bed, gazing down at me. The light swirled around them, mingled with warmth, these two fragile figures, the gaunt porcelain girl, the bruises gone from her milk-white skin, and the little Arab boy, the Bedouin boy, for I realized now that that is what he truly was. Fearlessly they stared at what must be un- speakable to behold for human eyes.

"You are so shiny!" said Benji. "Does it hurt you?"

"What can we do!" said Sybelle, so muted, as if her very voice might injure me. Her hands covered her lips. The unruly wisps of her full straight pale hair moved in the light, and her arms were bluc from the cold outside, and she could not help but shiver. Poor spare being, so delicate. Her nightdress was crumpled, thin white cot- ton, stitched with flowerets and trimmed with thin sturdy lace, a thing for a virgin. Her eyes brimmcd with sympathy.

"Know my soul, my angel," I said. "I'm an evil thing. God wouldn't take me. And the Devil wouldn't either. I went into the sun so they could have my soul. It was a loving thing, without fear of Hellfire or pain. But this Earth, this very Earth has been my purgatorial prison. I don't know how I came to you before. I don't know what power it was that gave me those brief seconds to stand here in your room and come between you and death that was looming like a shadow over you."

"Oh, no," she whispered fearfully, her eyes glistering in the dim lights of the room. "He would never have killed me."

"Oh, yes, he would!" I said, and Benjamin said the very same exact words in concert with me.

"He was drunk and he didn't care what he did," said Benji in instant rage, "and his hands were big and clumsy and mean, and he didn't care what he did, and after the last time he hit you, you lay still like the dead in this very bed for two hours without moving! Do you think a Dybbuk kills your own brother for nothing?"

"I think he's telling you the truth, my pretty girl," I said. It was so hard to talk. With each word I had to lift my chest. In crazy desperation, suddenly I wanted a mirror. I tossed and turned on the bed, and went rigid with pain.

The two were thrown into a panic.

"Don't move, Dybbuk, don't!" Benji pleaded. "Sybelle, the silk, all the silk scarves, get them out, wind them around him."

"No!" I whispered. "Put the cover up over me. If you must see my face, then leave it bare, but cover the rest of me. Or . . ."

"Or what, Dybbuk, tell me?"

"Lift me so that I can see myself and how I look. Stand me before a long mirror."

They fell silent in perplexity. Sybelle's long yellow hair lay flaxen and flat down over her large breasts. Benji chewed at his little lip.

All the room swam with colors. Behold the blue silk sealed to the plaster of the walls, the heaps of richly embellished pillows all around me, look at the golden fringe, and there beyond, the wobbling baubles of the chandelier, filled with the glistering colors of the spectrum. I fancied I heard the tinkling song of the glass as these baubles touched. It seemed in my feeble deranged mind that I had never seen such simple splendor, that I had forgotten in all my years just how shining and exquisite the world was.

I closed my eyes, taking with me to my heart an image of the room. I breathed in, fighting the scent of their blood, the sweet clean fragrance of the lilies. "Would you let me see those flowers?" I whispered. Were my lips charred? Could they see my fang teeth, and were they yellowed from the fire? I floated on the silks beneath me. I floated and it seemed that I could dream now, safe, truly safe. The lilies were close. I reached up again. I felt the petals against my hand, and the tears came down my face. Were they pure blood? Pray not, but I heard Benji's frank little gasp, and Sybelle making her soft sound to hush him.

"I was a boy of seventeen, I think, when it happened," I said. "It was hundreds of years ago. I was too young, really. My Master, he was a loving one; he didn't believe we were evil things. He thought we could feed off the badlings. If I hadn't been dying, it wouldn't have been done so soon. He wanted me to know things, to be ready."

I opened my eyes. They were spellbound! They saw again the boy I'd been. I had done it without intention.

"Oh, so handsome," said Benji. "So fine, Dybbuk."

"Little man," I said with a sigh, feeling the fragile illusion about me crumble to air, "call me by my name from now on; it's not Dybbuk. I think you picked up that one from the Hebrews of Palestine."

He laughed. He didn't flinch as I faded back into my horrid self.

"Then tell me your name," he said.

I did.

"Armand," said Sybelle. "Tell us, what can we do? If not silk scarves, ointments then, aloe, yes, aloe will heal your burns."

I laughed but only in a small soft way, meant to be purely kindly.

"My aloe is blood, child. I need an evil man, a man who deserves to die. Now, how will I find him?"

"What will this blood do?" asked Benji. He sat right down beside me, leaning over me as though I were the most fascinating specimen. "You know, Armand, you are black as pitch, you are made out of black leather, you are like those people they fish from the bogs in Europe, all shiny with all of you sealed inside. I could take a lesson in muscles from looking at you."

"Benji, stop," said Sybelle, struggling with her disapproval and her alarm. "We have to think how to get an evil man."

"You serious?" he said, looking up and across the bed at her. She stood with her hands clasped as if in prayer. "Sybelle, that's nothing. It's how to get rid of him afterwards that's so hard." He looked at me. "Do you know what we did with her brother?"

She put her hands over her ears and bowed her head. How many times had I done that very thing myself when it seemed a stream of words and images would utterly destroy me.

"You are so glossy, Armand," said Benji. "But I can get you an evil man, like that, it's nothing. You want an evil man? Let's make a plan." He bent down over me, as though trying to peer into my brain. I realized suddenly that he was looking at my fangs.

"Benji," I said, "don't come any closer. Sybelle, take him away."

"But what did I do?"

"Nothing," she said. She dropped her voice, and said desperately, "He's hungry."

"Lift the covers off again, will you do that?" I asked. "Lift them off and look at me and let me look into your eyes, and let that be my mirror. I want to see how very bad it is."

"Hmmm, Armand," said Benji. "I think you are crazy mad or something."

Sybelle bent down and with her two careful hands peeled the cover back and down, exposing the length of my body.

I went into her mind.

It was worse than I had ever imagined.

The glossy horror of a bog corpse, as Benji had said, was perfectly true, save for the horror of the full head of red-brown hair and huge, lidless bright brown eyes, and the white teeth arrayed perfectly below and above lips that had shriveled to nothing. Down the tightly drawn wrinkled black leather of the face were heavy red streaks of blood that had been my tears.

I whipped my head to the side and deep into the downy pillow. I felt the covers come up over me.

"This cannot go on for you, even if it could go on for me," I said. "It's not what I would have you see another moment, for the longer you live with this, the more like you are to live with anything. No. It cannot continue."

"Anything," Sybelle said. She crouched down beside me. "Is my hand cool if I lay it on your forehead? Is it gentle if I touch your hair?"

I looked at her from one narrow-slitted eye.

Her long thin neck was part of her shivering and emaciated loveliness. Her breasts were voluptuous and high. Beyond her in the lovely warm glow of the room, I saw the piano. I thought of these long gentle fingers touching the keys. I could hear in my head the throb of the *Appassionata*.

There came a loud flick, a crackle, a snap, and then the rich fragrance of fine tobacco.

Benji strode back and forth beyond her, with his black cigarette on his lip.

"I have a plan," he declared, effortlessly holding forth with the cigarette firmly grasped between his half-open lips. "I go down to the streets. I meet a bad, bad guy in no time. I tell him I'm alone here in this apartment, up here in the hotel, with a man who is drunk and drooling and crazy and we have all this cocaine to sell and I don't know what to do and I need help with it."

I started to laugh in spite of the pain.

The little Bedouin shrugged his shoulders and held up his palms, puffing away on the black cigarette, the smoke curling about him like a magical cloud.

"What you think? It will work. Look, I'm a good judge of character. Now, you, Sybelle, you get out of the way, and let me lead this miserable sack of filth, this bad guy whom I lure into my trap, right to the very bed, and pitch him down on his face, like this, I trip him with my foot, like this, and he falls, boink, right into your arms, Armand, what do you think of it?"

"And if it goes wrong?" I asked.

"Then my beautiful Sybelle cracks him over the head with her hammer."

"I have a better thought," I said, "though God knows that what you've just devised is unsurpassingly brilliant. You tell him of course that the cocaine is under the coverlet in neat little plastic sacks all stretched out, but if he doesn't take this bait and come here to see for himself, then let our beautiful Sybelle simply throw back the cover, and when he sees what truly lies in this bed, he'll be out of here with no thought to harm anyone!"

"That's it!" Sybelle cried. She clapped her hands together. Her pale luminous eyes were wide.

"That's perfect," Benji agreed.

"But mark, don't carry a copper penny into the streets with you. If only we had but a little bit of the evil white powder with which to bait the beast."

"But we do," said Sybelle. "We have just that, a little bit which we took from my brother's pockets." She looked down at me thoughtfully, not seeing me but running the plan through the tight coils of her soft and yielding mind. "We took everything out so that when we left him to be found, they'd find nothing with him. There are so many who are left that way in New York. Of course it was an unspeakable chore to drag him."

"But we have that evil white powder, yes!" said

Benji, clasping her shoulder suddenly and then bolting out of my sight to return within the instant with a small flat white cigarette case.

"Put it here, where I can smell what's inside," I said. I could see that neither of them knew for certain.

Benji snapped open the lid of the thin silver box. There, nestled in a small plastic bag, folded with impeccable neatness, was the powder with the very exact smell that I wanted it to have. I needn't put it to my tongue, on which sugar would have tasted just as alien.

"That's fine. Only empty out half of that at once down a drain, so that there's just a little left, and leave the silver case here, lest you run into some fool who'll kill you for it."

Sybelle shivered with obvious fear. "Benji, I'll go with you."

"No, that would be most unwise," I said. "He can get away from anyone much faster without you."

"Oh, so right you are!" said Benji, taking the last drag from his cigarette and then crushing it out in a big glass ashtray beside the bed, where a dozen other little white butts were curled waiting for it. "And how many times do I tell her that when I go out for cigarettes in the middle of the night? Does she listen?"

He was off without waiting for an answer. I heard the rush of water from the tap. He was washing away half the cocaine. I let my eyes roam the room, veering away from the soft blood-filled guardian angel.

"There are people innately good," I said, "who want to help others. You are one of them, Sybelle. I won't rest as long as you live. I'll be at your side. I'll be there always to guard you and to repay you."

She smiled.

I was astonished.

Her lean face, with its well-shaped pale lips, broke into the freshest and most robust smile, as if neglect and pain had never gnawed at her.

"You'll be a guardian angel to me, Armand?" she asked.

"Always."

"I'm off," Benji declared. With a crackle and snap, he lit another cigarette. His lungs must have been charcoal sacks. "I'm going out into the night. But what if this son of a bitch is sick or dirty or—."

"Means nothing to me. Blood's blood. Just bring him here. Don't try this fancy tripping with your foot. Wait till you have him right here beside the bed, and as he reaches to lift the cover, you, Sybelle, pull it back, and you, Benji, push on him with all your might, so the side of the bed trips his shins, and he'll fall into my arms. And after that, I'll have him."

He headed for the door.

"Wait," I whispered. What was I thinking of in my greed? I looked up at her mute smiling face, and then at him, the little engine puffing away on the black cigarette, with nothing on for the fierce winter outside but the damned djellaba.

"No, it has to be done," said Sybelle with wide eyes. "And Benji will choose a very bad man, won't you, Benji? An evil man who wants to rob and kill you."

"I know where to go," said Benji with a little twisted smile. "Just play your cards when I come back, both of you. Cover him up, Sybelle. Don't look at the clock. Don't worry about me!"

Off he went with the slam of the door, the big heavy lock slipping shut behind him automatically.

So it was coming. Blood, thick red blood. It was coming. It was coming, and it would be hot and delicious, and there would a manful of it, and it was coming, it was coming within seconds.

I closed my eyes, and opening them, I let the room take shape again with its sky-blue draperies on every window, hanging down in rich folds to the floor, and the carpet a great writhing oval of cabbage roses. And she, this stalk of a girl staring at me and smiling her simple sweet smile, as if the crime of the night would be nothing to her.

She came down on her knees next to me, perilously close, and again she touched my hair with delicate hand. Her soft unfettered breasts touched my arm. I read her thoughts as if I read her palm, pushing back through layer after layer of her conscious, seeing the dark winding road again whipping and turning through the Jordan Valley, and the parents driving too fast for the pitch dark and the hairpin curves and the Arab drivers who came on plunging at even greater speed so that each meeting of headlamps became a grueling contest.

"To eat the fish from the Sea of Galilee," she said, her eyes drifting away from me. "I wanted it. It was my idea we go there. We had one more day in the Holy Land, and they said it's a long drive from Jerusalem to Nazareth, and I said, 'But He walked on the water.' It was to me always the strangest tale. You know it?"

"I do," I said.

"That He was walking right on the water, as if He'd forgotten the Apostles were there or that anyone might see Him, and they from the boat, said, 'Lord!' and He was startled. Such a strange miracle, as if it was all . . . accidental. I was the one who wanted to go. I was the one who wanted to eat the fresh fish right out of the sea, the same water that Peter and the others had fished. It was my doing. Oh, I don't say it was my fault that they died. It was my doing. And we were all headed home for my big night at Carnegie Hall, and the record company was set up to record it, live. I'd made a recording before, you know. It had done much better than anyone ever expected. But that night . . . this night that never happened, that is, I was going to play the *Appassionata*. It was all that mattered to me. The other sonatas I love, the *Moonlight*, the *Pathétique*, but really for me . . . it was the *Appassionata*. My Father and Mother were so proud. But my brother, he was the one who always fought, always got me the time, the space, the good piano, the teachers I needed. He was the one who made them see, but then of course, he didn't have any life at all, and all of us saw what was coming. We'd talk about it round the table at night, that he had to get a life of his own, it was no good his working for me, but then he'd say that I would need him for years to come, I couldn't even imagine. He'd manage the recordings and the performances and the repertoire, and the fees we asked. The agents couldn't be trusted. I had no idea, he said, of how high I'd rise."

She paused, cocking her head to one side, her face earnest yet still simple.

"It wasn't a decision I made, you understand," she said. "I just wouldn't do anything else. They were dead. I just wouldn't go out. I just wouldn't answer the phone. I just wouldn't play anything else. I just wouldn't listen to what he said. I just wouldn't plan. I just wouldn't eat. I just wouldn't change my clothes. I just played the *Appassionata*."

"I understand," I said softly.

"He brought Benji back with us to take care of me. I always wondered how. I think Benji was bought, you know, bought with cold cash?"

"I know."

"I think that's what happened. He couldn't leave me alone, he said, not even at the King David, that was the hotel—."

"Yes."

"—because he said I'd stand in the window without my clothes, or I wouldn't let the maid come in, and I'd play the piano in the middle of the night and he couldn't sleep. So he got Benji. I love Benji."

"I know."

"I'd always do what Benji said. He never dared to hit Benji. Only towards the end he started to really hurt me. Before that it was slaps, you know, and kicks. Or he'd pull my hair. He'd grab me by the hair, all my hair in one hand, and he'd throw me down on the floor. He did that often. But he didn't dare to hit Benji. He knew if he hit Benji I'd scream and scream. But then sometimes, when Benji would try to make him stop—. But I'm not so sure about that because I would be so dizzy. My head would ache."

"I understand," I said. Of course, he had hit Benji.

She mused, quietly, her eyes large still, and so bright without tears or puckering.

"We're alike, you and I," she whispered, looking down at me. Her hand lay close to my cheek, and she very lightly pressed the soft upper part of her forefinger against me.

"Alike?" I asked. "What in the world can you be thinking of?"

"Monsters," she said. "Children."

I smiled. But she didn't smile. She looked dreamy.

"I was so glad when you came," she said. "I knew he was dead. I knew when you stood at the end of the piano and you looked at me. I knew when you stood there listening to me. I was so happy that there was someone who could kill him."

"Do this for me," I said.

"What?" she asked. "Armand, I'll do anything."

"Go to the piano now. Play it for me. Play the *Appassionata*."

"But the plan," she asked in a small wondering voice. "The evil man, he's coming."

"Leave this to Benji and me. Don't turn around to look. Just play the *Appassionata*."

"No, please," she asked gently.

"But why not?" I said. "Why must you put yourself through such an ordeal?"

"You don't understand," she said with the widest eyes. "I want to see it!"

22

BENJI HAD JUST RETURNED below. The distant sound of his voice, quite inaudible to Sybelle, instantly drove back the pain from all the surfaces of my limbs.

"That's what I mean, you see," he was talking away, "it's all underneath the dead body, and we don't wanna lift it, the dead body, and you being a cop, you know, you being Drug Enforcement, they said you would know how to take care of it . . ."

I started to laugh. He had really done himself proud. I looked again at Sybelle, who was staring at me with a quiet resolute expression, one of profound intelligence and reflection.

"Push this cover up over my face," I said, "and move away, far away. He's bringing us a regular prince of rogues. Hurry."

She snapped into action. I could smell the blood of this victim already, though he was still in the ascending elevator, talking to Benji in low guarded terms.

"And all this you just happen to have in this apartment, you and she, and there's nobody else in on this?"

Oh, he was a beauty. I heard the murderer in his voice.

"I told you everything," Benji said in the most natural of little voices. "You just help with this, you know, I can't have the police coming in here!" Whisper. "This is a fine hotel. How did I know this guy was going to die here! We don't use this stuff, you take the stuff, just get the body out of here. Now let me tell you—."

The elevator opened to our floor.

"—this body is pretty messed up, so don't go all slobbering on me when you see it."

"Slobbering on you," growled the victim under his breath. Their shoes made soft hastening sounds on the carpet.

Benji fumbled with his keys, pretending to be mixed up.

"Sybelle," he called out in warning. "Sybelle, open the door."

"Don't do it," I said in a low voice.

"Of course not," came her velvety answer.

The barrels of the big lock turned.

"And this guy just happens to come up here and die on you with all this stuff."

"Well, not exactly," said Benji, "but you made a bargain with me, no, I expect you to stick to it."

"Look, you little guttersnipe, I didn't make any bargain with you."

"Okay, then maybe I call the regular police then. I know you. Everybody in the bar knows you, who you are, you're always around. What are you going to do, big shot? Kill me?"

The door closed behind them. The smell of the man's blood flooded the apartment. He was besotted with brandy and had the poison cocaine in his veins

as well, but none of this would make a particle of difference to my cleansing thirst. I could scarce contain
myself. I felt my limbs tighten and try to flex beneath the
coverlet.

"Well, isn't she the perfect princess," he said, his
eyes obviously having fallen on Sybelle. Sybelle made
no answer.

"Never mind her, you look there, under the covers.
Sybelle, you come here by me. Come on, Sybelle."

"Under there? You're telling me the body's under
there, and the cocaine is under the body?"

"How many times I have to tell you?" asked Benji,
no doubt with his characteristic shrug. "Look, what part
don't you understand, I'd like to know. You don't want
this cocaine? I give it away. I'll be very popular in your
favorite bar. Come on, Sybelle, this man says he will
help, then he won't help, talk, talk, talk, typical government sleaze."

"Who are you calling a sleaze, kid?" demanded the
man with mock gentleness, the fragrance of the brandy
thickening. "That's some big vocabulary you have for
such a little body. How old are you, kid? How the Hell
did you get into this country? You go around in that
nightgown all the time?"

"Yeah, sure, just call me Lawrence of Arabia," said
Benji. "Sybelle, come over here."

I didn't want her to come. I wanted her as far away
from this as possible. She didn't move, and I was very
glad of it.

"I like my clothes," Benji chattered on. Puff of sweet
cigarette smoke. "I should dress like kids in this place, I

suppose, in blue jeans? As if. My people dressed like this when Mohammed was in the desert."

"Nothing like progress," said the man with a deep throaty laugh.

He approached the bed with quick crisp steps. The scent of blood was so rich I could feel the pores of my burnt skin opening for it.

I used the tiniest part of my strength to form a telepathic picture of him through their eyes—a tall brown-eyed man, sallow white skin, gaunt cheeks, receding brown hair, in a handmade Italian suit of shining black silk with flashing diamond cufflinks on his rich linen. He was antsy, fingers working at his sides, almost unable to stand still, his brain a riot of dizzy humor, cynicism and crazed curiosity. His eyes were greedy and playful. The ruthlessness underscored all, and there seemed in him a strong streak of genuine drug-nourished insanity. He wore his murders as proudly as he wore his princely suit and the shiny brown boots on his feet.

Sybelle came near the bed, the sharp sweet scent of her pure flesh mingling with the heavier richer scent of the man. But it was his blood I savored, his blood that brought the juices up into my parched mouth. I could barely keep from making a sigh beneath the covers. I felt my limbs about to dance right out of their painful paralysis.

The villain was sizing up the place, glancing left and right through open doors, listening for other voices, debating whether he should search this fancy overstuffed and rambling hotel apartment before he did anything else. His fingers would not be still. In a flash of wordless thought, I caught the quick realization that he'd snorted the cocaine Benji had brought, and he wanted more immediately.

"My, but you are a beautiful young lady," he said to Sybelle.

"Do you want me to lift the cover?" she asked.

I could smell the small handgun that was jammed in his high black leather boot, and the other gun, very fancy and modern, a distinctly different collection of metallic scents, in the holster under his arm. I could smell cash on him too, that unmistakable stale smell of filthy paper money.

"Come on, you chicken, buster?" asked Benji. "You want me to pull back the cover? Say when. You're gonna be real surprised, believe me!"

"There's no body under there," he said with a sneer. "Why don't we sit down and have a little talk? This isn't really your place, is it? I think you children need a little paternal guidance."

"The body's all burnt up," said Benji. "Don't get sick now."

"Burnt up!" said the man.

It was Sybelle's long hand that suddenly whipped the coverlet back. The cool air skidded across my skin. I stared up at the man who drew back, a half-strangled growl caught in his throat.

"For the love of God!"

My body sprang up, drawn by the plump fountain of blood like a hideous puppet on a score of whipping strings. I flailed against him, then anchored my burnt fingernails hard into his neck and wrapped the other arm around him in an agonizing embrace, my tongue flashing at the blood that spilled from the claw marks as I drew in and, ignoring the blazing pain in my face, opened my mouth wide and sank my fangs.

Now I had him.

His height, his strength, his powerful shoulders, his huge hands clamping to my hurt flesh, none of this could help him. I had him. I drew up the first thick swallow of blood and thought I would swoon. But my body wasn't about to allow it. My body had locked to him as if I were a thing of voracious tentacles.

At once, his crazed and luminous thoughts drew me down into a glitzy swirl of New York images, of careless cruelty and grotesque horror, of rampant drug-driven energy and sinister hilarity. I let the images flood me. I couldn't go for the quick death. I had to have every drop of blood inside him, and for that the heart must pump and pump; the heart must not give up.

If I had ever tasted blood this strong, this sweet and salty, I had no memory of it; there was no way in which memory could record such deliciousness, the absolute rapture of thirst slaked, of hunger cured, of loneliness dissolved in this hot and intimate embrace, in which the sound of my own seething, straining breath would have horrified me if I had cared about it.

Such a noise I made, such a dreadful feasting noise. My fingers massaged his thick muscles, my nostrils were pressed into his pampered soap-scented skin.

"Hmmm, love you, wouldn't hurt you for the world, you feel it, it's sweet, isn't it?" I whispered to him over the shallows of gorgeous blood. "Hmmm, yes, so sweet, better than the finest brandy, hmmm . . ."

In his shock and disbelief, he suddenly let go utterly,

surrendering to the delirium that I stoked with each word. I ripped at his neck, widening the wound, rupturing the artery more fully. The blood gushed anew.

An exquisite shiver ran down my back; it ran down the backs of my arms, and down my buttocks and legs. It was pain and pleasure commingled as the hot and lively blood forced itself into the microfibers of my shriveled flesh, as it plumped the muscles beneath the roasted skin, as it sank into the very marrow of my bones. More, I had to have more.

"Stay alive, you don't want to die, no, stay alive," I crooned, rubbing my fingers up through his hair, feeling that they were fingers now, not the pterodactyl digits they'd been moments before. Oh, they were hot; it was the fire all over again, it was the fire blazing in my scorched limbs, this time death had to come, I couldn't bear this any longer, but a pinnacle had been reached, and now it was past and a great soothing ache rushed through me.

My face was pumped and teeming, my mouth full again and again, and my throat now swallowing without effort.

"Ah, yes, alive, you're so strong, so wonderfully strong . . ." I whispered. "Hmmm, no, don't go . . . not yet, it's not time."

His knees buckled. He sank slowly to the carpet, and I with him, pulling him gently over with me against the side of the bed, and then letting him fall beside me, so that we lay like lovers entangled. There was more, much more, more than ever I could have drunk in my regular state, more than ever I could have wanted.

Even on those rare occasions when I was a fledgling

and greedy and new, and had taken two or three victims a night, I had never drunk so deeply from any one of them. I was now into the dark tasty dregs, pulling out the very vessels themselves in sweet clots that dissolved on my tongue.

"Oh, you are so precious, yes, yes."

But his heart could take no more. It was slowing to a lethal irretrievable pace. I closed my teeth on the skin of his face and ripped it open over his forehead, lapping at the rich tangle of bleeding vessels that covered his skull. There was so much blood here, so much blood behind the tissues of the face. I sucked up the fibers, and then spit them out bloodless and white, watching them drop to the floor like so much slop.

I wanted the heart and the brain. I had seen the ancients take it. I knew how. I'd seen the Roman Pandora once reach right into the chest.

I went for it. Astonished to see my hand fully formed though dark brown in color, I made my fingers rigid like a deadly spade and drove it into him, tearing linen and cracking breastbone, and then reaching his soft entrails until I had the heart and held it as I'd seen Pandora hold it. I drank from it. Oh, it had plenty of blood. This was magnificent. I sucked it to pulp and then let it fall.

I lay as still as he, at his side, my right hand on the back of his neck, my head bowed against his chest, my breath coming in heavy sighs. The blood danced in me. I felt my arms and legs jerking. Spasms ran through me, so that the sight of his white dead carcass blinkered in my gaze. The room flashed on and off.

"Oh, what a sweet brother," I whispered. "Sweet, sweet brother." I rolled on my back. I could hear the roar of his blood in my very ears, feel it moving over my scalp, feel it tingling in my cheeks and in the palms of my hands. Oh, good, too good, too lusciously good.

"Bad guy, hmmm?" It was Benji's voice, far away in the world of the living.

Far away in another realm where pianos ought to be played, and little boys should dance, they stood, the two like painted cutout figures against the swimming light of the room, merely gazing at me, he the little desert rogue with his fancy black cigarette, puffing away and smacking his lips and raising his eyebrows, and she merely floating it seemed, resolute and thoughtful as before, unshocked, untouched perhaps.

I sat up and pulled up my knees. I rose to my feet, with only a quick handhold on the side of the bed to steady myself. I stood naked looking at her.

Her eyes were filled with a deep rich gray light, and she smiled as she looked at me.

"Oh, magnificent," she whispered.

"Magnificent?" I said. I lifted my hands and pushed my hair back off my face. "Show me to the glass. Hurry. I'm thirsting. I'm thirsting again already."

It had begun, this was no lie. In a stupor of shock I stared into the mirror. I had seen such ruined specimens as this before, but each of us is ruined in our own way, and I, for alchemical reasons I couldn't proclaim, was a dark brown creature, the very perfect color of chocolate, with remarkably white opal eyes set with reddish-brown pupils. The nipples of my chest were black as raisins. My cheeks were painfully gaunt, my ribs perfectly defined beneath my shiny skin, and the veins, the veins that were so full of sizzling action, stood like ropes along my arms and the calves of my legs. My hair, of course, had never seemed so lustrous, so full, so much a thing of youth and natural beneficence.

I opened my mouth. I ached with thirst. All the awakened flesh sang with thirst or cursed me with it. It was as if a thousand crushed and muted cells were now chanting for blood.

"I have to have more. I have to. Stay away from me." I hurried past Benji, who all but danced at my side.

"What do you want, what can I do? I'll get another one."

"No, I'll get him for myself." I fell on the victim and slipped loose his silk tie. I quickly undid the buttons of his shirt.

Benji fell at once to unbuckling his belt. Sybelle, on her knees, tugged at his boots.

"The gun, beware of the gun," I said in alarm. "Sybelle, back away from him."

"I see the gun," she said reprovingly. She laid it aside carefully, as if it were a freshly caught fish and might flop from her hands. She peeled off his socks. "Armand, these clothes," she said, "they're too big."

"Benji, you have shoes?" I asked. "My feet are small."

I stood up and hastily put on the shirt, fastening the buttons with a speed that dazzled them.

"Don't watch me, get the shoes," I said. I pulled on the trousers, zipped them up, and with Sybelle's quick fingers to help, buckled the flapping leather belt. I pulled it as tight as I could. This would do.

She crouched before me, her dress a huge flowered circle of prettiness around her, as she rolled the pant legs over my brown bare feet.

I had slipped my hands through his fancy linked shirt cuffs without ever disturbing them.

Benji threw down the black dress shoes, fine Bally pumps, never even worn by him, divine little wretch. Sybelle held one sock for my foot. Benji gathered up the other.

When I put on the coat it was done. The sweet tingling in my veins had stopped. It was pain again, it was beginning to roar, as if I were threaded with fire, and the witch with the needle pulled on the thread, hard, to make me quiver.

"A towel, my dears, something old, common. No, don't, not in this day and age, don't think of it."

Full of loathing I gazed down at his livid flesh. He lay staring dully at the ceiling, the soft tiny hair in his nostrils very black against his drained and awful skin, his teeth yellow above his colorless lip. The hair on his chest was a matted swarm in the sweat of his death, and against the giant gaping slit lay the pulp that had been his heart, ah, this was the evil evidence which must be shut from the eyes of the world on general principles.

I reached down and slipped the ruins of his heart back into the cavity of his chest. I spit upon the wound and rubbed it with my fingers.

Benji gasped. "Look at it heal, Sybelle," he cried.

"Just barely," I said. "He's too cold, too empty." I looked about. There lay the man's wallet, papers, a bag in leather, lots of green bills in a fancy silver clip. I gathered all this up. I stuffed the folded money in one pocket, and all else in the other. What else did he have? Cigarette, a deadly switchblade knife, and the guns, ah, yes, the guns.

Into my coat pockets I put these items.

Swallowing my nausea, I reached down and scooped him up, horrid flaccid white man in his pitiable silk shorts and fancy gold wristwatch. My old strength was indeed coming back. He was heavy, but I could easily heave him over my shoulder.

"What will you do, where will you go?" Sybelle cried. "Armand, you can't leave us."

"You'll come back!" said Benji. "Here, gimme that watch, don't throw away that man's watch."

"Sshhh, Benji," Sybelle whispered. "You know damned good and well I've bought you the finest watches. Don't touch him. Armand, what can we do now to help you?" She drew close to me. "Look!" she said pointing to the dangling arm of the corpse which hung just below my right elbow. "He has manicured nails. How amazing."

"Oh, yeah, he always took very good care of himself," said Benji. "You know the watch is worth five thousand dollars."

"Hush up about the watch," she said. "We don't want his things." She looked at me again. "Armand, even now you're still changing. Your face, it's getting fuller."

"Yes, and it hurts," I said. "Wait for me. Prepare a dark room for me. I'll come back as soon as I've fed. I have to feed now, feed and feed to heal the scars that are left. Open the door for me."

"Let me see if there's anyone out there," said Benji with a quick dutiful rush to the door.

I went out into the hallway, easily carrying the poor corpse, its white arms hanging down, swinging and banging against me just a little.

What a sight I was in these big clothes. I must have looked like a mad poetical schoolboy who had raided the thrift stores for the finest threads and was off now in fancy new shoes to search out the rock bands.

"There isn't anyone out here, my little friend," I said. "It's three of the clock and the hotel's asleep. And if reason serves me right, that's the door of the fire stairs there, at the very end of the hall, correct? There isn't anyone in the fire stairs either."

"Oh, clever Armand, you delight me!" he said. He narrowed his little black eyes. He jumped up and down soundlessly on the hallway carpet. "Give me the watch!" he whispered.

"No," I said. "She's right. She's rich, and so am I, and so are you. Don't be a beggar."

"Armand, we'll wait for you," said Sybelle in the doorframe. "Benji, come inside immediately."

"Oh, listen to her now, how she wakes up! How she talks! 'Benji, come inside,' she says. Hey, sweetheart, don't you have something to do just now, like perhaps play the piano?"

She gave a tiny burst of laughter in spite of herself. I smiled. What a strange pair they were. They did not believe their own eyes. But that was typical enough in this century. I wondered when they would start to see, and having seen, start screaming.

"Goodbye, sweet loves," I said. "Be ready for me."

"Armand, you will come back." Her eyes were full of tears. "You promise me."

I was stunned. "Sybelle," I said. "What is it that women want so often to hear and wait so long to hear it? I love you."

I left them, racing down the stairs, hefting him to the other shoulder when the weight on the one side became too hurtful. The pain passed over me in waves. The shock of the outside cold air was scalding.

"Feed," I whispered. And what was I to do with him? He was far too naked to carry down Fifth Avenue.

I slipped off his watch because it was the only identification on him left, and almost vomiting with revulsion from my closeness to these fetid remains, I dragged him by one hand after me very fast through the back alley, and then across a small street, and down another sidewalk.

I ran into the face of the icy wind, not stopping to observe those few hulking shapes that hobbled by in the wet darkness, or to take stock of the one car that crept along on the shining wet asphalt.

Within seconds I had covered two blocks, and finding a likely alleyway, with a high gate to keep out the beggars of the night, I quickly mounted the bars and flung his carcass to the very far end of it. Down into the melting snow he fell. I was rid of him.

Now I had to have blood. There was no time for the old game, the game of drawing out those who wanted to die, those who truly craved my embrace, those in love already with the far country of death of which they knew nothing.

I had to shuffle and stumble along, the mark, in my floppy silk jacket and rolled pants, long hair veiling my face, poor dazzled kid, perfect for your knife, your gun, your fist.

It didn't take long.

The first was a drunken, sauntering wretch who plied me with questions before he revealed the flashing blade and went to sink it into me. I pushed him up against the side of the building, and fed like a glutton.

The next was a common desperate youth, full of festering sores, who had killed twice before for the heroin he needed as badly as I needed the doomed blood inside him.

I drank more slowly.

The thickest worst scars of my body yielded with much defense, itching, throbbing and only slowly melting away. But the thirst, the thirst would not stop. My bowels churned as if devouring themselves. My eyes pulsed with pain.

But the cold wet city, so full of rankling hollow noise, grew ever brighter before me. I could hear voices many blocks away, and small electronic speakers in high buildings. I could see beyond the breaking clouds the true and numberless stars.

I was almost myself again.

So who will come to me now, I thought, in this barren desolate hour before dawn, when the snow is melting in the warmer air, and neon lights have all died out, and the wet newspaper blows like leaves through a stripped and frozen forest?

I took all the precious articles which had belonged to my first victim, and dropped them here and there into deep hollow public trash cans.

One last killer, yes, please, fate, do give me this, while there's time, and indeed he came, blasted fool, out of a car as behind him the driver waited, the motor idling.

"What's taking you so damn long?" said the driver at last.

"Nothing," I said, dropping his friend. I leaned in to look at him. He was as vicious and stupid as his companion. He threw up his hand, but helplessly and too late. I pushed him over on the leather seat and drank now for rank pleasure, pure sweet crazed pleasure.

I walked slowly through the night, my arms out, my eyes directed Heavenward.

From the scattered black grates of the gleaming street there gushed the pure white steam of heated places below. Trash in shiny plastic sacks made a fantastical modern and glittering display on the curbs of the slate-gray sidewalks.

Tiny tender trees, with little year-round leaves like short pen strokes of bright green in the night, bent their stemlike trunks with the whining wind. Everywhere the high clean glass doors of granite-faced buildings contained the radiant splendor of rich lobbies. Shop windows displayed their sparkling diamonds, lustrous furs and smartly cut coats and gowns on grandly coiffed and faceless pewter mannequins.

The Cathedral was a lightless, soundless place of frost-rimmed turrets and ancient pointed arches, the pavement clean where I had stood on the morning when the sun caught me.

Lingering there, I closed my eyes, trying perhaps to recall the wonder and the zeal, the courage and the glorious expectation.

There came instead, clear and shining through the dark air, the pristine notes of the *Appassionata*. Roiling, rumbling, racing on, the crashing music came to call me home. I followed it.

The clock in the hotel foyer was striking six. The winter dark would break up in moments like the very ice that had once imprisoned me. The long polished desk was deserted in the muted lights.

In a wall mirror of dim glass framed in rococo gold, I saw myself, paled and waxen, and unblemished. Oh, what fun the sun and ice had had with me in turns, the fury of the one quick-frozen by the merciless grip of the other. Not a scar remained of where the skin had burnt to muscle. A sealed and solid thing with seamless agony within, I was, all of a piece, restored, with sparkling clear white fingernails, and curling lashes round my clear brown eyes, and clothes a wretched heap of stained, misfitted finery on the old familiar rugged cherub.

Never before had I been thankful to see my own too youthful face, too hairless chin, too soft and delicate hands. But I could have thanked the gods of old for wings at this moment.

Above, the music carried on, so grand, so legible of tragedy and lust and dauntless spirit. I loved it so. Who in the whole wide world could ever play that same Sonata as she did, each phrase as fresh as songs sung all their livelong life by birds who know but one such set of patterns.

I looked about. It was a fine, expensive place, of old wainscoting and a few deep chairs, and door keys ranged up a wall in tiny dark-stained wooden boxes.

A great vase of flowers, the infallible trademark of the vintage New York hotel, stood boldly and magnificently in the middle of the space, atop a round black marble table. I skirted the bouquet, snapping off one big pink lily with a deep red throat and petals curling to yellow at the outside, and then I went silently up the fire stairs to find my children.

She did not stop her playing when Benji let me in.

"You're looking really good, Angel," he said.

On and on she went, her head moving unaffectedly and perfectly with the rhythm of the Sonata.

He led me through a chain of finely decorated plastered chambers. Mine was too sumptuous by far, I whispered, seeing the tapestry spread and pillows of old gracious threadbare gold. I needed only perfect darkness.

"But this is the least we have," he said with a little shrug.

He had changed to a fresh white linen robe lined with a fine blue stripe, a kind I'd often seen in Arab lands. He wore white socks with his brown sandals. He puffed his little Turkish cigarette, and squinted up at me through the smoke.

"You brought me back the watch, didn't you!" He nodded his head, all sarcasm and amusement.

"No," I said. I reached into my pocket. "But you may have the money. Tell me, since your little mind is such a locket and I have no key, did anyone see you bring that badge-carrying, gun-toting villain up here?"

"I see him all the time," he said with a little weary wave of his hand. "We left the bar separately. I killed two birds with one stone. I'm very smart."

"How so?" I asked. I put the lily in his little hand.

"Sybelle's brother bought from him. That cop was the only guy ever missed him." He gave a little laugh. He tucked the lily in the thick curls above his left ear, then pulled it down and twirled its tiny ciborium in his fingers. "Clever, no? Now nobody asks where he is."

"Oh, indeed, two birds with one stone, you're quite right," I said. "Though I'm sure there's a great deal more to it."

"But you'll help us now, won't you?"

"I will indeed. I'm very rich, I told you. I'll patch things up. I have an instinct for it. I owned a great playhouse in a faraway city, and after that an island of fancy shops, and other such things. I am a monster in many realms, it seems. You'll never, ever have to fear again."

"You're truly beauty full, you know," he said raising one eyebrow and then giving me a quick wink. He drew on his tasty-looking little cigarette and then offered it to me. His left hand kept the lily safe.

"Can't. Only drink blood," I said. "A regular vampire out of the book in the main. Need deep darkness in the light of day, which is coming very soon. You mustn't touch this door."

"Ha!" he laughed with impish delight. "That's what I told her!" He rolled his eyes and glanced in the direction of the living room. "I said we had to steal a coffin for you right away, but she said, no, you'd think of that."

"How right she was. The room will do, but I like coffins well enough. I really do."

"And can you make us vampires too?"

"Oh, never. Absolutely not. You're pure of heart and

too alive, and I don't have such a power. It's never done. It can't be."

Again, he shrugged. "Then who made you?" he asked.

"I was born out of a black egg," I said. "We all are."

He gave a scoffing laugh.

"Well, you've seen all the rest," I said. "Why not believe the best part of it?"

He only smiled and puffed his smoke, and looked at me most knavishly.

The piano sang on in crashing cascades, the rapid notes melting as fast as they were born, so like the last thin snowflakes of the winter, vanishing before they strike the pavements.

"May I kiss her before I go to sleep?" I asked.

He cocked his head, and shrugged. "If she doesn't like it, she'll never stop playing long enough to say so."

I went back into the parlor. How clear it all was, the grand design of sumptuous French landscapes with their golden clouds and cobalt skies, the Chinese vases on their stands, the massed velvet tumbling from the high bronze rods of the narrow old windows. I saw it all of a piece, including the bed where I had lain, now heaped with fresh down-filled coverlets and pillowed with embroidered antique faces.

And she, the center diamond of it all, in long white flannel, flounced at wrists and hem with rich old Irish lace, playing her long lacquered grand with agile unerring fingers, her hair a broad smooth yellow glow about her shoulders.

I kissed her scented locks, and then her tender throat,

and caught her girlish smile and gleaming glance as she played on, her head tilting back to brush my coat front.

Down around her neck, I slipped my arms. She leant her gentle weight against me. With crossed arms, I clasped her waist. I felt her shoulders moving against my snug embrace with her darting fingers.

I dared in whisper-soft tones with sealed lips to hum the song, and she hummed with me.

"Appassionata," I whispered in her ear. I was crying. I didn't want to touch her with blood. She was too clean, too pretty. I turned my head.

She pitched forward. Her hands pounded into the stormy finish.

A silence fell, abrupt, and crystalline as the music before it.

She turned and threw her arms around me, and held me tight and said the words I'd never heard a mortal speak in all my long immortal life:

"Armand, I love you."

23

NEED I SAY they are the perfect companions?

Neither of them cared about the murders. I could not for the life of me understand it. They cared about other things, such as world peace, the poor suffering homeless in the waning winter cold of New York, the price of medicines for the sick, and how dreadful it was that Israel and Palestine were forever in battle with each other. But they did not care one whit about the horrors they'd beheld with their own eyes. They did not care that I killed every night for blood, that I lived off it and nothing else, and that I was a creature wed by my very nature to human destruction.

They did not care one whit about the dead brother (his name was Fox, by the way, and the last name of my beautiful child is best left unmentioned).

In fact if this text ever sees the light of the real world, you're bound to change both her first name and that of Benjamin.

However, that's not my concern now. I can't think of the fate of these pages, except that they are very much for her, as I mentioned to you before, and if I'm allowed to title them I think it will be *Symphony for Sybelle*.

Not, please understand, that I love Benji no less. It's only that I haven't the same overwhelming protective feeling for him. I know that Benji will live out a great and adventurous life, no matter what should befall me or Sybelle, or even the times. It's in his flexible and enduring Bedouin nature. He is a true child of the tents and the blowing sands, though in his case, the house was a dismal cinder block hovel on the outskirts of Jerusalem where he induced tourists to pose for overpriced pictures with him and a filthy snarling camel.

He'd been flat out kidnapped by Fox under the felonious terms of a long-term lease of bondage for which Fox paid Benji's father five thousand dollars. A fabricated emigration passport was thrown into the bargain. He'd been the genius of the tribe, without doubt, had mixed feelings about going home and had learnt in the New

York streets to steal, smoke and curse, in that order. Though he swore up and down he couldn't read, it turned out that he could, and began to do so obsessively just as soon as I started throwing books at him.

In fact, he could read English, Hebrew and Arabic, having read all three in the newspapers of his homeland since before he could remember.

He loved taking care of Sybelle. He saw to it that she ate, drank milk, bathed and changed her clothes when none of these routine tasks interested her. He prided himself on the fact that he could by his wits obtain for her whatever she needed, no matter what happened to her.

He was the front man for her with the hotel, tipping the maids, making normal talk at the front desk, which included remarkably fine-spun lies about the where-abouts of the dead Fox, who had become in Benji's never ending saga a fabulous world traveler and amateur photographer; he handled the piano tuner, who was called as often as once a week because the piano stood by the window, exposed to sun and cold, and also be-cause Sybelle did indeed pound it with the fury that would indeed have impressed the great Beethoven. He spoke on the phone to the bank, all of whose personnel thought he was his older brother, David, pronounced Dahveed, and then made the requisite calls at the teller's window for cash as little Benjamin.

I was convinced within nights of talking with him that I could give him as fine an education as Marius had ever given me, and that he would end up having his choice of universities, professions or amateur pursuits of mind-engaging substance. I didn't overplay my hand. But before the week was out I was dreaming of boarding schools for him from which he might emerge a gold-buttoned blue blazer–wearing American East Coast social conquistador.

I love him enough to tear limb from limb anyone who so much as lays a finger on him.

But between me and Sybelle there lies a sympathy which sometimes eludes mortals and immortals for the space of their entire lives. I know Sybelle. I know her. I knew her when I first heard her play, and I know her now, and I wouldn't be here with you if she were not under the protection of Marius. I will during the space of Sybelle's life never be parted from her, and there is nothing she can ever ask of me that I shall not give.

I will endure unspeakable anguish when Sybelle inevitably dies. But that has to be borne. I have no choice now in the matter. I am not the creature I was when I laid eyes on Veronica's Veil, when I stepped into the sun.

I am someone else, and that someone else has fallen deeply and completely in love with Sybelle and Benjamin and I cannot go back on it.

Of course I am keenly conscious that I thrive in this love; being happier than I have ever been in my entire immortal existence, I have gained great strength from having these two as my companions. The situation is too nearly perfect to be anything but utterly accidental.

Sybelle is not insane. She is nowhere near it, and I fancy that I understand her perfectly. Sybelle is obsessed with one thing, and that is playing the piano. From the first time she laid her hands on the keys she has wanted nothing else. And her "career," as so generously planned for her by her proud parents and by the burningly ambitious Fox, never meant much of anything to her.

Had she been poor and struggling perhaps recognition would have been indispensable to her love affair with the piano, as it would have given her the requisite escape from life's dreary domestic traps and routines. But she was never poor. And she is truly, in the very root of her soul, indifferent as to whether people hear her play her music or not.

She needs only to hear it herself, and to know that she is not disturbing other people.

In the old hotel, mostly full of rooms rented by the day, with only a handful of tenants rich enough to be lodged there year by year, as was Sybelle's family, she can play forever without disturbing anyone.

And after her parents' tragic death, after she lost the only two witnesses who had been intimate to her development, she simply could not cooperate with Fox's plans for her career any further.

Well, all this I understood, almost from the beginning. I understood it in her incessant repetition of the Sonata No. 23, and I think if you were to hear it, you would understand it too. I want you to hear it.

Understand, it will not at all faze Sybelle if other people do gather to listen to her. It won't bother her one whit if she's recorded. If other people enjoy her playing and tell her so, she's delighted. But it's a simple thing with her. "Ah, so you too love it," she thinks. "Isn't it beautiful?" This is what she said to me with her eyes and her smiles the very first time I ever approached her.

And I suppose before I go any further—and I do have more to put down about my children—I should address this question: How did I approach her? How did I come to be in her apartment on that fateful morning, when Dora stood in the Cathedral crying to the crowds about the miraculous Veil, and I, the blood in my veins having combusted, was in fact rocketing skyward?

I don't know. I have rather tiresome supernatural explanations that read like tomes by members of the Society for the Study of Psychic Phenomena, or the scripts for Mulder and Scully on the television show called *The X-Files*. Or like a secret file on the case in the archives of the order of psychic detectives called the Talamasca.

Bluntly, I see it this way. I have most-powerful abilities to cast spells, to dislocate my vision, and to transmit my image over distances, and to affect matter both at close range and matter which is out of sight. I must somehow, in this morning journey towards the clouds, have used this power. It might have been drawn from me in a moment of harrowing pain when I was for all purposes deranged and completely unaware of what was happening to me. It might have been a last desperate hysterical refusal to accept the possibility of death, or of the horrible predicament, so close to death, in which I found myself.

That is, having fallen on the roof, burnt and in unspeakable torment, I might have sought a desperate mental escape, projecting my image and my strength into Sybelle's apartment long enough to kill her brother. It certainly is possible for spirits to exert enough pressure on matter to change it. So perhaps that is exactly what I did—project myself in spirit form and lay hands upon the substance that was Fox, and kill him.

But I don't really believe all this. I'll tell you why.

First off, though Sybelle and Benjamin are no experts, for all their savvy and seeming detachment, on the subject of death and its subsequent forensic analysis, they both insisted that Fox's body was bloodless when they got rid of it. The puncture wounds were apparent on his neck. In sum, they believe to this very hour that I was there, in substantial form, and that I did indeed drink Fox's blood.

Now that a projected image cannot do, at least not insofar as I know it. No, it cannot devour the blood of an entire circulatory system and then dissolve itself, returning to the cicatricula of the mind from which it came. No, that is not possible.

Of course, Sybelle and Benji could be wrong. What do they know about blood and bodies? But the fact is, they let Fox lie there, quite dead for some two days, or so they said, while they waited for the return of the Dybbuk or Angel whom they were sure would help them. Now in that time, the blood of a human body sinks down to the very lowest part of the carcass, and such a change would have been visible to these children. They noted no such thing.

Ah, it makes my brain ache! The fact is, I don't know how I got to their apartment, or why. I don't know how it happened. And I do know, as I have already said, that as regards the entire experience—everything I saw and felt in the great restored Cathedral at Kiev, an impossible place—was as real as what I knew in Sybelle's apartment.

There is one other small point, and though it is small it is crucial. After I had slain Fox, Benji did see my burnt body falling from the sky. He did see me, just as I saw him, from the window.

There is one very terrible possibility. It is this. I was going to die that morning. It was going to happen. My ascent was driven by immense will and an immense love of God of which I have no doubt as I dictate these words now.

But perhaps at the crucial moment, my courage failed me. My body failed me. And seeking some refuge from the sun, some way to thwart my martyrdom, I struck upon the predicament of Sybelle and her brother, and feeling her great need of me, I commenced to fall towards the shelter of the roof on which the snow and ice quickly covered me. My visit to Sybelle could have been, according to this interpretation, only a passing illusion, a powerful projection of self, as I've said, a wish fulfillment of the need of this random and vulnerable girl about to be fatally beaten by her brother.

As for Fox, I killed him, without doubt. But he died from fear, from failure of the heart, perhaps, from the pressure of my illusory hands on his fragile throat, from the power of telekinesis or suggestion.

But as I stated before, I don't believe this.

I was there in the Cathedral in Kiev. I broke the egg with my thumbs. I saw the bird fly free.

I know my Mother stood at my side, and I know that my Father knocked over the chalice. I know because I know there is no part of me that could have imagined such a thing. And I know too because the colors I saw then and the music I heard were not made up of anything I had ever experienced.

Now, there is simply no other dream I have ever had about which I can say this. When I said the Mass in Vladimir's City, I was in a realm made up of ingredients which my imagination simply does not have at its disposal.

I don't want to say any more about it. It's too hurtful and awful to try to analyze it. I didn't will it, not with my conscious heart, and I had no conscious power over it. It simply happened.

I would, if I could, forget it entirely. I am so extraordinarily happy with Sybelle and Benji that surely I want to forget it all for the space of their lifetimes. I want only to be with them, as I have been since the night I described to you.

As you realize, I took my time in coming here. Having returned to the ranks of the dangerous Undead, it was very easy for me to discern from the roaming minds of other vampires that Lestat was safe in his prison here, and indeed was dictating to you the entire story of what had happened to him with God Incarnate and with Memnoch the Devil.

It was very easy for me to discern, without revealing my own presence, that an entire world of vampires mourned for me with greater anguish and tears than I could ever have predicted.

So, being confident of Lestat's safety, being baffled yet relieved by the mysterious fact that his stolen eye had been returned to him, I was at leisure to stay with Sybelle and Benji and I did so.

With Benji and Sybelle I rejoined the world in a way which I had not done since my fledgling, my one and only fledgling, Daniel Molloy, had left me. My love for Daniel had never been entirely honest, and always viciously possessive, and quite entangled with my own hatred of the world at large, and my confusion in the face of the baffling modern times which had begun to open up to me when I emerged in the late years of the Eighteenth Century from the catacombs beneath Paris.

Daniel himself had no use for the world, and had come to me hungering for our Dark Blood, his brain swimming with macabre, grotesque tales which Louis de Pointe du Lac had told him. Heaping every luxury upon him, I only sickened him with mortal sweets so that finally he turned away from the riches I offered, becoming a vagabond. Mad, roaming the streets in rags, he shut out the world almost to the point of death, and I, weak, muddled, tormented by his beauty, and lusting for the living man and not the vampire he might become, only brought him over to us through the working of the Dark Trick because he would have died otherwise.

I was no Marius to him afterwards. It was too exactly as I supposed: he loathed me in his heart for having initiated him into Living Death, for having made him in one night both an immortal and a regular killer.

As a mortal man, he had no real idea of the price we pay for what we are, and he did not want to learn the truth; he fled from it, in reckless dreams and spiteful wandering.

And so it was as I feared. Making him to be my mate, I made a minion who saw me all the more clearly as a monster.

There was never any innocence for us, there was never any springtime. There was never any chance, no matter how beautiful the twilight gardens in which we wandered. Our souls were out of tune, our desires crossed and our resentments too common and too well watered for the final flowering.

It's different now.

For two months I remained in New York with Sybelle and Benji, living as I've never lived before, not since those long-ago nights with Marius in Venice.

Sybelle is rich, as I think I've told you, but only in a tedious struggling sort of way, with an income that pays for her exorbitant apartment and daily room service meals, with a margin for fine clothes, tickets to the symphony and an occasional spending spree.

I am fabulously rich. So the first thing I did, with pleasure, was lavish upon Sybelle and Benjamin all the riches I had once lavished upon Daniel Molloy to much greater effect.

They loved it.

Sybelle, when she was not playing the piano, had no objections whatsoever to wandering to the picture shows with Benji and me, or to the symphony and the opera. She loved the ballet, and loved to take Benjamin to the finest restaurants, where he became a regular marvel to the waiters with his crisp enthusiastic little voice and his lilting way of rattling off the names of dishes, French or Italian, and ordering vintage wines which they poured for him, unquestioningly, despite all the good-intentioned laws that prohibit the serving of such strong spirits to children.

I loved all this too, of course, and was delighted to discover that Sybelle also took a sporadic and playful interest in dressing me, in choosing jackets, shirts and such from racks with a quick point of her finger, and in picking out for me from velvet trays all kinds of jeweled rings, cufflinks, neck chains and tiny crucifixes of rubies and gold, solid-gold clips for money and that sort of thing.

It was I who had played this masterly game with Daniel Molloy. Sybelle plays it with me in her own dreamy way, as I take care of the tiresome cash register details.

I in turn have the supreme pleasure of carrying Benji about like a doll and getting him to wear all the Western finery I purchase, at least now and then, for an hour or two.

We make a striking trio, the three of us dining at Lutèce or Sparks (of course I don't dine)—Benji in his immaculate little desert robe, or got up in a finely fitted little suit with narrow lapels, white button-down shirt and flash of tie; me in my highly acceptable antique velvet and chokers of old crumbling lace; and Sybelle in the lovely dresses that spill endlessly out of her closet, confections her Mother and Fox once bought for her, close cut around her large breasts and small waist and always flaring magically about her long legs, hem high enough to reveal the splendid curve of her calf and its tautness when she slips her dark-stockinged feet into dagger-heeled slippers. Benji's close-cropped cap of curls is always the Byzantine halo for his dark enigmatic little face, her flowing waves are free, and my hair is the Renaissance mop again of long unruly curls that used to be my secret vanity.

My deepest pleasure with Benji is education. Right off, we started having powerful conversations about history and the world, and found ourselves stretched out on the carpet of the apartment, poring over maps, as we discussed the entire progress of East and West and the inevitable influences upon human history of climate, culture and geography. Benji gabbles away all during television broadcasts of the news, calling each anchorperson intimately by his or her first name, slamming his fist in anger at the actions of world leaders and wailing loudly over the deaths of great princesses and humanitarians. Benji can watch the news, talk steadily, eat popcorn, smoke a cigarette and sing intermittently with Sybelle's playing, always on key—all more or less simultaneously.

If I fall to staring at the rain as if I've seen a ghost, it's Benji who beats on my arm and cries, "What shall we do, Armand? We have three splendid movies to see tonight. I'm vexed, I tell you, vexed, because if we go to any of these, we'll miss Pavarotti at the Met and I'll go pasty-white with sickness."

Many times the two of us dress Sybelle, who looks at us as if she doesn't know what we're doing. We always sit talking with her when she bathes, because if we don't she's likely to go to sleep in the bathtub, or simply stay in there for hours, sponging the water over her beautiful breasts.

Sometimes the only words she says all night are things like, "Benji, tie your shoes," or "Armand, he's stolen the silverware. Make him put it back," or with sudden astonishment, "It's warm, isn't it?"

I have never told anyone my life story as I've told it to you here and now, but in conversation with Benji I have caught myself telling him many things which Marius told me—about human nature, and the history of the law, about painting and even about music.

It was in these conversations, more than in anything else, that I came to realize in the last two months that I was a changed being.

Some stifling dark terror is gone from me. I do not see history as a panorama of disasters, as once I think I did; and often I find myself remembering Marius's generous and beautifully optimistic predictions—that the world is ever improving; that war, for all the strife we see around us, has nevertheless gone out of fashion with those in power, and will soon pass from the arenas of the Third World as it has passed from the arenas of the West; and we will truly feed the hungry and shelter the homeless and take care of those who need love.

With Sybelle, education and discussion are not the substance of our love. With Sybelle it is intimacy. I don't care if she never says anything. I don't go inside her mind. She doesn't want anybody to do that.

As completely as she accepts me and my nature, I accept her and her obsession with the *Appassionata*. Hour after hour, night after night, I listen to Sybelle play, and with each fresh start I hear the minute changes of intensity and expression which pour forth in her playing. Gradually, on account of this, I have become the only listener of whom Sybelle has ever been conscious.

Gradually, I have become part of Sybelle's music. I am there with her and the phrases and movements of the *Appassionata*. I am there and I am one who has never asked anything of Sybelle except that she do what she wants to do, and what she can do so perfectly.

That's all Sybelle ever has to do for me—is what she will.

If or when she wants to rise in "fortune and men's eyes," I'll clear the way for her. If or when she wants to be alone, she will not see or hear me. If or when she wants anything, I will get it for her.

And if or when she loves a mortal man or mortal woman, I'll do what she wants me to do. I can live in the shadows. Doting on her, I can live forever in gloom because there is no gloom when I am near her.

Sybelle often goes with me when I hunt. Sybelle likes to see me feed and kill. I don't think I have ever allowed a mortal to do that. She tries to help me dispose of the remains or confuse the evidence of the cause of death, but I'm very strong and swift and capable at this, so she is mostly the witness.

I try to avoid taking Benji on these escapades because he becomes wildly and childishly excited, and it does him no good. To Sybelle it simply does nothing.

There are other things I could tell you—how we handled the details of her brother's disappearance, how I transferred immense sums of money into her name and set up the appropriate and unbreakable trust funds for Benji, how I bought for her a substantial interest in the hotel in which she lives, and have put into her apartment, which is very huge for a hotel apartment, several other fine pianos which she enjoys, and how I have set aside for myself a safe distance from the apartment a lair with a coffin which is unfindable, unbreachable and indestructible, and to which I go on occasion, though I am more accustomed to sleeping in the little chamber they first gave to me, in which velvet curtains have been fitted tightly over the one window to the airwell.

But the hell with all that.

You know what I want you to know.

What remains for us but to bring it to the moment, to sunset on this night when I came here, entering the very den of the vampires with my brother and with my sister, one on either side to see Lestat at last.

24

THIS IS ALL a little too simple, isn't it? I mean by that, my transformation from the zealous child who stood on the porch of the Cathedral to the happy monster making up his mind one spring night in New York City that it was time to journey south and look in on his old friend.

You know why I came here.

Let me begin at the start of this evening. You were there in the chapel when I arrived.

You greeted me with undisguised good will, so pleased to see I was alive and unharmed. Louis almost wept.

Those others, those raggedy young ones who were clustered about, two boys, I believe, and a girl, I don't know who they were, and still don't, only that later they drifted off.

I was horrified to see him undefended, lying on the floor, and his mother, Gabrielle, far off in the corner merely staring at him, coldly, the way she stares at everything and everyone as though she never knew a human feeling for what it was.

I was horrified that the young tramps were about, and felt instantly protective of Sybelle and Benji. I had no fear of their seeing the classics among us, the legends, the warriors—you, beloved Louis, even Gabrielle, and certainly not Pandora or Marius, who were all there.

But I hadn't wanted my children to look on common trash infused with our blood, and I wondered, arrogantly and vainly perhaps, as I always do at such moments, how these roguish sophomoric slob vampires ever came to be. Who made them and why and when?

At such times, the fierce old Child of Darkness wakes in me, the Coven Master beneath the Paris Cemetery who decreed when and how the Dark Blood should be given and, above all, to whom. But that old habit of authority is fraudulent and just a nuisance at best.

I hated these hangers-on because they were there looking at Lestat as though he were a Carnival Curiosity, and I wouldn't have it. I felt a sudden temper, an urge to destroy.

But there are no rules among us now that authorize such rash actions. And who was I to make a mutiny here under your roof? I didn't know you lived here then, no, but you certainly had custody of the Master of the Place, and you allowed it, the ruffians, and the three or four more of them that came shortly after and dared to circle him, none of them, I noticed, getting any too close.

Of course everyone was most curious about Sybelle and Benjamin. I told them quietly to stay directly beside me and not to stray. Sybelle couldn't get it out of her mind that the piano was so near at hand, and it would have a whole new sound for her Sonata. As for Benji, he was striding along like a little Samurai, checking out monsters all around, with his eyes like saucers though his mouth was very puckered up and stern and proud.

The chapel struck me as beautiful. How could it not? The plaster walls are white and pure, and the ceiling is gently coved, as in the oldest churches, and there is a deep coved shell where once the altar stood, which makes a well for sound, so that one footfall there echoes softly throughout the entire place.

The stained glass I'd seen brilliantly lighted from the street. Unfigured, it was nevertheless lovely with its vivid colors of blue and red and yellow, and its simple serpentine designs. I liked the old black lettering of the mortals long gone in whose memory each window had been erected. I liked the old plaster statues scattered about, which I had helped you to clear from the New York apartment and send south.

I had not looked at them much; I had shielded myself from their glass eyes as if they were basilisks. But I certainly looked at them now.

There was sweet suffering St. Rita in her black habit and white wimple, with the fearful awful sore in her forehead like a third eye. There was lovely, smiling Thérèse of Lisieux, the Little Flower of Jesus with His Crucifix and the bouquet of pink roses in her arms.

There was St. Teresa of Avila, carved out of wood and finely painted, with her eyes turned upwards, the mystic, and the feather quill in her hand that marked her as a Doctor of the Church.

There was St. Louis of France with his royal crown; St. Francis, of course, in humble brown monk's robes, with his gathering of tamed animals; and some others whose names I'm ashamed to say I didn't know.

What struck me more perhaps even than these scattered statues, standing like so many guardians of an old and sacred history, were the pictures on the wall that marked Christ's road to Calvary: the Stations of the Cross. Someone had put them all in the proper order, maybe even before our coming into the world of this place.

I divined that they were painted in oil on copper, and they had a Renaissance style to them, imitative certainly, but one which I find normal and which I love.

Immediately, the fear that had been hovering inside me during all my happy weeks in New York came to the fore. No, it was not fear so much as it was dread.

My Lord, I whispered. I turned and looked up at the Face of Christ on the high Crucifix above Lestat's head.

This was an excruciating moment. I think the image on Veronica's Veil overlaid what I saw there in the carved wood. I know it did. I was back in New York, and Dora was holding up the cloth for us to see.

I saw His dark beautifully shadowed eyes perfectly fixed on the cloth, as though part of it but not in any way absorbed by it, and the dark streaks of His eyebrows and, above His steady unchallenging gaze, the tricklets of blood from His thorns. I saw His lips partway open as if He had volumes to speak.

With a shock, I realized that from far off by the altar steps Gabrielle had fixed her glacial gray eyes on me, and I locked up my mind and digested the key. I wouldn't have her touch me or my thoughts. And I felt a bristling hostility for all those gathered in the room.

Louis came then. He was so happy that I had not perished. Louis had something to say. He knew I was concerned and he was anxious about the presence of the others. He looked his usual ascetic self, got up in tired black clothes of beautiful cut but impossible dustiness and a shirt so thin and worn that it seemed an elfin web of threads rather than true lace and cloth.

"We let them in because if we don't, they circle like jackals, and wolves, and won't go away. As it is, they come, they see and they leave here. You know what they want."

I nodded. I didn't have the courage to admit to him that I wanted exactly the same thing. I had never stopped thinking about it, not really, not for one moment, beneath the grand rhythm of all that had befallen me since I'd spoken to him on that last night of my old life.

I wanted his blood. I wanted to drink it. Calmly, I let Louis know.

"He'll destroy you," Louis whispered. He was flushed suddenly with terror. He looked questioningly at gentle silent Sybelle, who held fast to my hand, and Benjamin, who was studying him with enthusiastic bright eyes. "Armand, you can't chance it. One of them got too close. He smashed the creature. The motion was quick, automatic. But it has an arm like living stone and he blasted the creature to fragments there on the floor. Don't go near him, don't try it."

"And the elders, the strong ones, have they never tried?"

Pandora spoke then. She had been watching us all

the while, playing in the shadows. I'd forgotten how very beautiful she was in a downplayed and very basic way.

Her long rich brown hair was combed back, a shadow behind her slender neck, and she looked glossy and pretty because she had smoothed into her face a fine dark oil to make herself more passably human. Her eyes were bold and flaming. She put her hand on me with a woman's liberty. She too was happy to see me alive.

"You know what Lestat is," she said pleadingly. "Armand, he's a furnace of power and no one knows what he might do."

"But have you never thought of it, Pandora? Has it never even entered your mind, to drink the blood from his throat and search for the vision of Christ when you drank it? What if inside him there is the infallible proof that he drank the blood of God?"

"But Armand," she said. "Christ was never my god."

It was so simple, so shocking, so final.

She sighed, but only out of concern for me. She smiled. "I wouldn't know your Christ if He were inside Lestat," she said gently.

"You don't understand," I said. "Something happened, something happened to him when we went with this spirit called Memnoch, and he came back with that Veil. I saw it. I saw the . . . power in it."

"You saw the illusion," said Louis kindly.

"No, I saw the power," I answered. Then in a moment I totally doubted myself. The long corridors of history wound back and away from me, and I saw myself plunged into darkness, carrying a single candle, searching for the ikons I had painted. And the pity of it, the triviality, the sheer hopelessness of it crushed my soul.

I realized I had frightened Sybelle and Benji. They had their eyes fastened on me. They had never seen me as I was now.

I closed my arms around them both and pulled them towards me. I had hunted before I'd come to them tonight, to be at my strongest, and I knew my skin was pleasingly warm. I kissed Sybelle on her pale pink lips, and then kissed Benji's head.

"Armand, you vex me, truly you do," said Benji. "You never told me that you believed in this Veil."

"And you, little man," I said in a hushed voice, not wishing to make a spectacle of us to the others. "Did you ever go into the Cathedral and look at it when it was on display there?"

"Yes, and I say to you what this great lady said." He shrugged, of course. "He was never my god."

"Look at them, prowling," said Louis softly. He was emaciated and shivering a little. He had neglected his own hunger to be here on guard. "I should throw them out now, Pandora," he said in a voice that couldn't have threatened the most timid soul.

"Let them see what they came for," she said coolly under her breath. "They may not have so long to enjoy their satisfaction. They make the world harder for us, and disgrace us, and do nothing for anything living or dead."

I thought it a lovely threat. I hoped she would clean out the lot of them, but I knew of course that many a Child of the Millennia thought the very same thing about those such as me. And what an impertinent creature I was to bring, without anyone's permission, my children to see my friend who lay on the floor.

"These two are safe with us," Pandora said, obviously reading my fretting mind. "You realize they are glad to see you, young and old," she said making a small gesture to include the entire room. "There are some who don't want to step out from the shadows, but they know of you. They didn't want for you to be gone."

"No, no one wanted it," said Louis rather emotionally. "And like a dream, you've come back. We all had inklings of it, wild whispers that you'd been seen in New York, as handsome and vigorous as you ever were. But I had to lay eyes on you to believe it."

I nodded in thanks for these kind words. But I was thinking of the Veil. I looked up at the wooden Christ on the tree again, and then down at the slumbering figure of Lestat.

It was then that Marius came. He was trembling. "Unburnt, whole," he whispered. "My son."

He had that wretched neglected old gray cloak over his shoulders, but I didn't notice then. He embraced me at once, which forced my girl and my boy to step away. They didn't go far, however. I think they were reassured when they saw me put my arms around him and kiss him several times on the face and mouth, as we had always done so many years ago. He was so splendid, so softly full of love.

"I'll keep these mortals safe if you're determined to try," he said. He had read the whole script from my heart. He knew I was bound to do it. "What can I say to prevent you?" he asked.

I only shook my head. Haste and anticipation

wouldn't let me do anything else. I gave Benji and Sybelle to his care.

I went over to Lestat and I walked up in front of him, that is, on the left side of him as he lay there to my right. I knelt down quickly, surprised at how cold the marble was, forgetting, I suppose, how very damp it is here in New Orleans and how stealthy the chills can be.

I knelt with my hands before me on the floor and I looked at him. He was placid, still, both blue eyes equally clear as if one had never been torn from his face. He stared through me, as we say, and on and on, and out of a mind that seemed as empty as a dead chrysalis.

His hair was mussed and full of dust. Not even his cold, hateful Mother had combed it, I supposed, and it infuriated me, but then in a frosty flash of emotion, she said hissingly:

"He will not let anyone touch him, Armand." Her distant voice echoed deeply in the hollow of the chapel. "If you try it, you will soon find out for yourself."

I looked up at her. She had her knees drawn up in a careless clasp of her arms, and her back against the wall. She wore her usual thick and frayed khaki, the narrow pants and the British safari coat for which she was more or less famous, stained from the wild outdoors, her blond hair as yellow and bright as his, braided and lying down her back.

She got up suddenly, angrily, and she came towards me letting her plain leather boots echo sharply and disrespectfully on the floor.

"What makes you think the spirits he saw were gods?" she demanded. "What makes you think the pranks of any of those lofty beings who play with us are any more than capers, and we no more than beasts, from the lowest to the very highest that walk the Earth?" She stood a few feet from him. She folded her arms. "He tempted something or something. That entity could not resist him. And what was the sum of it? Tell me. You ought to know."

"I don't," I said in a soft voice. "I wish you would leave me alone."

"Oh, do you, well, let me tell you what was the sum of it. A young woman, Dora by name, a leader of souls as they call it, who preached for the good that comes of tending to the weak who need it, was thrown off course! That was the sum of it—her preachings, grounded in charity and sung to a new tune so that people could hear them, were obliterated by the bloody face of a bloody god."

My eyes filled with tears. I hated that she saw it so clearly, but I couldn't answer her and I couldn't shut her up. I rose to my feet.

"Back to the cathedrals they flocked," she said scornfully, "the lot of them, and back to an archaic and ludicrous and utterly useless theology which it seems that you have plainly forgot."

"I know it well enough," I said softly. "You make me miserable. What do I do to you? I kneel beside him, that's all."

"Oh, but you mean to do more, and your tears offend me," she said.

I heard someone behind me speak out to her. I thought perhaps it was Pandora, but I was unsure. In a sudden evanescent flash I was aware of all those who made a recreation of my misery, but then I didn't care.

"What do you expect, Armand?" she asked me cunningly and mercilessly. Her narrow oval face was so like his and yet so not. He had never been so divorced from feeling, never so abstract in his anger as she was now. "You think you'll see what he saw, or that the Blood of Christ will still be there for you to savor on your tongue? Shall I quote the catechism for you?"

"No need, Gabrielle," I said again in a meek voice. My tears were blinding me.

"The bread and wine are the Body and Blood as long as they remain that species, Armand; but when it's bread and wine no more then no more is it Body and Blood. So what do you think of the Blood of Christ in him, that it has somehow retained its magical power, despite the engine of his heart that devours the blood of mortals as if it were mere air that he breathed?"

I didn't answer. I thought quietly in my soul. *It was not the bread and the wine; it was His Blood, His Sacred Blood and He gave it on the road to Calvary, and to this being who lies here.*

I swallowed hard on my grief and my fury that she had made me commit myself in these terms. I wanted to look back for my poor Sybelle and Benji, for I knew by their scent they were still in the room. Why didn't Marius take them away! Oh, but it was plain enough. Marius wanted to see what I meant to do.

"Don't tell me," Gabrielle said slurringly, "that it's a matter of faith." She sneered and shook her head. "You come like doubting Thomas to thrust your bloody fangs in the very wound."

"Oh, stop, please, I beg you," I whispered. I put up

my hands. "Let me try, and let him hurt me, and then be satisfied, and turn away."

I only meant it as I said it, and I felt no power in it, only meekness and unutterable sadness.

But it struck her hard, and for the first time her face became absolutely and totally sorrowful, and she too had moist and reddening eyes, and her lips even pressed together as she looked at me.

"Poor lost child, Armand," she said. "I am so sorry for you. I was so glad that you had survived the sun."

"Then that means I can forgive you, Gabrielle," I said, "for all the cruel things you've said to me."

She raised her eyebrows thoughtfully, and then slowly nodded in silent assent. Then putting up her hands, she backed away without a sound and took up her old station, sitting on the altar step, her head leaning back against the Communion rail. She brought up her knees as before, and she merely looked at me, her face in shadow.

I waited. She was still and quiet, and not a sound came from the occupants scattered about the chapel. I could hear the steady beat of Sybelle's heart and the anxious breath of Benji, but they were many yards away.

I looked down on Lestat, who was unchanged, his hair fallen as before, a little over his left eye. His right arm was out, and his fingers curling upwards, and there came from him not the slightest movement, not even a breath from his lungs or a sigh from his pores.

I knelt down beside him again. I reached out, and without flinching or hesitating, I brushed his hair back from his face.

I could feel the shock in the room. I heard the sighs, the gasps from the others. But Lestat himself didn't stir.

Slowly, I brushed his hair more tenderly, and I saw to my own mute shock one of my tears fall right onto his face.

It was red yet watery and transparent and it appeared to vanish as it moved down the curve of his cheekbone and into the natural hollow below.

I slipped down closer, turning on my side, facing him, my hand still on his hair. I stretched my legs out behind me, and alongside of him, and I lay there, letting my face rest right on his outstretched arm.

Again there came the shocked gasps and sighs, and I tried to keep my heart absolutely pure of pride and pure of anything but love.

It was not differentiated or defined, this love, but only love, the love I could feel perhaps for one I killed or one I succored, or one whom I passed in the street, or for one whom I knew and valued as much as him.

All the burden of his sorrows seemed unimaginable to me, and in my mind a notion of it expanded to include the tragedy of all of us, those who kill to live, and thrive on death even as the very Earth decrees it, and are cursed with consciousness to know it, and know by what inches all things that feed us slowly anguish and at last are no more. Sorrow. Sorrow so much greater than guilt, and so much more ready for accounting, sorrow too great for the wide world.

I climbed up. I rested my weight on my elbow, and I sent my right fingers slipping gently across his neck. Slowly I pressed my lips to his whitened silky skin and breathed in the old unmistakable taste and scent of him, something sweet and undefinable and utterly personal, something made up of all his physical gifts and those given him afterwards, and I pressed my sharp eyeteeth through his skin to taste his blood.

There was no chapel then for me, or outraged sighs or reverential cries. I heard nothing, and yet knew what was all around. I knew it as if the substantial place was but a phantasm, for what was real was his blood.

It was as thick as honey, deep and strong of taste, a syrup for the very angels.

I groaned aloud drinking it, feeling the searing heat of it, so unlike to any human blood. With each slow beat of his powerful heart there came another small surge of it, until my mouth was filled and my throat swallowed without my bidding, and the sound of his heart grew louder, ever louder, and a reddish shimmer filled my vision, and I saw through this shimmer a great swirling dust.

A wretched dreary din rose slowly out of nothingness, commingled with an acid sand that stung my eyes. It was a desert place, all right, and old and full of rank and common things, of sweat and filth and death. The din was voices crying out, and echoing up the close and grimy walls. Voices crowded upon voices, taunts and jeers and cries of horror, and gruff riffs of foul indifferent gossip rushing over the most poignant and terrible cries of outrage and alarm.

Against sweating bodies I was pressed, struggling, the slanting sun burning on my outstretched arm. I understood the babble all around me, the ancient tongue hollered and wailed in my ears as I fought to get ever closer to the source of all the wet and ugly commotion that swamped me and tried to hold me back.

It seemed they'd crush the very life out of me, these ragged, rough-skinned men and veiled women in their coarse homespun, thrusting elbows at me and stepping on my feet. I couldn't see what lay before me. I flung my arms out, deafened by the cries and the wicked boiling laughter, and suddenly, as if by decree, the crowd parted, and I beheld the lurid masterpiece itself.

He stood in His torn and bloody white robe, this very Figure whose Face I'd seen imprinted into the fibers of the Veil. Arms bound up with thick uneven iron chains to the heavy and monstrous crossbeam of His crucifix, He hunched beneath it, hair pouring down on either side of His bruised and lacerated face. The blood from the thorns flowed into His open and unflinching eyes.

He looked at me, quite startled, even faintly amazed. He stared with wide and open gaze as if the multitude didn't surround Him, and a whip did not crack over His very back and then His bowed head. He stared past the tangle of his clotted hair and from beneath His raw and bleeding lids.

"Lord!" I cried.

I must have reached out for Him, for those were my hands, my smallish and white hands that I saw! I saw them struggling to reach His Face.

"Lord!" I cried again.

And back He stared at me, unmoving, eyes meeting my eyes, hands dangling from the iron chains and mouth dripping with blood.

Suddenly a fierce and terrible blow struck me. It pitched me forward. His Face filled all my sight. Before my eyes it was the very measure of all that I could possibly see—His soiled and broken skin, the wetted, darkened tangle of His eyelashes, the great bright orbs of His dark-pupiled eyes.

Closer and closer it came, the blood flowing down and into His thick eyebrows, and dripping down His gaunt cheeks. His mouth opened. A sound came out of Him. It was a sigh at first and then a dull rising breath that grew louder and louder as His Face became even larger, losing its very lineaments, and became the sum of all its swimming colors, the sound now a positive and deafening roar.

In terror, I cried out. I was thrust back. Yet even as I saw His familiar Figure and the ancient frame of His Face with its Thorny Crown, the Face grew ever larger and larger and utterly indistinct and seemed again to bear down on me, and then suddenly to suffocate all my face with its immense and total weight.

I screamed. I was helpless, weightless, unable to draw breath.

I screamed as I've never in all my miserable years screamed, the scream so loud that it shut out the roar that filled my ears, but the vision pressed on, a great driving inescapable mass that had been His Face.

"Oh, Lord!" I screamed with all the power of my burning lungs. The very wind rushed in my ears.

Something struck the back of my head so hard that it cracked my skull. I heard the crack. I felt the wet splash of blood.

I opened my eyes. I was staring forward. I was far across the chapel, sprawled against the plaster wall, my legs out in front of me, my arms dangling, my head on fire with the pain of the great concussion where I had struck the wall.

Lestat had never moved. I knew he hadn't.

No one had to tell me. It was not he who threw me back.

I tumbled over onto my face, pulling my arm up under my head. I knew there were feet gathered all around me, that Louis was near, and that even Gabrielle had come, and I knew too that Marius was taking Sybelle and Benjamin away.

I could hear in the ringing silence only Benjamin's small sharp mortal voice. "But what happened to him. What happened? The blond one didn't hit him. I saw it. It didn't happen. He didn't—."

My face hidden, my face soaked with tears, I covered my head with my trembling hands, my bitter smile unseen, though my sobs were heard.

I cried and cried for a long time, and then gradually, as I knew it would, my scalp began to heal. The evil blood mounted to the surface of my skin and, tingling there, did its evil ministrations, sewing up the flesh like a little laser beam from Hell.

Someone gave me a napkin. It had the faint scent of Louis on it, but I couldn't be sure. It was a long long time, perhaps even so long as an hour before I finally clasped it and wiped all the blood off my face.

It was another hour, an hour of quiet and of people respectfully slipping away, before I turned over and rose and sat back against the wall. My head no longer hurt, the wound was gone, the blood that had dried there would soon flake away.

I stared at him for a long and quiet time.

I was cold and solitary and raw. Nothing anyone murmured penetrated my hearing. I did not note the gestures or the movements around me.

In the sanctum of my mind I went over, mostly slowly, exactly, what I had seen, what I had heard—all that I've told you here.

I rose finally. I went back to him and I looked down at him.

Gabrielle said something to me. It was harsh and mean. I didn't actually hear it. I heard only the sound of it, the cadence, that is, as if her old French, so familiar to me, was a language I didn't know.

I knelt down and I kissed his hair.

He didn't move. He didn't change. I wasn't the slightest bit afraid that he would, or hopeful that he would either. I kissed him one more time on the side of his face, and then I got up, and I wiped my hands on the napkin which I still had, and I went out.

I think I stood in a torpor for a long while, and then something came back to me, something Dora had said a long long time ago, about a child having died in the attic, about a little ghost and about old clothes.

Grasping that, clutching it tight, I managed to propel myself towards the stairs.

It was there that I met you a short time afterwards. Now you know, for better or worse, what I did or didn't see.

And so my symphony is finished. Let me write my name to it. When you're finished with your copying, I will give my transcript to Sybelle. And Benji too perhaps. And you may do with the rest what you will.

25

THIS IS NO EPILOGUE. It is the last chapter to a tale I thought was finished. I write it in my own hand. It will be brief, for I have no drama left me and must manipulate with the utmost care the bare bones of the tale.

Perhaps in some later time the proper words will come to me to deepen my depiction of what happened, but for now to record is all that I can do.

I did not leave the convent after I inscribed my name to the copy which David had so faithfully written out. It was too late.

The night had spent itself in language, and I had to retire to one of the secret brick chambers of the place which David showed me, a place where Lestat had once been imprisoned, and there sprawled on the floor in perfect darkness, overexcited by all that I'd told David, and, more completely exhausted than I'd ever been, I went into immediate sleep with the rise of the sun.

At twilight, I rose, straightened out my clothes and returned to the chapel. I knelt down and gave Lestat a kiss of unreserved affection, just as I had the night before. I took no notice of anyone and did not even know who was there.

Taking Marius at his word, I walked away from the convent, in a wash of early evening violet light, my eyes drifting trustingly over the flowers, and I listened for the chords of Sybelle's Sonata to lead me to the proper house.

Within seconds I heard the music, the distant but rapid phrases of the *Allegro assai*, or the First Movement, of Sybelle's familiar song.

It was played with an unusual ringing preciseness, indeed, a new languid cadence which gave it a powerful and ruby-red authority which I immediately loved.

So I hadn't scared my little girl out of her mind. She was well and prospering and perhaps falling in love with the drowsy humid loveliness of New Orleans as so many of us have.

I sped at once to the location, and found myself standing, only a little mussed by the wind, in front of a huge three-story redbrick house in Metairie, a countrified suburb of New Orleans which is actually very close to the city, with a feel that can be miraculously remote.

The giant oaks which Marius described were all around this new American mansion, and, as he had promised, all his French doors of shining clean panes were open to the early breeze.

The grass was long and soft beneath my shoes, and a splendid light, so very precious to Marius, poured forth from every window as did the music of the *Appassionata* now, which was just moving with exceptional grace into the Second Movement, *Andante con motto,* which promises to be a tame segment of the work but quickly works itself into the same madness as all the rest.

I stopped in my tracks to listen to it. I had never heard the notes quite as limpid and translucent, quite as flashing and exquisitely distinct. I tried for sheer pleasure to divine the differences between this performance and so many I'd heard in the past. They were all different, magical and profoundly affecting, but this was passing spectacular, helped in slight measure by the immense body of what I knew to be a concert grand.

For a moment, a misery swept over me, a terrible, gripping memory of what I'd seen when I drank Lestat's blood the night before. I let myself relive it, as we say so innocently, and then with a positive blush of pleasant shock, I realized that I didn't have to tell anyone about it, that it was all dictated to David and that when he gave me my copies, I could entrust them to whomever I loved, who would ever want to know what I'd seen.

As for myself, I wouldn't try to figure it out. I couldn't. The feeling was too strong that whom I had seen on the road to Calvary, whether He was real or a figment of my own guilty heart, had not wanted me to see Him and had monstrously turned me away. Indeed the feeling of rejection was so total that I could scarce believe that I had managed to describe it to David.

I had to get the thoughts out of my mind. I banished all reverberations of this experience and let myself fall into Sybelle's music again, merely standing under the oaks, with the eternal river breeze, which can reach you anywhere in this place, cooling me and soothing me and making me feel that the Earth itself was filled with irrepressible beauty, even for someone such as I.

The music of the Third Movement built to its most brilliant climax, and I thought my heart would break.

It was only then, as the final bars were played out, that I realized something which should have been obvious to me from the start.

It wasn't Sybelle playing this music. It couldn't be.

I knew every nuance of Sybelle's interpretations. I knew her modes of expression; I knew the tonal qualities that her particular touch invariably produced. Though her interpretations were infinitely spontaneous, nevertheless I knew her music, as one knows the writing of another or the style of a painter's work. This wasn't Sybelle.

And then the real truth dawned on me. It was Sybelle, but Sybelle was no longer Sybelle.

For a second I couldn't believe it. My heart stopped in my chest.

Then I walked into the house, a steady furious walk that would have stopped for nothing but to find the truth of what I believed.

In an instant I saw it with my own eyes. In a splendid room, they were gathered together, the beautiful lithe figure of Pandora in a gown of brown silk, girdled at the waist in the old Grecian style, Marius in a light velvet smoking jacket over silk trousers, and my children, my beautiful children, radiant Benji in his white gown, dancing barefoot and wildly around the room with his fingers flung out as if to grasp the air in them, and Sybelle, my gorgeous Sybelle, with her arms bare too in a dress of deep rose silk, at the piano, her long hair swept back over her shoulders, just striding into the First Movement again.

All of them vampires, every one.

I clenched my teeth hard, and covered my mouth lest my roars wake the world. I roared and roared into my collapsed hands.

I cried out the single defiant syllable No, No, No,

over and over again. I could say nothing else, scream nothing else, do nothing else.

I cried and cried.

I bit down so hard with my teeth that my jaw ached, and my hands shuddered like wings of a bird that wouldn't let me shut up my mouth tight enough, and once again the tears streamed out of my eyes as thickly as they had when I kissed Lestat.

No, No, No, No!

Then suddenly I flung out my hands, coiling them into fists, and the roar would have got loose, it would have burst from me like a raging stream, but Marius took hold of me with great force and flung me against his chest and buried my face against himself.

I struggled to get free. I kicked at him with all of my strength, and I beat at him with my fists.

"How could you do it!" I roared.

His hands enclosed my head in a hopeless trap, and his lips kept covering me with kisses I hated and detested and fought off with desperate flinging gestures.

"How could you? How dare you? How could you?"

At last I gained enough leverage to smash his face with blow after blow.

But what good did it do me? How weak and meaningless were my fists against his strength. How helpless and foolish and small were my gestures, and he stood there, bearing it all, his face unspeakably sad, and his own eyes dry yet full of caring.

"How could you do it, how could you do it!" I demanded. I would not cease.

But suddenly Sybelle rose from the piano, and with

her arms out ran to me. And Benji, who had been watching all the while, rushed to me also, and they imprisoned me gently in their tender arms.

"Oh, Armand, don't be angry, don't be, don't be sad," Sybelle cried softly against my ear. "Oh, my magnificent Armand, don't be sad, don't be. Don't be cross. We're with you forever."

"Armand, we are with you! He did the magic," cried Benji. "We didn't have to be born from black eggs, you Dybbuk, to tell us such a tale! Armand, we will never die now, we will never be sick, and never hurt and never afraid again." He jumped up and down with glee and spun in another mirthful circle, astonished and laughing at his new vigor, that he could leap so high and with such grace. "Armand, we are so happy."

"Oh, yes, please," cried Sybelle softly in her deeper gentler voice. "I love you so much, Armand, I love you so very very much. We had to do it. We had to. We had to do it, to always and forever be with you."

My fingers hovered about her, wanting to comfort her, and then, as she ground her forehead desperately into my neck, hugging me tight around the chest, I couldn't not touch her, couldn't not embrace her, couldn't not assure her.

"Armand, I love you, I adore you, Armand, I live only for you, and now with you always," she said.

I nodded, I tried to speak. She kissed my tears. She began to kiss them rapidly and desperately. "Stop it, stop crying, don't cry," she kept saying in her urgent low whisper. "Armand, we love you."

"Armand, we are so happy!" cried Benji. "Look, Armand, look! We can dance together now to her music.

We can do everything together. Armand, we have hunted already." He dashed up to me and bent his knees, poised to spring with excitement as if to emphasize his point. Then he sighed and flung out his arms to me again, "Ah, poor Armand, you are all wrong, all filled with wrong dreams. Armand, don't you see?"

"I love you," I whispered in a tiny voice into Sybelle's ear. I whispered it again, and then my resistance broke completely, and I crushed her gently to me and with rampant fingers felt her silky white skin and the zinging fineness of her shining hair.

Still holding her to me, I whispered, "Don't tremble, I love you, I love you."

I clasped Benji to me with my left hand. "And you, scamp, you can tell me all of it in time. Just let me hold you now. Let me hold you."

I was shivering. I was the one shivering. They enclosed me again with all their tenderness, seeking to keep me warm.

Finally, patting them both, taking my leave of them with kisses, I shrank away and fell down exhausted into a large old velvet chair.

My head throbbed and I felt my tears coming again, but with all my force I swallowed my tears for their sake. I had no choice.

Sybelle had gone back to the piano, and striking the keys she began the Sonata again. This time she sang out the notes in a beautiful low monosyllabic soprano, and Benji began dancing again, whirling, and prancing, and stomping with his bare feet, in lovely keeping with Sybelle's time.

I sat forward with my head in my hands. I wanted my

hair to come down and hide me from all eyes, but for all its thickness it was only a head of hair.

I felt a hand on my shoulder and I stiffened, but I could not say a word, lest I'd start crying again and cursing with all my might. I was silent.

"I don't expect you to understand," he said under his breath.

I sat up. He was beside me, seated on the arm of the chair. He looked down at me.

I made my face pleasant, all smiles even, and my voice so velvet and placid that no one could have thought I was talking to him of anything but love.

"How could you do it? Why did you do it? Do you hate me so much? Don't lie to me. Don't tell me stupid things that you know I will never, never believe. Don't lie to me for Pandora's sake or their sake. I'll care for them and love them forever. But don't lie. You did it for vengeance, didn't you, Master, you did it for hate?"

"How could I?" he asked in the same voice, expressive of pure love, and it seemed the very genuine voice of love talking to me from his sincere and pleading face. "If ever I did anything for love, I have done this for it. I did it for love and for you. I did it for all the wrongs done you, and the loneliness you've suffered, and the horrors that the world put upon you when you were too young and too untried to know how to fight them and then too vanquished to wage a battle with a full heart. I did it for you."

"Oh, you lie, you lie in your heart," I said, "if not with your tongue. You did it for spite, and you have just revealed it all too plainly to me. You did it for spite because I wasn't the fledgling you wanted to make of me. I wasn't the clever rebel who could stand up to Santino and his band of monsters, and I was the one, after all those centuries, that disappointed you yet again and horribly because I went into the sun after I saw the Veil. That's why you did it. You did it for vengeance and you did it for bitterness and you did it for disappointment, and the crowning horror is you don't know it yourself. You couldn't bear it that my heart swelled to burst when I saw His Face on the Veil. You couldn't bear it that this child you plucked from the Venetian brothel, and nursed with your own blood, this child you taught from your own books and with your hands, cried out to Him when he saw His Face on the Veil."

"No, that is so very very far from the truth it breaks my heart." He shook his head. And tearless and white as he was, his face was a perfect picture of sorrow as though it was a painting he had done with his own hands. "I did it because they love you as no one has ever loved you, and they are free and have within their generous hearts a deep cunning which doesn't shrink from you and all that you are. I did it because they were forged in the same furnace as myself, the two of them, keen to reason and strong to endure. I did it because madness had not defeated her, and poverty and ignorance had not defeated him. I did it because they were your chosen ones, utterly perfect, and I knew that you would not do it, and they would come to hate you for this, hate you, as you once hated me for withholding it, and you would lose them to alienation and death before you would give in.

"They are yours now. Nothing separates you. And it's my blood, ancient and powerful, that's filled them to the brim with power so that they can be your worthy companions and not the pale shadow of your soul which Louis always was.

"There is no barrier of Master and Fledgling between you, and you can learn the secrets of their hearts as they learn the secrets of yours."

I wanted to believe it.

I wanted to believe it so badly that I got up and left him, and making the gentlest smile at my Benjamin and kissing her silkily in passing, I withdrew to the garden and stood alone beneath and between a pair of massive oaks.

Their thunderous roots rose up out of the ground, forming hillocks of hard dark blistering wood. I rested my feet in this rocky place and my head against the nearer of the two trees.

The branches came down and made a veil for me, as I had wanted the hair of my own head to do. I felt shielded and safe in the shadows. I was quiet in my heart, but my heart was broken and my mind was shattered, and I had only to look through the open doorway into the brilliant glory of the light at my two white vampire angels for me to start crying again.

Marius stood for a long time in a distant door. He didn't look at me. And when I looked to Pandora, I saw her coiled up as if to defend herself from some terrible pain—possibly only our quarrel—in another large old velvet chair.

Finally Marius drew himself up and came towards me, and I think it took a force of will for him to do it. He seemed suddenly just a little angry and even proud.

I didn't give a damn.

He stood before me but he said nothing, and it seemed he was there to face whatever I had yet to say.

"Why didn't you let them have their lives!" I said. "You, of all people, whatever you felt for me and my follies, why didn't you let them have what nature gave them? Why did you interfere?"

He didn't answer, but I didn't allow for it. Softening my tone so as not to alarm them, I went on.

"In my darkest times," I said, "it was always your words that upheld me. Oh, I don't mean during those centuries when I was in bondage to a warped creed and morbid delusion. I mean long afterwards, after I had come out of the cellar, at Lestat's challenge, and I read what Lestat wrote of you, and then heard you for myself. It was you, Master, who let me see what little I could of the marvelous bright world unfolding around me in ways I couldn't have imagined in the land or time in which I was born."

I couldn't contain myself. I stopped for breath and to listen to her music, and realizing how lovely it was, how plaintive and expressive and newly mysterious, I almost cried again. But I couldn't allow such to happen. I had a great deal more to say, or so I thought.

"Master, it was you who said we were moving in a world where the old religions of superstition and violence were dying away. It was you who said we lived in a time when evil no longer aspired to any necessary place. Remember it, Master, you told Lestat that there was no creed or code that could justify our existence, for men knew now what was real evil, and real evil was hunger, and want, and ignorance and war, and cold. You said those things, Master, far more elegantly and fully than I could ever say them, but it was on this great rational basis that you argued, you, with the worst of us, for the sanctity and the precious glory of this natural and human world. It was you who championed the human soul, saying it had grown in depth and feeling, that men no longer lived for the glamour of war but knew the finer things which had once been the forte only of the richest, and could now be had by all. It was you who said that a new illumination, one of reason and ethics and genuine compassion, had come again, after dark centuries of bloody religion, to give forth not only its light but its warmth."

"Stop, Armand, don't say any more," he said. He was gentle but very stern. "I remember those words. I remember all of them. But I don't believe those things anymore."

I was stunned. I was stunned by the awesome simplicity of this disavowal. It was sweeping beyond my imagination, and yet I knew him well enough to know that he meant every word. He looked at me steadily.

"I believed it once, yes. But you see, it was not a belief based on reason and on observation of mankind as I told myself it was. It was never that, and I came to realize it and when I did, when I saw it for what it was—a blind desperate irrational prejudice—I felt it suddenly and completely collapse.

"Armand, I said those things because I had to hold them to be true. They were their own creed, the creed of the rational, the creed of the atheistic, the creed of the logical, the creed of the sophisticated Roman Senator who must turn a blind eye to the nauseating realities of the world around him, because if he were to admit what he saw in the wretchedness of his brothers and sisters, he would go mad."

He drew in his breath and continued, turning his back to the bright room as if to shield the fledglings from the heat of his words, as surely as I wanted him to do it.

"I know history, I read it as others read their Bibles, and I will not be satisfied until I have unearthed all stories that are written and knowable, and cracked the codes of all cultures that have left me any tantalizing evidence that I might pry loose from earth or stone or papyrus or clay.

"But I was wrong in my optimism, I was ignorant, as ignorant as I accused others of being, and refusing to see the very horrors that surrounded me, all the worse in this century, this reasonable century, than ever before in the world.

"Look back, child, if you care to, if you would argue the point. Look back to golden Kiev, which you knew only in songs after the raging Mongols had burnt its Cathedrals and slaughtered its population like so much cattle, as they did all through the Kiev Rus for two hundred years. Look back to the chronicles of all Europe and see the wars waged everywhere, in the Holy Land, in the forests of France or Germany, up and down the fertile soil of England, yes, blessed England, and in every Asian corner of the globe.

"Oh, why did I deceive myself for so long? Did I not see those Russian grasslands, those burnt cities. Why, all of Europe might have fallen to Ghenghis Khan. Think of the great English Cathedrals torn down to rubble by the arrogant King Henry.

"Think of the books of the Mayas heaved into the flames by Spanish priests. Incas, Aztecs, Olmec—peoples of all nations ground to oblivion—.

"It's horrors, horrors upon horrors, and it always was, and I can pretend no longer. When I see millions gassed to death for the whims of an Austrian madman, when I see whole African tribes massacred till the rivers are stuffed with their bloated bodies, when I see rank starvation claim whole countries in an age of gluttonous plenty, I can believe all these platitudes no more.

"I don't know what single event it was that destroyed my self-deception. I don't know what horror it was that ripped the mask from my lies. Was it the millions who starved in the Ukraine, imprisoned in it by their own dictator, or the thousands after who died from the nuclear poisoning spewing into the skies over the grasslands, unprotected by the same governing powers who had starved them before? Was it the monasteries of noble Nepal, citadels of meditation and grace that had stood for thousands of years, older even than myself and all my philosophy, destroyed by an army of greedy grasping militarists who waged war without quarter upon monks in their saffron robes, and priceless books which they heaved into the fire, and ancient bells which they melted down no more to call the gentle to prayer? And this, this within two decades of this very hour, while the nations of the West danced in their discos and swilled their liquor, lamenting in casual tones for the poor sad fate of the distant Dalai Lama, and turning the television dial.

"I don't know what it was. Perhaps it was all the millions—Chinese, Japanese, Cambodian, Hebrew,

Ukrainian, Polish, Russian, Kurdish, oh, God, the litany goes on without end. I have no faith, I have no optimism, I have no firm conviction in the ways of reason or ethics. I have no reproof for you as you stand on the Cathedral steps with your arms out to your all-knowing and all-perfect God.

"I know nothing, because I know too much, and understand not nearly enough and never will. But this you taught me as much as any other I've ever known, that love is necessary, as much as rain to the flowers and the trees, and food to the hungry child, and blood to the starving thirsting predators and scavengers that we are. Love we need, and love can make us forget and forgive all savagery, as perhaps nothing else can.

"And so I took them out of their fabulous promising modern world with its diseased and desperate masses. I took them out and gave them the only might I possess, and I did it for you. I gave them time, time perhaps to find an answer which those mortals living now may never know.

"That was it, all of it. And I knew you would cry, and I knew you would suffer, but I knew you would have them and love them when it was finished, and I knew that you needed them desperatcly. So there you are ... joined now with the serpent and the lion and the wolf, and far superior to the worst of men who have proved themselves in this time to be colossal monsters, and free to feed with care upon a world of evil that can swallow every bit of pruning they care to do."

A silence fell between us.

I thought for a long while, rather than plunge into my words.

Sybelle had stopped her playing, and I knew that she was concerned for me and needed me, I could feel it, feel the strong thrust of her vampire soul. I would have to go to her and soon.

But I took my time to say a few more words:

"You should have trusted them, Master, you should have let them have their chance. Whatever you thought of the world, you should have let them have their time with it. It was their world and their time."

He shook his head as though he was disappointed in me, and a little weary, and as he had resolved all these matters long ago in his mind, perhaps before I had even appeared last night, he seemed willing to let it all go.

"Armand, you are my child forever," he said with great dignity. "All that is magical and divine in me is bounded by the human and always was."

"You should have let them have their hour. No love of me should have written their death warrant, or their admission to our strange and inexplicable world. We may be no worse than humans in your estimation, but you could have kept your counsel. You could have let them alone."

It was enough.

Besides, David had appeared. He had a copy already of the transcript we'd labored on, but this was not his concern. He approached us slowly, announcing his presence obviously to give us the chance to become silent, which we did.

I turned to him, unable to restrain myself. "Did you know this was to happen? Did you know when it did?"

"No, I did not," he said solemnly.

"Thank you," I said.

"They need you, your young ones," David said. "Marius may be the Maker but they are utterly yours."

"I know," I said. "I'm going. I'll do what I'm bound to do."

Marius put his hand out and touched my shoulder. I realized suddenly that he was truly on the verge of losing his self-control.

When he spoke his voice was tremulous and lustrous with feeling. He hated the storm inside himself and he was overcome by my sorrow. I knew this plainly enough. It gave me no satisfaction at all.

"You despise me now, and perhaps you're right. I knew you would weep, but in a very profound way, I misjudged you. I didn't realize something about you. Perhaps I never have."

"What's that, Master," I said with acidic drama.

"You loved them selflessly," he whispered. "For all their strange faults, and wild evil, they were not compromised for you. You loved them perhaps more respectfully than I . . . than I ever loved you."

He seemed so amazed.

I could only nod. I wasn't so sure he was right. My need for them had never been tested, but I didn't want to tell him so.

"Armand," he said. "You know you can stay here as long as you like."

"Good, because I just might," I said. "They love it, and I'm weary. So thank you very much for that."

"But one thing more," he went on, "and I mean this with all my heart."

"What is it, Master?" I said.

David stood by, and I was happy for that, for it seemed to act as a certain curb upon my tears.

"I honestly don't know the answer to this, and I ask you in humility," Marius said. "When you saw the Veil, what was it you really saw? Oh, I don't mean was it Christ, or was it God, or was it a miracle. What I mean is this. There was the face of a being, drenched in blood, who had given birth to a religion guilty of more wars and more cruelty than any creed the world has ever known. Don't be angry with me, please, just explain to me. What was it you saw? Was it only a magnificent reminder of the ikons you once painted? Or was it truly something drenched in love and not in blood? Tell me. If it was love and not blood, I would honestly like to know."

"You ask an old and simple question," I said, "and from where I stand you don't really know a thing. You wonder how He could have been my Lord, given this world as you describe it, and knowing what you know of the Gospels and the Testaments printed in His name. You wonder how I could have believed all that because you don't believe it, isn't that so?"

He nodded. "Yes, I do wonder. Because I know you. And I know that faith is something which you simply do not have."

I was startled. But instantly I knew he was right.

I smiled. I felt a sort of tragic thrilling happiness suddenly.

"Well, I see what you mean," I said. "And I'll tell you my answer. I saw Christ. A kind of bloody light. A personality, a human, a presence that I felt I knew. And He wasn't the Lord God Father Almighty and He wasn't the maker of the universe and the whole world. And He wasn't the Savior or the Redeemer for sins inscribed on my soul before I was born. He wasn't the Second Person of the Holy Trinity, and He wasn't the Theologian expounding from the Holy Mount. He wasn't those things for me. Maybe for others, but not for me."

"But who was He, then, Armand?" David asked. "I have your story, full of marvels and suffering, yet I don't know. What *was* the concept of the *Lord* when you spoke the word?"

"*Lord,*" I repeated it. "It doesn't mean what you think. It's spoken with too much intimacy and too much warmth. It's like a secret and sacred name. Lord." I paused, and then continued:

"He is the Lord, yes, but only because He is the symbol of something infinitely more accessible, something infinitely more meaningful than a ruler or king or lord can ever be."

Again, I hesitated, wanting to find the right words since they were so sincere.

"He was . . . *my brother*." I said. "Yes. That is what He was, my brother, and the symbol of all brothers, and that is why He was the Lord, and that is why His core is simply love. You scorn it. You look askance at what I say. But you don't grasp the complexity of what He was. It's easy to feel, perhaps, but not so easy to really see. He was another man like me. And maybe for many of us, millions upon millions, that's all He's ever been! We're all somebody's sons and daughters and He was somebody's son. He was human, whether He was God or not, and He was suffering and He was doing it for things He thought were purely and universally good. And that meant that His blood might as well have been my blood too. Why, it had to be. And maybe that is the very source of His magnificence for thinkers such as me. You said I had no faith. I don't. Not in titles or in legends or in hierarchies made by other beings like ourselves. He didn't make a hierarchy, not really. He was *the very thing*. I saw in Him magnificence for simple reasons. There was flesh and blood to what He was! And it could be bread and wine to feed the whole Earth. You don't get it. You can't. Too many lies about Him swim in your ken. I saw Him before I heard so much about Him. I saw Him when I looked at the ikons in my house, and when I painted Him long before I even knew all His names. I can't get Him out of my head. I never have. I never will."

I had no more to say.

They were very amazed but not particularly respecting, pondering the words in all the wrong ways, perhaps, I couldn't absolutely know. It didn't matter what they felt anyway. It wasn't really so good that they had asked me or that I had tried so hard to tell them my truth. I saw the old ikon in my mind, the one my Mother had brought to me in the snow. *Incarnation.* Impossible to explain in their philosophy. I wondered. Perhaps the horror of my own life was that, no matter what I did or where I went, I always understood. *Incarnation.* A kind of bloody light.

I wanted to be left alone by them now.

Sybelle was waiting, which was of far greater importance, and I went to take her in my arms.

For many hours we talked together, Sybelle and Benji and me, and finally Pandora, who was very distraught but would say nothing of it, came to talk casually and gaily with us too. Marius joined us and also David.

We were gathered in a circle on the grass under the stars. For the young ones, I put on the bravest of faces and we spoke of beautiful things, and places we would wander, and wonders which Marius and Pandora had seen, and we argued now and then amiably about trivial things.

About two hours before dawn, we had broken up, with Sybelle sitting by herself deep in the garden, looking at one flower after another with great care. Benji had discovered that he could read at preternatural speed and was tearing through the library, which was very impressive indeed.

David, seated at Marius's desk, corrected his misspellings and abbreviations in the typescript, painstakingly correcting the copy he had made for me in haste.

Marius and I sat very close together against the same oak tree, my shoulder against his. We didn't talk. We were watching things, and listening perhaps to the same songs of the night.

I wanted Sybelle to play again. I had never known her to go so long without playing, and I wanted badly to hear her play the Sonata again.

It was Marius who first heard an unusual sound, and stiffened with alarm, only to give it up and rest back beside me again.

"What was it?" I asked.

"Only a little noise. I couldn't . . . I couldn't read it," he said. He rested his shoulder against me as he had before.

Almost immediately I saw David look up from his work. And then Pandora appeared, walking slowly but warily towards one of the lighted doors.

Now I heard the sound. And so did Sybelle, for she too looked in the direction of the garden gate. Even Benji had finally deigned to notice it, and he dropped his book in mid-sentence and came marching with a very stern little scowl to the door to take stock of this new situation and get it firmly under control.

At first I thought my eyes had deceived me, but very quickly I realized the identity of the figure who appeared as the gate opened and closed quietly behind his stiff and ungainly arm.

He limped as he approached, or seemed rather the victim of a weariness and a loss of practice at the simple act of walking as he came into the light that fell on the grass before our feet.

I was astonished. No one knew his intentions. No one moved.

It was Lestat, and he was tattered and dusty as he had been on the chapel floor. No thoughts emanated from his mind as far as I could figure, and his eyes looked vague and full of exhausting wonder. He stood before us, merely staring, and then as I rose to my feet, scrambled in fact, to embrace him; he came near to me, and whispered in my ear.

His voice was faltering and weak from lack of use, and he spoke very softly, his breath just touching my flesh.

"Sybelle," he said.

"Yes, Lestat, what is it, what about her, tell me," I said. I held his hands as firmly and lovingly as I could.

"Sybelle," he said again. "Do you think she would play the Sonata for me if you asked her? The *Appassionata*?"

I drew back and looked into his vague drifting blue eyes.

"Oh, yes," I said, near breathless with excitement, with overflowing feeling. "Lestat, I'm sure she would. Sybelle!"

She had already turned. She watched him in amazement as he made his way slowly across the lawn and into the house. Pandora stepped back for him, and we all watched in respectful silence as he sat down near the piano, his back to the front right leg of it, and his knees brought up and his head resting wearily on his folded arms. He closed his eyes.

"Sybelle," I asked, "would you play it for him? The *Appassionata*, again, if you would."

And of course, she did.

THE END

8:12 a.m.
January 6, 1998
Little Christmas

(continued)

James, P. D., *A Certain Justice*
Koontz, Dean, *Intensity*
Koontz, Dean, *Sole Survivor*
Koontz, Dean, *Ticktock*
Krantz, Judith, *Spring Collection*
Landers, Ann, *Wake Up and Smell the Coffee!*
le Carré, John, *The Tailor of Panama*
Lindbergh, Anne Morrow, *Gift from the Sea*
Masson, Jeffrey Moussaieff, *Dogs Never Lie About Love*
Mayle, Peter, *Chasing Cézanne*
Morrison, Toni, *Paradise*
Mother Teresa, *A Simple Path*
Patterson, Richard North, *The Final Judgment*
Patterson, Richard North, *Silent Witness*
Peck, M. Scott., M.D., *Denial of the Soul*
Phillips, Louis, editor, *The Random House Large Print Treasury of Best-Loved Poems*
Pope John Paul II, *Crossing the Threshold of Hope*
Pope John Paul II, *The Gospel of Life*
Powell, Colin with Joseph E. Persico, *My American Journey*
Preston, Richard, *The Cobra Event*
Rampersad, Arnold, *Jackie Robinson*
Rendell, Ruth, *The Keys to the Street*
Rendell, Ruth, *Road Rage*
Rice, Anne, *Violin*
Rice, Anne, *Pandora*
Shaara, Jeff, *Gods and Generals*
Smith, Martin Cruz, *Rose*
Snead, Sam with Fran Pirozzolo, *The Game I Love*
Truman, Margaret, *Murder at the National Gallery*
Truman, Margaret, *Murder in the House*
Tyler, Anne, *Ladder of Years*
Updike, John, *Golf Dreams*
Weil, Andrew, M.D., *Eight Weeks to Optimum Health*
Whitney, Phyllis A., *Amethyst Dreams*